DIAMONDS OUT OF COAL

DIAMONDS OUT OF COAL

A Novel

N.G. KRAIEM

Friedlich Golde Publishing

Diamonds Out of Coal

N.G. Kraiem

© 2023 Friedlich Golde Publishing.
All rights reserved. No part of this publication may be reproduced, stored in a retrieval system or transmited in any form or by any means, electronic, mechanical, photocopying, recording or otherwise without the prior permision of the publisher or in accordance with the provisions of the Copyright, Designs and Patents Act 1988 or under the terms of any licence permitting limited copying issued by the Copyright Licensing Angency.

DISCLAIMER: This novel is purely the product of creative invention. All characters, settings, and events are either born from the writer's imagination or are portrayed in a fictional manner. Any similarity to real-life incidents, locations, or individuals, whether they are alive or deceased, is purely unintentional or coincidental.

Published by:
Friedlich Golde Publishing
Typesetting: Joseph Kraiem
Cover Design: Seventh Star Art
ISBN-13: 979-8-218-26305-8

Printed in the USA

To my husband.

Ani l'dodi, v'dodi li

I am my beloved's and

my beloved is mine.

Mae

"So? Explain to me," he said, trying to garner her attention. Sitting across from her, he took in the woman who sat before him. He examined her face as she crinkled her nose and halfheartedly looked about the room. Although she seemed as if she were trying to find the right words, the look in her eyes showed that her thoughts were elsewhere. It was only midday, but she looked tired—it was the type of weariness you'd see when life handed one all its trials without the reward of glory.

Looking past her swollen eyes and disheveled appearance, he noted her attractiveness. Her beautiful copper-colored skin glistened against the backdrop of her wrinkled dress; the hues of orange and violet clung tightly against her skin and highlighted just how sweet and supple it was. Her small celestial nose was slightly upturned, which lent an elegance to her face. Despite not wearing any makeup, her complexion was flawless—a natural shimmer seemed to appear as the sun caressed her cheek through the window behind her. He couldn't help but admire her beauty, just as he could not ignore her pain. The sadness in her eyes was unmistaken, and yet she still did not speak. She just sat—quietly so.

Feeling the weight of his gaze, she continued to avoid eye contact with him. *How could I start to explain myself? My reason for being here? Has my life up until this point really been that bad? So bad that I've ended up... here? Like this?* Glancing at him, she knew based on his piercing eyes that she would have to break her silence. "Explain what exactly?" she asked him.

"Explain why you're here?"

"Why am I here?" she stated in a manner she hoped would hide her unease.

"Yes. Why are you here?" he asked. As she closed her eyes, he noticed just how thick and lush her lashes were. Her long fingers suddenly reached up and brushed against her cheek. *Is she crying? Are those tears?* Goodness, he hated when women cried. No matter how many times it happened, he couldn't get used to that aspect of his job. Occupational hazard, he shrugged inwardly.

As he waited for her to get her bearings, he couldn't help but note how full her lips were as they quivered—they seemed to naturally pucker as if waiting to be kissed. When she finally opened her eyes, he saw the amber flecks within their chestnut color shine brightly, as the cat like shape of them began to squint inquisitively as if questioning him. *He* then became nervous. Am I staring, he wondered. He decided to smile to reassure her, hoping that it would coax her into answering. To his relief she began to open her mouth.

"Call me… Mae," she said.

"Mae?" he asked, raising his brows.

"Yes, it was my great-grandmother's name. Margot Mae Laveaux—that was her. Very Southern, I know. She was just a Creole girl from New Orleans, that dreamt big and lived her life even bigger. Everyone says that I look like her. Tall and lanky. Nothing but legs. I'm not sure that I see it, though. She was far more glamourous than I will ever be. Regal even. There's no wonder men fell for her. They would literally fall at her feet, begging for a chance to speak with her. That's at least how the story was told to me," she said absently, in a flawless Louisianian drawl. Shifting, she peered upon the room, scanning it, as if trying to find the words to muster an excuse to get herself away from his prying eyes.

"I wasn't aware that Southern twangs were customary for Brooklyn girls," he stated questioningly.

Nervous, she began wringing her hands together, squeezing them harder and harder until her fingertips became pale in color from the pressure. "I'm sorry. I was rambling, I know. I think… I think I should go," she said quickly, as she stood gathering her things.

"Running away isn't going to solve anything," he said tightly.

She looked at him confused, causing him to note his mistake in addressing her. Adjusting his tone, he went on, "What I meant…look…can you just sit? Please…have a seat. We can't very well work on what you've come here for if you leave now. Can we?"

Slowly, she returned to her place. As she settled herself down, he observed as she licked her lips timidly and pushed her dark shoulder length hair behind her ears. Goodness! Those lips, he thought. She really was a beautiful woman—one whose eyes he could get lost in forever, if she'd let him.

Mae could feel his eyes on her, and it trapped a heat inside her she couldn't explain—as if she were somehow melting from within. It was a feeling that was painful for someone like her, which made her want to fade away from his scrutiny. Now, more than ever, she wished she could hide within herself as she'd always done when under pressure, but the intensity of his gaze held her from doing so. She went to that place often now—where she would close out the world around her and scream into the darkness to her heart's content. But now as she sat before him, she was unable to bring herself to that place. Instead, she was choked with fear that he would pull her back into her realm of pain and uncertainty, which was enough for her to disengage from his look upon her.

Although the room, from the pastel blue walls with photographs that ranged from scenic views of places traveled, to lilies placed tastefully about on accent furniture was decorated precisely to make one's visit to such a place comfortable, it did nothing to help her disposition.

"I love lilies," she blurted. The minute she said it, she regretted it—feeling as if she were an invalid, incapable of tackling the task at hand. She was there for a reason. Why speak of lilies when I must deal with the mess that is my life, she chided herself.

"I like them too. They're my wife's favorite," he said sarcastically.

"Your wife? What is she like?" she inquired.

"Mae, can we stay focused on why you're really here?"

"I just thought… forget it. I don't know what I was thinking."

"Look… *Mae...*" he began—pausing to capture the way her eyebrows arched as she waited to hear him finish his sentence. The act of it lent her an inquisitive look that he found endearing. However, it also made her look like a scared child waiting to be chastised for spilling milk that was obviously too heavy to carry. He knew by looking at her that he had to calm her. There was no way this would work if she didn't compose herself enough for them to start. And he was losing patience with her. He leaned over and instinctively placed his hand gently on her lap. "I'm ready whenever you are," he smiled at her, "Now, tell me why you're here today."

"I don't know how it's gotten to be this way. I just know that I need to be here," she said.

"What are you talking about? What has gotten to be what way, Mae?"

"I'm here to…"

"Go on, Mae. Continue, please" he encouraged.

She sighed. An exhaustive, elaborate sigh—one that said she longed to get the burden of the world, for which she carried for far too long, off her shoulders, and send it as far away as the stars could muster. "I'm here to save my marriage," came tumbling from her lips.

With the release of her words, she instantly became more relaxed. The tension she held within her body began to ease, loosening her muscles and changing her once rigid carriage.

"Save your marriage?" he asked confused.

"Yes. I want to save my marriage."

"I was under the impression that you were here for something else entirely."

"No. No, sir. I am here to save my marriage," she said emphatically.

As he felt his placidity thinning, he began to fidget in his chair, to which she took notice. "Okay then," he replied, "What exactly is it that you would like to fix in your marriage—"

Sitting up in her seat, her eyebrows arched wildly as if she'd reached an epiphany, "Would you like to hear a story?" she asked suddenly.

"A story?" he replied, trying hard to mask his irritation, as confusion draped swiftly across his face, taking over his rugged features. *Is that a smile behind her eyes? Is she amused by my growing discomfort of how tedious our interaction is becoming? What is with this woman? First, she's in borderline hysterics, now she is pleasantly amused. Is she mad?*

"I guess I should start at the beginning, as most stories do. It is a story of us. Of him and me—or rather, how we came to be. There is no story without the beginning, and it's my favorite part," she uttered.

Glancing at him, she gaged his reaction as she played with the words, allowing them to flow from her lips slowly, as if dancing an elaborate waltz that only she knew. When she felt that she had his attention, she carried on, "We met as most kids do. In school. First year of secondary school to be exact."

"Look, um… Mae—"

"Just wait, Doc. Please let me start. Our story is more than just a story. It's a love story. One of the greatest you'll ever hear if you'd listen."

He sighed, visibly annoyed at how things were progressing, "Okay. If this is how you want our session to go, then carry on."

"Sessions, Doc. We'll need plenty more of these sessions to fix this debacle. I guess I should welcome you to the start of a beautiful partnership," she said smugly. Finally comfortable, she relaxed against the plush cushions of the grey couch she sat upon, which was situated in the center of the room across from the chair he sat in, and as he looked upon her with pen in hand and his notepad on his lap, she began her story, “He called me, Cole…”

Brooklyn

The very first memory I have, is the fear I saw in my mother's eyes as she stared down the barrel of a gun. We were lucky, they said, that the man who robbed her behind our building had enough heart to spare our family our loss. I was born into that world. A world where nightmares became reality, and boogeymen didn't hide beneath one's bed or behind closed doors. As a kid growing up in the ghetto, I realized quickly that a life lived behind a white picket fence, was never meant to be. It was seen as an unattainable dream. You see, the hood had a funny way of reminding you of just how meaningless you are to the world. And the older I became, the more aware I was of what growing up there meant for me.

The heroin epidemic that came as a byproduct of The Vietnam War, and the crack boom of the 80s made only a few things certain growing up in my neighborhood—drugs were plentiful, we were expendable, and love didn't exist. Fairytales were for the weak and there were no happy endings on my streets of Brooklyn. And though I realized that then, there was no other place that held my heart as strong as she. Her concrete jungle and gritty streets meant everything to me. She made me who I am—shaping and teaching me how to endure a life I never thought possible.

I didn't need much then. I was too busy being captivated by her power. The annual Summer parties of my childhood seemed to make *my* city, *my* borough, *my* block, come alive. And in those moments, just for that night, we hoped that the sounds of bullets flying, we so often heard, would litter the sky in place of fireworks, instead of in someone we knew.

Summer nights were filled with double-Dutch and Skelly, while our days were spent dancing, unabandoned in the middle of the street, as fire hydrants blazed cold water onto our backs to fend off the heat. We crept and listened to the old heads speak, and if we were careful of not being seen, we learned what life truly was about, and how to cultivate it for ourselves. It didn't matter how trash littered our block. The crack needles found in alley ways and in the grass as we played touch football never troubled us. None of it did. We still ran around for hours, climbing the walls of our concrete jungle until the streetlights came on, signifying that it was time to head home—the old heads now relieved of their duty of keeping watch. Those are the memories that speak to the nostalgic delusions of my childhood. And, yes, I was captivated then. Still, while proud of my beginnings, I knew that it was no place for me. As time went on, the spell that she had on me dissipated and the reality of her cruelty consumed me and led me to my now. It led me to him.

"I don't want to go to a family. I want to go to camp!" the seven-year-old me pouted.

"You shut your mouth right now. You go where I say you go. And who you think you talking to like that?"

I could see her irritation rising as we walked from the clinic with a pamphlet in hand, explaining all the adventures I was to have with a family from Upstate, New York. The Black and Brown children filled with laughter in the arms of well to do White families on glossed pages, did nothing to rouse my curiosity. It was different from the sea of people I had grown accustomed to seeing in my daily surroundings; after all, the only White people I ever saw, were the few at my school or the ones who worked at the clinic. It was often some poor soul who happened to draw the shortest straw and ended up in our world, for which they were unable to survive. The altruistic fantasies they conjured were in stark contrast to my living reality, making them transient beings who never stayed long in our sphere. Their world was foreign to me—frightening even. And I couldn't muster the courage to go to a place where everyone and everything was so different from my home… and me. I wanted to go to Summer camp, where the familiar was going to be, but my mother had other plans.

"They might have chickens and puppies," she said to me, trying to quell my fears and her growing frustration.

"I don't like puppies," I replied, "They scare me."

That was truth. Up until that point in my young life, I had only two encounters with them, both of which were terrifying. The first, I was chased by the little critter, and the other, well, it was an unfortunate experience seeing what happened to that woman. No. Dogs of any kind were not for me. As for chickens? Well, the only thing they were meant for in my mind, was to eat. I couldn't possibly go.

"I wanna go to the big camp with all the other kids," I said, referring to the six-week camp that was offered in place of the two-week family stay.

"Listen here, gal," my mother spoke against my ear, reciting the words in the light Southern drawl mixed with the coolness of Brooklyn that she picked up from my grandmother. A trace of my great grandmother's Southern beginnings, effortlessly flowed from her lips, "You ain't going to no big camp for that long, where too many people gon be handling you! Where them people probably don't even know what they doing! You going to one of them families, so I can call and check-up on you whenever I want! Now, you ain't gon sit here and keep sniveling and opening your mouth. Shut it up! You going!"

And that was the end of that. I said no more. It went on like this for years. Every Summer it was the same—I was to go to the family she'd chosen.. With every Summer I spent with them, I changed. I became more disheartened with the grittiness of my world. And the changes in my carriage and mannerisms became evident with each passing visit, morphing and solidifying me into this other—no longer of my home. My mother's work done.

By Middle School, the harsh realities of my world began to magnify, causing an unhappiness I couldn't seem to assuage. The calmness I felt within the lakes and farmlands that were only a few hours from home, and yet lightyears away, brought forth a desire within me. An urgency brewed, and I had a growing need to set my life apart from my urban playground. Her buildings began to enclose around me, stealing my breath and draining the hope I'd once held. Its bars and steel slab doors no longer resembled home, but a prison I desperately needed to escape. Despite my love for my city, she cut inside me like barbed wire, bleeding me from within. And I knew I no longer belonged to her, and everyone else began to see it too.

"They keep saying that I speak like a White girl. That I act like a White girl. I can't understand what I'm doing wrong," I said to my mother in the principal's office. The bruise on my lip aching and echoing the consequence of responding sarcastically to another day of constant ridicule.

"Look, I'm not gonna keep coming up to this school because these little wenches keep putting their hands on my daughter."

Shifting in her seat with a look of admonition mixed with controlled disgust, she began to speak, "Miss Johnson—"

"Brown. *Mrs.* Brown. Just because I didn't marry *her* daddy, don't mean I didn't marry somebody, and you need to stop acting like you don't know this. She's been here since kindergarten, and just because you came in here three-years ago, don't mean you without that knowledge, *Miss* Swanson," my mother replied snidely.

"That would be, Mrs. Swanson."

"Humph. I see you don't like it," my mother fumed, "Anyway, like I said, I'm tired of coming up here for these little bitches."

Her pale face began to contort, and her tan brows furrowed, showing her growing disdain for my mother's use of language. I always wondered what brought her to our school—it was clear that she was one of those who drew the short straw. She was not only out of place, but she didn't seem to care much for the people within my community. Her long, thin fingers ran through her chin length blonde hair, as she let out a wary sigh before addressing my mother, "Mrs. Brown, can you please refrain from using words that are detrimental and cutting to our students."

"Detrimental to your students? What about this girl here?" she said pointing in my direction, "What about her? So, you telling me that my daughter has to put up with their shit?"

"Mrs. Brown, really! I do wish you would control yourself!"

Glancing at my mother, I realized that she was close to losing it. I began to shrink in my seat, hoping that I would somehow get lost in it and shield myself from the ordeal I was sure would ensue. I looked over at Mrs. Swanson and noted the displeasure on her face in having to deal with yet another misfit. It was what I'd often heard her refer to us as—misfits. That's what we were to her, and it was something I tried hard to disprove. Yet my mother was there, in her office again, showing herself to be just that. I could only wonder what was truly going through Mrs. Swanson's mind as she braced herself for my mother's onslaught, while I sat quietly trying to mask my shame and embarrassment. In that moment, I hoped that whatever she would say and do, would be done quickly, so that she would leave as hastily as she'd barged in. But to my surprise, my mother's face softened, and her body relaxed, leaving behind the intensity of her burning need to rage.

"All I'm saying is that I really need for y'all to keep them girls off her. She's a good girl. She don't give y'all no trouble. She barely stands up for herself," she stated calmly.

"Mrs. Brown, I am aware of what kind of student she is. She's a dream to have. I know that you're upset, and we are trying our best to get things under control. Honestly, she doesn't belong in this place. It's part of the reason I called you in today."

"What you mean?" my mother asked, now at full attention. Straightening herself up in her seat, she watched as Mrs. Swanson reached into her desk and pulled out a small booklet.

"I've been watching your girl for some time now, and we both can agree that academically, she's exceptional. So, I looked into a few things. There is a program that meets once a week during school hours and twice more afterschool, and if she does well, she will be able to go here, for secondary school," Mrs. Swanson said, as she nodded towards the booklet excitedly.

My mother glanced down and looked at the school on the cover. As she skimmed through the glossy pages, I could see her eyes light up at the pictures of cobblestone walkways, stone buildings, and adolescents dressed smartly in their uniforms. But just as quickly as it appeared, the flicker of light that resembled hope, dimmed, and was replaced with the disappointment I had grown accustomed to seeing.

"How much this gonna cost me?" my mother said with mild irritation.

"Well…nothing. It's a new program. The school is trying to…well… expand its diversity, by giving kids like her a chance at a real future," Mrs. Swanson fumbled."

"How she supposed to get in?" my mother asked.

"If she does well in the program, which I expect her to, and succeeds in both completing it and passing their entry exams at the percentage stated in the admissions section, here," she pointed and then continued, "She'll be eligible for a full scholarship.

"Okay. She gon go."

"Keep in mind that you will be responsible for getting her to the sessions and the program's events after school. She can't miss anything at all," said Mrs. Swanson.

"I said, she going," my mother responded ardently.

"Okay then. Listen, we'll try to help her be as successful as possible. I know boarding school isn't what you are used to, but she won't be very far. This will be a wonderful opportunity for her."

"She'll be there. She gon make it to every session. You tell them she'll take her spot in this here program, and she gon get into that school," my mother replied with bolstered confidence.

Like a hellcat at a poker game, my mother waged her bets, and she placed all odds on me, knowing that I would do anything not to let her down. Leaning forward in her chair and with a cross of her legs, she sat as if waiting for Mrs. Swanson to call her bluff on her proclamation. Finally satisfied in her perception of setting things in motion, my mother asked, "Anything else?" The shake of Mrs. Swanson's head prompted her to stand, and I followed suit, rising from my seat as I waited to be dismissed.

"No. That is all. I will phone them as soon as you leave. Be sure to note the start date. It begins next week," she replied to my mother. Turning her attention to me, Mrs. Swanson said, "Make sure you get to where you belong, young lady. The day isn't over."

"Oh…okay…I will," I stammered, as my mother made her way towards the door—sauntering out as sensually as she'd come in. Following behind her, I slowed my pace to allow distance between her and me, so that I could get Mrs. Swanson's attention. As I mouthed my thanks, she shooed me out with a wink and smile, before picking up the phone.

"Hello, Stacey? Yes. She'll take the spot," came faintly to my ears, as I crossed the threshold of her door.

Walking past the secretaries' cubicles into the hall, I was on cloud nine, until I felt a harsh jerk towards the wall. Pain instantly wracked my body as I felt my back hit the concrete slab. Flinching, I opened my eyes to see my mother hovering over me— in my moment of bliss, I had forgotten her. Grabbing my arm to bring me closer to her, she whispered in my ear menacingly, "Make this the last time I have to come up here. If one of them little bitches put their hands on you again, you better knock them the fuck out. I'm not playing this game no more! Do you hear me? You either fight back, or I'm gonna whoop your ass. You up for two ass whoopins?" Biting back tears, I shook my head in reply, to which she loosened her grip. "I didn't think so. You don't let them beat you down. You hear me? Now you better work and get your ass into that school. Don't you disappoint me, now. Ain't nothing here that you want or need, you hear? You fuck up, you know what's gon be waiting for you, right?"

"Yes, ma'am."

"Now get your ass where you need to be," she said.

As she strolled down the hall, I, in turn, went where I always go when I wanted to escape. Crossing the threshold into the large space, I found my usual spot amongst the sea of books that sprawled across the walls. Opening my place in my current selection, I began reading the pages. It wasn't long before it carried me off away from my worries that surrounded me. I was right where I belonged. In my refuge.

Him

It was Fall. My time spent in the program prepared me well. The year went by as quickly as a Summer rain, filled with memories and goodbyes I kept close to my heart. Soon, I found myself walking the very cobblestone walkways that led to the entryway of stone buildings, I'd dreamt of every night. The architectural walls and ceilings seemed to engulf me as soon as I stepped within them. It was as I imagined them to be. Ever since, Mrs. Swanson's office, those pages, this place that I now found myself in, became my motivation. It was a driving force that took on a life of its own. In my eyes, I found my escape. And I felt strangely home.

It had been a week since my arrival. And as I acclimated to my new home a sense of calm washed over me. Its sprawling lawns and beautification gave me hope—I finally began to see a future outside the grief my home afforded. Yet, there was something that gnawed at me. No matter how I moved about my days, the sense that something bigger awaited would not leave me. And though I'd yet to understand what it meant then, my anxiety peaked as I maneuvered through my school's unsullied walls—unaware of who I was to them.

Despite my mother's grooming, I knew that I was still considerably inept in comparison to the creatures I now found myself surrounded by. After all, I was not the perfect diamond that so many of my peers seemed to be—flawless and pristine. There was a roughness about me I was not yet attune to. Setting me apart from the delicateness that seemed to consume the walls of my dormitory. It was during my first week, one night, that I realized just how different I was. Standing outside my room after showering, I heard them speak.

"Who is she?" said Cordelia Carmichael. She was of medium build with an aggressive gaze from sparkling blue eyes that always seemed to penetrate you, no matter her mood. She was familiar with the finer things in life and loved to relish in her prestige. Her family had been sending offspring from the Carmichael clan to our school since its humble beginnings; and her presence as a legacy, was overbearing and without regard for those around her. It was as if the world be damned, she was all that it encompassed— you were either a part of her landscape or a weed she'd snuff out.

"I'm not sure. I've never seen her before. Not until this year's orientation," came from Mia. Fiorella Rose Romano wasn't like the other girls. Her Mediterranean looks showcased dark hair that complimented her bronzed skin, and her expressive dark eyes spoke of adventure. She didn't care for the excitement within our halls. The constant banter of teenage girls did nothing to amuse her. She had her sights set elsewhere. Later, it was found that her interests lied within the arms of a professor from a nearby college, whom she later married.

She preferred to be called Mia; explaining that it gave her an edge in an atmosphere where she seemed to require its full attention. However, I knew better. Watching her cringe at the sound of her given name being called during orientation, was enough to surmise that she disliked her family name. A name that was passed down from grandmother to granddaughter and revealed her Italian heritage.

"Well, I don't like her."

"Why not? She seems fun enough. Better than the boring dribble we've seen for the past few years," Mia stated matter-of-factly.

"Still, something doesn't seem… right. Like, did you see her shoes? Her clothes? She's so…pedestrian. I bet she's a scholarship kid," Cordelia said snidely.

"Perhaps, she's just not as vain as you are, Cordie," Mia said with a shrug.

"Don't call me that. You know I hate that name."

"Cordelia, why do you care so much? She's honestly cool. She's kind of quiet… and…different. But she's nice enough. And it's only the first week. Give her a chance," said Gwyn, so quietly, she was barely audible.

She was a full-figured girl with deep-set hazel eyes that gazed from behind round glasses that always fell to the tip of her nose. A mousy girl around the others, she and I eventually grew to become fast friends. Despite the way she behaved with Cordelia and Mia, she was spirited and wild whenever she wasn't under their thumb. Her eyes would come to life with mischief, and we would spend hours laughing and planning our next venture. I guess it was because she was like me—a scholarship kid. The difference for Cordelia was that Gwyn understood her place in the hierarchy. To her, I, on the other hand, had not.

"I didn't ask you, Gwyn Fisher!" she snapped at her.

"I was only trying to say that she's a nice girl."

"I don't care what you were trying to say. She doesn't belong here. Even the way she speaks is weird. Everything about her is an obvious indication of what class she's churned from," Cordelia said incredulously.

"Oh, Cordelia, give it a rest. As Gwyn said, it's only been a week. Give her a chance. For me?" Mia replied.

At that moment, I chose to walk in. Feeling like an intruder, I strode with my head hung low, as I made a beeline to my bed. Hoping all the while that they would ignore my presence. But to my dismay, I heard her. Her words came sweetly, as if coated in honey to mask her malice, "Colette, we were just talking about you," Cordelia said.

I turned over from my position facing the wall to look at her—her words pouring over me as if they had been doused with acid. My eyes washed over her questioningly, "Why?"

"We were just saying how great it is to have you with us. I do hope that you have a great time while here. And I…well, we… look forward to getting to know you. Don't we girls?" Cordelia said coyly. Her smile never reaching her eyes.

Turning away from her to face the wall again, I learned from that day forward to watch more and speak less—eventually acquiring the correct ways in which the young ladies of such carriage carried themselves. By the time classes began, no one suspected or questioned if I belonged. My mother's words, "Keep your friends close and your enemies closer, gal. You hear? Not everyone gon be your friend. You there for a reason. Don't let those rich brats play you," played over and over in my mind. I was ready.

The first day of classes started like any other day. The hustle and bustle of students scurrying down corridors invigorated me. Lecture halls stood in grand rooms fitted with a lavishness I'd only seen on television. Still, some maintained the intimacies of classrooms I had grown inured to. The earthiness of the walls was decorated with pennants from classes past. Their frayed edges indicating the age of the school, as they vibrated the energies of students of yesteryear.

It was Latin class where we first crossed paths. Happenstance had conjured a recipe that placed me in his path—for I was slated to attend French and he Spanish. However, both classes were full. So, there we were, two people, worlds apart, destined to meet.

Nothing about my initial meeting with him was extraordinary; in fact, it was mundane. I walked into the small classroom and settled myself in front as I normally did in my other classes. There were no bells and whistles. No feelings of need or longing. The idea of love at first sight was still seen as a delusional pastime to me. And so, my first encounter with him was as ordinary as a setting sun.

"You dropped your pencil," a voice called from behind.

Not realizing whom the comment was addressed to, I continued looking forward, waiting for the teacher to arrive and began the day's lesson.

"Hey. You. Upfront. You dropped your pencil," the voice came again.

At this, I turned my body. There in the hand of a dark-haired boy, one row over and two seats back, was my pencil. Waving it to and fro, he didn't stop until it captured my attention.

Rising from my seat, I walked over to the boy that held it. "Sorry. I didn't realize I lost it," I said to him, "Thank you."

"Don't mention it," he said as he handed it to me. "Hey, what's your name?"

Looking down at him, I noted how large his deep brown eyes were. They were the kind you'd find on Greek statues in museums peering down at you. His prominent Roman nose sat upon full lips that seemed to plant themselves in a constant smirk. It was as if he held a secret no one else was privy to. His jaw was strong and came together into a chin that held a slight cleft—all of which complimented his dark olive skin. He was decidedly handsome. His looks resembled that of an Arabian prince—dignified and noble.

"Colette. Colette Johnson," I replied, extending my hand.

"Benjamin Lati. But everyone calls me Ben."

"Nice to meet you, Ben," I said as I turned to walk back to my seat, once again readying myself for the start of the lesson.

The months went by seamlessly, and I adjusted to my life as a boarder, fitting neatly within its gates as if I had always been part of their world. Like a chameleon, I learned to blend in with the stylishly dressed young men and women and became what they needed me to be. Despite this, there was still an unspoken distance that remained, creating a loneliness that was crippling. And then there was him. He allowed me to be myself. His kindness and laughter were infectious, and I had grown forward to seeing his sly smile.

We only interacted in class. Often, we'd find ourselves speaking candidly about our plans and the life we desired—never once alluding to who we were outside of our stone fortress. Despite our limited time together, a spark ignited between us that left me wanting more moments with the boy with large Greek eyes. However, time ticked by the way it always does, leaving me breathless. Soon, the end of that year brought on the summer months. And though it brought freedom from my studies, the harrowing realization of the differences between my two worlds was apparent. I was home, and within the enclosure of bodegas and sweet Italian ice. I could not think of cobblestone walkways. And I could not think of Benjamin Lati.

The Kiss

Sophomore year began as the first year did. However, an increased interest in Latin required the need for more classes, placing Ben with one teacher and myself with another. It wasn't until mid-year that we began to see each other again, due to my study hall coinciding with his volunteer hours at the library.

"Hey. You. Pencil dropper," he whispered, sneaking up behind me as I sat enthralled in a book.

"Jeez, Ben," I said as I adjusted myself in my seat trying to calm my nerves.

Noting that he had startled me, he offered his apologies while taking the seat across from me.

"Sorry. Didn't mean to scare you?" he began. "How are you? How was your Summer? I miss you in Latin."

"I'm fine. Summer was okay. Didn't do much. Only worked."

"Worked?"

"Yes. Worked. Some of us do that sometimes."

"Obviously," he said smiling. "How do you like the new Latin teacher, Mr. Jefferies?"

"He's nice," I answered dreamily, "I like him a lot."

"Oh, my goodness. Do you have a crush?" he asked. His smile was warm and inviting, as it widened with amusement.

"So. What is it to you?"

"Nothing. I just didn't expect you to be interested...in I don't know…that type of thing."

"And what is that supposed to mean?"

"I mean, I didn't expect you to be interested in the opposite sex like that," he replied.

I must have looked at him strangely, conveying my irritation, because he backpedaled, saying cautiously, "What I meant… is that… you've always seemed to be more interested in your studies than dating."

"Well, I am, but it doesn't mean I can't look," I answered tightly. "Also, I am hardly in the business of trying to pursue a relationship with a teacher."

"Well, that makes you different than some of our counterparts."

"No!" I squealed loudly, garnering the attention of the people around us. The look from the librarian was audible, translating loud and clear that I needed to be quiet.

"Shh," he chastised. "We don't need everyone knowing our conversation, do we?"

"Well excuse me. It's not my fault that you couldn't think of a better place to discuss something so absurd and crass, than in a library," I stated.

"Because we see each other so often, Colette?"

"Fine," I said conceding, "But really? Why are you surprised by my reaction?"

"Perhaps, it is because you would have to live under a rock to miss it. Come on, you don't see the flirtation around campus? Stolen glances everywhere? It's obvious."

"Flirtation doesn't equate to sex or a relationship, Ben," I said whispering to him.

"Why are we whispering?"

"I don't want people to know that we're talking about… you know…that."

His eyes widened as he asked, "You're a virgin, aren't you?"

"Shh," I snapped at him, "Not so loud."

"Why are you getting so touchy? It's just sex. It's not that serious."

It wasn't just sex to me. Where I grew up, sex got you in trouble. It was your sentence into that world, repeating the unrelenting cycle of generations before. My mother was aware of that fact, and the slap across my face she gave me the Summer before returning to school, still resonated her gruff words, "Stay away from them damn boys. I don't need no nappy headed little brats running around here. You be stupid if you want, and you'll find yourself getting worse."

Despite her forcefulness, it wasn't the physicality of her words that drove her point home. Like many girls from my neighborhood, I had already gotten a taste of what the sexual desires of boys and men could be, and that lesson was the deciding factor in making myself a promise to keep chaste. Finding my resolve, I sat up straighter in my chair and leaned in closer before saying to him, “That’s because its none of anyone’s damn business.”

He was a little taken aback and visibly flinched at my comment, which forced his speedy reply. “Touchy. Touchy. Touchy,” he said.

“Aren’t you one? A virgin, I mean?” I asked annoyed.

“Can you keep a secret?” he said, leaning in closer to me.

Rolling my eyes, I said, “Who am I going to tell, Ben?”

“I don’t know. Cordelia seems to be a safe bet. And we both know that if she knows, she’ll tell everyone. Goodness, I can’t stand the girl. She really is a bitch.”

“I won’t tell her anything. Not even the other girls, and they’re basically the only friends I have here,” I said shyly.

“You have me,” he said with a smile.

Looking into my eyes, his veil lifted, and he grew serious as he said, “Yes. I am. Contrary to what I said before, sex is a very big deal to me, and I think it should be shared with someone you love—and that will be my wife. So, I want to wait until I find the one I want to spend the rest of my life with. Is that strange?”

“Nope. Not strange at all. I could see that. I feel the same way.”

“Cool. That’s good to hear,” he smiled and brushed my hand lightly, and with a long elaborate sigh he said, “At least I’m not the only one who feels this way. Sometimes it seems like everyone is way too…”

“Stuck on sex and stupid,” I said finishing his sentence.

“Yes!” he exclaimed. Relaxing back in his chair, he waved towards the book in my possession. Changing the subject he asked, “So, what are you reading anyway?”

“One of the greatest books known to man—written by *Charlotte Brontë*, of course,” I said as I handed it to him.

Opening to one of the pages, he read a bit of the words etched across the page, “How can you read this?”

“Um…it’s a book and I’ve already learned to read, so—”

“Har. Har. Very funny. I meant that the use of language is so different than ours. It’s hard to follow.”

“Says you,” I said smugly.

“Meh. I can’t get into it,” he said, handing it back to me.

“Too bad. It’s positively lovely. She’s one of the greatest writers I’ve ever read. I love all her work,” I said as I opened back to the page I was on before he arrived. Looking down at the pages, I heard him shuffle in his seat in attempt to get my attention.

"So… you think I'm crass?" he said as he raised his eyebrows up and down suggestively. I couldn't help but laugh at him.

"Gosh, Ben. You're such a booger sometimes."

"But a very likable booger, right?"

"Yes, Ben. You are without a doubt, a very likable booger," I chuckled.

We went on like this for the rest of the year. From that day forward, I made sure that my study hall overlapped with his hours at the library. In those moments spent together, talking during his breaks, and helping him sort books, he and I developed a friendship unlike any other I had before. As the attraction for the other grew, it was clear that we enjoyed each other's company. Still, we said nothing of our growing affection for one another. Instead, our innocence blissfully led us into building the foundation for what was to come, as Summer came again, beckoning us home.

Junior year for Ben and me saw us without our usual talks. Our time spent in the library were no more, as our schedules divided us. On a campus so large, it was easy not to find one another. Our dormitories were on opposite ends, and without classes shared, we found ourselves missing opportunities to be together. It wasn't until our last year, when the reins of our studious life began to loosen, did we finally see each other.

It was in our school theatre house that Ben and I crossed paths again. I was reading over my lines when I felt the faint heat of someone breathing down my neck. I turned suddenly, spinning around in my seat, to come face to face with his smirked lips.

"Jesus, Ben!"

"My pencil dropper. I thought that was you," he said, embracing me.

"Why do you always have to scare me?"

"Because it's fun," he said plainly. "I missed you."

"I missed you too. Where have you been?!"

"Um… here. At school. Like you," he said. The laughter and mirth in his voice could not be missed.

"Don't be such a smartass, Ben. You know what I meant," I chided.

He had changed. Gone was the young boy of medium height I'd first met. While still slender, he was replaced by a young man, who now stood well over six feet tall. His shoulders were now thick and broadened, tapering down to full arms and abs that filtered through his school uniform. He had filled out nicely. His voice, once light and boyish, had become huskier and silky, morphing into a baritone that was not only calming, but commanding. The smooth baby skin he once sported, was now replaced with stubble growing across his chiseled olive face. Yes. He had changed.

"Well, I've been around. I saw you once, but you were moving so fast through the crowds I couldn't catch up to you. I tried every day for a week to see if I could spot you there again. No luck," he said with a shrug.

"Oh. I'm sorry," I said disappointed, wishing I had seen him.

"It's cool. We're with each other now. So, how have you been? How was life without me around?"

"Horrid. Boring. Abysmal," I said as I waved my hands about dramatically, hoping he would get how much I missed his presence.

"Good. I'm glad you missed me."

"How could I not?" I asked.

A tinge of red spread across his cheeks, lending a sparkle in his eyes he tried desperately to hide. Clearing his throat, he ran his hands nervously over his face before asking, "Did you work this Summer?"

"Affirmative. How about you? What did you do?"

"Oh nothing—I only threw a major bitch fit about moving to L.A. and having to leave here."

"Wait. You're leaving school?!"

"No. I convinced my parents to let me stay. Why leave when I'm already on my way out anyway, right? Plus, it would look really stupid on those pesky college applications if I transferred now."

"Oh. Well, I'm glad you're staying," I said sincerely.

"Me too. Why are you down here anyway? It's almost curfew."

Picking up the papers before me I said, "I was running lines after chorus. You?"

"Sweet. You're doing the play! I guess I would have seen you eventually anyway, since Akal is in it. Must be fate." he exclaimed. "As for me, I just came to get some peace. The guys are being annoying."

The guys, as he referred to them, were his best-friends—Paul, Jackson, and Akal. They were typical teenage boys. Their lives consisted of sports, girls, and computer games. However, Paul Hassan stood out from the rest of them. His parents were Kenyan ambassadors, who thought the world of their only son. He was built from lean muscle with carob hued skin, which gleamed in the sunlight. And he loved showing it off. He was always the fancy of some girl who sought a place on his arm.

Unlike Paul, Jackson McQueen was timid in nature. He only came to life when in the presence of the other boys, otherwise, he was rather reclusive. His pale features and fiery red hair descriptively illustrated his English and Scottish roots. He had wide set green eyes that seemed to be in a permanent look of perplexity. Always genteel, there was no denying his WASP up-bringing.

Then there was Akal Bayard-Patel. He was a sweet boy whose mother came from England and father from Gujarat. He was always considerate in the way he treated others. Lively, he was quite tall and muscular, with thick dark brows and light brown hair. One would have thought he would have been on some team or another, but he preferred the stage. As my interests lay there as well, I saw him often, and it was how I kept up with the rest of the boys, especially Ben. While they were all his friends, they also happened to be his dormmates, and they could be wild. Looking at him, I said, "I understand. I'm sure they're rapt in their own great game of jokes or that computer stuff I've overheard you boys talking about."

"Yeah, well, I need some quiet. Are you going to be here every night?"

"Probably. Why?"

"You mind if I sit with you sometime? Maybe hang out and talk like we used to?

Nodding my head, I replied, "I'd like that."

Sometimes became every night. From that evening forward, after rehearsals, while the theatre was empty, Ben and I would sit quipping about teachers and students alike. We spoke about our plans after graduation, which at that time, seemed so far away. Still, we didn't divulge our home life. It seemed to be a sensitive subject for us both, but that all changed the night we came to be. It was a night that would live on in our history and one that culminated in our life together.

That day began like any other day—unassuming in its monotony and mundanity. Nothing gave way to what was to come. I navigated the halls and walkways of campus as I always did, darting from one lecture to another wishing time would pass quickly, so that I could see Ben.

That night, he and I settled into our usual seats in the middle of the theatre, when our moment of solitude was interrupted by the sounds of chatter around us. As some of the crowd of pseudo and novice thespians left the room, and we took our usual place to begin what we thought would be another evening of tongue-in-cheek banter, we saw that some of our counterparts had other plans. It was then, that people-watching became more intriguing.

We watched as they bounced around the hall, taking on acts of daring play. It wasn't long before they noticed our presence, and Melanie, the play's lighting master decided to invite us to join them. We all played along, rousing each other up with games that we knew if caught, detention would be inevitable. Then it happened. The evening grew somber as couples began sneaking off into dark spaces, and the audible sounds of their teenage passion filled the air. I'm not sure what came over me in that moment, but I blurted, "You want to go make out?"

Glancing quizzically at me, he answered, "Really? Sure…I mean… if you want to."

Standing up from the edge of the stage that we'd been sitting on, he held out his hand until I gave him my own. Leading us backstage to where the old piano sat, he gestured for me to sit on top of it with him. Climbing up, I couldn't help the wave of anxiety that washed over me. I didn't understand why I felt that way. Afterall, Ben wasn't the first boy I'd kissed. By then, despite my mother's insistence, and my apprehension, I had had my fair share of kisses from boys who adorned themselves in dockers and cardigans. But I couldn't understand my nerves. It was Ben after all. My good friend. It should have been nothing to kiss him. But there I was, my heart racing and palms sweating, engulfed in the light darkness of heavy stage curtains—afraid of one, Benjamin Lati.

As we sat in silence in anticipation of a teenage triste, he finally spoke. His voice raspy and shaky, betrayed the uneasiness he tried desperately to hide. "Do you want to talk?" he asked.

I nodded to answer him. Noting his parted legs, I scooted between them until I felt my back hit his chest. We sat quietly for a moment. And as his breathing quickened, he slowly raised his arms and wrapped them around me, forcing me to lean into his warmth. "Can I tell you something?" he whispered, "I don't feel like I belong here. Or anywhere for that matter."

Staring up at him, I noted that for the first time, Ben didn't seem like himself. Gone was the laughter that often filled his eyes. It was replaced with something I couldn't quite identify, as if he were trying to mask the feelings rising within him. Even the touch of humor that always danced across his smirked mouth, seemed to fade. Looking up, deeply into his eyes, I smiled, hoping to coax him into going on. Sensing my intent, he said, "I just want to go home and have people actually care."

"Where is home by the way?" I asked.

In all my time spent with Ben, I never learned where he came from. And although I never spoke about such things, it never occurred to me that Ben didn't either. Our talks had been lively— rooted in fun, which was typical for Ben, a practical joker. Shifting a bit, he answered, "Brooklyn."

"Brooklyn?! I'm from Brooklyn!" I exclaimed. I knew my city, and Ben didn't behave like the boys from the Brooklyn I knew. So, in my curiosity I asked, "What part?"

"Crown Heights," he said cautiously.

I knew of Crown Heights. And I also knew that Ben wasn't like the Island or Latin boys that dwelled there. So, it could only mean one thing. I remember the day the rioting started; heated and passionate words of anger filled the air and spread through my home like wildfire. My family's words, which expressed a rage and grief over the loss of a child not their own, had resonated within my eleven-year-old body. When the riots began, anti-Jewish sentiment ran like blood through one's veins, with blind fury being at its epicenter. It fueled a destruction between our people, just as one's heart fuels the body. I remember feeling it course through me, for I felt my people's pain.

"You're Jewish?" I asked him, needing confirmation of what I already knew.

"Yeah," he replied. He went on to explain that his family was orthodox, and although his father owned a few small businesses, real estate was where the family had been most successful. He came from a strict conservative household, and his parents had high expectations for him and his siblings, which is why, Ben was sent to our school. He was being groomed for a life of running what his father fostered for their family. It was something that he didn't want for himself, but was imposed upon him, nonetheless. His family's move from The City was supposed to be an opportunity to expand their ventures, but it was one that Ben couldn't bring himself to concede to, especially if it meant leaving the city, we both loved.

Although he was his father's second son, having come from nothing, his father, as Ben put it, poured his heart and soul into whom he considered to be his most promising child. Unfortunately for Ben, that happened to be him. As I listened to Ben speak, I couldn't see the people I once saw as an enemy so long ago—I could only see him. Benjamin Lati. A kid from Brooklyn, just like me, trying to navigate his world the best way he knew how.

"It's just so much pressure, you know?" he asked rhetorically.

Of course, I knew what he meant. I knew what it was like for a parent to put so much into making you a success, you felt you would crack from the weight of their desires. I saw Ben's father and my mother as the same. From the time I was old enough to understand, I felt as though my mother poured into me, so I could be who she needed for the future. At times, I felt more like a retirement plan than I did her child. Still, she had given up her life and youth for me, and I felt I owed her in return.

"I know how that goes," I said in agreement.

"You do? But you always seem so… put together," he said, struggling to find the words.

"I'm not. My mother has decided that I am to become a doctor. Once upon a time it was her dream…until I ruined it," I said resentfully, "She had me when she was fourteen. Sometimes it feels like she's on a mission to live her life vicariously through me. Kind of like a second chance, I guess. You know?"

"What part of Brooklyn are you from?" he asked curiously.

"I'm from East New York."

He nodded his head as if he were finally understanding, and slowly tumbled out the words I had grown accustomed to hearing, "But you don't seem like you're… you know… not like those people," he fumbled, "What I mean is…you don't seem like you're from there."

Anger rose within me, shifting my once reserved nature into a prowling lioness. By this time in my life, I had grown used to such statements about my place of birth. Truthfully, I also judged the likeness and character of the people who made up the place I called home. I was guilty of the thoughts that were probably running rampant through his head. Despite this, I was also the witness of people coming together. I was part of a community who helped each other as much as we could. And as the positive memories of my childhood and visits home took hold, I found myself saying, "You know, you don't seem like a Jew either."

He stiffened. His body grew rigid, and it beckoned a strange sense of protection in me, making me regret my words.

"Touché. I'm sorry," he said sincerely.

"You know, there are hardworking people where I come from too. People who are kind and peaceful. My parents are that way. I'm that way. Perhaps you should learn more about those people," I stated heatedly as indignation began to rear its ugly head.

"Again, I'm sorry. Forgive me, Colette? I'm willing to learn if you teach me, as I hope you would learn about who I am and where I come from."

"I know about Jews," I said, as I felt the tension leave my body.

"Oh, you do? And what do you know about Jews?" he asked cautiously.

"I know about the *Sabbath*. I also know about *Hanukah*. It's the one where you give each other gifts—kind of like Christmas, right?" I spoke. He nodded, amused. Continuing, I expounded, "After the riots, I used to read books about you guys—your culture. The holocaust. Things like that. At the school I was in before coming here. You know…I always wondered what it was like to be one of you. You all seem so…insular. I guess I find that part intriguing."

This seemed to please him. He began to squeeze me more tightly, as he scooted himself lower, forcing my body to sink more into his, to which I obliged.

"We don't talk about the riots, you know? It wasn't easy for us either… what happened. Honestly, I wish it would have all gone differently. That none of it ever happened. It really caused a rift between our people, didn't it?"

"Yeah. It did. I can admit it changed my perception of you all. I was almost…I don't know, fearful to some extent," I reflected. "Hey…but look at us. At least we're friends."

"Yes. We're friends. Also, to backtrack a little, we're not all insular, as you say," he said thoughtfully. "Some are more liberal and open than others."

"I think I read that somewhere before. But, I don't remember exactly. It was some time ago."

"I'm glad that you know something about my people. At least you took the time to learn a bit about us. That says a lot. So often here, when I've spoken about who I am, I've gotten nothing but nastiness from many I thought were my friends. They try to brush it off as jokes and games, but I know better. Look…again…I'm sorry that I only thought about the bad in respect to where you come from."

"It's okay. As you probably have, I've grown used to it."

"But we shouldn't have to. God knows it's not easy for people like us here."

Looking up at him curiously I asked, "And what might that be?"

"Others," he replied, "Regardless of what people believe, I've learned that being Jewish is just as accepted as being Black in this place. Neither one of us truly belong here, do we? I know you've heard the things our Waspy friends have said, when they think we're not listening. That's why I've always liked you, Colette. You were always different from them… different to me," he said genuinely.

Leaning his head tenderly against mine, he went on to tell me about his life prior to arriving at our school. How he started out at *yeshiva*, but it wasn't right for him. He always felt like an outsider there, very much the same way I did at my previous school at home.

Growing quiet, we took in the silence around us, and listened to each other's breathing, completely relaxed in the tranquility of our surroundings. I was the first to speak, "Why do you feel as if no one cares?"

"Because they don't," he answered with unbound anger. "My parents only seem to care about business. Nothing else. Nothing more. It's the only thing my father ever talks to me about, or rather yells at me for."

"Sounds like most of the kids here. Comes with the territory, I guess. The life of the affluent. Everyone seems to be drowning in their parent's expectations of them becoming some fierce mogul; as if it's some sort of weird *manifest destiny* or something," I stated. "Honestly, I don't think you're alone. If I were to wager, I don't think most of our classmates want it—their future. They seem to be more like you, in that aspect. You're all pushed so hard. Why is that?"

"Rich people nepotism bullshit is why? I don't know. But I don't want any part of it. I want to do my own thing. Live my own life, you know? Not hear shit like, 'why are you not watching the stores? Did you check the shipments? You're so useless,'" he said, mimicking his father's words. "You know my eldest brother is there with me when I go home on weekends, while they're in L.A., right? But does he handle things? Nope. Instead, he uses up all the money my father sends us on the stupid girls he constantly brings home. There's never any food in the house, and I basically starve until I come back here."

"I'm so sorry, Ben. I didn't know."

"Don't be. Talking with you these past few weeks has made me forget about things at home. I feel whole when I'm with you, Colette," he revealed hesitantly.

"I'm glad," I replied, feeling at ease in his comfort.

As we sat back in the dark and serene silence, relaxing into each other once again, we heard the doors slam. It was followed by the loud, brash voice of the janitor, Mr. Edwards, "What are you kids doing in here?! You have until the count of ten to get back to your rooms, or I'm heading straight to the headmaster."

"What should we do?" I whispered frantically. As time got away from us, I hadn't realized how late it had gotten.

"Shh. Stay calm. Just wait here. He doesn't know we're behind here."

"But what if he catches us?"

"We'll be fine," he soothed.

I couldn't afford to get into trouble for breaking curfew. There was no recourse for me if I did anything to warrant my dismissal or tarnish my record. And although I knew I should get up and leave, there was something about Ben that made me want to throw caution to the wind. He had a way of making me feel strangely protected—and alive.

"Okay," I whispered.

We sat, frozen in place as we waited for the chaos to diminish. After hearing nothing, we slowly moved off the piano, making our way towards the end of the stage. Ben went down first, and then lifted me onto the floor.

"As always, my pencil dropper, it was great talking to you," he said playfully.

"Could you stop with that. I'm sure you can come up with a better nickname for me than pencil dropper," I said, feigning irritation.

"Hmm," he said. Putting his hand to his chin dramatically, he pretended to be in deep thought. "I got it. But if I give you one, you have to give one to me too."

"Okay. What about, Benny?"

"That quick, huh?"

"Well, I've sat on it for some time now," I said timidly.

"Really now? That's interesting. Why Benny?" he asked.

"I don't know. Ben just seems so…grown-up. And you're not an old man yet. You're playful. Fun. Kind of a clown," I rushed, "You look more like a Benny anyway."

Smiling and looking me over, as if he were looking at me for the first time he said, "I like it…Cole."

"Cole?"

"Yes. Cole. Because only when you put a lump of coal under pressure, do you get a diamond as rare and beautiful as you," he said sweetly.

I could see the earnestness in his eyes, and it made my knees weak, rendering me speechless. "Well, I'll see you. Same time tomorrow?" he said as he came in for our usual parting embrace. But at that moment my world went blank. I felt as if I were in a trance. It was as if we were being driven by a force and will not of our own. I don't remember the moments before it happened, I only remember the charge of electricity that crashed through my body when our lips touched, jolting me from my dream like state and forcing me back from him.

He spoke first, "I wasn't trying to… were you?"

"No. I… I have to go," I said as I frantically rushed toward the doors, leaving him where he stood. I rushed across campus—heading back to my dorm room, as I tried to understand what took place. My mind waging a war against me. *Did I kiss Ben? Oh, my goodness you kissed Ben! What does it mean? Does he like me? Of course, he likes you, stupid, he's your friend. But, no... I mean, does he like me, like me? Well, he called you beautiful, so obviously he likes you. He was just being nice. Shit, I kissed Ben!*

I didn't notice when I reached my room, nor did I feel myself opening the door. It wasn't until I heard Gwyn call out to me, that I realized where I was. The look on my face must have startled her because she asked, "Colette! Is everything alright?" Her words came faintly over the ringing in my ears.

"I kissed Ben," I said, still in shock.

I must have been unclear, because I could hear Mia saying, "What?"

Finally calming myself, I walked to my bed and sat before I spoke, "I kissed Ben!"

It was as if I were at confession. It didn't feel wrong, but something that felt so good—so right—well, it had to be sinful.

"Oh, big deal!" Cordelia exclaimed, "You act like he's the first boy you've ever kissed.

"This was different," I said to her contorted face. For some reason, she seemed angry at the news.

"Wait. You kissed, Ben? As in Benjamin Lati? Gross. Him? The Jew?" Mia stated. She could barely mask her disgust.

Instead of answering, I decided to lay in the safety of my bed. Turning my body away from them, I allowed myself to drift back to the night's events. I could still feel his lips on mine, and it was only then that I registered the taste of them—like sweet honey dew. Later, we would say that it was surely fate that brought us together.

Drifting to a sleep that would unquestionably be tormented, I heard our phone ring. Feeling a hard tap on my shoulder, I turned to see Cordelia thrusting the phone towards my face. "Here you are, *Cole*," she said incensed, "It's *Benny* on the line for you."

And so began my life with him, and the end to a not so ordinary day.

A Woman Lost

Placing his notepad beside him, he sighed deeply as his mind raked over the purpose of her story. "From the tale you tell, I'm not sure why you're here," he said.

"That was only our beginning, Doc. If it were the whole story, I wouldn't be here," she stated.

She seemed calmer now. Somehow, the story of their beginning had eased her anxiety. Her demeanor changed—she no longer sat like she wanted to fold within herself and hide from his gaze. With posture now straightened and legs crossed alluringly, she indicated a confidence that wasn't present upon her arrival into his office.

"I guess, I should try this again—your marriage seems to have a decent foundation, so what is actually lacking?" he asked.

"I think the better question is: What changed? And to answer your question? Well, that is another story. For another session," she said lightly.

Watching him, she noted his vexation. And she wondered if she should answer his question, but just as quickly as the idea popped into her head, it left. She needed this. She needed to take charge and commit to something that would make her feel good. This was her time, and she wouldn't allow anyone to rush it. If he knew the road she'd traveled, and truly understood the suffering she faced, he wouldn't be so quick to hurry this process she had undertaken. Leaning forward in her seat, she said to him, "Is there anything else?"

"Why, Mae? Why that name?" he asked after a painful pause; his body was slumped forward, and his eyes were glazed over with the same perplexity and suspicion he had during her story.

"Mae is everything I am not. I need her. I need her to get through… this."

"What's wrong with being you?"

Closing her eyes and breathing in deeply, she gained the strength needed to face her reality, "She is neither confident nor able. She has neither strength nor courage. She is nothing. At least nothing… to him."

"Mrs. Lati—"

"Mae. I really would prefer if you called me Mae, Doctor."

"Mae," he said correcting himself, "I believe that perhaps we should focus on you. The *real* you."

Staring at him blankly, her mind drifted as she began to consider his question, when she noticed the time on the clock sitting on his desk in her periphery. "Oh no. I have to go," she stated as she stood abruptly, and made her way towards the door.

"But we still have more time for our session."

"I'm so sorry. I really must run. I forgot that it's the Sabbath. I must get home and get everything ready. See you next week, okay," she said on her way out.

Riding the subway had always given her peace. The roaring sounds of the train as it passed through tunnels, put her at ease. She'd focus on the feel of its vibrations as it moved along the tracks. It made her feel like a child being comforted by the smooth rocking of their mother's arms, as they were lulled to sleep. On her rides, she'd watch the other patrons. She would observe as they jostled their way through the city—assigning stories to them to distract her from her life. She hoped that wherever they ended up, they would find a happiness she couldn't seem to obtain.

She watched a mother across from her struggle with her toddler. The young child seemed over his subway adventure. Twisting and writhing his body about, he attempted to free himself from the confines of his stroller. She smiled at his mother reassuringly, hoping that it would give her the resilience to endure her son's tantrum. At that moment, a group of young street performers came by—their music, dancing, and flips and turns became a welcomed distraction that pacified the once screaming child. The city had a way of doing that. Coming to one's rescue when you least expected it. As Colette approached her stop, one of the young men tipped his hat in front of her, and she placed a few bills inside.

Gathering her groceries, she walked to the door and waited for the train to slow and its doors to open. Feeling a tap on her shoulder, she turned to see the young man she'd given money to. His red baseball cap was now planted firmly on his head, and doelike eyes peered from underneath its brim. The color of his cap and matching jersey, highlighted the redness in his brown skin. While the rest of the boys gathered their things to head to the next car, he decided to approach her.

"Thank you so much! What you did means a lot," he said sincerely. She hadn't meant for him to see how much she'd given him, but she was glad that she was able to help.

"You are very welcome. You boys did an excellent job."

"You don't understand, Miss. This is money to help me pay for college," he replied.

His accent played like music to her ears. It had been a long time since she'd been to that side of Brooklyn—the place that once held her heart. She didn't think about it often, but sometimes, on days like today, she missed it. Hearing the young man speak, dredged up memories of her humble beginnings, putting a smile on her face.

"No. I do understand. I appreciate what you guys are doing."

"Thank you. You need any help with your things?" he offered as the train stopped.

"No. But, thank you. Now, you go make that money," she said with a wink, and stepped off. The women selling *churros* she spotted was the only thing on her mind before heading toward the stairs that would carry her home.

Exiting the station, as she walked, she marveled at the tree-lined city blocks. The vibrancy of its greenery never ceased to amaze her. The transformations that happened during Spring, filled the concrete space with such beauty, she couldn't help but be transfixed by it. She always loved walking this part of the city growing up—the white, caramel, and penny-colored splashed brownstones had always seemed out of place to her. Yet she always wished she'd have a place amid the beautifully built buildings. Now, there she was, walking along the immaculate row of homes until she reached her own.

Approaching her steps with keys in hand, she was stopped by a familiar voice, "Colette. Oh, Colette, honey."

Letting out a tense sigh, she braced herself for the conversation she knew would ensue. It was her neighbor—Mrs. Feinstein. She was a woman who had come into their lives blazing with energy. Although an elder, Miriam Feinstein was a force to be reckoned with. She had honey-blonde hair that was always perfectly coiffed; while her green eyes appeared deep in thought and complimented an aquiline nose that sat above full lips. She reminded Colette of an old Hollywood starlet—elegant and beautiful. And she was as picturesque as the trees lining their neighborhood.

They had met the day Colette moved into their home. Unlike their neighbors, Miriam had made it a point to introduce herself. Noting the *mezuzah* on the door when she entered to have a spot of tea, she invited Colette to her *shul*. From then on, she took the young woman under her wing, never once judging her for her upbringing the way others had done. With her only child living in Israel and her husband Perceval frequently away, Miriam was always around to keep watch of Colette and Benny's brood.

In truth, although Miriam could irritate her, Colette recognized how remarkable she was. As a child, she watched her father, a rabbi, and her artist mother, become part of the Civil Rights Movement. They marched side by side thousands of others, who wanted nothing more, as Miriam put it, than to have the freedom to choose the life they desired. Her parents' walk from Selma to Montgomery had been harrowing—still, it never deterred them from fighting. It was something that had a profound effect on Miriam. By the time she reached eighteen, she'd become quite familiar with the inside of a jail cell. Her activism eventually led her in protest of the Vietnam War and in becoming a leading advocate for the Women's Rights Movement. Later in life, she became a successful author, whom Colette read frequently and thoroughly enjoyed.

In the years that followed their initial encounter, she'd become a surrogate mother to Colette and acted as a grandmother to her children, who called her *Bubbe*. They loved on her as grandchildren would. Yes, Miriam Feinstein was wonderful. She was a constant beam of light when Colette could feel nothing but darkness. However, it was her motherly intuition, Colette could not stand. It was as if she could smell when something was wrong with her, and today wasn't the day she wanted to be told, what she could be doing to make things better. It was something she couldn't bear, even if it were done with loving kindness.

Turning to her with a forced smile she said, "Hello, Miriam."

Miriam stood quietly for a moment as she studied Colette like a locksmith trying to pick a stubborn lock, making her grow anxious. "I spoke to Sarah today," Miriam charged.

"Oh? And how did that go?"

"She said she's worried about you."

"Miriam, why don't you get on with it," Colette said smartly. She had not meant to be gruff, but she didn't have the energy to deal with their encounter. After all, she had dinner to make before the Sabbath began, and she was already behind.

With a raise of her perfectly sculpted brows, Miriam began to say something, but thought better of it. She was going to dismiss the slight from the woman she considered a daughter. Instead, she started again, treading lightly this time, "Well… Sarah said that…why she said that… you were seeing someone for counseling."

"I am. I'm seeing someone," Colette replied tightly, as she made a mental note to rip Sarah to shreds. Their exchange was to be confidential, and she did not appreciate her talking to anyone about her current state—especially if that someone was Miriam.

"Why did you not come to me first?"

"I didn't want to worry you."

"Oh darling, you could never be a worry to me," she said, placing her hand gently on Colette's shoulder.

This was why she had not come to her. One look into those piercing eyes and gentle way in which Miriam handled her, so very much like her grandmother, made Colette want to hide in shame.

"I know that I am not, but you shouldn't have to come to my rescue."

"You're my family. You are the daughter I always wished *HaShem* would send me," said Miriam. "I bet it's that Benjamin again. Goodness, I've always told Perceval that I wish you would have crossed paths with my Joshua, instead of the menace he's married to," she said heatedly.

"Miriam! She isn't that bad," Colette chuckled.

"You know very well that she is! Now don't try to change the subject. Are things still going badly between you two?"

"Yes. They are. But I assure you, Miriam, I have it handled."

"The hell you do. You should be turning to your husband instead of Sarah. He should be your confidante. Not her," Miriam chided. "Are you two still not sharing a bed? I bet that's what you need."

"Miriam! Really?! Not everything can be fixed with sex," she said taken aback. Colette could never get used to the forwardness of the woman she considered a second mother.

"It's a start. Intimacy is important, darling. Why, Perceval and I—"

"I'm going to stop you right there," Colette interrupted.

Looking her over, Miriam couldn't understand how a man like Benjamin didn't have the beautiful woman in front of her in his arms every night. But they weren't always this way. There were times where he absolutely adored Colette; their love, true and unbridled, would set a glow upon her that resonated through her entire being. Still, over the years, Miriam had witnessed moments where Benjamin would take a pronounced disinterest in his bride. In most cases, it came on suddenly—his mood would shift as quickly as a changing wind; bringing on a melancholy that would fill the Lati household with fretfulness and fear.

Although it had been years since his tide had changed, this year had been far worse than others. He seemed to fixate, as Miriam observed, on working himself hard; as if he were purging some demon within himself.

While Miriam did not dislike Benny, per se, he grated at her nerves because she thought the world of Colette. She was stunning. In truth, her Joshua was in-love with her, and she couldn't blame him. The young woman before her was everything she could ever want in a daughter. She had class and grace. And was filled with compassion for everyone, no matter their station. Her girl had worked hard for the success she shared with her husband. But there she stood, with the same look of defeat she now often saw on her face. A beauty this rare should not wear a look of sadness like a crown, Miriam thought. No matter how hard Colette tried to mask it, Miriam knew misery when she saw it. Trying to lighten the mood she said, "Oh honey—what do you think keeps my marriage alive and great?"

"Miriam, you're too much," Colette laughed.

"I'll tell you one thing… you young girls forget that its good for you too—"

"I am hardly a young girl, Miriam. And I am not without the experience of it."

"Considering your age, you are not beyond the need for wisdom, my dear. You're a baby. At least you are to me," Miriam said lovingly. Reaching down for one of the bags, she said, "Now come. I'll help you make dinner for *Shabbos*. Percy and I are having dinner with you. You know, Kami is in too."

"You don't have to carry it. I will."

"My sweet girl—I know that I am old, but I am not decrepit. Now let go of the bag."

Colette couldn't help but smile and wish that she were as strong as the small woman beside her. Releasing the bag to her, they walked together up the stairs to prepare the house for the holy night. As she approached the threshold, her apprehension began to build. She knew that with her husband's arrival, she was in for a night of heated tension. And with Miriam now in attendance, after the days he had of late, she knew the distance she'd face from him. It made her wish she could hide away from it all, until the morrow.

Home

Walking into the home of Benjamin and Colette Lati, one would think that the couple who resided in such opulence would have it all. The brightly colored walls, painted a creamy white hue, gave a sense of openness and airiness to their well-maintained residence. Entering the foyer, you'd find a beautiful rounding staircase with black wrought-iron bannisters lined atop white marble stairs. To the right of the entryway, housed the family's formal living room. It was adorned with the furnishings and fixtures the couple acquired over the years during their travels. And their grand dining room was dressed in acacia wooden furniture, they had fallen in-love with during a trip to Zambia.

Walking through the open space of the entryway toward the kitchen and family room, one would find photos of their life together placed strategically along the wall. The laughter and love captured in time, spoke of moments, Colette no longer held with esteem. She couldn't recognize the faces that peered out from them. They sat, mockingly so, of what once was. And no matter how much she tried to feel the pleasure of the couple gazing back at her, she felt nothing—especially not that of a woman who had it all.

As she put her groceries on the venetian gold countertops, she spotted her younger sister, Kami. She was named after their father, Kevin. And although he was not Colette's biological father, he was the only father she'd ever known. The one who sired her, desired the pipe that housed his addiction more than he loved her.

The day her parents brought home the screaming little girl with jet black hair, was the day, Colette first learned what it meant to love. She always wanted a sister; and when her parents told her that she was to have one, she waited as patiently as a ten-year old girl could for her arrival. The moment she held Kami her heart swelled. Staring down at her face, she knew instantly who the little girl was to be—her baby. From that day forward, she spoiled Kami, and not much had changed since then.

Finally noticing her presence, her sister began to make her way to her, filling Colette with love and admiration at the woman she'd become. Her curly afro adorned her head like a crown, framing her oval shaped face, that housed a perfectly round nose atop a smirked full mouth. Like Colette, she stood tall, with long legs that trailed up to a firm and ample backside, which extended from a tiny, cinched waist. She had taken on the richness of their mother's coloring—its dark mahogany tone made her skin gleam and bright, as if it'd been kissed by the sun. She was as beautiful as Colette knew she would be.

"Lee-Lee," Kami said as she ran into her arms, using the pet-name she had for her since babyhood. "I need your help!"

Never wanting to see her sister in distress, Colette asked, "What's wrong, Kami?"

"The restaurant called and said they can't accommodate us for the bridal shower," she said in a panic.

Colette still couldn't believe that the little baby her mother placed in her arms so long ago was getting married. She couldn't wait to see her walk down the aisle. "I'll call them. Don't you worry. I'll take care of it by weeks end," she said soothingly.

"Thanks, Colette," she heard in the distance. "See, honey. I told you she would fix it," came from Akal.

Never would she imagine that he would be the one to sweep her baby sister off her feet. After graduating secondary school, they'd lost track of each other. Like most, college and life had sent them down different paths—forcing them apart. Later, a chance business venture would forge their reconnection, and place him in proximity to her sister.

Afraid that their age difference would cause strife in the family, Kami and Akal had kept their romance secret, until their love toppled over into an engagement, Colette now found herself preparing for. She and her parents were apprehensive at first, but Akal proved himself to be who he'd always been. He handled her sister with such patience and kindness, it moved her. Colette was thrilled for them.

Akal sat, planted in her family room, watching television with her girls and youngest son, as if he had always been part of their family. He hadn't changed much since their formative years. His handsome face still expressed an air of mystery, while his demeanor still commanded calm and tranquility. He adjusted his position, languidly so, to not disturb the peace of the children who sat comfortably in his arms. Nodding his greetings to Colette, they exchanged amused glances over the poutiness of his future bride.

Turning to face her fiancé, Kami shouted, "No thanks to you."

"You really do worry too much, honey," he said as he rose from his place on the sofa, rousing the little ones. They really did love their Uncle Akal.

"I… really, no like really…need you to be a bit more serious about things," Kami said through gritted teeth. "It's your wedding too. You know?"

Taking her into his arms, he said playfully, "You really are becoming one of those crazy brides. I believe I've spoiled you too much."

"We. We have all spoiled her. Lord knows, my Colette does," Miriam said, looking up from her preparations of the *challah*. She was a master at it. They all loved the sweet tastiness of the bread and other treats she baked.

"Why is everyone picking on me today? I am not spoiled, Momma Miriam," Kami said with a stomp of her foot, before burying her head into Akal's chest, causing them all to let out a laugh at her inflated display of testiness. With feelings hurt, her pout became more exaggerated, capturing Colette's attention. Seeing her little sister sulk always struck a nerve with her, and it prompted her need to defend her.

"You guys, leave my Kami alone," she said as she made her way back to the kitchen.

"You see what I mean?" Miriam said with a pointed finger. "May HaShem help you, Akal, my dear. You have your work cut out for you, son."

"I am well aware," he said. "However, I am more than prepared to tame the beast that is my fiancée."

At this, Kami swatted at him, "You're not funny," she snapped.

"Ouch. That hurt!" Akal reacted, rubbing his arm dramatically as if in pain. Her ego bruised, Kami decided it was better to join her nieces and nephew, to which her fiancé followed not far behind.

"Are you guys staying for *Shabbat*, Akal?" Colette called to him.

"We sure are," he replied.

"Are your parents back, hun?" Miriam asked Colette. "I wanted to see if your mom wanted to have dinner with me next week. There's this new place, I know she'll love."

"No. And you know what? She's been rather weird lately. Now that I think of it. Both she and Dad have been."

"I must agree with you there, sis. Mom has been rather weird the last few months. I've never in my life had to play telephone tag with her this much. And she looked off the last time I saw her. That is, when she's allowed a visit. It feels like she's ghosting us, to be honest," Kami said.

It was strange the way in which her mother had become suddenly unavailable. Throughout their lives, she had always made herself accessible to her and Kami. Although her parents had entered a new stage in life, there was something about their mysterious bouts of travel and seclusion that pestered her. "I'll check in with them when they get back," Colette replied.

"I'll give her a call also, when Shabbos is over," Miriam said, turning her focus back to preparing the bread. Colette dug in following suit. And as they began working together to create the lavish meal that would accompany a night of prayer and family, her mind returned to him. Dread washing over her, once again.

By the time he arrived, the women of the house had transformed the Lati home into blissful serenity. Kami had come out of her funk long enough to assist the older children in finishing up the cleaning. The large dining table was draped in a beautiful ivory Moroccan lace runner, which complimented its Jacobean-stained color. And the lights were dimmed, so that the only illumination stemmed from the Shabbat candles, that sat elegantly in the middle of the dining buffet.

They had worked hard in preparing the night's meal, and the perfume of lamb with raisins, apricot, vegetables, and spices cooked in *tagine*, accompanied by *couscous*, salad, and asparagus soup, permeated through the house. The fragrant scent of the bread, Miriam baked, helped to complete a symphony of aromas that tickled their senses. It was intoxicating. Grabbing wine from the cellar, Colette placed it on the table to finish its dressing. While admiring her handy work, a sense of calm washed over her. The ritual of preparation on this night had always brought her peace.

Noting the hour, it was when she decided to hand over the reins to Perceval to begin the night's blessings, that he walked through the door. The rush of pounding feet and laughter coming from the foyer, as the girls came tumbling in, indicated his arrival. "*Abba* is here!" they screamed simultaneously, as he strolled up behind them, scooping Charlotte, eight, into his arms.

Colette watched him closely as he planted light kisses on their daughter's caramel-colored cheeks, making her almond-shaped dark brown eyes light up with laughter from his beard tickling her. As their daughter pulled away from his attack, Benny looked deeply into her eyes, admiring her beautiful face. Touching his head to hers, he played with the soft, silky curls of her auburn-colored hair, which fell to her waist, and whispered tenderly against her cheek, "*Neshama sheli.*"

"Hey. You're forgetting someone," said Nala, their twelve-year-old daughter. She had come to them during a time of inexplicable need. From the moment they picked her up from the hospital where she was born, he'd adored her without reservation. Touching the smoothness of her dark brown skin, with loving eyes, he planted a light kiss upon her forehead, and said to her, "You know, I could never forget my beautiful doll. You look magnificent today."

Palming the tight, jet-black coils on her head that framed her delicate face, he walked her forward toward the family room as he carried Charlotte in his arms and said, "Come. Tell me about your day."

As he passed, he glanced at her. Leaving her in place, without so much as a sound passing from his lips. His face, now contorted with tension, told Colette what her night would hold. "*Shabbat Shalom* to you too," she said solemnly to his back, as she walked slowly behind him; uncertainty now, filling her core.

After his arrival, they all settled into their places at the table for dinner. She only faintly heard the prayers as they were being said. Instead, she watched his expressions and movements from her seat, as she sat quietly at the other end of their dining room table. It wasn't until Miriam leaned in, telling her it was time to serve, that she realized just how distracted she'd become. Rising, she called to her eldest daughter, so that she could help pass the plates of salad to the men, while the women prepped the other dishes.

Entering the kitchen, Colette felt their eyes on her. Waiting until Nala was out the door with her second plate, she yelled in frustration, "What?! Why are you two gawking at me?"

It was Miriam who spoke first, "Dear, I am so worried about you two, I don't know what to do with myself."

"It's fine. Everything is fine. Stop worrying."

"It's fine? Your marriage is not an 'it,' my girl," Miriam replied passionately.

"Lee-Lee… you know how much I love Ben…and you know that I'd be the first to say if Momma Miriam was being her meddling self again," Kami said playfully, smiling at the older woman, "But things haven't been…I don't know…right? Sis, what's going on?"

"Nothing is going on," Colette said tightly, feeling herself grow tense.

"Nonsense. In what world is it okay for a man to not greet his wife as he enters their home?" said Miriam.

"Him not greeting me is not the end of the world—"

"I'll tell you what kind," Miriam interrupted, but stopped herself as Nala entered the kitchen to grab another plate. Watching as the girl left once more, she brought her voice down to a whisper, "Listen, when a man is neglecting his wife in such a way, you cannot fault those who are in wonder as to why. I mean… look at how late he strolled in. On the most important night of the week, at that! What was he doing that was so important? And does he say anything once he is home? No. The chutzpah!"

"He could have been at shul, Miriam," Colette responded, becoming exhausted from it all.

"You and I both know that he was not. Unless shul is serving rounds of whiskey, which I would know, he was not there. I have it in my right mind to ask him," she said impetuously.

"Oh goodness, Miriam. Please don't."

At that moment, Colette knew she would have no peace that night. She had it in her right mind to beg her, but she knew that Miriam was in a mood. With dinner plated in its entirety, she inwardly prayed that she could hold on to the ride to come.

"That was splendid!" Colette heard Perceval say from his seat. It was seating that was normally occupied by her eldest son, Judah. She missed his presence in their home. He'd just completed his first year of college, but the contention between him and his father made visits rare. Lately, he'd taken to finding comfort at Leila's home—his high school sweetheart. She knew that he was likely sharing this night with her family instead. The longer she was without her son, the more her anger towards her husband grew. She wanted her son home. Their meetings once a week at the little café near his studio apartment, were not enough. If he weren't so hard on him, Judah would be here, where he belongs, Colette thought.

Glancing over at the Feinsteins, she watched as Perceval caressed his wife's arm lovingly. "My compliments to you dazzling beauties. I can't believe how lucky we are to have such fine cooks on our hands," he said as he took a sip of his coffee—his eyes never leaving his wife. He seemed spellbound, as if he were admiring her beauty for the first time. She loved the way they looked at each other. They made her believe that their kind of love could be possible for her again. And she hoped with all her might, that her plan would work.

Despite the company of her family, Colette had never felt more alone. She watched as Akal whispered something sweetly in her sister's ear, igniting a smile that spread across her face. Her son, Luke, seventeen, was tickling her youngest son Zachary, who was three-years old, making him squeal. His face reddened by laughter, normally the color of a baby fawn, was caressed by soft ringlets of golden-brown curls that bounced as he giggled from his brother's onslaught. She loved how close the two of them were.

Then there was him. He had settled in his place at the head of their table with their two girls at his side, basking in their adoration and trying his best to give each of them his full attention. He was always so gentle and loving in respect to them; it was a way in which he had not been with her in some time. In truth, she was jealous of the affection he had for their daughters, which made her even more broken by her growing shame. It wasn't just his aloofness that made her feel the distance between them; it was the lack of care and kindness he no longer granted her. A tenderness he still possessed and she could clearly see in the way he managed their children.

As if sensing her discomfort, Miriam cleared her throat, signaling that she was about to speak, making Colette brace herself for her words, "So, Ben," she heard Miriam say in preparation. "Do tell…why were you so late to dinner this evening?"

He looked up at Miriam with a look that was usually reserved for her, and Colette knew that it was going to be an unpleasant affair. Even Perceval began to shift uncomfortably in his seat, as tension replaced the smile Benjamin had just moments before when speaking with their daughters. Straightening up in his seat he said to her, "While you are certainly a light in our lives, Miriam…where I was prior to entering my home, is none of your concern."

Colette could feel his hostility brewing, and at that moment she wished she were anywhere but there. She watched as Miriam coolly looked him over. Her soft green eyes, narrowed in suspicion. The room was so quiet that you could hear a pin drop. Sensing that what was to follow would not be for young eyes and ears, Akal and her sister stood, and asked the children to follow them to the family room.

As Perceval and Colette watched them leave, Miriam and Benny's eyes never left each other. He was the first to speak, "Look, Miriam, I'm not going to do this with you tonight."

"Do what exactly? I just asked a simple question, dear. You see, I find it incredibly odd that you were so late," she said coyly.

That had done it. His entire demeanor changed. Colette could see his jaw tighten as he tried to control himself. His smirked mouth, once relaxed, became menacing. "I was at the bar with some colleagues, but again that isn't any of your business, now is it?" Benny replied through clinched teeth.

"Well, it is the business of your wife, and since she can't seem to muster enough moxie to ask you, I'm doing it for her. There isn't any reason for a married man with children, on a night like tonight, to stroll in smelling like a bar," Miriam spat.

"Perceval," said Benny, as he nodded his head toward Miriam. His warning was subtle, but his message was clear. He needed the older man to get control of his wife.

Understanding his intent, Perceval cleared his throat trying to gain Miriam's attention, "Honey, perhaps we should leave this to the two of them." Rising from his seat, he hoped that his wife would follow suit.

"No. I. Will. Not!" Miriam stated firmly. It was clear that she had no interest in backing down.

"Miriam. It's okay. Really. I can handle it. Just let it be."

"I'm sorry, Colette. But I will not sit by and watch this train wreck," she replied. Turning her attention to Benny, she said with a pointed finger, "And, you?! The least you could have done was give your wife a call. What about saying hello to her when you entered? Can you not do that anymore, even?"

"I didn't realize I needed permission to go to the bar for a fucking drink. Excuse the hell out of me," Benny replied nonchalantly. "In fact, I think I could use a drink right now. *May* I please have a fucking drink?"

"Don't you use that language with me, young man," Miriam chastised.

"Oh. I'm sorry, didn't ask the wife's permission first. May I please use the word 'fuck'?" he said looking towards Colette, who was mortified. She hated when he behaved this way. Although she knew that Miriam could sometimes speak out of turn, she knew she meant well, and he knew the same.

"Benny, please—" Colette pled.

"Please, what?! All I want to know is if I have your permission to use the word 'fuck' in my home. Or do I need permission to even do that? Fine. May I please have permission to ask your permission to use the word fuck?"

"Ben, really. Calm down, son," said Perceval, trying to choke the flame that was now burning within the young man before him. "I know that you're angry, but there is no need for—"

"And there really isn't a need for your wife to interfere. My wife and I are fine," Benny retorted.

Colette closed her eyes at his denial of their current state. She didn't understand why he didn't want help, or at the very least, talk about why things had changed so much.

"Oh, really? Do you know that she's seeing a shrink? I had to hear that from Sarah Cohen, for crying out loud," Colette heard Miriam say.

Why did she have to tell him? Especially that Sarah knew, Colette thought, flinching inwardly. She could feel his eyes on her, and as she opened them slowly, the glare on his face made her want to shut them again. Looking into his eyes, she hoped that the regret she felt would translate to him and deter him from acting out. To her relief, Perceval spoke, and broke the trance of contention between them, "Ben, why don't we go into the study, son? I'm sure a bit of scotch could do us both some good. Give everyone a moment to cool off. What do you say?"

Benny didn't say a word. Instead, he stood, fists down on the table assisting in lifting him from his seat, while he stared Colette down. She lowered her head and stared at the palms of her hands. She could hear his feet shuffle out the room, and a few moments later, the sound of the front door slamming, vibrated through their home. Still, she sat in her seat, unable to move—defeated.

Severed

It was well into the witching hours when she heard him walk through the door. The sound of him stumbling through the foyer and up the stairs to their bedroom awakened her from her slumber on the couch in the family room. She thought back to his exit from their home just hours before. Leaving her in the wake of his rage, Miriam and Perceval came to her rescue and comforted her, making her reel from embarrassment. Still, Colette was happy that they stayed to keep everything in order. They both worked with her sister and Akal to settle the children and finish what little chores there were to do; they were a welcomed distraction to her young ones. They tried not to look at their mother—neither of them wanted to come to her aid, for fear of what they may find.

She waited in silence and watched as time ticked by on the clock above the mantel. If she played her cards right and waited long enough, she knew that she would find him peacefully asleep; the night's drink taking him to slumber. If true, it would help her avoid the confrontation she'd dreaded having, once she realized Miriam would be joining them for dinner earlier that evening.

With the hour passing, she listened carefully to the sounds of the house to ensure that sleep had consumed him. Finding only the sound of water trickling down into the kitchen sink, she headed upstairs towards the room she shared with him. Stopping, she looked at the pictures that adorned the walls and couldn't help but think herself a fake. How long had she been planting the perfect smile on her face, to create the perfect picture, which would sit in a perfect frame? All of which masked just how imperfect things truly were.

So many things seemed to plague her as she wondered what went wrong in her life. At this point, she could hardly stand to look at herself in the mirror anymore. She wondered if he knew—if he knew how much of a phony she truly was. *Is that why he doesn't love me anymore? Can't love me? Has he finally realized that I wasn't worth the trouble?*

Finally arriving at their bedroom door, she took hold of the knob. Turning it slowly, she pushed forward with care, so that she would not wake him. Passing the bed, she tiptoed toward the bathroom to shower, with hope that the warmth of the water would relax her enough to brave a night next to him. Turning the water on, she waved her hand through to test the temperature and played with the pressure with her fingertips. The sound of the water mesmerized and placed her in a trance, bringing her back to the time she met the boy with large Greek eyes. She thought about their life together and the way it had changed over the years. She knew that those who knew them in passing would certainly shun her for the way she viewed her life with him. But if only they knew. If they truly knew what the years had brought her, they wouldn't be so quick to judge her despair.

Stepping into the heat of the water, she worked to wash her body and hoped to cleanse her mind, so that sleep would claim her once more. She tilted her head back and allowed the waves of balminess to run over her, making her feel anew. Forcing herself to relinquish the need to stay in the safety of the water, she reached for her towel that always hung next to his. Unable to find it, she waited for the steam to lift, so that she could see better, when she came face to face with him, holding her towel in his hand. By the look in his eyes, he was not over the clash between him and Miriam. And by the smell of him, he had had more than his fair share. As his eyes wandered over her salaciously, she suddenly felt self-conscious and quickly placed her arms around herself to cover her body. This seemed to anger him. With narrowed eyes, he tossed her towel in her face, and watched as she quickly wrapped herself in it.

"Why did you invite that woman here?" he asked harshly. Walking past him, she headed toward the vanity that connected to the entryway of their walk-in closet. Before she could pull out her chair to sit, he grabbed her gruffly by the arm, drawing her near to him, unimpressed by her rebuff. "Why. Did. You. Invite. Her. Here?" he bit out again.

Saying nothing, she glanced at his hand on her arm and brought her gaze back to his eyes, bidding him to let her go. Taking heed, he released her slowly. Sitting, she began her nightly routine as she tried to gain her composure. Feeling his eyes on her through the mirror, she didn't dare look at him. Instead, she continued the process of readying herself for bed, and hoped that she would find the strength to combat him.

"When do I ever invite her? She invites herself. And it's not like she's not welcomed here," Colette said gently.

"Says who?! Who says she's welcomed here?"

"Come on, Benny. Not tonight," she said trying to soothe him.

"Don't fucking 'come on, Benny', me. For once I would like to come into my home without some bullshit. With some peace."

"It's not me who disturbs the peace in our home, Benjamin," she snapped.

The moment she said it, she regretted it. She had not meant to be snarky, but she was growing wary of battling the man who held her heart. Looking toward him, she found him staring at her with such crossness she couldn't help but flinch. "What I mean to say is that we all want you home, Benny. It would be nice if you would just spend a bit more time—"

"I spend time with our kids, Colette," he said cutting her off.

"Well, then, it would be nice if you'd come home and spend time with me. I need… I need you too, you know?"

"Here we go. Here. We. Go. Go on. Tell me how I'm being such a shit to you," Benny sneered.

"I don't mean it like that!" she cried, "I just want to have my husband. You don't talk to me anymore, and you're drinking again—"

"Don't fucking start that shit, Colette!" he roared.

"Can you calm down please. You're going to wake the kids," she said as she walked through their closet, with him fast on her heels. Grabbing her night gown, she began placing it over her head as she said, "Why do you always have to yell at me? I'm not asking for much, Benjamin."

"You shouldn't be asking for anything. You want for nothing. You have a beautiful home, cars, an expense account."

"That's not what's important. I want you," she said.

She reached to caress his face, but he pulled away from her. Dropping her hand, she felt ashamed that she attempted the gesture. Walking into their room, she made her way towards their bed, and turned down the sheets so that she could get in. She felt as he climbed in after her, and whether it was a half-hearted attempt to regain some sense of dignity or a moment of passioned indignation, she turned and said through clenched teeth, "You know, it's not like you got all of this by yourself. If it weren't for me, you'd still be a snot-nosed little punk trying to figure out a way to get from under his father's thumb! I shouldn't have to beg my husband to want me!"

For a moment, she thought she saw an inkling of remorse in his eyes, but just as quickly as it passed across his face, it was replaced with unobscured rage, and she knew then that she was in for it.

"You're right. No wife of mine should have to beg to be fucked," he said to her in such a hushed tone, it sent chills down her spine.

"Benjamin?"

The terror in her voice could not be mistaken. Slowly, she began to rise—for fear that any sudden movement would disturb whatever calm was left in him. As intuition took control of her, she tried to make a run for the door, when she felt his hands tugging her forcefully back toward the bed. Pushing back against him with the palms of her hands, she said with labored breath, "Benjamin, please. Let go of me."

Her pleas seemed to entice him more. As he tried to gain access to her mouth, the smell of alcohol on his breath burned her nostrils, making her nauseous. She struggled against the weight of him and the growing panic rumbling inside her caused her to forget herself. It wasn't until she felt the sting of her hand and observed the redness of his cheek, did she realize what she had done. "You hit me? Are you out of your fucking mind?!" he howled.

"Benjamin, please. Just let me go," she pleaded.

For a moment, she thought he'd regain control of himself, but the escalation of the day's events and the whiskey he consumed would not let him stop. It consumed him; allowing him to take hold of her wrists within his hands, pinning them back above her head with such forcefulness, she was sure she would bruise. While he held her hands with one hand, he worked to collect the bottom of her night gown with the other. She bucked against him to no avail; it only seemed to aid him more in his quest to take her. He did not hear her pleas, and soon she felt the dull tip of his erection against her entry, forcing itself within her. Feeling her body begin to split in two, the burning and aching between her thighs registered what was taking place.

As he pushed inside her with angered hunger, Colette went numb. She was no longer there. And although she felt her body, in that moment, she couldn't feel herself. She couldn't feel her weakness. The self-doubt. The need to be wanted by him. She could only feel the throbbing taking hold within her center.

His drunkenness made his assault more forceful and labored, making her feel as though the pain would shatter her. The roughness of his beard that once tickled her neck during passionate trysts, now stung her face as it scraped against her cheek. The anguish she felt tumbled from her lips as she let out an agonizing whimper, alerting him to her discomfort, caused him to stop. Finally looking down at her, it was the vacant look in her eyes and the tears streaming down her face that knocked him to his senses. Wrenching himself from her body, he sunk into his mounting mortification, as he realized the degradation, he subjected her to.

Lifting herself from the bed, she walked into their washroom. The tenderness between her thighs, although faint, tried to force her consciousness to come to terms with what had happened. Reaching the shower, she turned the water on, and begin to wave her hands beneath the heat. Testing the temperature, she once again measured the pressure against her fingertips. Stepping in, she allowed the water to crash over her body and unwind the tension that racked her bones. And as she tilted her head back, the heat knocked her from her daze. It wasn't until she heard the crashing of furniture and his crying out in a shrill of pain that she felt herself fall to her knees. While wrapping her arms around her body, tears fell once more.

The night ended with both sitting within the comforts of their heartache, basking in the familiarity of nothingness that continued to sever the bond between them.

The Morning After

The morning hours crept upon her like an assault to her senses. The same sun that she once met with hope became a mockery. As the brightness of daybreak tapered through the windows, she already knew what the waking hours would have in store for her.

Colette stared at the light as it bounced across the room, and it tortured her. Its brightness, a confirmation of a new beginning, was an affront to her fragility, and etched away at her sanity. The emptiness she suffered encouraged a listlessness she'd never felt before, weighing her down and forcing her to delay starting her day. She was happy he had left their home when she was cleansing her body of the indecency he afforded her. She couldn't face him; in fact, at present, she'd rather ignore what happened. It was easier to let it go. With how unpredictable he'd become, she couldn't risk agitating him more.

She didn't need the affirmation of the previous night's event to confirm the violation she felt. "What did I do?" she asked herself. Colette couldn't understand what she had done to provoke him. She had slapped him, yes. But surely it didn't warrant his reaction—it didn't warrant what he'd done.

It was moments like this she noticed just how cowardly she was. The differences between the two, his strength in contrast to hers, made her feel small. He had always been different. His ability to navigate the world at his leisure, allowed him privileges and pleasures he had grown accustomed to—one of which being her. In retrospect, she wondered if she should count herself lucky in having the honor of receiving him. In giving him pleasure.

"He could have been with someone else," she rationalized as she sat festering at the brightness of the light beaming through the window. Its rays effortlessly taunted her, as it drew out her fragility. However, despite her attempt to justify his actions, she could not. She would not allow herself to acknowledge this episode as some form of acceptance of what lovemaking would now become.

He was unlike the man she'd grown to love. He'd become a predator in the night, seeking her out to endure his madness. And through the cruelty he bestowed her, he tore what little hope of reconciliation apart; sending her need of being husband and wife once more to shame. She was humiliated. Still, in truth, she'd found some solace in the way he claimed her.

Festering in her despair, she wondered, *hadn't he taken me in the way a husband is entitled to his wife? Who am I to complain? What would I even call last night? I'm married. We're married. He's just hurting. I know he is. We both are. No need to cry is there? It's not like it would do any good.*

Despite her desire to stifle her pain, tears began to rage again, as her humiliation piled, drowning her in sadness. She was so desperate for the feel of him—for his love, that she'd begun to accept his violation against her. He'd taken a piece of her soul, claiming her to a part of himself that for a moment brought him back to her, but nevertheless had split her in two. Cutting her into pieces that she was sure would never allow her to be whole again.

Last night was not the only time she had experienced such a violation; she just never thought it would come at his hands. The touch of predators on the urban streets of her childhood, constantly seeking the warmth and suppleness of young bodies to feel and press against, was something she could never forget and had grown accustomed to. Truthfully, she was happy that unlike some she knew, the harm that they committed against her was limited to taking what they believed was their right in touching her and not in stripping her of her innocence completely. And just as she now held relief that she was able to hold on to her virginity in trade for the molestation of her being, she was also relieved in the fact that he had not been able to complete the act in its entirety; that his inability to finish proved that there was something still within him that cared for her. She could at least afford herself that sense of dignity from the mounting misery she seemed unable to rescue herself from.

She was drained. And although she wanted to bury herself beneath the warmth and darkness of her blankets, she was no quitter. Despite her husband's assault against her, she knew him—she knew that the previous night's actions didn't reflect him. What he had done was not a representation of the boy she'd fallen in-love with. There had to be a reason for the way he was treating her—especially last night. She wouldn't forgive him just yet. No, she would not. However, something within her couldn't give up on reconciling. At the very least, she wanted to understand how things had gone so badly. There was only one man who could help her figure it out. At best, he could help her muster the courage to either sink the idea of resolving her marriage, or swim to aid in its survival. Luckily, he held office hours on the weekends. And she hoped he wouldn't mind an emergency visit.

Playing with the gloves in her hands as she stood in the lobby trying to pull herself together, she hoped her frailty wouldn't betray her, and she would be able to channel strength again, by becoming Mae. It took everything in her not to pace about the area as her mind frantically raced. Coming there seemed to make her more nervous than she had been when she was home alone with her thoughts. Given the madness she escaped, she was lucky she didn't have a panic attack on the way to his office.

As she tightened her grip around her gold leather gloves, she thought of their last encounter. How becoming Mae made her feel powerful and sure of herself. It allowed her to find the fire she once had—a fire she hoped would eventually tell her story—their story. Standing in front of his door now, she brushed imaginary dust from her vintage cream-colored swing skirt, as it magnified her new persona as a sweet southern belle; allowing her grandmother's fighting spirit to flow through her. Giving a tap, she opened the door and gave a slight nod to the secretary seated to the left of the entry way.

"Hello, Mrs. Lati. Don't we look nice today?"

Placing a self-conscious pat to her perfectly styled hair with one hand, and with a wave of her gloves in the other, she replied, "Thank you so much for noticing, Anne. It does a girl good to get spruced up every now and again."

The peculiar look she received from Anne upon opening her mouth and releasing the southern drawl she had mastered so long ago, almost made her retreat.

"Well, we don't see women dress as fashionably as you anymore, Mrs. Lati. Honestly, you look like you stepped off a runaway from the 50s," she said admiringly, as she took in the ensemble.

"I am trying something new," Colette stated as she glanced about her person, ensuring that no detail was left unturned.

"It suits you. And those gloves?! I think I need you to take me shopping. You look absolutely divine," Anne gushed.

"Oh, thank you. Flattery will get you everywhere," she replied playfully. "Do you know when he will be ready for me?"

"Let me check for you."

Reaching for the phone, Anne dialed into the room and smiled as she waited for a reply on the other line. "Hello? Yes. She's here now. Send her right in? Will do." Placing the phone down and reaching for the buzzer, she gave Colette the nod to head inside.

Colette never noticed how bright the room was before. Taking in the way the light played against its pastel hues and paintings on the wall, caused her anxiety to peak. Distracted by the cheerfulness of the room, she didn't notice him right away, but once she had, she was immediately intimidated by his gaze. Slowly, his line of sight traced her face and down the lines of her body, making her shiver. "Sink or swim," she whispered to herself.

Taking a breath, she walked slowly, deliberately swaying her hips in a manner that exuded confidence and grace to the seat across from him. Watching his mouth slightly part in anticipation of her steps, let her know that she could get through their session, as long as Mae stayed with her.

"Would you care for another story, Doc?"

In all the time he'd spent in his profession, he had never seen a patient transform before his eyes as she did. He didn't know whether to be in awe of her or concerned for her mental state. Either way, he did know that she was mesmerizing under the light of the room. The way she crossed her legs just so and parted her cherry painted red lips slightly as she leaned forward in her seat awaiting his answer, caused an unconscious pull of his body.

Despite her allure, after dealing with the catastrophe that was his life, he was in no mood for storytelling. He wanted to get down to the bottom of why she felt the need for their sessions.

"Doc?" she said inquisitively, as she awaited his response.

"In all honesty, *Mae*, I would much rather get to the root of…whatever is ailing you. It would make our sessions go more… smoothly," he stated, unable to mask his crossness.

Hearing the irritation in his voice, she sat up straighter in her seat feeling the heat rise to her face as she felt her temper swell, and with pure indignation she stated, "Well, isn't it your job as my…counselor to allow me to get to things as my comfort allows? To delve into the deepest thoughts of my very being, as I see fit?"

Evaluating what she said, he knew that he was being particularly short with her. He had always taken pride in his ability to keep personal grievances out of the office, and he knew that this time shouldn't be any different. It was time for him to be the professional she sought; at least until he could fully understand her reasoning for seeking him out in the first place.

"You're right," he admitted. "I'm having some difficulties myself, but that is no reason to try to rush things with you. I will leave personal business at the door from now on. However, I'm curious… how will these…stories of yours help with our sessions? Or you, for that matter."

"Why don't you just wait and see, Doc? Deal?" she said with an outstretched hand.

Taking her hand into his, he noticed its warmth and how delicate it was. It was like a lily, unfolded, sitting delicately and daintily within his hands. The very same flower, his love, loved very much. He consciously measured how small they were in comparison to his own and tested its softness against his skin. The feel of them made him draw from her quickly. Taking his pen in hand he said, "Shall we begin then? You may start when you're ready, Mae."

"Sex has always been difficult for me. At least the idea of it. Being raised in a home that did more than its fair share of confusing me on the matter, it wasn't until Benny that I ever seriously considered it. The act of it was the beginning… it was the beginning of my true understanding of the lustful ways of men. And…well…just how broken I was. How broken I guess…we both were…

Free

The weeks following Benny and my first kiss had been mystifying. At the time, we didn't know what our moment meant, and we delved into our curiosity to see if the kiss we shared was one-time magic. We learned a lot about each other as our friendship flourished; growing steadily as it solidified a bond I never imagined. There were moments when it felt as if we were the only ones in the world. And it was during one of our conversations, while I lay in bed and he lay in his across campus, that he finally worked up the courage to make me his.

"You know, I heard that she's really a serpent," Benny said mischievously.

I couldn't help but squeal with laughter as he continued his attack on Cordelia. It never ceased to amaze me just how much he despised her. As if she were somehow a chain into a world, he had no interest in being part of.

"Come now. She isn't that bad—"

"The lies you tell, Cole," he sighed. "You know, I really wish that our parents weren't friends, so that I didn't have to see her ugly face outside of school."

"You really should be nicer, Benny."

"Me? Be nice? You must have me confused with someone else."

"You can pretend to be an asshole with other people, Benjamin Lati, but I know better."

"Benjamin? Ouch. I must be in trouble," he joshed.

"It's not that. I'm just calling you out on your bullshit. You're a sweetheart, and you know it."

"To be fair, I am only nice to you. So, it's not really bullshit."

"I'm sure," I said, laughing at his antics. At that moment, I noticed the look of testiness plastered on Cordelia's face. For some reason, she had begun to become increasingly hostile towards me in those weeks following the kiss Benny and I shared. I knew that I was never her most favorite person; however, I didn't understand why the budding relationship transpiring between Benny and me, shook her so. And in my teenage angst and ego, I had not the patience then, to deal with her growing disdain. The feeling of warmth from hearing his voice was all I craved. So, in all my youthful wantonness, I bit out, "What do you want, Cordelia?"

"Ah. The serpent is at it again I see?" I heard Benny say, as Cordelia and I stared each other down.

The sound of my heartbeat rushed through my ears. Being with Benny had conjured a change in me. With him, I had found a sense of strength. Yet, despite how brave I had become, I was no fool. Cordelia could ruin everything I worked hard for. In my mind, she had the ability to shatter one's dreams. Her privilege and standing translated beyond our school walls; and although I knew I should be careful, I couldn't muster sense enough to care.

I had spent my time in stone buildings, learning the languages and ideas of ancient scholars—latching on to those whom I believed would change my world. Changes I hoped would allow me to break away from the shackles of my home. However, I found myself no longer able to breathe. It was as if I were suffocating from within. I began to feel smothered by its unsullied walls that were surrounded by the ideas of the likes of *Aristotle* and *Descartes*. I felt stifled by the realization that I would never be part of the world she was born into, and by that time, I had started to give up. And I no longer desired their acceptance—I had Benny.

Perhaps it wasn't Benny alone. It could have been my own feelings of drowning that helped me stand up to the idiocrasies and politics of my surroundings. A war had begun to rage within me. And it had found an enemy in the hierarchy our school seemed to form amid the teenage egos of young boys and girls playing at adulthood. Power plays and games were forged, based on the ideals and entitlements their parents etched into them. They didn't understand that glory wasn't given but earned; and one rarely garners a taste of its sweet splendor at the glorious age of adolescence. Cordelia didn't realize this. She saw me in those following weeks, as no longer a stain on her perception of what her world meant, but what her world would become, if someone like me were able to infiltrate their ranks.

I watched as her mouth twisted into a foul shape of contempt and ire, as she registered the words that escaped my lips. Standing up with hands on hips and hatred in her eyes, she said to me, "You know, some people don't want to hear you throw yourself at the first boy who pays someone like you, attention. I know that where you're from, class and self-respect is... nonexistent. But for goodness sakes, find some."

"You mean, the same self-respect you have? If I'm not mistaken, didn't you screw two of our classmates in the same week?" I snapped.

"How dare you?! Who do you think you're talking to?!"

Feeling the heat of anger rush to my face, I sat up on my bed to face my adversary, "I'm talking to you. I'm so sick of you! I don't know what your problem is, but I haven't done anything to warrant your contempt. So, I wish you would leave me the hell alone!"

"My problem? My problem is stupid girls like you who don't seem to know their place. And thinking that they can take things that don't belong to them," she seethed. "It's bad enough that our school allows your kind to roam here, but I'll be damned if you think you're going to use us to get ahead. There is nothing more pathetic than a gold-digging social climber. You will never be one of us."

It finally made sense why she suddenly tolerated me less those past few weeks. And as I watched her mull over what the implications of my acceptance into her sphere meant, I felt sorry for her. Her entire identity and existence rested in her exclusivity in a world that ultimately shunned her. It had been two years since Cordelia's father's addiction aided him in squandering their family's money. If it weren't for her name and legacy, she wouldn't have been able to finish our last year. In fact, the only chance Cordelia had in continuing the life she had become accustomed to, was to snag one of our schoolmates. As many of the families had begun to ignore the Carmichaels, she was finding it to be an impossible feat. I finally understood. She didn't want Benny—she needed him. And I had become the one person standing in the way of what she considered easy prey.

Although I had no claims over Benny, I felt protective of him. His friendship and kindness meant the world to me, and despite not establishing what we were to one another, I wasn't going to let someone like Cordelia stop me from getting a taste of happiness either.

"Oh, I'm sorry. I didn't realize that Ben belonged to you," I retorted.

"Well, he doesn't belong to your kind. You shouldn't even be here. You know, when my father and granddad went here, people like you knew better. They took their time and education and went on with their lives. They didn't try to be us and take more than what was offered."

"Oh. I see. You mean us poor scholarship kids? We should be appreciative of what is…offered to us? Not take what doesn't belong to us? After all, we wouldn't want to be accused of climbing the social ladder, now, would we? If that's the case, I think you should lead by example, Cordelia."

"Excuse me?" she stated with eyes wide, and arms crossed.

"You're not part of them anymore! You are the one that should be facing facts. You sit here and spew your rhetoric at me, but you are the one who, save for the grace of your family's name, would never be allowed into our school. You're broke! And academically, you have no leg to stand on. It's a wonder how you even made it to senior year. You think we don't know why you've made it your mission to try to date and bed every guy in our graduating class? You're hoping that one of them will take you home to their family for keeps. But the jokes on you, because I'm sure that at this point, they're just using your desperation in their favor. The only one you haven't been able to get your grubby hands on is Ben, and it just irks your nerves that he has an interest in me, doesn't it? Tell me if I'm right, Cordie, dear. I'm guessing that your family is so determined to be back in the good graces of polite society that they're using you to do so!"

With lightning speed, she approached my bed and hovered over me. I suppose she intended to intimidate me. However, it only inflamed my anger more. Fueled by my fury, I snapped from my position sitting on my bed to face off with her. I had no idea what I would do, but what I did know, was that I would not allow Cordelia to have the opportunity to best me. With furrowing brows, bulging veins, and skin so red, it looked as if it had been tortured by a vengeful sun god, she said menacingly, "You are going to wish you never met me. I'm going to finish you. You are done here."

"Careful, Cordie. Careful now. We both know that us scholarship kids are on thin ice—need I remind you that you're place here isn't a solid one. One wrong move, and that's it. *Your* time is done. Just like that," I stated with the snap of my finger. "You hold just as much weight as I do now. If not, less so, considering I'm not the one prancing around with my legs open for everyone to have a turn."

Like a cartoon character playing on screen, I could see her blood boiling like an erupting volcano, signaling her explosion. "I'm going to kill you, you fucking bitch!" Within seconds, her hand rose, as if to slap me. Standing nose to nose with her, I hoped the look in my eyes conveyed my intent.

"I really wish you would. You must forget where I come from, Cordelia, or you wouldn't dare raise your hand to me. I will mop the fucking floor with you."

It was a low for me—utilizing the perception she had of me. I hated that she had taken me there, but there was something about her trying to come between Benny and me, that drove me to assert myself. Regardless of her anger and bravado, Cordelia was no fool. She may have been able to bully her way through life, but this was one of those moments she didn't want to know what consequences awaited her assault. Backing away, she eyed me up and down before saying, "You're lucky I don't want to waste my time with gutter trash. Just stay in your place. God, forbid I have to see you beyond graduation."

"Sure. The minute you stop being an incessant brat, I'll get right on that."

And with that, she headed out of the room with the door slamming behind her, leaving my body wracked with tension.

"She deserved it you know," I heard Gwyn say meekly, as she pretended to read her book that sat lamely on her desk.

It didn't matter if Cordelia deserved it. What mattered was that I allowed her, or rather, had allowed myself, to delve into that part of me I relentlessly fought to be free of. I knew what privilege I had in being in such a place. I didn't need reminding of my true position. I didn't need to be reminded of what I was. Just as she saw me as a threat to her station, her intention was a threat to my escape. No one understood me the way Benny did—and although I was unsure of how I felt, I was certain of how he made me feel. He liberated me. And I needed to be free. It was something I would have fought for, forever.

The need to fight against Mia's sharp glance and judging eyes burned me. Heat seized my body as rage threatened to erupt. Closing my eyes, I choked back my climbing emotions, so that I did not further injure the image I had cultivated for so long. No matter my disinterest in belonging, I disappointed myself. I'd done what I promised I would never do—I had shown myself to be the girl who was too uncouth to be in their world. It made me feel as though I'd lost myself, even though I didn't quite know who that was.

I turned to Mia in hopes that I may receive empathy. However, I was greeted with distance. It was clear that she did not want to be involved, nor did she want to approve of Gwyn's assessment of what transpired between Cordelia and me. Sitting back down, I heard my name being called in the distance. In my exchange with Cordelia, I had forgotten Benny on the line. Putting the phone to my ear, I braced myself for the potential lashing I felt certain I would receive from him, for my unbecoming behavior. Instead, I was met with such excitement, I thought I'd imagined it.

"Hell yeah! Look at you. You annihilated that bitch! Nicely done. I knew there was a reason why I love you."

"Love me?" I whispered, uncertain of what I'd just heard.

"Hey…can we meet somewhere?" he asked. His voice was frantic and burned with excitement.

"Meet? Where? When?"

"Now. I need to see you…now."

Growing concerned by his urgency, I asked, "Is everything okay, Benny?"

"I just need to see you, Colette. Meet me at the grove? You know the one in town? Behind the drive-in movie theatre? Can you get there?"

"Not everyone owns a car like you, Benjamin."

"Pick you up outside the gate then?

"Benny," I whined. It was late, and the altercation with Cordelia had left me spent. Yet somehow, I couldn't convince myself to say no. His silky, deep baritone voice had a way of luring me to him. "Fine. I'll meet you."

"I'll be there in five. Okay?"

"Okay. I'll see you there."

Sitting up, I braced myself for the possibilities and quietly left my roommates in wonder of my departure.

So, This is Love?

The ride we shared was painfully quiet, and it was hard to read Benny. His face, although softened, was masked in deep thought with a remnant of fear. I had never seen him afraid before. And despite my overwhelming sense of panic, I wanted only to comfort and hold him close to me.

As we got closer to our destination, I watched as his apprehension played out through the circling of his thumb against his index finger; a nervous tick of his that seemed to happen more frequently now. Reaching out to him, I took his hand in mine to bring him ease. Although he did not look at me, I could feel the calm wash over his body.

"You know, you're the only one who could make me feel this way, Colette," he said, breaking the silence between us.

"Feel what way?" I asked, turning my attention to him. Squeezing my hand gently, he let silence fall over us again. He seemed to find comfort in its tranquility, as if he needed it to fuel his courage.

It wasn't long before we stopped. And I realized that we had reached an area of the grove I had not seen before. A natural clearing seemed to part the large trees that hung over us—painting a picture and caressing the land in a way that was inviting. The light from the moon accentuated their color, causing a serenity that quelled my tension. It was like peering through rainfall. Despite my desires to lay within the empty clearing and engulf myself in the dangling leaves and branches, the intense gaze, emanating from Benny made me feel unsettled; shrinking me and forcing a timidness I didn't recognize.

Sensing my apprehension, he embraced me from behind. The strength of his body pressed against mine gave me comfort, as I relished in his warmth. Breaking his hold on me, he reached into the trunk of his car and pulled out a slew of heavy blankets.

"Don't worry. We're okay here. There's a cabin up ahead that the guys and I usually go to when we want to get away, but I thought we could sit outside, if you don't mind," he said to me.

I nodded as I watched him spread one of the blankets across the ground. His attentiveness was jarring—it was as if it were warning me of what was to come. Approaching me now, he laid his hand lightly at the small of my back and guided me to sit beside him on the outstretched coverlet. "You must be cold. You're shivering," he stated.

Shaking my head absently, I allowed him to draw me near to him and cover us carefully with the blankets he settled beside himself. I couldn't admit that my shivering was due to the waves of emotion that seemed to grow between us.

"What are we doing here, Benny?" I asked, trying to search his face as he stared into the distance. I waited for what felt like an eternity for him to turn and meet my gaze, but he didn't answer. Instead, with a flick of his hand, he cupped my face gently, kissing me deeply. I accepted him shamelessly, as heat rose within, guiding me in seeking a closeness to him I did not yet understand. And as he lowered me down, I basked in the liberties I allowed him to take with my body.

His touch was tender and careful, as if he were afraid I would startle. Slowly, his confidence peaked, and he began to explore my body mercilessly, sending signals throughout that were foreign to me. My desire rising, I grabbed his hand and guided it up my thigh and down my pants to the place I knew we both wanted him to feel. As Benny worked his hands against me, the dampness and heat between my thighs grew, while an involuntary thrust of my hips began to match his rhythmic movements. My breathing increased as the tightness I felt mounting finally erupted, making me scream his name. Opening my eyes, I found him peering down at me.

"God, you're perfect. You're fucking incredible," he whispered.

The sincerity and weight of his words made me overcome with emotion. Never had I received such a proclamation from someone. And despite my embarrassment at having surrendered myself to him and wanting him, I thought, perhaps, I truly was worth the care he took with me.

"Make love to me," I said breathlessly.

"What?" he asked. Bewildered. My words not yet registering. "Make love to me, Benny," I said again.

Caressing his cheek, I brought his face down to mine, so that I could taste him again. I had spent my entire life until that point trying to escape the advances of young men—and yet with Benny, his touch, the feel of his lips, made me desire more. It felt right.

As we undressed each other, despite the cool early November air against our bare skin, I only felt heat radiating between us. Pulling his body on top of mine, I waited to feel the hardness grow between his legs I'd heard about in passing; but it never came. Feelings of insecurity rushed me as quickly as the fog that enveloped us in a cover of white mist. Sensing my uncertainty, he rolled away from me in frustration.

"It's okay if you don't want to. You don't have to force yourself to be with me in that way, Benny," I said, unable to hide my dejection.

"Force myself?! I would give anything to make love to you right now, Colette."

"Then what's wrong?" I asked, as I observed his mounting frustration. His large eyes were no longer drowsy with desire, but seemed transfixed, as his expression harbored growing disdain.

"Talk to me. You can always talk to me, Benny," I said in earnest.

"I… um…I can't get it up."

"Excuse me?"

"I. Can't. Get. *It*. Up."

"You mean… it won't get… you know?" I said, pointing my index finger towards the sky.

"It's not you," he said fervently, "I'm just so nervous. I want it… I want it to be perfect, Colette. I want to do this right."

Climbing on top of him, I stroked his hair and searched his eyes. "I don't need perfect, Benny. I just need you. We can just lay here if you want," I said laying my head in the nook of his neck, while continuing to stroke his hair. "I can sing you a song," I quipped.

"I'm in no mood to hear a song, Cole."

Trying to lighten the mood, I cheerfully began to recite the lyrics of an old nursery rhyme, to which he feigned mild irritation. "Colette. Seriously? How is this supposed to help?" he whined.

Ignoring him, I proceeded to sing, raising my voice in time with the words as I did as a child, causing his body to tense as he tried to restrain his laughter. Rising enough to glide my hand over his torso, I began tickling him, and in turn, he turned to position himself on top of me, "Quite the comedienne you are, I see. You think you're funny?"

"Actually, I'm hilarious," I stated with an air of haughtiness, as I stared up at him, watching as his eyes began to grow serious once more. Unconsciously, I touched his face and allowed my hands to graze over the light stubble gracing his skin.

"Ah, motek. Cute you may be, but hilarious you are not," he said with a chuckle.

"*Motek*? What does that mean?"

"It means sweetheart in Hebrew—"

"Oh. I didn't realize you spoke Hebrew," I said as I realized there was still more to learn about the boy before me.

"I speak Arabic also," he said matter-of-factly.

"Wait. You do? Isn't that not supposed to be a thing? You know… you being Jewish and all?"

"It is a thing if you're *Mizrahi*," he said.

The look I must have given him caused him to laugh, as he prepared to offer an explanation to the expression I conveyed. "Mizrahi Jews are Jews of North African and Middle Eastern descent."

"Oh. I didn't know. Learn something new every day, I guess," I responded, "Wait, then where is your family originally from?"

"My family were originally from Iraq. They left before the pogrom of June 1941," he began.

It was a story that had been told to him many times as a child, and now he told it to me with the same fortitude one would, when explaining their family's tale.

"My great-grandparents went first to Syria, and then eventually ended up in Israel, some years after the Arab-Israeli War, in…1948, if I remember correctly. So, I grew up speaking Hebrew, and learned Arabic from my father's mother," he said proudly.

"Oh. Well, the more you know," I said impressed. "How do you say it in Arabic then?"

"How do I say what?" he asked absently.

"Sweetheart, silly," I responded, "How do you say it?"

"*Habiba*," he said. His eyes shone brightly as he said it. And then he looked at me—peering beyond my flesh, with something I couldn't quite put my finger on.

"Habiba" I whispered. Letting the words roll off my tongue, I took delight in the way it played across my lips. "You know… this whole thing… tonight…will be a funny story we can laugh about later," I said to him.

"This will be a hell of a story to tell our grandchildren someday," he said more to himself than me.

"Grandchildren?" I spat.

I could hardly contain the laughter trying to escape me. Despite the way I felt about him, I never saw Benny in my future. How could I? Even though we came from similar stomping grounds, my urban playground was starkly different from his. We came from two separate worlds—he from a circle of grandeur, and I from a sphere who could no longer dream.

Regardless of how far away we were from home, our lives on campus were nothing but an illusion. There was no possibility of a life with Benny. Sure, we were outsiders. Our otherness is what drew us together. But in the real world, in our lives back home, we were others to each other. Yet, the look in his eyes captured his adoration, igniting a flame of passion and need, I'd never known. It was like his temperature was rising with each passing second, emitting the commitment he would soon promise me.

"Yes. Grandchildren. You and me. I'm going to marry you someday, Cole. You wait and see. You're going to be my wife," he said seriously.

"You're tripping," I said, slipping back into the words of my block, as panic rose like a tidal wave. Turning away from him, I mulled over the words he said to me, and I wondered, how could he make such promises? How could he forget who we were? School was our refuge, yes—we could be anything we wanted to be to each other there. I couldn't understand why he couldn't enjoy it, instead of making things complicated. Why did he have to make me hopeful for something I knew could never be?

It didn't matter how we felt; I had come to terms with the fact that we would never be more than two people in a place, for a finite amount of time, joined together to see each other through. But then he turned my head to face him, and looked deeply into my eyes as he whispered, "I love you, Colette." And it made me feel whole.

Stroking my cheek, he wiped away moisture from the misty fog that continued to engulf us. Closing my eyes to the heat of his touch, I allowed myself to relish in the depths of his affection. He kissed me—gently at first. But as I began to accept him more, his kisses became deeper and eager, as if he were trying to possess me. And as my body relaxed, reacting to the warmth of his breath against my mouth, I began to dream of a future with him. With each passing moment our kissing intensified, and his caresses burned an impassioned yearning within me.

Liquid warmth seeped from my center, conveying my readiness for him. Knowingly, he traced his right hand from along my side and up my thigh, coaxing me to open wider for him as he settled his pelvis between my legs.

"God, I need you so badly, Colette," he whispered at the side of my cheek, as he worked the sheath of protection onto his member.

As he positioned himself to enter me, I touched my lips to his and arched my pelvis forward until I was met with the tip of him, and grinded against his hardness as my need for him grew. Feeling my wetness gliding over him, I moaned, melting into him, "I want you."

"I love you. You're mine, Colette. Forever and always," he said gruffly, as he pushed himself inside me, claiming me as his. The sound that escaped him projected his need, which would eventually become my addiction.

Like a shock to my system, pain washed over me with a force that left me breathless. Of course, I'd heard my friends speak of their first time—of the pain they assured themselves was nothing. But this was different. The feeling of being torn confirmed the loss of my virginity. The pain, sharp and true, radiated deep into my belly. In that moment, with Benny's member nestled tautly inside me, I wondered if I'd made a mistake. Feeling my flesh tearing, with closed eyes, I couldn't help the cries that followed.

Sensing my discomfort, Benny began wiping tears that snuck past my closed lids. "Are you okay? Do you want me to stop, Cole?" he asked. Shaking my head, no, I hoped that he would press on.

"I'm going to stop," he said.

I could hear the tension in his voice; it was racked with masked desire. And it was at that moment that I knew— I loved him. I loved Benjamin Lati. His tenderness—the care he took with me, made me fall in-love with the boy who would become the man who would eventually hold my heart.

"Don't stop," I said reassuringly.

"You sure?" he asked breathlessly.

"Please…Benny. It's okay."

"I need to move, Colette. I feel like I'm going to burst if I don't, but I don't want to hurt you."

Wanting only to please him, I tucked his head into the crevice of my shoulder, where I could listen to the heaviness of his breathing. Bringing my mouth to his ears, with my eyes squeezed tight, I stated ardently, "I'm yours. I want you to."

"I'll go slow," he whispered.

His movements flowed rhythmically, as he gripped my hip, moving slowly in and out of my flesh. Soon, I began to grow accustomed to his fullness. The sharpness I initially felt was replaced by a dull ache, that allowed me to move with him. I didn't feel the same pleasure I did when he touched me, but it no longer pained me so, and I found myself matching his rhythm, causing him to sink deeper inside me.

"Please don't move like that," he groaned, biting his bottom lip.

"What? Am I not doing it right?"

"No. Too good. You're doing it way too good. I want to savor you, but you're going to make me finish, Colette."

Increasing his pace, his face once relaxed, became distorted with pleasure. Seeing him that way sent a rush of heat, and I couldn't help the wave of carnality that swept over me. "Benny," I cried. Bliss now flowed through my body as we moved in time against each other, dancing to a harmonious tune all our own. No longer in control, his body arched inward as his strokes became more fervent.

"Say my name again, Cole," he said.

"Benny," I called out, as the tightness between my thighs began to mount.

"Fuck. Colette! I'm sorry" he bellowed, as he removed himself from my person, his seed, now sitting warm against my thigh in the condom he wore.

"What for?" I asked.

"I finished," he said winded, "I didn't mean to. I wanted you to enjoy it too."

"But I did enjoy it."

"Did it hurt… I mean, did I hurt you?"

"Only a little at first," I soothed, "But then, it started to feel like before, when you touched me."

"I wish it were better for you," he stated.

"There's always later. Practice makes perfect, right?" I said, smiling at him.

"I love you, Colette. Truly. I do," he said with such promise, I almost believed we had a chance.

"Benny?" I started. But with his face filled with hope, I couldn't finish what needed to be said. "Never mind."

"Look, it's okay. You don't have to say it if you don't want to. I just want you to know that I do," he said sadly.

"It's not that Benny."

"Then what is it?"

"Can you…can we just lie here for a while?" I asked.

He didn't understand. The problem was that I did love him. I had fallen for him effortlessly in the moment we just shared. In truth, I'd fallen for him long ago. But I hadn't the heart to tell him that we were high on a love that wouldn't come to fruition. That it was wishful thinking. Because as much as I wanted to believe and fold into his love for me, I knew that we were just two kids, unfit for the true reality of our worlds. Instead, I allowed myself to melt into his embrace, as we settled in a comforting silence, savoring the feel and closeness of our bodies together, his member rising once more.

"So, this is what the guys meant. I didn't think it would be like this," he said.

Repositioning himself, he settled between my legs and touched his nose to mine. Whispering against my lips, he asked, "Can I have you again?"

Closing my eyes and with the arch of my back, I opened wider to show my acceptance of him, as I wished to God that the night would not end, and that the cruelness of our reality wouldn't punish us in the morning.

The Cruelties of Lust

Swallowing my trepidation, I kneeled before him following his gaze to his unzipped trousers. "I don't know if I can do this, Benny. I don't feel comfortable," I said as my apprehension grew. It had been a few months since our first time together and with each passing day we had grown closer and yet miles apart.

As with most teenage boys who had found the secret to life between the warm mound of flesh within womanly thighs, every spare moment that we had together, I found myself in some uncompromising position or another. By this point, I had become resentful. Although I enjoyed the awakening our new-found intimacy gave me, I missed our long talks that were now few and far between. And as I stared down at his erect member waiting to be engulfed by my mouth, I could not help but be irritated that I was missing yet another moment of our senior year.

"Please, motek. Just a little bit."

"But I don't know what to do. You act as if I've done this before," I whined.

"I've done it to you," he said matter-of-factly.

"You didn't give me much of a choice," I stated indignantly. Not exactly thrilled by how that incident came to be.

"Still. You enjoyed it," he retorted smugly. The look on his face made me want to pummel him.

"That doesn't change how it happened. It doesn't matter if I enjoyed it in the end, I would have liked to have a say."

Despite the pleasure that came from the experience, I didn't appreciate his forcefulness. Ripping my clothes off and putting his mouth on me despite my protest, wasn't my idea of fun.

"Look, just try it, Colette. I don't see why it's such a big deal. It's not like we haven't done it," he said, barely harnessing his frustration.

I couldn't tell him that I found it revolting. I was already struggling with the guilt of losing my virginity. I couldn't possibly allow myself to do this. Giving pleasure to a man this way was sinful. For me, it was described as something becoming of loose women—a teaching that was given by my mother, who I could barely look in the eye now—now that I was unclean.

"Can't we just go back to the group and enjoy our senior trip, Benny? I'm not like you guys, I don't just get to go skiing on a whim," I pled. "I just want to enjoy this time with our friends. I want to actually see what a slope looks like."

My eyes closed at the thought of feeling the crunch of snow beneath my feet, as the crisp February air, playfully glided across my skin. The feel of hot chocolate draining to the back of my throat danced across my mind. The warm liquid was sure to be refreshing after being whipped by the wintery wind—I was sure of it, when I suddenly felt a tap on my shoulder.

"Did you hear me, Colette?" he asked, incensed.

"No. I'm sorry. What did you say?"

"I said that you can't use the fact that I have money and you don't as an excuse for everything."

"How is me telling you that I want to see and enjoy something that I've never experienced before, an excuse? You know I worked hard for this, Benny."

"Like no one else works hard except for you, Colette?"

"That's not what I meant and you know it," I said as I stood.

He stared at me with fiery eyes filled with anger, making me shutter. Having had enough of the exchange, I began to head towards the door when I felt his hand grip my wrist pulling me back.

"I thought you loved me, Cole."

"Love? What does love have to do with giving you a fucking blow job, when I don't feel comfortable, Benjamin?" I said, my frustration mounting.

"Why don't you want to please me, Colette?" he asked.

He sat with quiet indignation, and for the first time, I truly felt intimidated by Benny. The entitlement to my body and his growing possessiveness, created a distance he didn't seem to want to see. I had never seen this side of him before—it throttled me, stirring my senses, and ignited a hyper-vigilance that would never leave me.

"So, now I don't please you?" I asked timidly.

"You don't care to try."

"That's not fair! All I do is try to please you."

"Then why won't you do it? All I'm asking is for you to try."

"You know why!" I said through clenched teeth as I began to bite back tears.

"I'm not them. I'm not those people. You can't punish me for something someone else did to you, Colette," he lambasted.

Part of me knew that he was right. While he shouldn't have to pay penance for the acts of others, the turmoil I endured should have been reason enough to leave well enough alone. He was the only one I ever told and felt trusting enough to share the assault that was committed against me. And while I never sought to escape his love, his need for me scraped at the lesion of hurt vibrating and coiling inside me, threatening to tear me apart. The wound, despite how old, seeped within me—its venomous poison leaching into our love like a treacherous serpent, and I found myself wishing to be far away from him, as the memory of my pain deepened.

Proximity. A noun that means nearness in time, space, or relationships—synonym to propinquity. It could either breed love or contempt; but in my case, it signified the end of my childhood. For it was proximity that allowed me to see the world for what it truly was. And it was proximity that found me by his side. Who knew that a word could be so powerful in its ability to design my descent into feelings of nothingness?

I had taken comfort in the attention he bequeathed me. His consideration had overtaken my wits, causing me to falter from my delusions. My days were spent enraptured by daydreams of brown skin dressed smartly in a suit, standing by my side, as we stood in front of an altar designed by God, uniting our households into one. I was smitten. I had garnered the notice of the young man who conjured dreams of who my forever was to be. It was this era, my desire for worthiness, that detached me from my instincts, and blinded me of his wickedness.

I was a child then. And I possessed the innocence and naivety that an eleven-year-old would. Despite the sounds of sirens blaring, lulling me to sleep, the world wasn't terrifying. It was my oyster. Until the moment I lost myself, I held out hope. I believed that I would be released from the bars of my prison. The enchantment of his care made me anticipate my release, for I was sure that I had found my prince. I had long awaited him, and I was ready to be whisked away from the lure of my gritty streets and placed within the safety of the white picket fence, I was sure he would bestow me. But I was wrong. He wasn't there to save me—he was there to take my soul.

Although I knew the evils of death by another wielding a weapon, I didn't truly understand its power. It snaked around you, curling itself tightly, crushing your life force. Its control was unrelenting and haunted your very being, as it waited patiently for your pleas for liberation. You become imprisoned by an illusion of your former self; forever a ghostly figure, a shell unable to find your essence. That is what he did to me. Like a thief in the night, he had taken everything from me, and caused me to pray for a death that never came.

He was a boy of fifteen, and his smooth brown skin with reddish undertones were in stark contrast from the yellow hues his younger brother sported. At that age of innocent admiration, I felt as if I were always floating when around him. His presence was magnetic. It lured me to him and consumed me with its sorcery. When his parents had succumbed to the same disease that ravaged many in my community, my parents took him and his brother in. They felt for them, and their compassion couldn't fathom seeing the siblings apart. So, in the space of our small two-bedroom apartment, we added two more, and it wasn't long before my dream boy became my living nightmare.

Even at that age, I felt I should have known better. The slight touches that sent shivers of uneasiness down my spine were not meant to show care but were testing my resolve. He was assessing my acceptance of his advances and my willingness to tell. Even though I felt discomfort in the feel of his stolen caresses, I ignored them. For ignoring it meant that I could keep living in my dream world, away from the shadows that plagued me. And despite my apprehension, it wasn't until that day that I realized that I had flirted with danger. I was the one that allowed the final break of my spirit, for which I would never be the same.

It had been an uneventful day until it happened. I'd spent my time at school, bolstering through my studies as usual. I watched time pass with anticipation, as it got closer to school's end. I couldn't wait to see the chiseled-face boy with hair that waved like the ocean and tell him about my day. Although usually lighter in step and spirit on my walk home, I couldn't help the restlessness I felt upon reaching my door. It was as if something in me knew that things were about to change. Despite my reservations, I never thought the hurt I would experience, would come at the hands of the boy with adoring, piercing hazel eyes.

"Your mom and dad had to take your little sistah to the hospital, so I'm gonna watch you until they get back," he said.

"Is Kami, okay?" I asked worried. Even back then, she was my world.

"When they called, it looked like they might keep her, so they gon be there for at least a couple of hours."

"Oh," I replied. My anxiety not easily masked, as I felt him tug me into his arms.

"Don't worry, Nugget. She'll be fine. We got pizza for dinner, and I already rented some movies for us to watch," he said, leading me toward the living room, where I saw his brother watching images play across the screen.

Taking a seat across from them in my dad's lazy chair, I sat solemnly. Watching the television blankly, I wondered about my baby sister. My interest in the quest for buried treasure dancing across the monitor became non-existent, as I delved deeper into worry.

"Come sit next to us," he said. His voice came in flat, as his words filtered through my thoughts and discontent. As they registered, I glanced at the empty space he patted. Walking to them, I nudged myself within the small space and tugged down my skirt, as I tried to sit comfortably. "I feel bad too, you know," he said, as he played listlessly with the edge of my skirt, causing my anxiety to rise.

"You do?" I asked.

"Of course. Y'all are like family to me. And family never wanna see someone hurt or sad, right?" he stated simply, his hands now gliding up my thigh.

Fear struck instantly. It shattered my nerves and forced me to pull away from him. "Do you think Kami is okay?" I asked.

"I think Kami is doing just fine. But if you're feeling down, I have a way to cheer us up," he said.

The coolness in his voice made me shiver. Looking into his eyes, I saw it; and although not the first time I had seen lust peering back at me, I didn't know what it could mean, until then. I didn't understand that the desire I saw, could be so impure and would lead to the carnage and devastation of my being. It was a look I had never wanted to see again—until Benny. Growing tense, I began to rise from my seat when I felt his strong hands gripping me closer to him, "Where you going?"

"I think I should go to my room now," I stated.

My mouth dry, the hold that he had on me, ignited a panic I could no longer ease. The intensity of his gaze spoke of a viciousness I had no desire to see. And with each pass of his hand beneath my skirt, as his other held me gruffly around my waist, the need to flee hit me full force.

"I think you need to stay here…with us."

"But I really should go. I have homework to do and—"

"Come on, girl. I'm sad. Aren't we friends? Don't you want to help me?" he asked, awaiting my nod of affirmation. Upon receiving it, he leaned in closely and whispered, "Then let me see you."

"Huh? See me how?"

"Take off your clothes," he said coolly.

Looking at him blankly, I stared confused, as I tried to process what he said. My body stiffened as I understood his meaning, forcing me to sprint from my place on the sofa. I didn't make it far before I felt my body lift roughly from the floor. His words were menacing, as he spoke forcefully in my ear, "Take your clothes off, now!"

"Khai, I don't want to. My mommy—"

"Listen, I don't wanna hurt you, Colette. But I will if I have to. Don't make me angry. Shawn just wanna see how pretty you look without your clothes on, that's all. Don't you, Shawn?" he said as he lifted my shirt, exposing my budding breast.

Planting me firmly on the floor, he wrapped his arms around me to hold me in place, as he turned me to face his brother who smiled knowingly. My embarrassment weighed upon me, shackling me to his imprisoning grasp. "Shawn, pull down her skirt and underwear," Khai ordered his brother, causing me to writhe in his arms.

"Please. Don't. Just let me go," I pleaded.

"Fight me and I will hurt you. You don't want that do you?" he said. Guiding his hand languidly to my neck, he gripped my throat effortlessly, leaving me gasping for air. The physical pain of my labored breath distracted me from the agony of my growing humiliation, as I felt my underwear being removed.

"She got hair down there," Shawn said, stroking the fine hairs that had begun to shadow my pubic region.

"You wanna feel virgin pussy, bro?" Khai asked. The venom in his words and demeanor now played mockingly against me, as I began to come to terms with the egotist, I once thought my prince.

"Please, stop." I whimpered. The dread I felt was insurmountable, and I'd began to fear every second that passed, as I wondered if his torment would ever end.

"Shut the fuck up," he said gruffly.

"Khai, please," I begged. Pushing me down to the floor, he spread my legs widely, hovering between them, as my mortification grew.

"If you say something again or don't do as I say, you gonna regret it?" he replied coldly. The look in his eyes was enough to attain my compliance.

"Ay yo, Shawn. Come here. Stick your fingers right there. Yeah, like that."

Pain swept through me, as inexperienced fingers poked and prodded me like a hot iron poker, attempting to rouse a fire that couldn't be ignited. As tears burned hot against my cheeks, he laughed maniacally, mocking my pain of their torture against me.

"I bet you she can't suck dick," Shawn said.

"Look at you, little homie. You trying to get your dick sucked, huh? Sit up, Colette," Khai demanded.

Tears continued to stream down my face, blurring my vision and enhancing the sound of their zippers coming undone. The dull tip of their members sliding against my face, forced me to taste the saltiness of my tears as they glided against my lips. In that moment of my despair, I wondered how I could have been so stupid. How did I not understand that his interest wasn't the start of budding love, but to groom me for my anguish. And as I felt the swell of them continuing to play against me, I couldn't help the sickness surging within me, causing me to retch all over them.

"Yo, what da fuck! You little bitch! I should smack the shit out you, man!"

"Yo, Khai. Let's just leave her. She's boring anyway. And with the way she acting, she probably gon tell," said Shawn.

"She better not. I swear you better not, yo. If you say a word, Colette, I'll fucking kill you," Khai raged, as his voice drifted toward the back rooms, and I sat festering in the consequences of my naivete. In time, I heard them leave my parents' home; and while I should have been relieved, the possibility of my mother finding out what I had done, brought sickness once again.

As I cleaned myself and the mess I'd made, I wished for peace. I wondered if God would forgive me for what I had done—for what I'd allowed to happen. I wanted to go back to the way things were; when the thought of him made me blush with excitement, instead of the tremor of humiliation that now consumed me. Although I never received the cleansing of my memory I desired, my prayers were answered. Later that night, they were booked for robbing someone with a knife they had taken from my parents' kitchen. But to me, it should have been for murder—for he killed my spark for life and robbed me of hope and my strength along with it. And although my innocence was unequivocally stolen, I was still somehow one of the lucky ones. I had never told anyone what happened to me until Benny, and yet, there I stood again, my anxiety rising as the feeling of losing another part of me emerged.

Noting the look of irritation growing steadily on his face, I kneeled before him as I waited for him to take his seat. Closing the lid to support his weight, he released his member from his jeans, showing himself ready to feel the warmth of my mouth. Peering at him, its rosewood color began to mock me, as I tried my best to garner courage. As if sensing my apprehension, Benny worked his fingers through my hair before resting his hand on the base of my neck, "Come on, babe," he whined. Lust danced in his eyes, and brought back memories of my molesters, as a knot formed in my stomach I couldn't unbind. And with each push of my neck, guiding me towards him, panic struck, viciously eating away at my core.

"I don't know if I can," I whimpered. Looking into his eyes, I hoped he would see my desperation. Instead, I found him glaring at me unsympathetically with a surmounting frustration that was building rapidly, which I was afraid to see through.

"I don't have time for this, Colette," he said.

Applying pressure once again, he arched himself upward until the tip of him met my lips. With teeth bared, I tried to conceal my growing discomfort. Opening my mouth, I squeezed my eyes shut from the tears threatening to fall, as feelings from the past and present swirled together like an angry storm at sea. The shock of his smoothness did nothing to soothe the suffocation I endured from my overwhelming sense of shame.

Up and down I went, as I allowed him to guide me; his moans of pleasure and direction were muffled as waves of indignity continued to wash over me. It wasn't until I felt him pull away abruptly, releasing himself in the sink beside us, did I begin to breathe again. The waves settled as I returned myself to safety—and shame enveloped me like a blanket as I returned buried secrets back to their rightful place.

"That was amazing. See, I knew you'd be…great," he complimented.

Meeting my eyes, his voice trailed off as his face distorted with guilt. But just as quickly as it crossed his handsome face, it receded. Reaching for my hand and pulling me close to him, he nuzzled his face against mine and whispered in my ear, "You know I love you. Don't you? Never forget that. Now let's go hit those slopes."

Nodding my head against his cheek, I swallowed the burning need to lash out against him, as I began to no longer see him as the comfort I once held so dear. Swallowing my resentment, I allowed him to take hold of me as we walked into the night. The cold air seemed warm against his coolness. I saw him differently now— and for the first time, I felt no consolation in being with him. Instead, I found solace in the warmth of my hot chocolate draining against the back of my throat, as it washed away the taste of him— my vision of undying love.

Without Her

Bringing herself back to the present, she began her normal routine of trying to calm and release herself from the violations committed against her. Closing her eyes, darkness consumed her, taking her away from the light, so that she could free herself from her sorrow. Closing the door against the memories that plagued her, she screamed them shut. Peace now overtaking her body.

Glancing at him, she noticed that he was no longer scribbling on his pad. Instead, she found him staring at her with such intensity that she began to squirm under the weight of his scrutiny. Beneath his veiled neutral expression, she could see the solemnness that stood brightly behind his eyes; along with something else she couldn't quite put her finger on. It was at this moment that she really took a good look at him—although he seemed fatigued from his own woes, he was rather good looking. His full lips sat in a heavy pout. Its flesh-toned color looked soft and glistened with anticipation. There was something about his eyes that was captivating and made her feel bare underneath his gaze. He looked to be reeling from his own internal suffering, which gave him an alluring air. Stay focused, she chastised herself.

She realized then that it had been a long time since she'd been made love to. The experience with her husband the previous evening was a nightmare—one she hadn't fully awakened from. There were no longer nights spent entangled with desire; filled with a love that was pure and true. She couldn't remember the last time they were captured by a longing that left her breathless or trapped her in love's aftermath. She missed it. And despite what he had done, she missed him.

He couldn't help it. He couldn't help that when he looked at her, he felt guilty from the demons that plagued him. Unlike his other clients, his ability to maintain distance with her was becoming increasingly difficult. Sure, he had empathy for the others, but her story resonated through his soul. It was too much for him to bear, and he found himself lashing out at her, "If you felt that way, then why stay?" he asked coldly.

His words tempered and harsh, startled her, which made him recoil with embarrassment. Finding himself, he tried to mind his vexation and regain his composure; it wasn't her fault that he was in the predicament he found himself in, so it was time that he acted accordingly. "I'm sorry, Mae. Forgive my tone. I'm just trying to understand."

"What is love to you, Doc?" she asked absently.

"Sorry?"

"Well, most people think that love is a matter of…well…falling. We see it all the time in movies—girl meets boy. Boy meets girl. They see each other in the distance, and they just know. It's so easy. And I mean… that's the way it was at first for Benny and me; however, I don't know anymore. You know? I don't know why I chose him, but I do know that I stay because I love him. And yet, I'm not even sure what love is, sometimes," she said. "Last night he did something to me—something I never thought him capable of. But after sharing our story with you, I wonder if it's been part of him all along. Yet, a part of me knows that that is foolish to even think. That it isn't true. I'm sorry. I'm rambling again, aren't I?"

"No. You're not rambling," he assured. "Maybe you're right. Perhaps the kind of cruelty he paid you has been part of him all along."

"You know what, Doc? I feel like I'm going crazy," she shuddered.

"You're not going crazy," he replied, "But I do wonder…what exactly do you see in him?"

"There's always light in darkness, isn't there?" she muttered.

The uncertainty she felt manifested in her demeanor, as tension began to overwhelm her body once more. "You see…it wasn't…well, it hasn't always been hard between us. And I know that things will get better. They always do. What I mean to say is, what else am I supposed to do? He's the only love I've ever known, even if it hasn't always been good. I can't…"

"Leave him," he whispered, finishing her sentence. "It's what you should have done. It's what you should do. Save yourself the misery."

His response took her aback, forcing her to defend the man who'd once loved her fiercely, "Why? He can't help who he is, just as much as I can't help who I am."

"It doesn't mean you have to—"

"Look, Doc… I realize that my husband's way of being has long been a nuisance to our love. There were many reasons why I should have left—why I should have let him go. However, we started with something different. Something special. Magical even. It was the kind of love that moves you and makes you feel as if you live and breathe that person. I realize that realistically, we never had a chance with all the outside noise to begin with. And life hasn't exactly been kind to us, nor our marriage. But I can't help it. I can't help how much I love that man. I can't give him up. I've tried. And there isn't a moment or place in this world, where I could be without him, despite what he's done in the past, or even now," she confessed. "And, while I know…I know that he has done wrong—that he's not always the *best* man. I know that he is much more than his mistakes. That he is just as imperfect as I am.

"I think I understand what you mean," he replied.

Swallowing the lump in his throat, he thought back to his past and how it changed the person he'd become. She was right in her assessment. Like her, he was a manifestation of all he had endured; and it almost shattered him. Now, watching as she tried to work out her pain, he wanted nothing more than to reach out and find comfort in her.

She sat, with a look in her eyes that had become all too familiar; and as she sighed exhaustedly, she said, reflecting, "You know, Doc? I never thought of it this way before. I never realized that everything that has happened to me, set the tone for my entire existence. The only thing my life has taught me is that happiness is fleeting. It's all I've ever known, and maybe… I don't deserve anything better. I mean, after all this time of expecting something different, why should I be hopeful? Right? Maybe this is it. This is all I'll ever have," she shrugged. Glancing at the clock, she began to gather her things. The need to bolt had become overwhelming. And as she rushed towards the door—or rather, from the pain of her truth, she said, "I'm sorry. We went over time today. I must go anyway. I'll see you at our next session."

She didn't wait for him to respond. And as he watched her leave with her purse and gloves in hand, he noted that she no longer walked with the confidence she'd entered with. The hunch of her shoulders and the hesitation in her stride, as she mulled over the gravity of her words, let him know that Mae had left her. The depletion of her strength struck him with sadness and led to his escaped confession, "You do deserve better, Colette."

After leaving her session, Colette wondered about her future with Benny. She questioned if they would ever restore what they once had, or would they forever be crippled by the pain of their past. And as the weight of their quandary hit her, she thought, *what am I supposed to do now?* In truth, up until last night, she believed that they could somehow be saved, but as her session invoked troubling memories of their past, she questioned why she didn't leave, and what exactly was she holding onto.

It wasn't long before storefronts turned into tree lined streets; and before she knew it, she reached the place that had become a prison. She was home.

"Ma'am, we're here," the driver called out to her.

"I know. Just... just give me a minute."

"There are other fares I need to take, Ma'am."

"Listen, I will compensate you greatly, if you let me sit for a bit," Colette replied languidly.

She wished she'd let Marlo drive her. But after the evening she had, she needed the sounds of the subway to soothe her and help her in becoming Mae. However, as she sat in front of her home, she realized her mistake in the route she had taken. With Marlo, she would have been able to take her time before entering the dwelling that now held so much pain. She needed a moment to compose herself. It was that time again; when she had to put on her mask and paint herself into the wife and mother that was expected of her. Always pretending—perfect and pristine, for the life she'd fabricated. She wondered if she would have been better suited as an actress with the number of feigned smiles and family moments, she was able to stomach, while she died from loneliness.

"That kind of day, huh?" he asked, peering at her from his rearview mirror. His eyes were warm and kind, like Marlo's always seemed to be when tending to her.

"Unfortunately, it's been that kind of day...week...month...year. But who's counting," Colette replied.

Turning towards her, he adjusted his turban as he looked her over. Seeing the sadness in her eyes, his heavily mustached mouth turned into a smile, illuminating his brown almond eyes. "I understand," he said, "These kinds of moments happen to the best of us. Take all the time you need."

Nodding, she turned her head towards the window and watched as other cars whizzed by. Moments passed before she felt well enough to commit to her transformation. Stepping out the car, she handed the driver his money, "Here. For your trouble. Thank you for your kindness."

Grasping hold of her hand he said, "I don't know what it is that's plaguing you. But it'll all work out. I have a feeling about these things."

Her feet now firmly planted on the curb in front of her whitewashed townhouse, she waved at the man who had given her temporary refuge, as apprehension began to rear its ugly head. The steps leading up to her doorway seemed an impossible feat, for which she found herself lacking. To go back inside the home they shared, after what happened, felt as if she were inviting the devil back to take what was left of her. She doubted that even God could save her from the overwhelming emotions boiling within and threatening to surface. "Sink or swim," she whispered.

She had to get it together. After all, what was the purpose of going through all this, if she were just going to throw in the towel. She had gone through the trouble of conjuring feelings from the past to ensure a brighter future—she had to see it through. *Be brave, Colette. You can do this.* Closing her eyes, she took long, deep labored breaths before making her way to the stairs that led to her home, when she felt a light tap on her shoulder.

"Colette, I thought that was you," the voice said, piercing her thoughts and grating at her nerves, as it caused her body to tense. She recognized the sing song voice tormenting her ears, and she was in no mood for her intrusion.

"Hello, Sarah," she replied sharply. At one point, she thought the woman she'd known for some time, a friend. But lately, Colette was beginning to think that a torch, she had long thought extinguished, was very much alive and blazing in the heart of the woman before her.

With wispy boxed-dyed blonde hair and green eyes, Sarah Cohen had a way of making one uncomfortable, while simultaneously revealing all within themselves, in one interchangeable moment. Her glasses, which sat on the brim of her prominent snubbed nose, seemed to allow her round beady eyes to peer into your soul. She was slight—yet demanding, and always on the prowl for news. It was the only thing she'd take in exchange for her pardon. Due to her nature, the years hadn't been kind to her. Her skin, once supple and vibrant, had become pale and translucent. She wore a permanent scowl, accompanied by a smile on her small thin lips, that never reached her eyes. Ignoring her curt tone, with pursed lips, Sarah released her high-pitched wail, intruding Colette's thoughts once again.

"You know, Colette…I wanted to drop by to see how you were doing since we last spoke. You didn't seem well. You really had me worried."

"There is no need for you to worry. Really, Sarah. I'm fine."

"Well, Miriam doesn't seem to think so. In fact, she agrees with me," she said snidely.

Colette bit the inside of her cheeks to keep from being what she was sure would be seen as crude. She was having a time of it. And the revelations she'd acquired during her session did nothing to lighten her mood. She couldn't seem to catch a break. In that moment, Sarah was the last person she wanted to deal with. Her very existence grated at Colette's nerves to no end—perhaps that is why she shared so much the last time she was in her company. She needed her to go away. But today was not the day that she would over share, to release her from the unpleasant encounter that was Sarah Cohen. This time, she wanted to relish in her misery in peace.

"Really, Sarah. It's been a rough day. And I don't have time to chat—"

"Rough? You know you can always talk to me."

"And then what? You'll disclose whatever I say and use it for your arsenal and personal entertainment? No thank you."

"I don't understand. How could you think that of me? I've always had nothing but the best intensions when it comes to you and your family," she replied sneakily. The smirk that lingered on her pale face was too much for Colette to bear.

"Sarah, is there ever a time that you choose to just mind your own fucking business? Seriously, are you so miserable in your own life that you seek out the misery of others to make yourself feel better? Or is it just with me you do this to?" Colette responded, unable to control herself. The dealings of her day and the impending doom that seemed to loom over her marriage was too much to undertake; she didn't have the time, nor the head to deal with Sarah Cohen.

"I beg your pardon?" Sarah questioned. Her tone now barely audible, she was visibly shaken and taken aback by the outburst of the women in front of her. "Miriam and I are only trying to help you, Colette—"

"While Miriam has and will always look out for my well-being, you're only trying to get your fill of gossip, Sarah. You always have. Or is pestering me just some sort of vendetta for you?"

"I don't know what I have done to make you so angry, but—"

"Spare me your bullshit. All you've done is spread my business, just like you've done with everyone else. You're not a friend. There's a reason why no one speaks to you, and stupidly, I invited you in. I tried to give you the benefit of the doubt, but you've proven yourself, just as you always have, to be nothing more than a conniving bitch!" Colette exploded.

Anger washed over her, translating into words she never had the nerve to say before. She was tired of constantly restraining herself to suit the needs of others. If she were a contributor to the façade she maintained, it was because she'd permitted it, to which she could do no longer. Turning on her heel and walking towards her door, she addressed the woman whose face was now etched with harnessed fury, "Don't think I don't know what you're trying to do here. Stay away from me and my family, or you'll regret it. You have a good day now, Sarah."

As Colette opened the door, a smile danced across her face. It beamed brightly, and for the first time, she didn't care about the consequences their encounter would ensue. Closing the door behind her, she allowed the noise of her children's play to engulf her. The laughter in their voices seemed to mesmerize her, carrying her down the hall and giving her a moment of bliss before she was stricken by the realities of her life. While she loved and adored her children, she felt the weight of their presence. They were an anchor to him. Shackling her to the edge of drowning. *I stopped feeling close to him long ago*, she admitted to herself. It seemed that her sessions were becoming more of a truth teller than anything else. It opened old wounds that were threatening to expose her, forcing her to sink into the abyss it was creating.

"Momma," sounded brightly through her thoughts. It was the tiny voice of her youngest beckoning her to him. She hadn't realized that she'd reached them. She had placed herself, lazily against the threshold of the doorway, when he noticed her. "When did you get home? Where were you?"

"You look pretty, Momma," said Charlotte, tugging the hem of her dress that now seemed so out of place. Looking down at her person, she wanted to release herself from the armor that was Mae.

"Let me go change," Colette said more to herself than to her children.

"But where were you?" asked Zachary again. His bright eyes tried hard to seize her attention. He could always capture her heart with just one smile. At his age, he was a ball of love and heartwarming embraces that were always comforting. He never wanted to be without her, just as his father once had.

"Momma doesn't have to tell you where she goes, Zack. She's a grown woman," Nala stated, without taking her eyes from her book. The amount of sass in her voice caused Colette to chuckle. She dreaded the teenage years with both her daughters, because she knew that they would be certified divas, as her grandmother would say.

"Honey, I'm going to go upstairs and change, and then I will tell you all about my day. Is that okay?" Colette said to her little man. As she stroked his cheeks and stared into his eyes, she couldn't help but think how identical they were to his father's. They had a way of mesmerizing her, just as Benny's did, making her love their son even more.

After placing a kiss on the squishy cheeks between her palms, she made her way upstairs to disrobe her shield, and her apprehension grew. Her senses came alive; circling her like bees to honeycomb. Her breathing increased, as the fine hairs along her body stood on end, making her feel as though she were traveling down a dark alley alone. Reaching her door, she hesitated, and with that she knew—*he* was home. But why was he home? He should still be at the office, she wondered.

Steadying her nerves, she opened the French doors to their bedroom to find him lying in the bed that seemed so inimical just hours before. His arms hung lazily over his eyes, and he did not stir upon her entering. Closing the doors quietly behind her so that she would not disturb him, she went into their closet to change. Placing each item gently in their place, without turning she said, "I thought you were sleeping."

"How do you do that?"

"Do what?" she asked timidly.

"You know what I mean. How do you know when I'm next to you?"

"I don't know. Practice? It isn't always that way. Sometimes I know. Sometimes I don't," she lied. She always knew. The one thing she was sure of, was the feel of his presence. And glancing at him, she could tell that he wasn't buying it.

"Benny senses, then" he joked nervously.

"If you say so," she replied.

After rushing home from work, he had seen her sitting in the car outside. Noting the time before coming to her, he wondered if she realized that she was out there for over an hour—just sitting. Looking her over, he noticed how drained she looked. He didn't like to see this side of her, yet he always seemed to be the cause. No matter how many times he promised himself that things would be better—that he would be better, it always ended the same.

"Colette?" he spoke; uncertainty now beginning to grip him.

Her eyes, still lowered toward the ground, made him tense, and he could feel himself becoming defensive, which he knew was not what they needed. He too was tired. He was tired of feeling incomplete in his marriage—rejected. He was tired of feeling like a failure, when he knew that he was only trying to do what was right. All he wanted was his wife—the woman he loved. The woman who used to light up at the sight of him. And the girl who saw past his flaws. He knew that when she asked for his time, she expected the man he once was, and it saddened him that he could not be that for her, especially now, after the year they had.

Time has a way of changing people. And like his wife, he had been altered by life's unrelenting suffering. It had been unkind; hardening him as his experiences snaked their way around his heart in a merciless hold. It pulled him into its grasp, forcing him to submit to its suffocation of misery, and made him into someone he barely recognized.

The past year had been the most taxing on him—moving him along in a state of constant anger and secrecy that caused him to be distant from her and lash out. This wasn't the first time his struggles had gotten the better of him; but in the past, he had her to see him through. Now he felt alone, because through no fault of her own, he couldn't have her. She was the one person that made him feel safe and whole. She was his best friend. But he couldn't risk her knowing the pain he'd endured the past year, for he knew that it would break her. It could sever the bond between them. And because of it, all he had was a vacant fragment of the love of his life, due to the secret he harbored.

He knew he wasn't innocent. He understood his role in the current state of their marriage, but the fact that she never truly saw him—the part of him that when he looked at her, his heart skipped a beat, plagued him. How could she not know how much he truly loved her. Why couldn't she see that anymore, and pull him back from the ledge he was teetering on, he wondered. He knew that he had to fix things to mend the bond between them, especially with what was to come; but he had no idea how to tell her. Truthfully, he had been struggling with it for so long, a part of him was glad that things were coming to a head, so that he wouldn't be strained by carrying the load on his own.

Staring at her, he didn't understand why he allowed things to evolve into what they were now. Although he couldn't blame her, it hurt that she wouldn't look at him. That she wouldn't meet his gaze with those pretty chestnut eyes of hers. He missed the illumination of their amber flecks—it was one of the ways he could tell her mood.

"Colette, please look at me," he felt himself say. At this point, he was not opposed to surrendering to begging.

"I have to get dinner—"

"Please, just wait a minute," he said, reaching out to her. She flinched against his touch, making him draw back quickly, as if he were struck by a hot flame. The sight of her fear made him wince with shame. *How could I allow her to become fearful of me again? And this time, I don't think I could even forgive myself, so how could I expect her to?*

Dropping his hand from her, he averted his eyes because he could no longer stomach looking at her disappointed gaze. Coward. Don't stop now.

How do you think she feels? he chided himself, as he tried to gather his words and bravado. "I don't… I don't want you to be afraid of me, Colette. I didn't mean… I didn't mean for it to be like that. I never meant to hurt you in that way."

"In *that* way?" she scoffed.

"In any way, Colette. I never mean to hurt you. Ever."

"But you did."

"I know I did, but it wasn't my intent—"

"Your intent? What *was* your intent, exactly, Benjamin?"

"I just wanted… I just. It's just that I miss you so much, Colette. I miss *us* too."

"Well, you have a funny way of showing it," she said, choking back tears as her emotions began to get the better of her.

"Look, I know that what I did was… it was," he began, but the words wouldn't come out. There was nothing he could say to remove the pain he inflicted upon her. And although he had reconciled himself to this fact, he hoped with all his might that she could somehow forgive him. If only he could find the right words.

"You hurt me, Benny! You! *You…hurt...me*!" she exclaimed. Tears began to stream down her face uncontrollably, as she folded within herself and said, "You know… never in a million years did I think that it would be you that would do that to me."

Moving past his outreached arms, she walked toward their bed, fighting the urge to accept the olive branch he placed before her. Walking behind her, he stood in the doorway of their closet as she settled herself on her side of their bed. It took everything in him not to rush to console her. But he was no fool. Despite what she believed he still knew her. And coming to her in this moment would do nothing more but incite her fury against him. It was best, he assured himself, to keep his distance.

"I know what I did was wrong, Colette. You just…you don't understand what it's been like—"

"What it's been like? What it's been like for you, huh? I haven't had my husband in a fucking year, Benjamin. And when I do… oh when I do…look what I get," she said exasperated. She didn't know what came over her, but for once she didn't care.

"You speak as if I meant to do this, Colette. Like I meant for any of this to happen. For last night to happen."

"So, please… do explain, Benjamin…what did you mean to do?"

"I wanted to have my wife. You don't know how much I've wanted you.

To be with you…hold you. Then it happened…and I wanted to feel you. I needed to feel my wife… without. Without—"

"Without what, Benjamin?!" she growled.

"Without you treating me like this! Questioning everything! What my touches mean? Whether or not I love you? Don't you think I know that I'm different? That I'm not the same? That it's like…before? If only you knew what I've been through. What it's been like."

"With what what's been like? For once, talk to me. Please," she begged.

She felt crazy. Even after all he had done, she was still allowing him to explain himself. Her desperation had led her to what she could only believe, was a period of temporary insanity, to which she didn't want to succumb to anymore. "I don't know if I can do this right now, Benjamin. I'm tired," she said, finally turning to face him. Meeting his eyes, she could see the guilt plastered across his face, and for a moment, she had an incessant need to go to him. But before she could react, they were startled by the sound of her phone ringing.

"Don't answer that," he said.

The intensity of his tone startled her, making her hand jerk back suddenly, causing her phone to drop to the floor. It landed face-up, which allowed her to view the screen. Glancing at the name flashing, she noticed the rigidity that now afflicted his body, which began to fill her own with unease, "But it's my mother," she replied.

"Listen, can we just talk for a bit? There's something I need to tell you," he said frantically.

"Now you want to talk? You've had a year to talk to me and tell me what's wrong with you—"

"I've been going through some things, Colette. That's all. I know that what I've done is wrong, but we've gotten through before—"

"This isn't like before, Benjamin. This is different. You are different. I know what that part of you looks like, and this isn't it," she snapped. "Anyway, I haven't heard from my mother in a while. She's been dodging my calls, which isn't like her. So, since she's finally decided to grace me with her presence, I'm going to answer it, okay? Now, if you'll excuse me."

"Cole. Motek. Please. Don't answer that now."

"You haven't called me that in ages. Benjamin, what's going on? You're scaring me."

The clanging of her mother's call ended. And he began pacing back and forth, nervously about, causing her to take pause. His movements, erratic and wild, were unlike his typically smooth and calculating nature. She stared at him, until the sounds of the chimes coming from her mother's call resounded once more, ending a standoff neither realized they were in.

"I need more time," he said. His voice came in a pained whimper, so faintly, she barely heard him, which threatened her resolve. Cautiously, she held the phone in her hand as she braced herself for what was to come.

"Hello," she answered.

Her words, although her own, sounded strange. It was without its melodious air of excitement Colette often had when hearing from the woman she adored. Instead, it was claimed by fear, making her mouth dry. She suddenly felt the urge to ask him for a glass of water, but nothing came out. Her mind went blank. The woman on the other end of the line tormented her with her airy breathing and silence, making her regret taking the call. Something in Colette knew that her life would soon change and leave her broken-hearted, "Mommy, are you there?" she said.

"Coco-bean," her mother called out.

On most occasions, the endearing way in which her mother beckoned her using her childhood name, would be met with affection that she wasn't always sure how to give, but enveloped Colette all the same. Then there were other times it was used to ease pain that would soon follow. Given her mother's tone, Colette knew in her heart that it would be the latter. And when she was threatened by the reality of what was to come, she wanted nothing more than to escape to that place where she could scream within.

"Mommy, can we talk later? Now is not a good time. I need to start dinner soon, and—"

"Colette, this can't wait," chimed her stepfather. His booming voice, always infectious with laughter, now held a tone of uncertainty and sadness that made her weak in the knees.

"Daddy, what's going on? All of you are starting to scare me," she questioned. The vibration of her phone did nothing to relieve her anxiety, as the flash of her sister's name came into view. "Shoot, Kami is beeping through. Let me take her call, and I'll call you back, okay?" Colette rushed out.

"Just tell her, honey! Tell her now, before you lose your nerve," her step-father chided her mother.

"Daddy, I don't think I want to hear this—"

"Baby girl, you need to listen to what your mother has to say."

"Kevin, I don't think I can do this," her mother cried.

"I already done talk to Kami, now. Anita-Mae, you need to tell her! It ain't right to keep this from her anymore. Tell her!"

"It's cancer. I have cancer, Colette. I'm sorry, baby," said her mother.

Those words—although it sounded like her mother said them, the ringing that commenced in her ears made her think that she must have misheard. *Cancer? What did she mean? Cancer? No. She must be mistaken.* "You know, you guys almost got me. You're a riot. Truly, you are. Hysterical actually," she said, laughter filling her voice.

"Colette, honey…I'm sorry, but it's true," said Kevin.

"Look, you two. I don't have time for games. I'm hanging up now. Call me when you're ready to behave," Colette quipped. Tossing the phone on the bed, she turned to her husband with a shake of her head, as laughter began to build once more, "Cancer? Can you believe them? That's not a very funny joke. I mean seriously, what do they take me for? They're really not funny, you know."

The look on his face as he began to close the space between them, told her all she needed to know, forcing her to crumble onto the floor. The hilarity she'd once found in her parents' disclosure, had now turned into a crushing pain. What am I supposed to do without her, sprang to her mind as her phone went off once more. And with his strong arms now wrapped about her, she hadn't the heart to fight him anymore. The searing anguish left from the lashing of her mother's words, were more than she could bear; so, she allowed herself to relish in his embrace. She didn't want to think of his transgressions against her. Nor did she want to be cloaked in the strength that being Mae afforded her. She needed him—his strength. Sinking into him, she let it be, unsure if she would be able to swim another day.

Powerless

Colette lay undisturbed from her place. It had been days, still she'd been unable to stir. Her bed was now her refuge. A place where she could wallow in her misery in relative peace. She was in a constant state of rage and perplexity that she was unwilling to part with. "How did I not see it sooner?" she vexed again and again.

"Mommy? Abba said that it's time to get ready. Mommy? Are you listening?" Nala said, calling out to her from her doorway. Her sweet voice pervaded the silence Colette wanted to sweep herself in. While she knew that her children missed her, she could not bring herself to face them this way. The pain she felt was immeasurable; and she found herself unable to breathe from the weight of it. Giving up on trying to coax her from bed, her daughter shuffled down the hall and called out to her husband, "She still won't move, Abba."

This wasn't the first time she mourned a loss. Growing up in a place where funerals were more common than celebrations of births, made her very familiar with losing someone she loved. She spent many nights thinking of the things she'd lost between her and Benny. And though the loss of one of their children had been shattering, nothing prepared her for what she had to inevitably face— her mother was gone.

"Colette?" Benny called out, "You need to get ready, motek. It's time."

"Go away," she responded begrudgingly.

"Colette, you can't stay in this bed forever. You have to get ready and say your goodbyes," he said.

Coming to her, he sat next to her and caressed her cheek. Smacking his hand away, she sat up to face him, "Don't you touch me."

If looks could kill, he would have been a dead man. He knew that what he did was wrong, but he hoped that she wouldn't still be this angry with him. He loved her mother, and it was hard for him too. Exasperated, he walked to the door to see to their children. "Just be ready in an hour. Everyone is expecting you downstairs. You've already missed her viewing," he said, closing the door behind him. Her earth-shattering scream that followed pierced through the doorway, constricted his heart.

If one were to guess, they wouldn't have known what an egregious day it was. The sun shone brightly as any other summer day, annoying her to no end. The warmer weather brought out young couples walking hand-in-hand, and children playing noisily on the sidewalk. Even the birds were chirping cheerfully about her window. Yet, all she wanted to do was scream—she wanted to scream at them all for being so happy. Their happiness was torment—picking away at her, as one would a canker sore. Unmasking the woman she pretended to be. Taking another swig of her drink, she tipped her glass to them as she staggered away from their harassing glow. "Fuck 'em all."

"I think you've had enough," Benny said.

She didn't notice him enter, and as he gripped her wrist, trying to catch the glass in her hand, she had it in her right mind to pummel him with it.

"Great. Now there's two of you here to annoy me," Colette slurred.

"Yup. Definitely enough."

"Get your fucking hands off me!" she shouted, jerking herself away from him, "No one bothered you when you were getting plastered. Didn't even bother you when you stuck your dick in me when I didn't want you to, now did I?"

Standing toe to toe with him, she allowed her words to play mockingly against his lips. The look on his face incited her mischievousness more. In the passing months, as she watched her mother's steady decline, she had grown fond of amusing herself with his discomfort. In her mind, she was only paying it forward for what he had done. Spotting an open bottle of vodka on the table, she swayed her way toward it—grabbing it in hand, she began to chug.

"Now, that's enough, baby girl," Kevin's voice boomed.

"Yes, honey. I think it's best that you put this down and go upstairs and sleep it off," said Miriam. Her hands were now protectively squeezing the sides of Colette's arms as she tried to walk her out the kitchen.

"Kami, darling, give me a hand. All the guests are gone anyway. Help me get her upstairs where she can rest."

"You know what I'm tired of?" Colette asked. Her words were now barely coherent, and her eyes, that were once glazed over in despair, were now icy with anger. "I'm tired of y'all telling me what to do all the time."

"Colette, please. Just go to bed," Benny pleaded.

"Shut up, Benjamin. No one was talking to you."

He was growing tired. The constant scorn and insults thrown at him, were taking their toll. He was trying to be patient with her. Although he knew what he'd done may not have been right, he didn't have a choice. What was he supposed to do? He didn't mean to keep their secret from her for so long—neither of them could've anticipated this outcome, so why was he being punished? He couldn't keep apologizing for something he'd done out of love. Trying to mask his growing irritation, he addressed her as sweetly as he could muster, "Look, Colette, I'm trying here. But you're making it difficult—"

"I'm making things difficult?" she sneered. "Why don't you tell them, Benjamin? You tell them what you did?"

"Tell us what?" asked Akal from his place behind her sister.

"It's nothing. Why don't you guys let me handle it," Benny replied.

"It's nothing? Nothing he says," Colette laughed maniacally. The more she looked at him, the more the urge to do him bodily harm grew. The lies he spewed from his mouth left a taste in hers so sour she could spit. "He knew. He knew she was sick."

"What do you mean he knew she was sick?" Kami asked.

"He knew that our mother was sick the entire time," she croaked, "For a year he knew, and he said nothing!"

"Are you fucking kidding me?!" Kami screeched.

Like their mother, her sister had a vivacious temper and short fuse. Her ebony features were now marred with furrowed brows. Pulling her against him, Akal applied pressure firmly against her belly in hope of keeping her cool.

"Oh, Ben. You didn't?" Miriam cried.

"Colette, now is not the time. If everyone would please go. I'll see to my wife."

"I think not, Ben," Kami said heatedly, "I want an explanation right now. Go on, sis."

Despite everything, there was still a part of Colette that needed to maintain control—her kneejerk reaction to protect her sister began to kick in, creating a fire of confliction inside her. She deserves to know, she rationalized. The drink she'd consumed didn't help; it only made it easier to release the knowledge that plagued her, in the weeks leading up to her mother's death.

"*He* decided that it would be a good idea to keep mom's illness a secret from us. *He* was the one that got to be there for her. Not me! Not you! Not us! You took that away from me! You took the last moments I could've had with… with my mother… away from me," she said to him in anguish. "You see, daddy? Your perfect son in-law didn't even have the decency to tell us—"

"It wasn't his fault, baby girl," Kevin said. The apprehension in his voice was telling. He couldn't stand to see his daughters this way, but he also couldn't let Benny take the fall for what their mother decided to do. "Your mother decided a long time ago that she didn't want you girls to know that she was sick. She didn't want to worry you. She was sure… well, she was sure that she would beat it this time. And when I couldn't be there for her, she asked Ben if he would. It was your mother who made him promise to keep it from you. He didn't want to do it."

The weight of his words crushed her. The tightness that began to fill Colette's chest was overwhelming as she felt her temperature rise with anger that was threatening to boil over. In a sober mind, she would have been able to contain herself. But as she stood there seething, the heat of her anger with her loosened tongue over-powered her, and with a scream that quaked them all, she turned on her heels and walked out the door with only her purse in hand.

Damsels Save Themselves

Grief is an imposter. It disguises itself as a blanket of comfort and consumes you with its power. Like a mother concealing her child from a harsh wind, it shields you from the realities of your life without the one you lost. Isolating and true to only her misery, its protection offered her nothing, besides company in her despair. The six weeks since Colette left home were filled with emptiness—she felt nothing as she drowned herself in bottles. Crudely trying to numb her pain.

The first few hours away from her family were a blur; she couldn't remember how she ended up in the shoddy hotel she now found herself in, but she welcomed her new home all the same. The room wasn't the best she stayed in, but it's ruddy colored walls and faded sheets fit her mood, and she wasn't quite ready to part with it. The dated décor and yellowing of paintings past, solidified the company in which she needed to keep her misery. It offered the solitude she needed to dwell on the loss she faced.

The shock of the revelations that passed between her and the men she held dear, rocked her to her core; and she couldn't stomach being near them. She was happy that in her drunken stupor, she had sense enough to grab her purse. And since he had not yet canceled her cards to draw her in, she chose to remain in the comfort of her despair.

She groaned inwardly as her phone rang. She had not the energy, nor desire to answer it. She knew that it was likely one of her children calling to see when she would return home. As disclosed by Luke, they were tired of living off a diet of pasta and take-out. And her eldest, Judah, was over missing their weekly visits. Despite their complaints, she knew that it was their way of conveying their worry for her, unlike their father. Her husband was the only person she hadn't heard from. And with his detachment from their current state, compounded with her loss and guilt, she sought the bottom of the bottle more times than she cared to admit.

She was growing weary of the numbness she allowed to consume her. She needed to feel something, anything at all, besides the pain that permeated the air. Its scent was stifling and threatened to seize her senses as it lingered in wait, readying for her to faulter and succumb to its cruelty. Thankful that Miriam brought her things, she decided it was time to seek the sanctuary she desired. Getting up with bottle in hand, she took a sip and walked over to her hotel closet to pick out something to wear, as she prepared herself to transform once again.

The grey pencil skirt she wore clung tightly to her round hips and accentuated her firm backside. Walking into his office, she sashayed past him with a confidence that only Mae could bring. Although his demeanor was cool and collected, his eyes betrayed him. She watched as he took in the fullness of her breast in the fitted cashmere cardigan she wore. The softness of the army green fabric brightened the red undertones of her skin, making her breast appear supple and inviting. She smiled at him coyly, and watched as he shifted uncomfortably beneath her gaze, "Hello, Doc. It's been a while," she said.

Her amusement at his discomfort was clear, and the poise she garnered when entering the room, was enough to haunt his dreams. He realized that he was smitten by this character she conjured, whomever she may be. Uneasy with this revelation, he considered the consequence this posed to their relationship. He knew that it was in their best interest to transfer her to one of his colleagues; yet something within him could not find solace in committing to the idea. No. He needed to see where this would lead. He couldn't seem to tame his curiosity when it came to this creature before him, despite his irritation with her need to mask her true self.

In her absence, he had thought of her often. The way her smile lit up her beautiful face, plagued him. The sound of her voice, melodious and calming, played over and over in his mind like a soft tune, forcing him away from his duties more than he cared to admit. In truth, he was glad he hadn't heard from her. As she was already haunting his dreams, he didn't need sight of her, so that she could be his walking fantasy. He knew that he was playing a dangerous game with his attraction to her, but like any temptress, she had a way of reeling him in. She gripped his desire with a need so powerful, he wanted nothing more than to meld into her.

She sat before him; filled with a sensualism that beckoned him to her seduction, as she angled her body in a way that teased his senses and drew him in. Stroking her fingers lightly against the firmness of her breast, he knew that she was doing everything in her power to entice him. *God this woman will be the end of me.*

"It has been quite some time since you've been in, Mae. I was getting worried—"

"Worried, huh?" she scoffed. "Is that why you've been so dutiful in inquiring about my well-being, Doc?"

"I do have other patients, Mae."

"Well, isn't that a pity? And here I thought that you really cared for me," she said, feigning disappointment.

The look on his face was priceless. She couldn't tell if he wanted to mount her or throw her out of his office, but she was loving every minute of it. For once, she felt in control. It had been a long time since she'd felt like a woman, and she welcomed this newfound sense of sensuality she embodied, with ease. Shedding the skin of insecurity that long consumed her and shadowed her ability to command the body of a man, awakened the seductress within her—moving and guiding the flirtation she now invoked against him. And now, with how he sat before her, visibly shaken by her allure, she found a sense of power that exhilarated her. With the vodka she consumed still piloting her convictions, her boldness devoured her rationale and led her to give into her desires. Kneeling before him, she placed her hands firmly on his thighs and said, "Well, Doc. I guess I should leave. Since, you know…you have other patients. All of whom seem to be far more important than little ole me. However, if I leave…I was wondering how you planned on making it up to me. You do care for me, Doc—don't you?"

"Have you been drinking, Mae?"

"Are we really going to discuss that or are we going to do something else?" she asked.

As her eyes locked with his, she lazily ran her hands up his thighs, threatening to stroke the member between his legs that was growing harder by the minute. Grabbing her hands, he struggled under the intensity of her gaze, as the need for her welled within him. He didn't know why he allowed things to get this far, but he felt compelled to take her in his arms and taste the sweetness of her lips. He missed this feeling. It'd been some time since he felt the heat of the chase, and he wanted nothing more than to devour her—consume her, in a way that would dissolve the agony neither of them wanted to face. And her magnetism and feminine prowess made it harder for him to deny his longing for her.

"Mae. This isn't appropriate," he said tautly.

Although he'd meant to be authoritative, his voice and body betrayed his true desires, "I think…I think we should end our session."

"Please, Doc. I need to feel you. I just need to feel you," she said.

"Mae," he said breathlessly reaching out to her, "I…"

Her craving was so great, her body ached with anticipation. This was never part of her plan. However, she needed to feel something, anything, outside the pain that stifled her—choking her, until everything went numb. And yet, somehow it bellowed so loudly that it heightened her senses, pushing and pulling her in different directions until she felt lost in her grief. She needed this. She needed *him*. Everything before no longer mattered. In that moment, she only wanted to feel the heat of him.

"Fuck me," she said, so faintly she wasn't sure he heard her. But when she felt the press of his lips against hers, she allowed herself to be swept up by his passion.

He couldn't help himself. He had been without the feel of a woman against him for so long, he fell to his desires. His yearning, carnal and true, pushed him over the edge, making him her prey. The feel and taste of her as he undid the buttons of her cardigan inflamed him; and when he realized there was nothing beneath, but the beauty of her exposed breast, it sent him reeling. He was intoxicated by her and had to remind himself to slow down, so that he could savor her syrupy sweetness.

Now straddled upon him, her soft moans as he caressed the curvature of her back side and placed one hardened nipple into the wetness of his mouth, encouraged him to go on. Lust rose between them—coaxing him to slide the lace that encompassed the mound he wanted to bury himself in, aside. The dampness that over-took his finger as he stroked her heat, made it hard for him to maintain control. His voice was raspy and croaked with desire, "Please…let me taste you," he whimpered.

She didn't say a word as she stood to remove her lacy underwear. Hiking up her skirt, she made her way to his desk and sat upon it. Laying back, she opened her legs wide to show her acceptance of him. It wasn't long before she felt the balminess of his tongue, steadied on that part of her that was overwhelmed with need. His bearded face tickled her center; and the feeling that rose between her thighs caused her to cry out, igniting a flame she'd long thought snuffed out. The sound of his moans uniting with hers as he drank from her, increased a hunger that only he could fill, and she found herself begging to be released from his torturous play.

He needed her like the air he breathed; and she brought out a fervor in him that was boundless. Her legs draped over his shoulders, trembled as he groaned in agony with a need to quench a thirst that seemed endless, forcing his member to constrict under the constraints of his pants. As if reading his mind, he heard her whimper with desire for him, to which he was more than happy to oblige. Leveling himself to enter her, he could do nothing but admire the vision before him—from the arch of her back as she sought him, to the way she drew in her bottom lip, she stirred him until he could wait no more. Sucking in a breath as he plunged inside her, he listened to her cries of pleasure as she called out his name. He could do nothing more but be enraptured by the feel and sight of her. She was sensational, and her eagerness to have him, aroused him even more.

He moved, slowly at first and masterfully against her, as he lured her to match his hunger and guided their rhythm. His hardness filled her to capacity, drawing out a heat she'd long been without. And as they worked together, passions rising, the tightness of her threw them into a frenzy they willingly fell to—letting it consume them as they reached a crescendo of ecstasy that drove them over the edge.

It took a moment before they caught their breath, and as the dust settled, he became perturbed by the look in her eyes. The once bright amber flecks began to darken, warning him of an impending storm that wanted to spill over. She stood, averting her eyes away from him, as she forced her skirt down and turned her back to him. Frantically, she looked for her underwear, to which he'd already gathered in his hands. "I have them," he said, clearing his throat of the growing tension that gathered between them. "Right here."

"Thank you," she whispered.

The high of her climax was fleeting, leaving her once again with emptiness and pain, that was now shrouded in the indecency of their intimacy. At that moment, Colette wondered what *she* would have thought of her. What would she think of the drunkard she had allowed herself to become in the weeks that followed her death.

"I should have fought harder for her," she chastised herself. Her sobriety peaking, she could no longer shield herself against the sorrow that rushed to engulf her—forever encroaching on the solitude she so desperately needed, and for that she found it harder and harder to breath. As the moments between each breath decreased, and the air seemed to remain trapped with no means to escape, she found herself gripping him tightly, and collapsed against him as she struggled for air.

"Be calm. You're having a panic attack. Just try to remain calm and catch your breath. Come on. Watch me. Do it just like this," she heard him say, but she was trapped in a fog she couldn't find her way out of. And while she knew that she should try to calm herself, a part of her didn't want to. She wanted to fall into the abyss she was sure held promise, to take her to the woman she wanted to hold again, but nothing happened.

"Why isn't it happening?" she questioned between gulps of air, "Why can't I get to her!"

"Why can't you what?" he said, "Listen, you have to calm down, okay?"

"I…want…her…back!" she bit out.

The words between each gulp became more consistent. And as her breathing stabilized, her feelings began to pour out in an expulsion of words that seemed to have a mind of their own. "It's…my… fault. I shouldn't… have agreed …to it. I shouldn't have …let it happen. I should have *known.* I needed more time. More time…with her. But it was stolen from me. And all I have left? All I have left is the memory of watching her leave me—and having to take her life away. Why did I do that? I should have… just let her go on her own. Many people last on life-support, don't they?" she asked heatedly.

"It wasn't your fault. It wasn't anyone's fault. She was sick," he soothed. She couldn't listen. She didn't have the heart to heed his rationale, and as the tears streamed down her face, she realized that she couldn't do it anymore. She didn't want to. She needed to be with her.

"I want to go with her," she said abruptly. Calm washed over her so suddenly, it sent shivers down his spine.

"What do you mean, you want to go with her?" he asked cautiously.

"I need to see her again. It'll only be for a moment," she said pulling away from him.

His grasp around her that once swaddled her with sympathy, was now drenched with fear. *Go with her? Did I hear her correctly?* "What are you saying, Colette?" he replied. There were no more formalities. He needed to let go of their façade.

"Would you let go of me? I need to go. She's waiting for me," she said to him, so composed, that he himself was almost convinced to let her go.

"Colette…listen to me. You can't go with her," he said, trying to mask his growing anxiety. Her body now tense, he braced himself for the coming change of tide he knew would follow.

"You're not making any sense. I need to go with her, now! Don't you see she's waiting for me. I promised her—I promised her that she wouldn't be alone. She needs me," she cried. Her frustration mounting, her movements became erratic as she struggled to free herself from him, "Let me go. What are you doing? I need to go!"

"Colette! Please. Let me help you—"

"I don't want your help! I want to go to her. Why won't you let me go to her?!"

"There's nowhere to go. She's not here. You can't go to her because she's… she's gone," he said solemnly.

"Gone?" she asked.

"Yes. She's gone."

His words no longer made sense. She wasn't gone. How could she be gone if she just saw her. Now where did she go? She was just leaning against the wall, she wondered. "You scared her away! Ugh! How could you?!" she accused.

"I didn't scare her away. She *died*, Colette. Your mother is dead!" he roared. He couldn't do it anymore. He couldn't play pretend. Not while she was like this.

"No!" she said emphatically as she caught a glimpse of her mother's face peering through the light of the moon in the glass. "You're wrong. She's waiting for me outside the window. All I have to do is go out there, and we can be together. Don't you see her? Why won't you let me go? Please. Let go of me!"

"Colette, please. Stop this!"

"I need to be with my mother. Let. Go. Of. Me!" she said, growing impatient with his arms holding her firmly against him. "I need my mom. Mommy. Mommy!!!! Please come get me! I can't do this anymore. I can't do it without you! Let me go! I need my mother! Mommy!"

Amid her pleas, the world slowed around her as everything became muffled. She faintly heard him call for help in subduing her. It wasn't until she felt the drowsiness of sleep overpowering her, that she knew she wouldn't get the chance to go with her mother. Her smiling face in the window, with outstretched arms reaching out to her, was the last thing she saw before darkness fell over her.

Captive

The room spinning, she waited for the vertigo that plagued her every morning to pass—a side effect of the medication she had been forced to take. Bracing herself to rise from her bed, she shrank against the brightness of the empty walls of her room. They sat, white and untouched, goading her with their purity. It invoked a madness, that were at times hard to contain. However, the silence she forced upon herself aided in muffling her dread—for she knew that it wasn't their treatment that roused her sanity, but the darkness she placed herself in.

The weeks she had spent in hospital had gone by in a blur. She spent her days in sessions meant to air out her grievances of discretions past; but she couldn't let go. She didn't want to be released from the cruelty of her grief. She would not allow herself to delve deep behind the mask that formed the flesh of numbness glaring back at her. Conceding was not an option. She preferred the darkness—she took comfort in it, and its ability to lull her. Her mother's arms felt tight around her there; and as long as she stayed, sunken in and calmed by her despair, she could feel her touch again.

Hearing the shuffle of feet outside her door, she knew that it was time to go to that place again. The place where she was supposed to exhaust herself with the realities of her world. With feet planted, she waited silently until she heard the familiar knock, beckoning her to follow the trudge of somnolent souls. Joining their line of weariness, she walked down the sunny halls as they mocked her inability to face the life that was now her own. It was in that moment of solemn solitude that she saw his face in the sea of white walls surrounding grey clad hesitant legs, that her heart sank.

The sudden wave of embarrassment was too strong, and she found herself unable to flee to the sunken depths she'd taken to drifting to. It had been weeks since it happened. "Why is he here?" she whispered to herself. His large brown eyes, muddled with concern, seemed to peer right through her. Eyes that she could not escape, seemed to pry within—calling her to him. When looking into them, she wanted nothing more than to open herself up, but the animosity growing inside, due to his absence, prevented her from pushing past her desire to leave the protection of her veil of darkness. Yet still, with the strength of an inexplicable force, she felt her body draw near to him.

Seeing her there was agonizing. The feel of her so close invoked a longing he had long tried to stifle. The scent of her pushed past his senses, conjuring memories of familiarity that caused his knees to buckle. He couldn't believe that she was willing to stand before him—and despite the gauntness that plagued her face, she was still as beautiful as ever. All he wanted to do was hold on to her and allow himself to be intoxicated by the impression of her body molded against his, but he knew that with the tide that placed itself between them, he was no longer able to have her the way they once were.

His gaze was captivating. And as much as she wanted to peal her eyes from his, she couldn't find it in herself to do so. Never did she think that her body and soul could be riddled with such hate and lustful hunger; its pain and beauty rushed her, carrying her into the purgatory she now sank into. She couldn't withstand the torment swirling inside her. What is wrong with me, she asked herself. She was so at ease with the sight of him, yet it drained her all the same. Her soul cried out for him. Compelling her to end the damnation she felt. And as she stared into his eyes, she realized that it wasn't him she wanted. It wasn't him she needed at all. It was them—she needed them, together.

The range of perplexity washing over her face made him want to reach out to her; but their current environment stopped him in his tracks. This was not what he was there for. He needed to be brave for her—for them. Bracing himself for their interaction, he searched her eyes to see if there was a semblance of her left. In that moment, he wished the once strong girl he knew, would appear, and take over the shell of the woman he saw now. Looking at her sheepishly and exhaling the breath he felt he'd held for a lifetime, he said, "Is it okay if we talk for a moment?"

The eruption of laughter that escaped her, startled her just as much as it was disconcerting to him. She took pleasure in his distress, igniting a mischievousness that caused her to react recklessly. Without thought, she brought her body in proximity to his, ensuring that he could feel the heat emanating from her. Drawing near, with her lips almost touching his, she whispered to him, "Kiss me first, *Benjamin.*"

"Can you just step inside here, please?" he said, gesturing toward the open door, praying that she would cooperate.

Contempt rushed her as she made her way into the room. Moving boldly, she sashayed toward the long couch sitting in the middle of its space—it's luxuriousness calling out to her. The hospital bed and chair in her room did nothing to comfort her, and it had been so long since she'd placed her body against anything inviting. She wanted nothing more than to drown in its softness. For the first time since being there, she allowed herself some semblance of feeling human—even if only for a moment. The way the sofa yielded and molded to her body like a cloud ready to carry her off, made her feel secure, and she relished in its simplicity.

He watched as she splayed her body across the couch, legs hanging daintily and opened in such a way, he couldn't help but stir. She had no clue what she did to him. Since the moment she walked into their classroom, he thought of nothing but her. He yearned for her, desperately. He needed her just as he needed air. And he wanted nothing more than to change their current state, so that he could have her completely again. However, in that instant, the way she laid her body across the sofa, rocked his senses. She was toying with him. And her display against him was as inviting as a cold glass of water waiting to be savored in the desert sun. "Must you sit like that?"

"Please… tell me. How should I sit?"

"I don't know. Just not like…that," he said, swallowing hard. The urge to take her became more and more over-powering and fogged his memory of why he was there.

She noted his torment as he tried to maintain his restraint, and it made her want to make him suffer more. She wanted him to feel the pain he inflicted upon her, by forcing her away from their family. Their children were her only means of strength; and although she knew that she had part in her own pain, she could only see his doing. "Isn't this how you want me anyway? On my back?" she asked with eyebrows raised conspicuously.

"Why do you always make me out to be a horrible person?" he asked.

Taking the seat across from her, he felt his anger rising. While he knew he hadn't been the man she needed him to be, he was trying. He couldn't understand why she wouldn't see that. He wondered if there was any hope for them. The road that led them here was a harsh one, but he'd always been able to seek out the girl that loved him. Yet now, all he saw was emptiness behind her almond-shaped eyes, and it tore him apart. "Listen, Colette—"

"I heard. You know?"

"Heard what? What are you talking about?"

"I heard what he did. Even now, you keep secrets from me."

"Who told you?" he questioned, exasperated. He hadn't told her for a reason. Keeping it secret was the last thing he intended, all things considered. He just didn't want her to suffer more than she already had. He knew that she wouldn't be able to forgive him—he barely forgave him himself.

"What difference does it make as to who told me? The real issue is why do you always do this to me? You treat me like a child. Like a fragile piece of glass that only you have the privilege of breaking when *you* deem fit. Why is it that you're the only one that's allowed to hurt me?" she retorted. "It would have been nice if you were the one to tell me that that man is nothing but a lying piece of shit. How long? How long did it take for him to move her into my mother's home? Into my mother's bed?"

Seeing the tears forming in her eyes, he couldn't say it. He couldn't break her heart that way. "I don't think it's a good idea to discuss that under the circumstances. It will do nothing to help—"

"Like you care? You put me here. You haven't even bothered coming to see me. How I'm doing—"

"You think I want to be away from you? You don't think this is hard for me too?" he exclaimed, "Look, I didn't know what to do. How to…I didn't know how to—"

"You didn't know how to what?!" she charged. Her anger now unbridled. She wanted nothing more than to take her fist and thrash against him—to sear his flesh with blows filled with her anger. "It's not about me. It was about you. You couldn't bare it, so you never came. You don't care about me and what I need. You took me away from my home…my children—"

"You aren't well! You had a nervous break-down for fuck's sakes. What was I supposed to do?"

"Do what I did for you! Not stick me here. Do you know what this is doing to me—or is that the point?" she charged, "You just always need to be in control, don't you? So that I can't leave your ass!"

"Why do you always have to think the worst of me?" he asked. He hated when she got this way. When she voided his affection for her. "I love you and I always want what's best for you. For us." He went to caress her face, and instead of the soft touch of her smooth cheek underneath his palm, he felt the harsh sting of her hand hitting his away.

"The only person you care about is yourself. It's always been about you. Always."

"You know that's not true. I've done everything in my power to make you happy. Everything I've done has always been for you."

"Everything you've done was designed to keep me in a cage! Like a little bird you only let out when you're ready to play," she fumed. Bitterness tore away at her. And she found herself wanting to be released from all she had locked inside her.

"Why didn't you fucking leave then, huh?" he raged. He grew close to her, his nose menacingly touching hers. "I didn't force you to stay, did I? Here I am trying to fix this… this mess we're in. And all you do is reject me?! I never forced you to fucking stay!"

"Oh. There he is now," she said smugly, "There's the Benjamin I was waiting to see. I was wondering when you'd stop by."

"You provoked me, and you know it! You gave me no choice with your antics, Colette."

"You mean, like you gave me a choice in marrying you, huh? If you had left me alone, we wouldn't even be here. I wouldn't have to live this nightmare with you!"

"That's not even remotely true! Nor is it fair!" he exclaimed. He couldn't stomach it—he couldn't take her dismissal of their love. And if she felt forced to live in her regret with him, then he knew there was no way to save them.

"Really? Not true you say? Well, I beg to differ," she huffed. In the time she had been held, caged within the walls of the facility she now found herself in, she had a lot of time to think on her life with Benjamin Lati. And if he could not see the truth of what they were—in the life he'd bestowed upon her, she was going to make him see it.

"I don't have to listen to this shit," he said, rising from his seat. The knob on the door now calling out to him.

"Doing what you do best, Benjamin? Just go and run away like you always do," she said to his back, causing him to stop before reaching the door. Despite his need to flee, he couldn't let her win. He couldn't allow her to make a mockery of everything they were. Making his way back to his chair, he braced himself for what she was about to say.

"Go on. Speak," he said. Her smile grew larger, as a look of satisfaction spread across her beautiful face, "You know, my doctor said that I have a knack for storytelling. Do you mind if I tell you one?"

"Do I have a choice?" he scoffed.

"Okay," she said, relaxing into the comfort of the soft airy couch, "Let's play."

The Meeting

The time leading up to graduation went by in a whirlwind. Benny and I spent our time in hidden passageways that seemed designed to mask our passion and need to explore our desire for each other. I could do nothing but give in to him. And while his promise of forever hung heavily on my mind, I did not hope. Still, I tried my best to become immersed in the moments we shared, for I knew that my time with him was coming to an end.

While everyone around me seemed to be elated by their future, I was limited in what mine held. Sure, I had gotten into the same institutions as my peers, but the scholarships afforded to me did nothing to ensure my place—it wasn't enough. And I hadn't the means to get what seemed to be at my fingertips. Two years was the plan— two years of city college, and I would work and save to claim my place among stone buildings once more. It was the only thing that made going back to the place I no longer belonged, bearable.

I didn't know how to return to her again. I was no longer the girl I once was. The transformation I'd experienced in my new home made me fearful of her urban streets, and what I would be forced to endure. I knew I wouldn't be able to stand the expectations being home would bestow upon me—and yet, I had no other choice but to go back to her.

I could hear them already—the snide remarks of contentment, as they basked in my failure—the same way in which, Cordelia had. She'd become the bane of my existence the last few weeks of school. Mocking—she was thoroughly elated by the embarrassment I sported. I felt I had wasted time. That all my efforts had been for naught. And although I'd succeeded in completing my time there, I had not gained the prize I so desperately sought. I wasn't to become the butterfly I'd hope to become; instead, I stood trapped in my chrysalis, forever forgotten in a world that wouldn't allow me to be.

In the weeks that passed, I became disconcerted, as my time became more evanescent. The months passed and graduation crept upon me like a thief in the night—ready to steal the security I had found in my new world. It took my breath away. And then it came. The day in which he joyously awaited, and I dreaded most. For he could not see what I knew to be.

"They're going to love you!" he exclaimed.

His eyes lit up with an excitement I'd never seen before. His cheeks, flushed and rosy, made him look like a young cherub, ready to show off a new discovery. It was unfortunate for him, that that discovery was me. Although I loved Benny, his lack of acceptance of what we were, added to the brewing pressure I faced. I needed him to understand that there wasn't a place for me in his ever after, just as he had no place in mine. *Why can't he see it? Why was he prolonging the inevitable?*

I was so distracted by my thoughts; I didn't realize we'd arrived until I heard him speak. "Are you ready?" he asked.

His smile—it was a smile filled with such hopefulness I didn't dare crush it with my own. So, with a nod of my head, I trudged forward, trying my hardest not to reveal the rumble of uncertainty building within me. And with a well-placed hand on the small of my back, he pulled me closer to him as we walked toward the table. Willing my anxiety away, I melted into him, and allowed myself to accept his strength—that is, until I saw her.

She sat with the indignation and coolness of a lioness ready to pounce on her prey. Her hair was arranged menacingly. Her intent, threatening. She knew my modest appearance would be no match for her well-manicured attire, and she relished in my quiet uncertainty. Watching as she exchanged knowing glances to the strangers at the table, my hands went unconsciously down the front of my dress. The material, though clean and crisp, didn't stand a chance to the satin and cashmere that adorned her body.

Despite being roommates, I'd never met the man and woman who I'd come to know as Cordelia's parents. Yet there her mother sat, in a pink tweed suit that was two sizes too small for her plump torso. Her green eyes were weary and void of vivacity. And she appeared as any other woman unable to let go of the girl and life she'd grown accustomed to. If it weren't for her offending glare, I would have felt sorry for her. Instead, I saw only her daughter's future sitting before me, and could find no pity, as she piled another empty glass of whiskey onto the table.

As Cordelia's mother's resentment of my presence rose, I felt the eyes of the middle-aged man next to her on me. Turning my focus to him, the notation of his appearance was muddled by the disgust I felt upon acknowledging his gaze. The lust in his icy blue eyes made me shrink; an action that didn't fare well with Benny. Tension began to build in his lean frame, making his hold protective and hostile, to which I shifted uncomfortably in his arms.

"Abba. *Ima.* I didn't know we were having company," Benny said. Unable to mask his irritation.

"Come, son. You remember Mr. and Mrs. Carmichael, don't you?" said his father. His voice was loud and booming. It came like a rolling thunder—commanding and steady. Its light accent from his native home, complimented his intense demeanor, and was illuminated by the deep brown eyes he sported on his serious face.

"You know as well as I do, I know who they are. Mr. and Mrs. Carmichael. While always a pleasure, I didn't expect to see you here."

"Your father and I had some business to attend to and thought it would be great to get the families together again for dinner, before you two kids go off and leave us for college," Mr. Carmichael said, ignoring the growing friction between our dinner party.

"Abba, can I talk to you for a minute? Please?" Benny asked.

"Whatever it is, it can wait. It would be rude to ignore our guest, Benjamin," his father replied. "Why don't you take a seat next to Cordelia. And your friend… what is your name? Can sit next to your mother."

This was the first time during their exchange, that I was addressed. His father's dismissal of me, peaked Benny's embarrassment. As he festered in his humiliation, Benny stood quietly brewing in his anger. His jaw clenched and fist tightened as he tried to restrain his growing fury.

Trying to will peace into him, I said, "I would love to sit next to you, Mrs. Lati."

"Cole, you don't have to do that—"

"It's okay. I want to. Go sit beside Cordelia and your father."

"Why don't we go?" he whispered to me.

Fear crept into his once buoyant eyes, crippling the rage that recently radiated behind them. And he began to grip me with a desperation that left me winded. In that moment, he knew that if we stayed, he would lose me, and it was this admission that made him want to escape.

There was no use in leaving. We were now locked in a song and dance that would only prolong the inevitable. And while this was not the way I'd wanted things to end, I knew it was bound to come. I had planned a perfect day spent intertwined in each other's arms. We were to be enraptured by the glory of our love making, which would carry the strength to see us through. But they wouldn't allow it, and I had to make him see sense and truth.

"Let's just get this over with. I don't mind sitting next to your mom," I said to him, trying my best to pacify him.

As I waited for him to take his place between Cordelia and his father, I made my way to Mrs. Lati. "Hello. I'm Colette. It's nice to finally meet you." Taking my hand into her own, she gripped it reassuringly.

"Hello, Colette. It is nice to meet you too," she said lightly. And so began my meeting with the Latis.

Dinner commenced acrimoniously. And I sat, immobilized by my anxiety, acting as a spectator to a game I had no interest in playing. I found myself dissociating with the trauma of losing my love. I watched and ignored the chiding of Cordelia's advances, and buried myself in my plate, which didn't appeal to me. The way she caressed Benny fell emptily against me. Her hands brushing lightly against his forearm as the air vibrated with her laughter, made me wither. She'd won. He no longer belonged to me, nor I to him.

"You haven't touched any of your food, my dear," said Mrs. Lati. Her heavy accent played sympathetically against my ear. As though she knew my pain. "Is it not to your liking?"

"No. I'm not very hungry," I replied. Attention now on me, I shifted nervously from the sudden scrutiny of my dinner companions.

"I heard that you got several acceptances," said Mrs. Lati, changing the subject, "Your parents must be very proud."

"Her *mother* would be proud if she were going. Colette's father left her before she was born," Cordelia revealed. The smugness in her eyes sent heat rushing to my face, as my body tensed with rage. It wasn't enough to humiliate me by staking her claim on Benny, but she had to rub my failure in my face.

"You're not going?" asked Mrs. Lati, now granting me her full attention. Her deep hazel eyes rested inquisitively upon me.

"Some of us aren't as fortunate to be able to pay for college, Mrs. Lati. And while I am not going to any of the schools I'd hoped to attend, I will be attending a city college until I save enough to transfer to the school of my choice," I said, hot with anger. My eyes never leaving Cordelia.

"I thought you said she was top of your class, Benjamin? What happened to her scholarship?" came from Mr. Lati, his curiosity now roused. My gaze in-turn, shifted to Benny, as I wondered what other untruths he disclosed to his parents.

"Unlike two of us here, I am within the top five percent of our graduating class, Mr. Lati. However, I didn't get a full scholarship to any of my choices, so as I mentioned, my plan is as stated. Now, if you will excuse me. I need to go to the ladies' room," I said, trying to steady myself, for a much-needed respite.

Entering the refuge of the restroom, my anger began to brim like a fiery volcano. *How dare he? Why wasn't what I'd accomplished enough? Why did I have to appear as someone else for them? For him.* Peering at myself in the mirror, I realized I had done the same. During my time spent immersed in their sphere, I'd bent and molded myself into someone else—someone whose only desire was to appease…them. "Who are you?" I asked myself.

Soon a knock rumbled against the door and I heard the faint sound of his voice, "Cole, are you okay?" he asked. The regret in his speech was poignant. But before I could answer, the gruff tone of another pulsed through. Putting my ear closer, I heard them.

"What are you doing, Benjamin? You can't leave our guests sitting there like that."

"*Our* guest, Abba? Ours? I asked you to dinner to meet my girlfriend. Not to be bombarded by Cordelia and her parents."

"Your girlfriend? Look…I get that you've had a great time with her. I mean…we've all dabbled and had our fair share of fun, but she—"

"Abba, this is serious! I love her!"

"Love her? You don't know what love is," he scoffed, "What? Do you think that she's going to be your wife? Do you really believe this girl is good enough for you? For the life you're going to lead. She's not even Jewish!"

"And Cordelia is? Last time I checked, she's nothing more than a WASP brat!" Benny said harshly, through hushed tones.

"She is willing to learn and commit to our ways. And we've known Cordelia and her family since you started school here. They are wonderful people. What do you even know about this girl? Her family?"

"What does her family have to do with anything? It's her I want."

"Benjamin, when you marry a woman, you marry her family. After what Cordelia revealed, how am I supposed to feel? How can I… how can I even sit down with her father to have a cup of coffee, if she doesn't have a father to begin with?"

"She has a stepfather if you're so pressed to have coffee with someone," Benny retorted.

"And her mother? She had her at fourteen years-old, Benjamin? Really?! What kind of values does this family have?!" his father questioned.

"Where did you hear that from? Did, Ima tell you?"

"Your mother didn't say anything. And I'll have a talk with her later about keeping something like that away from me. Unfortunately, I had to learn this from Cordelia, as well."

"Cordelia needs to learn how to mind her business," Benny mumbled. "I can't stand that bitch!"

"You watch yourself," said his father, "You don't speak about a young woman in that manner."

"You really think I give a shit about her?" Benny seethed, "You know… let me ask you something, Abba. Truthfully now. Is this really about her 'family values'… or do you have an issue with Colette because she's Black?"

"Now you listen to me, Benjamin, and you listen good—her color doesn't matter to me. Do you think I don't know what people think about us, just because of who we are? What we look like?" his father began. "And this isn't about money either. So don't you dare. This is about family. Our heritage and legacy! I didn't come to this country with your mother with nothing… not even two nickels to rub together… to see it all go down the drain. I made a promise to your mother that I intend to keep. She believed in me when no one else would. She deserves to be surrounded by all the good in the world—a great family. A daughter-in-law she would be proud to have; and a son who is willing to put the family first! Who will take care of her when I leave this earth?! We both know that your brother and sister won't do it. Nor will they protect what I've worked hard to build."

"Abba, that isn't fair. I shouldn't have to carry that load. It's not my responsibility to—"

"It's not just that, Ben. I want more for you son—more than I ever had or could dream of."

"Colette is everything I've ever dreamed of."

"Be realistic, Benjamin! How could a girl like that, help you have the life you deserve? What could she bring you—to our family? How would she raise your children? My grandchildren! A girl who comes from the family—the life that she does, could never raise a family in our way," his father reasoned.

"What makes you think I want to raise my kids how you raised me, anyway? Who says I want to raise good little Jewish boys and girls? Huh? I was never made for that life, Abba. I don't belong! And I don't want it!"

"If you think that you're going to shirk thousands of years of culture and tradition, you are sorely mistaken."

"Screw tradition! If I can't have her, I don't care about tradition. I don't care about what or whom you deem to be 'a proper wife.' I want *her*. I love *her*. I want her to be my wife!" Benny exclaimed.

Tensions flared between father and son, and I sat in turmoil awaiting the outcome of Benny's declaration. Although he always professed his love and intention for me to be his, he had never said those words out loud to the world. It made my heart stricken with pain. For I knew that it was a love and wish that could never be.

"Son, I know this is hard for you to understand, but Cordelia is smart and refined," his father responded, "She was raised to be a lady and would fit easily into the fold—"

"Cordelia is no lady, Abba. She's a skank!"

"Stop with the insults, Benjamin. Whether you want to admit it or not, Cordelia is sophisticated and well raised. She's also going places. And this girl—"

"Colette," Benny seethed, "Her fucking name is Colette!"

"Whatever," his father dismissed, "How do you know she's not just using you, because of what our family has?"

"You mean like you're doing with Cordelia and her family?" Benny retorted.

"Watch yourself, Benjamin! It is not the same."

"How so? Please, tell me, Abba… how is it not the same?" Benny asked. "You spew nonsense like this to me on one hand, and then with the other, you're ready to throw me to the wolves. And for what?"

"If I allow this delusion you have of love and a life with that girl to go on, I will be throwing you to the wolves. I understand that times have changed, and things are changing. I know that you are not of the old country, so I can bend. But there are some things I cannot abide," he exclaimed. "I will always make sure that at the very least, the people my children choose to bring into my family—our family, are worth it. That they at least share similar values! Come from a good home. And Cordelia is a good match in that respect, no matter what you think."

"She and her family aren't who you think they are!"

"Look, I've explained myself already. I will not do it any further."

"And I won't entertain being with a girl I despise, when I have a woman that I love and who loves me back," said Benny. "And for the record, Colette isn't like that. She doesn't care about what *you* have, Abba. She cares about me. It's the other one and her family you should be worried about."

They stood for a moment. In a silence so heavy that it rendered a punch to my gut. His father was the first to break, "Please, Benjamin," he pleaded, "You're my pride, son—everything I've ever wanted. Don't ruin things with Cordelia, for someone who isn't a fit for you."

"You have another son. Let him date her," Benny whined with the vigor of an enraged toddler.

"Cordelia wants you! And with the way you're behaving, I can't understand why!" his father fumed, "Why aren't you listening to me? What kind of spell does this girl have on you, that you would blatantly defy me? It's as if you've gone mad. And for someone who's nothing more than gutter trash. She has her own life to lead. You have yours. Okay...okay…don't look at me that way. If you really want her, then keep her on the side and at arm's length, if you must. But she is not the one for you. I won't accept a girl like her as your wife. Do you understand me?"

The silence that followed signified my exit. It wasn't until I felt the weight of his hand against my cheek, that I realized I was crying. "No, Benny," I whimpered, "Don't."

"I'm so sorry. I don't know why my dad is acting—"

Tears streamed down my face uncontrollably, blurring my vision, "It's fine. You know…I knew letting you go would be hard, but I didn't think it would hurt this much," I said.

"What are you saying?"

"I'm saying I'll make this easy for you."

"Please, Colette. Don't do this now."

"I won't be second to anyone, Benny. Not for anyone. Not even for you. And especially to someone like Cordelia. I'm worth more than that. No matter how unsure I may seem, I at least know that."

"I love you," he said with such intensity I almost faltered. "I need you, Colette. You know that I can't be without you."

"You already are."

"At least let me drive you back to campus so we can talk about this," he begged.

"I'm not getting in any car with you. I'll take a cab, thanks."

"Why are you being this way? Just let me take you back, so that we can talk."

"There is nothing for us to talk about. My mind is made up. We were never meant to be together anyway. Things were never meant to go this far. But you took it there. Why did you push so hard? Why did you make me love you?!" I cried. "Look. We've felt and have gotten more than most people have ever been lucky to have in a lifetime. Let's be glad of that, okay?"

Turning away from him, I walked towards the taxi stand into an awaiting car, unsure if I'd ever be whole again. While he stood with his heart breaking—tearing him apart.

The Cafe

No one tells you about the pain heartbreak causes you to endure. And although it had been two-years before I saw him again, the hurt that entranced me, left me reeling. The humiliation upon seeing him, walking hand-in-hand with Cordelia on graduation day, was more than I could bear. I could do nothing more. My only recourse was to stay away. He didn't contact me. I guess he realized just as I did, that there was nothing more to say. So, I left him behind, and went back to my concreate jungle. My wounds unable to heal.

Going back home had been a living nightmare. The truth of my failure cost me more than I accounted for. Soon, the realities of my former home, began to compress me tightly. So tightly that I found myself unable to breathe. The chaos of my home choked me like quicksand as I floated around in this new dream—my nightmare. Where the sound of silence was replaced with sirens. And the serenity of being captured in his arms were replaced by the lure of the streets. I was no longer someone. Soon, my grief wracked me. Hollowing me out and imprinting a powerlessness, I now wore like a coarse blanket. That is, until I saw him.

I had resigned to not seeing him in the crowds of dark-haired men that crossed my path. Although I had dreamed of a time he would walk through the doors of my café, I knew he'd made a new life. Somewhere with Cordelia. Where he could do his duty and make his family proud. Where there was no place for me.

My first six months without Benny, dragged along. Like a ghost, I trapsed silently and listlessly throughout my days. And although I found myself within the depths of obscurity, I uncovered a refuge in the little café that offered me solace; where I found solitude in my studies and worked toward my escape. It was in a blissful moment on a brisk Fall day, where I was wrapped in the security of my books and the smell of cocoa beans, that he walked into my life again.

He didn't notice me at first. While he walked in seemingly oblivious to me, his mere presence sparked an awareness I thought I'd long forgotten. He seemed taller than I remembered. And time had somehow replaced him with a man. Proud and strong. No longer the boy I once knew. His hair, longer now, was thick with loose curls that framed his bearded face.

Walking in with a girl by his side and new friends in tow, he seemed weary behind the smile he sported. A sense of sorrow overcast his once delicate face, lending him an air of crudeness and ruggedness, that was somehow endearing.

It was a moment before he saw me. The smile plastered across his face, faded away in awe. Like magnets, we pulled towards each other. Closing the space of time that kept us a part. Soon, I felt the warmth of his sweet embrace. The familiarity of his scent permeated my senses; bringing back a rush of memories that overpowered me and weakened my knees. I was back in our place. Where soft kisses in alleyways, and feet planted firmly on the cobblestone beneath us, was all that mattered. The feel of his hand underneath my chin brought me back, coaxing my gaze to his large brown eyes. We didn't say a word—just stared. Entranced by the heat rising between us, pulling us closer until our lips glided together in an urgency and fervor beyond our control. It wasn't until the sound of an unfamiliar voice came screeching like a cracking whip, did we force ourselves apart.

Bracing myself, I turned to face the young woman who was visibly shaken by our heated exchange. The look in her eyes conveyed her displeasure with my presence. And I knew that I intruded on a happiness she'd desired with the man standing between us, "Who is this, Benjamin?" she asked. Her voice laced with ice, sent shivers down my spine.

"What happened to Cordelia?" I mustered.

She stood there brewing. Yet, I did not care about the girl with green eyes, hot with anger. She had long dark hair that cascaded around her alabaster skin. Her tone, although pitchy, was heavily accented the same as Benny's mother. Her full figure and stance, which was intended to be menacing, made her legs look like tree trunks. Her round glasses sat atop her round snubbed nose, which was pointed high towards the ceiling, signifying her disdain for me. Later, I would learn what kind of person she truly was capable of being.

"How does she know about Cordelia, Benjamin?" she asked.

"Benny and I went to school with her," I replied in his place. It was then that I noticed, just as she did, that he hadn't taken his eyes off me. And like a light bulb being turned on, it finally hit her. She knew exactly who I was.

"You're her, aren't you? You're Colette," she said. And as her mind grappled with the information before her, her body began to render defeat and replaced itself with a timid creature, unsure of herself.

"Sarah. Could you give us some time, please?" he finally said.

"Sure, Ben. I'll be over there. Don't be too long," she replied solemnly.

He followed me to my table I had reserved for slow days. After seating himself, he sat quietly as I busied myself with moving my books out of our way. Once I settled, he took my hands into his and inspected them, as if feeling the weight of them for the first time.

"Sarah, huh?" I spoke.

"Yeah. Sarah Cohen. My father and her dad knew each other when they were kids, in Israel, and caught up with each other again. She just moved to The City. So, my dad asked me to show her around."

"Oh," I replied, unable to mask my skepticism.

"That's not the whole truth. I'm sorry. It's just that, I can't believe you're here."

"Where else am I supposed to be?"

"You know what I mean. I didn't expect you to be here. Why aren't you in Brooklyn?"

"There something wrong with The City?"

"No. I don't mean that, Cole," he said.

His words came naturally. Spinning melodiously around my heart. "I haven't heard that in ages," I whispered.

"I'm sorry. I shouldn't have called you that. I don't have the right to call you that."

"It's okay. I still like it," I said, "But to answer your question, I go to school up here, and since this place wasn't too far, I applied for the job, and here am I.

"You work here?" he said, mulling over my words in disbelief.

"Yup. I've worked here for some time now."

"You work *here*?" he asked again. The laughter that followed was erratic and boisterous.

"What's so funny?" I asked, "Seriously, Benny. What's wrong with you?"

"Do you know how many times I've looked for you? How many times

I've been home… and to East New York, no less, and you're here?" he replied.

"Colette, this is my uncle's place. This is his café. That's why I brought Sarah and my friends here. All this time, I've looked for you, and you were here. Do you know how many times I've been here? When did you start working here?"

"I started soon after returning home," I stated.

The universe was remarkable. All the time I'd been wracked by my despair, I'd been crossing his path. Perhaps that is why I felt so safe in my little café—there was a level of comfort in seeing his family there. The familiarity in their faces only now became evident as I stared at his face in shock. He hadn't forgotten me. He hadn't placed me on a shelf of memories of lovers past. He longed for me, just as much as I longed for him.

"I can't believe this," he said, placing his hand gently on my cheek, "I missed you, Cole."

"You never called," I said heatedly. Pain washed over me in waves, as I recalled the moments we missed. And I found myself sinking. It gripped me harshly. Setting me ablaze, burning my cheeks hotly, and ringing noisily in my ears.

"I know…. I… I couldn't. I thought you hated me because of what happened with Cordelia."

"And what exactly was that?"

"It's Cordelia. You know I despise her—"

"Not enough to not date her for daddy, though?" I said callously. The scar tissue of his betrayal now exposed, began to ooze the rage I still contained.

"Look… I know I fucked up, Colette. And while I tried to please them, I couldn't stop thinking about you and that's why things ended with her. Not that it lasted long anyway. After things ended with Cordelia, I thought about contacting you, but I couldn't find the courage to call. Instead, I started going into your neighborhood during my time off, hoping to bump into you and let fate do the talking. When it didn't happen, I agreed to meet with Sarah, per my father's insistence. Never in a million years did I expect to find you here."

"How long did it last with you and Cordelia?"

"Why does it matter, Colette?"

"It matters to me, Benjamin!" I exclaimed.

"Cordelia and I…. well, we… we broke up…um… it's not that easy to explain," he stammered.

"Just spit it out already!"

"We broke up six months ago," he said. His face suddenly filled with shame, and he was unable to meet my eyes.

"Six months, huh? You were with her for a year and half! How much love could you possibly have for me if you were with her for that long, Benjamin?"

"It's not that simple."

"Simple would have been leaving me alone and accepting our relationship for what it was," I said. Images of them together invaded my thoughts, *did he make love to her the way he did to me? Did the taste of her set fire to his very being the way he did me? How could he be with her and still think of me?*

"That's not fair! You have no idea what it's been like for me—"

"For you? It's been hard for you? You had *her*?"

"And I left!" he said defensively.

"Is that before or after you stopped playing between her legs? There's no way you could be with her that long and never—"

"I never fucked her," he whispered angrily, "Don't you dare accuse me of that. That's one of the reasons it never worked. I couldn't do it. Because all I could think about was you."

"You expect me to believe that?" I scoffed, "You expect me to believe that in all that time, you never had her?"

"Look, she sucked my dick…or at least tried to. I tried touching her, but even that, I barely stomached. But I *never* fucked her. I couldn't rise to the occasion," he said.

I visibly flinched, shaken by his honesty and vulgarity. "I've never been with Sarah either, if that's what you're wondering. I can't. And it's because of you. You're like a drug to me, Colette. You're my only dream and desire. That's why Sarah knows about you. They both knew I could never love them because I'm still in-love with you."

He spoke vehemently of a love, I swore to myself, I would never become victim of again. Yet there I was, looking into the eyes of the man who captured my heart, unable to peel myself away from him. "You being in-love with me doesn't mean anything, Benny. You know how your—"

"Don't even finish that sentence. I made a promise to myself a long time ago that if given the chance, I wouldn't ruin this with you. It would be all or nothing."

"What about, Sarah?"

"She knows how I feel about you. And I told you a long time ago, Colette, that you were going to be my wife one day, and I meant every word. From the moment I had you, you became mine. Forever and always."

"Benny. Please," I pleaded, as tears threatened to fall. Although I wanted him back, I knew I couldn't stand against all that came with having him. Yet here he stood in front of me, steadfast in our love of imperfect perfection, ready to make us whole again.

"Hey…uh, Ben? Sarah's getting kind of irritated, and I think she's complaining to your uncle. Maybe you should come back and sit for a while."

"I'm staying here, Lisa," he said to a dark-haired young woman with deep-set hazel eyes, sporting a rainbow *kippa* on her head.

"Benny, maybe you should go," I tried to defuse, as the world already began crashing down on us.

"I said, I'm staying. I'm not going anywhere. It's you and me now, Colette. You. Are. Mine."

Forever Bound

It wasn't long before our relationship was thwarted by the pressures of family. The heavy hand of his father came crashing down like a Tsunami. The onslaught of his attacks against our union turned Benny's agitation with their lack of approval into cruelty. I couldn't tell if he blamed them or me. The love he once had, so sweet and pure, turned rancid and burned my heart like acid. It wasn't long before I began to go to that place again. Where darkness was comforting and welcoming. Feelings of doubt echoed through me like thunder. Still, he held on to me—unable to let go of our love. And as our certainty of each other began to chip away under the scrutiny and strain of its captors, we faltered. Yet, the burden we had undertaken did not bequeath our end, but secured our life together, forever.

It was a dark, chilly night. The crisp Winter air circled around us in his small studio apartment, whispering what I thought would be our end. Christmas lights beamed through his window, twirling and swaying against the walls like fireflies. It was a dance that usually soothed me and brought joy to my heart, but I could no longer find happiness in its tranquility. I'd come there to let him go; for we were no longer under the protection of our naivete and could no longer ignore the invasion of familial duties and sensibilities.

"Why are you so quiet?" he asked. His body taut from another family call. A shouting match I'd heard from my seat on his bed, as I pretended to watch TV.

"No reason," I said evenly. "I was wondering if you wanted to go out to dinner tonight."

"How? The bastard is cutting me off," he exclaimed as he raked his hands through his mass of curls.

"I didn't say you have to pay. It'll be my treat. In fact, you don't have to be the one paying all the time, love," I said cheerfully, as I reached out to caress his cheek.

"I don't need your fucking charity," he fumed, smacking my hand away.

"Fine. How about I make dinner? Then we can binge on movies and junk. What do you say?" I said, trying to offer him an escape. Leaning my head against his, I tried wrapping my arms about his waist, as I willed him peace, only to be met with callousness.

"I thought I made it clear that I didn't want to be touched by you."

"I'm sorry. I'm only trying to help—"

"Trying to help? You think a night of fun is what I need? My life is ruined! How am I supposed to pay for school? This place?" he retorted with such viciousness, I felt myself shrink. "You know what I need? I need you to shut up for a minute, so I can fucking think!"

"You don't have to be so mean—"

"And perhaps you should stop being so fucking sensitive and live in reality for a moment. This isn't about you right now."

"You know, what? Look, Benny," I said apprehensively. "I think it's time we talked. Seriously this time."

"I hate it when you say it that way," he replied. He was drained— like a fighter at the end of his rope. And I could no longer stand to see him that way.

"This is too much, Benny. All this fighting and arguing is just too much."

"You're starting to sound like them."

"Well, maybe they're right. You ever think of that?"

"What is that supposed to mean, Colette?"

"You know what I mean."

"Don't start that shit! Why do you always have to bring this up? Why? Don't you think I have enough to deal with—with them? I don't want to do this with you too."

"Why can't you see that this is tearing us apart, Benjamin? You apart!"

"Why aren't you willing to fight for us?!" he began to rage.

"What us? You think we can keep going on like this? Every time you get into it with them, you change. You're not the same person, Benny."

"How am I supposed to be, exactly? You haven't a clue what this is doing to me. And now you come with this?" he said.

"You're not supposed to be an asshole! You're not supposed to take everything out on me, like I forced you to be with me. I never asked you to be with me, not even in the beginning—"

"So, what? You're saying that you never wanted me? Is that it? You never wanted to be with me?"

"That's not what I meant!" I exclaimed. I was tired. Tired of the same conversation. Tired of the constant war that seemed to wage between us. A war with so many battles lost.

"So, please… stop this. Can you drop it? I don't need to hear this from you. You're all I have," he pleaded.

"I can still be there for you, Benny. We can always be friends—"

"I don't want to be friends!" he roared. His fury ready to boil over, unbridled, he exclaimed, "Why can't you understand that I just want you! Huh?! That there will never be a point in time where I will want to be without you?!"

"Stop yelling at me. Please. This is what I mean. I can't do this constant fighting with you."

"If you would stop saying that you want to leave me, then it wouldn't be a problem," he replied.

"That's not it, Benny. You know it's not about me wanting to leave you. I just can't stand to see you hurting. I don't want to be the cause of your pain. Not ever."

"You haven't caused anything. It's them."

"Then why do you take it out on me? Don't you see that it can't work like this? It's hard to feel like you love me when you're constantly badgering me, especially after you talk to them," I said, trying to reason with him.

"I'm sorry. I'm just under a lot of stress, okay?"

"Perhaps you should find a better way to deal with that, because I—"

"I am sorry, Colette. From the depths of my soul. I am sorry. I never want to hurt you. It's never my intention to hurt you. Ever. This is just… so hard," he said. His forehead now pressed against mine. "I want you, Cole. I *need* you."

"I do love you, Benny. I do," I whispered.

Placing his hands on my face, he kissed me deeply. "I want a life with you. A family," he said between each tender kiss. Willing me into a submission he knew only he could bring.

"Benny, don't," I begged.

He was meticulous in his caresses; and my resolve weakened with each kiss he placed on my body. As his hands glided over me, sliding, and coiling around me with a warmth so powerful, it drifted me deeper into a slumber, that only the pleasure of his touch could give me. With each flick of his tongue against the heat of my flesh, the aching and dampness between my legs grew, and I knew I had to be his. If only once more.

"Condom," I said breathlessly.

My request was not met with the usual reach into his nightstand. Instead, I felt his hands removing my underwear. Soon the heat of his mouth sunk deeply into the warmth of my tunnel, causing me to swell with need. Gripping my hands, he worked rhythmically against me, as I moved my hips to his manipulative play. Soon, I found myself reaching the peak my body sought, crashing into a crescendo of carnality he took pleasure in watching.

"I love you so much, Colette," he whispered, kissing a trail up my body. Making his way back to my lips, he kissed me with such vigor, I felt that he wanted to devour my soul. And as I felt the weight of his body upon me, I opened widely with an eagerness that made him groan deeply against my ear. His hardness pulsated against me, and soon, I felt the dull tip of him rubbing gently and teasingly against my center, setting me ablaze again.

"Wait, Benny. Wait a minute."

"I can't. I need to feel you," he whimpered.

Pushing himself inside me, he molded himself against me as if willing our bodies into one. His kisses were lit with an eagerness that made me quiver, as he urged my body to move with his. He began, slowly at first, coaxing me to bend to his will. Like a wizard, he was filled with a sorcery I couldn't conquer. Caving in, I allowed myself to meld into him and become his instrument of pleasure, reaching my peak once more.

The rush of life flowed from his body into mine. In my drunken desire, I didn't realize that Benny had passed a point of no return, I now found myself becoming victim to. "Did you just...?" I spoke, trying to grasp the consequence of our lovemaking.

"I couldn't help it, Colette," he moaned.

"Why didn't you pull out, Benny?" I questioned. Frantic, I became immobilized. The shock of what just occurred wracked my body with fear.

"I didn't mean to. It felt… it just felt…right."

"What if I get—"

"I'm pretty sure that you are," he said with such certainty, it drained the color from my face.

Admission

The room was spinning. He couldn't believe what he heard from the love of his life. The woman who was his passion. The one he thought loved him. Although he knew their relationship had its faults, he always believed that their love was what bound them together. He couldn't help but fret. The shift in her perspective made him wonder, *what was she implying? Does she not love me? Has she ever wanted me? No, couldn't be. Not my Colette.*

Despite his fears, he couldn't rationalize her truth. For the woman he knew and shared a life with, wanted him as much as he wanted her. She was the one who brought him out of darkness, through a love that had become his lifeline. She was his everything—his remedy. She couldn't mean what he was thinking.

"Are you trying to say…are you saying that the only reason you married me is because you got pregnant?" he asked, searching her eyes. And the coldness that peered back at him, caused a pain he never thought possible.

"What do you think?" she replied.

"I don't know what to think anymore."

"Did you really think I wanted to get married, then? With everything that was going on. And with everything we were going through?" she spewed. Her voice was icy and laced with a malice she didn't recognize herself. Venom swelled within her, coiling around her heart like a cobra ready to attack, "You did it on purpose—you took my dreams from me—just like you do everything else!"

"So, you're saying that you don't love me? That you didn't love me? That our first born is the only reason why you ever married me? I guess the ones that came after, are the only reason you've stayed, then. Is this what you're trying to tell me, Colette?" he charged. His words bleeding out from him, pleading with her to tell him that he was wrong.

Why did he always do this? Why did he always bring it to this point? As if love was the only thing that mattered, she thought. For her, it no longer mattered at all. Love was the reason she fell head over heels for a man she should have never hoped for. Love was the reason she stayed, even when she felt the final threads of herself pluck away. It wasn't kind. It was painful. When felt truly and wholly, love tore away at your soul. She was done with love.

"Love?" she snorted. "You still live in a fantasy world, don't you? How quaint."

"You don't have to patronize me. Just say it already," he pled.

Her words hit him like a ton of bricks—penetrating him, with an iron ring, weighing around his heart. And although her words ripped away at his resolve, he wouldn't believe them. He couldn't accept this show of her.

"You answer me first."

"Answer what?"

"Did you do it on purpose?"

"Do what on purpose, Colette? Stop speaking in riddles," he steamed, as his nerves began to jumble into a ball that made his belly ache. Of course, he knew what she meant. However, he'd never evaluated whether there was any truth to her accusation. He had wanted a child with her then, more than anything. Hell, he knew she would be the mother of his children the first time his lips touched hers. If he were honest with himself, he wanted her with child the night they conceived their first born, but he had no real intent, or rather, he didn't think that it would happen—really. But in that moment, with the heat of her around him, he couldn't negate the fact that there was hope—that their encounter would secure and bind them as one, forever. Watching the skepticism grow in her eyes at his feigned naivete, he decided to acknowledge her question, "I didn't do it the way you're implying, Colette."

And he hadn't. He wouldn't pretend that he wasn't happy that that night brought the very essence of their love into fruition. When it happened, it felt as though he had finally gotten what he had longed for with her. Even now, he knew it was right to do—as if some divine hand played a role in solidifying their life together, the night they conceived their son. And he believed in his heart that it was the same hand that forged their kiss in their school's theatre, so long ago. They were always meant to be with each other.

Whether she wanted to believe it or not.

"You're full of shit, Benjamin!"

"What difference does it make now, Colette?"
he whimpered. Kneeling in front of her, his hands desperately grasped her face, as he tried to will her back to him—to his love.

"What difference does it make? What difference does it make? Were you the one that had to give up everything to be his mother? Were you the one that had to sacrifice themselves, and everything they'd worked hard for and wanted?" she fumed. Drawing away from him, she got up to create distance between them. She didn't want his touch. She couldn't have his touch. She needed to get this out. It was time.

"Sacrifice? You act as if you were some sacrificial lamb being brought to slaughter. The one and only, Colette, who was the only one who lost in the process of marrying, The Big Bad Wolf, Benjamin Lati. Come on. I didn't lose too?"

"Don't start, Benjamin—"

"Oh. Now it's 'don't start, Benjamin?' You know, I'm sick of your self-righteous bullshit, Colette. You act like you're some saint that took me in. Poor, Benjamin! Look at his lovely and courageous wife. Who took her unstable husband into her bosom and salvaged him into the man he is today. His savior."

"Are you mocking me now? Here's the difference, Benjamin. You had a fucking choice. You chose to be with me. You chose to defy them. You chose to release in me and make me a mother, so that I would never leave you!" she said heatedly.

"I didn't choose to love you!" he roared, as he beat his palms hard against the floor, causing her to fall back onto the chair behind her. Noting how his anger startled her, he sat down on the floor to face her. Closing his eyes, he fought back the tears threatening to escape. "You think I had a choice? I never had a choice when it came to you. From the moment I laid eyes on you, I knew I was in-love with you. There was never a choice for me. I just learned not to fight it. Why would I, huh? And why do you?"

"Benny…I—"

"No. For the first time in my life I felt loved. I felt like I could be myself. There was no pressure with you. You believed in me. And I wasn't going to give that up. But now you tell me it was a lie?"

"It wasn't a lie—"

They were silenced by a knock at the door. Their emotions harnessed, they awaited the appearance of a stranger, only to be met with a familiar face. His thick mass of dark, tight curls complimented his bronze skin. He had long lashes that dressed eyes that were like his father's—large and proud. The Semitic nose he sported inherited from his father's heritage, danced gracefully above a mouth that held a familiar smirk, shared by one, Benjamin Lati.

"Judah," Colette called out to him. He had taken to having their weekly meetups with her at the hospital. Was it that time already, she wondered. "What are you doing here?"

"I know it's not our regular day, but I just wanted to see you, Mother."

"Oh, come here. Come in. Come in," she said. Pulling him into her, she took in his familiar scent and became intoxicated by his warmth. No matter how he came to be, the young man she held conjured a love within her so strong, it stole her breath away—just as his siblings did.

"What is *he* doing here?" he asked. Nodding in his father's direction.

"I came to see my wife," replied Benny.

"That's a first," Judah scoffed.

"Why are *you* here? Shouldn't you be at school?" Benny questioned, unable to hide his irritation. As much as he tried to ignore his son's baiting, it wasn't easy. He knew that he'd made mistakes, but the sting of his son's bitterness towards him, never went away. And he couldn't help but react.

"I don't need permission to visit my mother," Judah replied tersely.

Feeling the growing tension between father and son, Colette tried to emanate calm from her body into the young man who held her heart. Rubbing his back gently, she beckoned him to take a seat next to her. However, his mother's tranquility did nothing to calm the beast within. He hated seeing her like this. And he hated seeing his mother in this place. Week after week he had come to visit with the woman who was his everything, and he couldn't wait to have her home again.

He knew his mother worked hard to care for him and his siblings. She was constantly trying to make up for what his father lacked. In truth, he loved his father dearly. However, like his brother, Luke, he was very much aware of the toll that being married to him had taken on his mother over the years. And for that, he could not forgive him.

The animosity Judah held for him was something Benjamin wished would dissipate. All he wanted to do was move forward with his family and heal from the scars that were so deeply engrained from the onset of their existence. But they wouldn't let him. If he were honest, the rejection he felt from his son is what caused him to be harder on him.

"You may not need permission to see your mother, but you definitely owe us an explanation as to why you're not at school," Benny said, heatedly.

Deciding to ignore his father and get to the point of his visit, Judah turned to his mother instead, "I have someone for you to meet, Mother."

"Meet? Who?" Benny asked.

"I was talking to my mother—"

"And I'm talking to you, Judah! I'm still your father—"

"Don't remind me," Judah replied snidely.

"Judah, please. Can you just answer his questions?" Colette said gently. After the afternoon she just had, she was not ready to play referee to another clash between the two.

"Fine," he stated. He could see the strain in his mother's eyes, and this caused him to snuff the fire burning within him. "It's a girl…or should I say…a woman."

"I'm not following. What happened to Leila?" Colette asked.

"We're not together anymore."

"Why? What happened?" Benjamin stated, just as shocked as his wife.

Sighing inwardly, Judah worked hard to stifle the sarcasm that always brewed when dealing with his father, "As I was saying, *Mother,* we're not together anymore. I met Rose…and…well, I didn't feel a connection with Leila anyway—"

"So, her name is Rose, huh?" Colette asked. In that moment, he reminded her of his father. The light in his eyes took her back to their early years. The signs of new love blossoming was infectious to her—causing her to smile at his joy.

"Yeah. She's great. She's smart. Has a good head on her shoulders…and she's absolutely gorgeous."

"Well, when do we get to meet her?" said Colette. His excitement for the girl fostered her interest. She had never seen him this animated about Leila.

"I was hoping that…well… you would meet her now?" he said, running his hands nervously through the curly mass atop his head.

"You've got to be kidding me," Benny stated.

"Benjamin…please. Don't," she begged. Her senses now heightened by her husband's changed demeanor. She knew that an eruption was imminent if she didn't rein him in.

"What do you mean, please don't? Why would he think this was an appropriate time to bring someone here? Someone we don't even know. To meet you. Now? Of all times?" he seethed. Turning to his son, who sat arrogantly awaiting his wrath, he said, "If you haven't noticed, son, your mother isn't exactly on vacation in the fucking Bahamas!"

"Perhaps, Abba, I invited Rose here to meet Mother, because I asked her to marry me," Judah responded smugly.

"Marry you?!" Benny raged.

It wasn't long before he could feel the synapses short circuiting in his brain, summoning him to snap. He may not have been privy to everything going on in his son's life, but he knew at the very least that just three months prior, at his grandmother's funeral, Leila Swartz was on his arm. But now he was getting married. And to a girl that he knew nothing about.

"Yes, Abba. I asked her to marry me because she is—"

"I don't care what she is! You're only twenty -years old. You're a child! You are not marrying some girl that your mother and I have never met," he replied vehemently.

"You think you can tell me what to do? You two were the same age when you married."

"I'd known your mother, backward and forward by then. We were friends when we were nothing more than wet-behind the ear teenagers, and then things progressed!"

"So, you're saying what? You guys are somehow special? It's not like your so-called friendship has done anything to stop you from getting to where you guys are now—"

"Don't you dare speak on things you have no idea about, boy!"

His voice was now low and drenched with anger, and it sent chills down her spine. "Benjamin, please. Calm down. Why don't we just meet the girl?" Colette soothed. To her, it cost nothing to meet the young woman who might become their daughter in-law. And with her hand on his arm, she willed him to bend to her command.

"Fine… bring her in, I guess," Benny relented.

They stood watch as their son walked out the room to bring in the woman who they may now have to welcome as their own. As she filtered through, they sat, stunned by her beauty. She was tall, and her stature melded perfectly to their son's six-foot-two frame. Her umber-colored skin complimented a face that sported full lips and high cheek bones. She had almond shaped eyes that were piercing as they peered over shades that sat upon a delicate nose. Her short, cropped, tightly coiled hair framed her face, just as smartly and fittingly as her crop top and mini skirt hugged her hourglass figure. She reminded Colette of some of the Ethiopian models she'd seen walking the runways—just stunning.

"Hey. I'm Primrose...Primrose Kimani. But most people call me, Prim… minus your son. It's nice to meet you," she said lightly. Her soft voice and accent echoed through the room, as she held out her hand to Colette, taking it gently.

"A bit of an accent, I see. Where is it from?" asked Benny. He looked her over like a detective going over a crime scene with a fine-tooth comb. And if his instincts were right, and he knew they were, the beauty that stood before them was going to be trouble.

"My parents are Kenyan," Prim replied with a smile. "My mother was raised in London, while my father was reared in Kenya. I, however, was born and raised in Kenya. And I came to New York when I was about eight-years old, however."

"Oh. How interesting," Benny stated dismissively, causing tension to build in his son's face, "Please, have a seat."

"Yes. Have a seat. Tell us more about yourself. How did you two meet?" Colette asked excitedly, trying to counter her husband's unwelcomeness.

"We met when he came into my place of work."

"And what might that be? Your work, I mean," asked Benny.

"She's a waitress," Judah answered quickly.

Cutting her eyes at her new fiancé, she was irritated by his lack of transparency. If she wasn't bothered by where she worked, neither should he be."What my handsome man is trying to say, is that I am a bottle girl at Stilettos Gentlemen's Club."

"Oh," said Colette. A gentlemen's club? Had she heard her correctly, she wondered. "You go…to…gentlemen's clubs, Judah?"

"It's not that serious, Mother," he said, shrugging her off.

"So, you're a stripper?" asked Benny.

"No, sir. As I said before, I am a bottle girl," she corrected haughtily. "But if push comes to shove, who knows what the future might hold. Right?"

"Judah, can we speak to you for a moment? In private." Benny said to his son.

"Whatever you need to say to me, you can say it in front of my fiancée," Judah replied heatedly.

"It's okay, darling," Prim said, rising to leave, "You go on and talk to your folks."

"If you're going then I'm going," Judah replied.

"I'll be out in the waiting area, baby. Mrs. Lati it was very nice to meet you," she said sweetly, strutting towards the door. Upon reaching the handle, she made a quick turnaround to face the family that would become her own, and with a mischievous knowing smile and nod of her head, she gave a terse, "Sir," to the man that would become her father-in-law.

"Why did you have to act that way towards her?!" Judah exploded.

"You bring a stripper—"

"She's not a stripper. Unless you're being willfully deaf, she's a bottle girl. And if you had given her a chance, you would know that she only works there to take care of her younger sisters, along with trying to pay for school," he responded emphatically.

"I don't care about the *why*. The fact remains, that she has no place with you or in our family," Benny said, slapping his thigh for emphasis.

"You sound so much like, *Sabba*, it's not even funny," Judah said more to himself than to his father. "Isn't that the same attitude he had towards my mother? Because she was different?"

"You can't compare the two, son!"

"How so? They're from similar backgrounds. Mom finished school…no thanks to you by the way, and made something of herself…and Rose is—"

"Your mother wasn't a bottle girl at a fucking strip club, prancing around half naked for the whole world to see, Judah!"

"No. You're right. She was too busy being both mother and father to two little boys, taking care of a home, and trying to deal with you," he retorted angrily.

He was growing wary, and he was trying his best to maintain control when dealing with his son, but he was not making it easy. "Look," Benny stated evenly, "Regardless of what you say, it doesn't change the fact that you've brought her here, during this time, into a place where your mother is trying to heal."

"You mean into a place that she's in because of you?"

"You better watch yourself, son."

"Judah… please," Colette implored.

"No! Enough is enough, Mother," he cried.

"What the fuck did your mother say, boy!"

"And you… you think we're stupid? Like we don't know you two are one step from ending it all. And it's all because of you. *You*," Judah said turning his attention toward his father.

He had enough! There was no way he was going to allow his child to speak to him in that manner—something had to give. Standing now, Benny moved to close the space between them. It wasn't until he felt the gentle hand of his wife come between them, willing him to calm himself, that he even noticed she was there. All he saw was the growing indignation in his son's eyes as he puffed out his chest, ready to square off, and it enraged him.

"I don't know what your problem is, but I'm sick of your shit, Judah. I have tried to be a good father to you—to all of you."

"A good father? When? Was it when you were over there away from us? Or was it when she had to pick up the pieces for you when you came back home?"

"I did the best I could under the circumstances, son. You have no idea what hell I've been through. Not even a fraction," he said. His wife's hands, still steady in between them.

"I don't care! It's always about you!" cried Judah.

"It was never about me. It was what I had to do to make a way for our family, and I paid a heavy price for it."

"Whatever," Judah said. He was not yet ready to deal with his father rationally. "At the end of the day, you've stuck her in here, when she would have never done that to you, and you can add it to the list of things I'll never forgive you for. Now if you'll excuse, I've kept my fiancée long enough."

"Judah, don't go," Colette begged, as she trailed behind him to the door.

Turning to her with a hug and kiss he said, "Don't worry, Mother. I'll be back to see you and get you out of this shit hole, soon."

Closing the door behind their son, she looked at her husband with a look so heated, he quivered. "Don't look at me like that."

"How could I not? Why do you always have to drive him away?"

"Me? Why do you let him act like a spoiled brat?!"

"It's not like he doesn't have a right to be angry, Benjamin."

"So, you agree with him, then? Alright. Let's have a go at Benjamin. The shitty father and husband,"Benny said defeated.

"Can you just calm down, please?"

"No. All I've learned today is that you agree with our son that I am a terrible husband and father, and despite me loving and wanting you, the only reason you ever married me was because of our son, who does everything in his power to show me just how much he resents and hates me."

"That's not even remotely true," she said quietly. She hated seeing him in pain.

"Then what is it? You resent me too, don't you? Us? Do you regret your life with me?"

"That wasn't what I meant."

"Then what?!" he yelled.

"Are you going to let me speak or not?" she said incensed.

"I'm sorry." he said, as he repositioned himself. The movement gave his body something to do, as he tried to force patience that he didn't have.

"I…" she began slowly. She didn't want to trip around her words because she wanted them to be clear. She wanted the words to come out in the way she intended. Most importantly, she didn't want her words to hurt him. "I did love you then, Benjamin. But I would be lying if I said that I married you for only that reason. If it weren't for Judah, we wouldn't be together now."

"That's not true. You can't say that—"

"Let me finish. Please. You know how things were. You know how we were," she tried reasoning with him.

"I've apologized for that, Colette. I was a kid. We were kids."

"And that's exactly my point! I was a child, Benjamin. I was a child that was trying to get out of the fucked-up situation I was in. I had a plan. I wasn't equipped to deal with—"

"You're saying this like you're still stuck there. Like you didn't get out. As if you don't have a nice home. A beautiful family—"

"I didn't want to get it off your back!" she exclaimed. Running her hands through her hair, she tried to calm the wave of frustration mounting within her, "I wanted to do it on my own. That was important to me."

"How can you say you didn't do anything on your own? Did you not finish school? Are you not successful in your own right?"

"It's not the same. I became everything they expected of me. How many of them now think that I did any of those things without you? That everything I worked for didn't come from you?" she questioned. Tears now flowing freely down her cheeks.

He couldn't stand to see her in this state. The tears that streamed down her face were like a knife wound to his heart, and he couldn't help but go to her and kiss them away. Although the resentment she and his son held hurt him, it was nothing compared to seeing her in pain. That's why he held the secret of her mother's illness from her for so long, even though he knew it was right to tell her. He couldn't bear watching her drain herself trying to hold it all together. He'd seen her do so, so many times before, and refused to let her do it again for her sake… or was it for his?

Looking into her eyes now, he couldn't understand how someone so beautiful, and everything he could ever hope for, didn't know her worth. "Why do you have the need to prove yourself all the time, Cole? What is wrong with us building together the way we did? Do you think I got to where I am without you?"

"You don't understand," she said between sniffles.

And he didn't. He was designed in a world that would take his success with grace and wouldn't question his place, while she had to always fight for hers. She was aware of their glances—the way in which colleagues and peers alike noted her position as a reflection of the men around her. The assumption was sealed and signed the moment she conceived their son. "How could you sit there and forget how I was treated when I got pregnant with Judah?"

Yes. How could he? He wished he could forget. His father made it perfectly clear that he thought she was nothing more than a scheming whore. People they thought were their friends shunned her—attributing her pregnancy as her way to secure her life. If only they knew that he had purchased a ring, the day after they reunited in the café. He was only waiting for the right time to give it to her. The constant war with his parents made the timing impossible. It wasn't until she came with the check his uncle had given her, courtesy of his father, to go away and terminate their son, that he realized what he needed to do. They eloped a week later, and he realized now, that she did so, begrudgingly, "Why do they get more consideration in our relationship than I do?" Benny asked, trying to mask his irritation.

"You don't get it. You never have."

"I do get it. Of course, I do. I know how they and others treated you. How they all made you feel. But for the life of me, I can't say that I know why it matters. Why they matter now. Now? After everything we've accomplished and been through?"

"It's because every time people see me, all they see is who I'm married to. They don't see me. No one ever does."

"I see you. I see you, Colette. I've always seen the wonderful person you truly are. It's the reason I fell in-love with you in the first place," he said with such intensity, he hoped she felt it. "Goodness, woman, if you felt this way… so…resentful, why didn't you just say it?"

"Because you would have listened to me if I did? I tried. I tried when you asked me to stay home to raise our children, because no wife of yours should be made to work. I tried when you got mad at me for deciding to go back to school. I tried, Benjamin. I've always tried. You just weren't willing to listen."

"Okay. That's fair. I could see that," he said hesitantly.

"You can?" she asked skeptically.

"If you hadn't noticed, I can be an asshole when I want to be. Especially back then," he said sheepishly.

For the first time, she laughed with ease. She was right. He pushed her into being someone he thought his family would accept. *And it's the same way I push our son—all for image's sake. How can my wife and son ever feel loved, if I'm constantly pushing them to be something they're not*. He realized that he wasn't any different.

"Yeah. You can be quite the asshole, when you want to be," she agreed.

"Hey, you're not immune. You can be quite the asshole yourself."

"I never said I was a saint, now did I?" she chuckled.

Although he loved her for who she was, he knew that his family's acceptance lied heavily on her ability to play the role. All of which came at a price he didn't anticipate paying. *What if everything I tried to do to keep her with me, is the reason she's pulling away now?* He shuddered at the thought.

"Honestly?" she said with a sigh. Bringing his attention back to her, "You were just not an easy person to talk to. And then *it* happened."

Just the thought of it made her mouth go dry, and her body tremor. The elusive "it." The "it" they did not speak of—and nonetheless, it hung in the air like a rancid piece of flesh, choking them both with its hostility.

"I know. And I'm thankful every day that you stuck by me through it all."

"I thought I was going to lose you."

"Yet you saved me…again and again," he said sincerely.

"I'm your wife. Most importantly, I'm your friend. I'll always be there for you."

"Colette, can you at least think about how I feel? Why I wanted you both? And everything we have now," he asked, changing pace. "I didn't see your pregnancy as something terrible. I could never. I saw it as something… as something. You know what, never mind. I don't want to misconstrue anything."

"It's okay. You can tell me."

"I don't know how," he said, "I can't find the words."

"I find stories to be a great way," she said. Her eyebrows rose encouragingly, as she awaited his tale, "Just pretend like you're talking to someone else. Like I'm someone you don't know."

"Okay. I guess I can do that. You've done it already. Although, I'm not very good at stories. But I'll try. Do I need to start it like a fairytale?" he jested.

"No," she laughed, "You keep asking me 'how to do it,' like I didn't learn from the best. Or have you forgotten? Just start it, however you feel comfortable."

"Okay. I already knew you…well…*she* was pregnant…"

I Do

I didn't need her confirmation that she was pregnant. The moment I released inside her, I already knew what the outcome would be. As we made love, I felt nothing but certainty; it was the same way I felt the first time we kissed. Despite the way she looked on the night she broke the news to me, I knew that the life she carried would make us become who we were always meant to be—a family.

She came to me with tears of apprehension streaming down her face, and despite the fear projecting through her eyes, I could feel nothing but joy at the possibility of our future together. Our son's conception solidified all that we were and who we were to become. Yet there she stood, distressed, instead of marveling at the beautiful life we could have, and it split me in two.

"What are we going to do, Benjamin?" she asked hotly.

It had been eight weeks since I'd last seen her. The bliss I felt upon her call to meet back at my apartment, had initially made me feel that she was coming to her senses. Instead, I was met with the woman whose fortitude I once admired, slap me in the face with a reality I did not want to see.

"My mom is going to kill me."

"Cole, it'll be okay," I said. My attempt to soothe her was for naught.

"You know what? It was a mistake. And mistakes can be fixed," she rambled.

"What are you saying?"

"What do you think I'm saying, Benjamin? We don't have to—"

"You would get rid of our child?"

"What do you expect me to do? How can we support a child?

"We can make it work, Colette. I will make it work. I will figure it out, but you can't get rid of this baby. Our baby. You have to promise me."

"Promise you what? Do you think we're going to end up being some happy family? News flash, Mr. Lati, but if you haven't noticed, we have nothing! Plus, your family hates me. And it doesn't take a rocket scientist to figure out why!"

"It's not like that," I replied.

"Then how is it, Benjamin?"

"I don't…I don't know. They're just particular. Snobs, sure. But it's not how you think," I said skeptically. Despite what I told her, I wasn't truly sure myself.

"Get real already. People don't treat others the way that I've been treated unless they are bigots!"

"Now that's not fair. My mother has been nothing but kind to you, and—"

"Not fair? Not fair?! Are you fucking kidding me?" she raged, "You're really delusional! Just, fucking delusional! Your father won't even allow me in his home. And although your precious mother hasn't been like him, she never goes against his word. So, if you think they're going to welcome me and this baby into your family, when the family dog is treated better than I am… I mean, at least he's able to go in the house… then you have another thing coming to you!"

"That can be fixed" I said to her. "If you convert, I bet it won't be a problem—"

"Who says I want to convert?"

"I mean you've always spoke about how you thought about it before, and I always assumed that if we married, you'd convert so that we'd raise our kids—"

"Always like you…just assuming away. I thought you didn't want that?"

"I changed my mind. It is important to me. I didn't realize it then, but I do now," I replied. With the possibility of being a father, reality set in. There was no way I could step away from who I was—my heritage.

"But can we stay on topic, please," I said, "Haven't you thought about it?"

"Yes. I thought about it. And I probably would have done it, had I not had the displeasure of meeting your family. Either way… I shouldn't convert just to make them feel better," she fumed. "Like, at what point do you even think about me, or what I want? You know what? It's a good thing that we're not getting married. And we're damn sure not having any kids!"

Her words were like a dagger to my heart. The anger that rose within me made me crazed. And there was no way I was going to lose my family. "If you'd just listen to me, please, Colette? I'm sure that everything will work itself out. And I'm going to do my best to provide for you and our baby," I said, hoping she would see sense.

"What makes you think converting would solve our problems with your family?" she said absently.

"Why wouldn't it? That's the only reason why they're like that with you," I lied.

"Uh huh," she scoffed. "Just my religion, huh? Not because I'm 'gutter trash,' as your father so eloquently put it."

"You're right. He's an ass. But I know him. Family and tradition are what's important to him," I said. "Also, it's not like I wouldn't want it that way either, Colette."

"Oh, so now it's you too that would need me to convert. Tell me… did me being Jewish matter when you befriended me? When you professed your love to me? How about when you fucked and released in me, without my permission to create this baby!"

"Don't be crass," I chided.

"I'm sorry. Made love to? Is that better?"

"Yes, it is. Because despite what you want to believe, our baby was made by us and with love, Colette."

"Love? You didn't even love me enough to give me a choice," she said. Tears once again cascaded down her cheeks, marring her face in turmoil. "You say you love me, but you're trying to change me. To suit you! How is that love? How does this show me that you love me? If I were good enough to be with… and you wanted to marry me before this… then why do I have to become something that I am not?"

"I'm only trying to make it easier on us, motek. That's all. And it's what I want, either way, my love—"

"Bullshit!"

"It's not bullshit."

"It is! Never once have you spoken to me about it. Never once did you say that converting was a requirement to be with you. To love you. To potentially be your wife," she seethed. "You know…maybe this was your plan all along. Make me fall in-love with you—"

"So, you do love me?" I said trying to lighten the mood.

"Shut up, Benjamin! I don't have time for your jokes right now. This isn't a game. You can't get through this one with your fucking humor," she stated emphatically, "You can't say that you love *me*, and then try to mold me into someone else, to please others."

"I'm sorry. Look, we can discuss it a little down the line, but I know that—"

"You know nothing!" she said.

Pulling a piece of paper from her pocket, she slammed it down on the counter. Picking it up, it's shape and print took hold of me and made me shiver. And the familiar name and numbers sprawled neatly across, made my breath go still.

"When did he give this to you?"

"Your uncle, Ezra gave it to me, along with my final paycheck. I'm not supposed to contact you, or your family ever again."

"How does Ezra know?" I asked.

"I confided in Yael. I guess she told her father. I thought she was my friend," she sneered.

"So that means that my dad knows," I whispered.

My chest constricted. He knew. They all did. How long had they known? The fear that skated across my face must have resonated, because whatever glimmer of care she had toward me throughout our exchange, was replaced immediately with disgust.

"Of course, he knows. How else do you think I got the check, Benjamin? It doesn't matter anyway…I'm good."

"What does that mean?" I asked, as panic rose deep within my belly.

"It means…I'm good. I won't be a bother to you and your family, Benjamin."

"Oh no you don't," I said heatedly, "You're not going anywhere until you clarify what that means."

She took a moment to find her words and find her sense of calm, "Look. My home life is trash—always has been, always will be. And…I realize that I don't want to bring a baby into that…that place. It has a way of eating you alive. I have a chance now. Let me take it," she whispered, as her voice quivered with pain that gripped me just as tightly as she gripped the check that was now back in her hand, making my heart hurt.

"Don't do this, Colette. If you do, it will break us."

"We're already broken! We are never going to happen," she said with the same fire and passion that usually made me quake. I knew that she was trying to make me see reason, but I couldn't. How could I accept that she was throwing away our future—our life together? And like trumpets sounding, my heartbeat began to ring loudly in my ears. Its pace increased, and with fists clenched tightly, I couldn't stop the rage beating within me. She was not going to take my child away from me. Nor would I let her leave me.

"If you think you're going to walk out of here with *my* child inside your womb, you're out of your fucking mind! Do you think I'd let you sacrifice my child?"

"Two hundred and fifty thousand dollars would go a long way for me, Benjamin. I could finish school—"

"Are you fucking dense?!" I cried. At this point all reason had left me. Grabbing her mindlessly, my hands wrapped around her arms effortlessly and with strength I didn't know I had.

"You're hurting me!" she yelled, jerking her body from my grasp.

A sharp sting radiated throughout my face, as her hand collided against me—losing sense of myself, I began to slap and beat at my face and chest again and again as I felt myself drown in a pain so powerful, my body ached. Collapsing onto the floor and giving into my agony, I allowed my body to release the swell of despair that had overtaken me, leaving my cries echoing throughout.

"Do you think that you're not hurting me?" I exclaimed in a voice not of my own.

Her arms enclosed around me. And I let my body relax in her embrace, as I tried to come to terms with my new reality. We sat in each other's arms for what felt like an eternity—cheek to cheek, as our tears melded as one, before I finally had the strength to speak, "I'm sorry I hurt you."

"I know," she whispered. "But—"

"No. Please, Colette, don't," I whispered. I couldn't bear to listen to her shatter my dreams once more, "Can you answer a question for me?"

"What is it?"

"Why did you come here?" I asked, as my resolve began to return. I didn't realize it before, but something was off.

"I thought you deserved to know."

"No… you're lying to me. I know you," I replied. My mind raced with the epiphany that hit like a beam of light. "You didn't have to tell me anything. You could have taken the money quietly and gone, Colette. I would have been none the wiser. You're here because you know ending this…ending us…is wrong. And because, you know that I would fight for us the way you don't have the strength to. Look at me and tell me that I'm wrong."

The look on her face told me everything I needed to know. And with a nervous sigh and shrug of her shoulders, she said, "I don't know what to do."

"The only thing you need to do is trust me."

"I don't know if I can."

"Do you love me?"

"Yes. Of course, I do," she said with such admonition, I felt like a child being chastised. "If I didn't love you, I wouldn't be trying to do what's best for you. I wouldn't be trying to leave you, Benny. You know that."

"If you love me, you would be doing what's best for us, which includes you…as well as what you truly want to do," I stated. "You were never going to get rid of this baby…were you? The only person you were going to leave out of this equation was me."

"No…I," she began, "I thought you at least had the right to know, and I don't think… I can't do this by myself, Benny. I can't have this baby alone… but I don't want you to have to give up—"

"I won't give you up, Cole. *Enti 'umri*," I said with heated passion. "You are my life."

"We're not even together," she whined.

"Last time I checked, we were together just fine, and it got us here," I said slyly. Lifting her cautiously onto my lap, I placed my palm against her belly. As I rested my head against hers, I prayed that she would give life to dreams I couldn't believe were just my own. "Please. I want this baby more than you will ever know—just like I want you—both of you. Please?"

"I don't know," she said. Her apprehension clear.

"Come with me," I said.

Getting up, I led her to sit beside me on the bed. Leaning over, I reached into my nightstand to grab the small box I didn't have the heart to throw away. I'd always had hope that she would come back to me. Opening it, I placed the velvet box in her hand, "I got this as soon as I saw you that day at Ezra's café. I was just waiting for the right time to give it to you."

"We can't, Benny," she said, "We just…can't."

"We can. And we will. It will be hard, but we'll make it work. It's you, me, and the baby now. Us against the world," I said.

Taking the ring out the box, I placed the slight and elegant jewel on her hand. Its sparkle put a smile on my face, as I looked at it encompass her delicate finger—signifying the hope I had for our future. Cupping her cheeks, I willed her eyes to look into mine, "Marry me, Colette."

And with a nod of her head, I sealed our pending union with a kiss that spiraled into the throws of passion that only two lovers can create. Spending the night with her in my arms, I rested easy knowing that I would have the family I always wanted. And with a trip to the courthouse a week later, she became my wife—forever mine.

Triggered

Taking him into her embrace, she tried her best to extinguish the battle that raged within him. And as she molded her body into the tension radiating through his, she hoped that the softness of her love would guide him through the angst he was feeling.

Bringing his head away from her comfort, he searched her over. He knew in his heart that she didn't regret their life together. Yet, the resentment that traipsed across her face previously, did nothing to quell his fears. "You agreed to our marriage just as I did. You could have said, 'no'. Just as I wasn't forced, no one forced you to marry me either."

She was tired. He needed to realize that their union didn't change how things transpired. "Can you at least see things from my perspective? Please?"

"Why would I? I mean, how could I? If I give in to what you're implying, I would basically be saying that our entire marriage is a lie, and I can't accept that."

"But why can't both be true, Benjamin?"

"Meaning what?!"

Wrenching his body away from her harshly in frustration, he rubbed his hands tensely together and sighed heavily. Defeated he said, "You know, sometimes I wonder if loving you…I mean truly loving you, would have been best shown by letting you go. Because you make it seem as if I'm not worth it. Like all that we've become…grown together, wasn't worth it."

"Benny, now that isn't fair. I just need you to understand…for you to get…look…I don't feel like I had a choice, okay? In marrying you. In becoming who we are. Now wait…hear me out," she said, as the friction in his face returned, causing her to wait a moment before continuing. "As I was saying…I did not have a choice in Judah's conception…that was taken from me when you did what you did. But I would be remiss and dishonest if I said that his conception was the reason, I married you. Did it speed up the process? Felt as if my hand was forced? Yes, to both. But I wanted to marry you for you. Not because I was pregnant, but for *you*. I wanted nothing more than to be your wife…but I wasn't resilient enough to endure the things we've gone through— honestly, neither of us were. We were children! We just…we just needed more time. To grow. To know ourselves. To become… strong enough to deal with…life."

He allowed her to pull him back to her. He knew in his heart that she was right. The things they experienced; he wouldn't wish on his worst enemy. But he couldn't shake the feeling that based on this reality, there was no purity in her choice to be with him. It would forever be marred by the inception of what made them a family—and he was the reason for it.

"I didn't feel as though we had time," he stated honestly. The truth hitting him like a ton of bricks.

"I know, but we were too young. We barely made it a few months before things got chaotic again."

"I was willing, Colette. I didn't care about any of that. I just wanted you."

"But you had that luxury. You had the ability not to care. My whole life was spent trying to get out of there, and the moment I got pregnant with Judah, it was jeopardized. Plus…never mind," she said with a shrug. She wasn't ready to go there just yet.

"I know, but I knew that we could make it work. I just knew that we would. I felt it in my heart and soul, and all I needed was for you to believe in us. It doesn't matter anyway because you still…"

"Benny. I know how it seems to you. But trust me, it doesn't change the fact—"

"Look, I know that I messed up, but we—"

Putting her hands to his lips, she said, "Attempting to finish my sentence I see. What I was going to say was… it doesn't change the fact that we built something great, despite how it all happened. And despite how our marriage came to be, it never changed the fact that I wanted you. I just didn't think I could have you…that I…that I deserved you," she whispered. Her head was cast low, as she averted his gaze, unable to meet his eyes.

"Are you kidding me? It was me who didn't deserve you," he said heatedly.

"I just thought…that I needed to be perfect for you, Benny. I wanted to finish school and be somebody, so that I could be good enough for you. And then I got pregnant."

"Oh, no…no…no, motek," he said. Bringing them down to the floor, he planted her between his legs with her back against him, his arms wrapped around her, in the way they had first started their journey. "You were everything I ever wanted…everything I needed."

"Then why try so hard, Benny? Why push me?"

He knew what she meant. Although the conversion eventually became her idea, he never stopped trying to cultivate an image for her that would be accepted by them. Instead of congratulating her for her accolades, he lamented about her lack of care in being a dutiful wife. It wasn't because he cared. In fact, he was proud of her. Truthfully, her accomplishments then, made him afraid that she would eventually see reason and find someone more worthy of her. Yet despite the verity that she was everything he needed, he tried to force her to meet a standard she never needed to.

"I'm sorry. I've accused you of caring what others think, and I did the same. I didn't want to make it easy for my family—hell, the community even, to dislike or mistreat you. I now realize that I only made it harder for us. Their approval meant nothing in the long run. Not just because they didn't care either way, but because you were perfect for me. And overall, everything worked out in the end, with you just being you. I worried for nothing."

She was taken aback. He had never said those things to her before. Hearing him speak candidly about what she always felt was true, put her heart at ease. It made her feel as though they had a chance. A sense of calm washed over her, causing her to nestle deeper into him. They laid motionless and took in the serenity of their closeness and the quiet around them. After some time, she spoke. Turning to him, she asked, "Do you think we can fix this?"

"We always do, motek. We always do," he said, caressing her cheek.

"I hope so. I know what has happened these past few months—this past year, maybe difficult to bounce back from. But I hope that we can fix it. That we can fix us. I mean, it hasn't been all bad, right?" she shrugged.

"Look, as much as we've been through, yet here we still stand…we'll be fine," he smiled.

"Sometimes I just don't know, Benny. It's like the world keeps coming at us. It just won't stop!"

"You don't understand. Do you, Colette? There is nothing that will keep me from you, but you. As long as you love and want me, I will always be your husband," he said fervently, taking her back into his arms.

"My love for you knows no bounds, Benny. You know that. Right?"

"I know. I just never realized how much resentment you held for me. It stings," he sighed, "Who knew this year would bring up so much…we've obviously left unspoken."

"Yes. We need to do better. And I'm ready to do better, if you are," she said.

"Good. Then we're in agreement. It's still you, me, and our family, against the world," he said. "From childhood until forever, motek. Always."

"I suppose so. Besides, who else would be able to tolerate you?"

"Hey!" he laughed. "I take offense to that. I was thinking more along the lines of, who else would I have found to be my wife, and mother to my children?"

"I miss them terribly. The kids, I mean. I miss them so much," she spoke softly.

"I know you do, and I'm sorry you haven't been able to be with them."

"It's not like I deserve to be with them."

It was his turn to break away, as he tried to fathom how she came to such an asinine conclusion. "What do you mean?"

"I left them. I locked myself away in that motel. Ended up here," her voice trailed, as she tried to gain control of her emotions. The grasp of his hands enclosing her own, and the patience he displayed in his eyes, gave her the confidence to continue. "I don't know…I mean…I don't think I'm fit to be their mother."

Tears gleamed in her eyes and his heart ached for her. The one thing he knew for certain, was that his wife prided herself in the way she took care of them—her family. Despite the way she felt, he knew that her assessment of her status as a mother to their children was ludicrous. The only thing she ever thought of was their children, and how to make them happy. So much so, he now realized that she gave too much of herself.

He got it. He finally understood the reason for her break down. The secrets, and his distance because of it, made her work herself even harder. She pushed and pulled past the uncertainty he afforded her, to ensure peace in their home—for their children. She'd lost herself—her strength. In the midst of trying to keep everything perfect, and his aloofness under wraps, she had dwindled into nothingness. He realized now that she didn't have the fight needed to get through losing her mother. She never had a chance to get through the past year—not any of it. *Why didn't I just tell her sooner? Because you wanted to protect her, like you always do, you fool.*

One thing was certain now—the woman that made him a husband and father—his wife, was only human. And for that he could not fault her, without faulting himself.

"Colette, the kids understand. You were grieving…you still are. And if I were to judge you for this, I might as well pass judgement on myself. You didn't get here alone, motek. If I were…if I were honest with you from the beginning…we wouldn't be here right now. I shouldn't have kept that from you. And it all brought me back…back to that place. It kept me away from you. For that, I am so sorry," he said.

Although she appreciated his honesty, it couldn't sweep away the guilt she felt in allowing herself to become someone she didn't recognize. "It doesn't matter, Benny. I'm supposed to be there."

"It does matter. It matters, because you can't always be perfect for us, Cole. And I realize that now," he stated, "Besides, you are there, even while being in here. You don't think I know that you speak to them every night? Or that, even from here, you're still making sure that everything from school functions to doctor's appointments, go along seamlessly? To which I might I add…and I should have said this long ago…I've got it handled."

"But it's not that simple."

"What's not simple about letting me take some of the load while you're here? Or at all?"

"The last time you called yourself taking a bit off my plate, you kept a secret from me for an entire year," she said lightheartedly.

"Ouch," he said, "That one burned. But it doesn't change the fact that you should be focusing on getting better."

"I know…I know. It's just that I feel…I feel connected to them when I take care of things. And I…well… I don't want them to hate me for leaving them and being here," she said, wiping a tear away.

"I see," he said. His sigh was audible and filled with unmasked pain. "You don't want them to hate you, the way that Judah hates me?"

"I'm so sorry. I didn't mean it like—"

"It's okay. I get it. But I assure you… they won't hate you. They think you're on a wonderful vacation because you needed time for …well…you know," he spoke.

He hadn't had the heart to say it. She meant a lot to him too. It was she who helped them get through the trials of being young parents. She was the one who helped care for his wife and children when he couldn't be there, and for that, he would always love his mother in-law dearly.

"They do?" she asked. Her amusement was evident, because there was nothing more she would have rather been doing.

"Yes. And they know nothing about what happened. Plus, the fact that you still do all that you do for them, the only thing they're missing is your physical presence."

"Ugh! I just miss them so much."

"I offered to bring them here, but that's always been your choice."

"I don't want them to see me like this," she whispered. "I can't. It's best that they think that I'm on a vacation on some tropical island. At least I have Judah to visit me."

He understood. There were times he wished he would have been where she was sitting now—perhaps that was why he opted to commit her there. It would have saved him from the grief he felt over the relationship he now shared with their son, "Why do you think he hates me so much?" he asked.

Sighing deeply, she searched for a way to tell the man she loved, that he was and would always be, loved by them all. She had not meant to dredge up his pain, and for that she owed him this. And although she knew he needed the truth, her love for him could never force her heart to speak against him cruelly, no matter the cost. For that reason, she wanted to find the right words.

"Because…um…he didn't have a chance to know you. The real you. You know…before…"

The past tumbled its way to the forefront of her mind, causing her to reach absently towards the scar that lightly shone under the thickness of his beard—parting it like the red sea. It was a reminder of the things they dared not speak. She shuddered as the weight of the past hit her like a ton of bricks. I almost lost him, she thought. And she realized then, that despite her pain, given his past, he had handled things the best way he knew how.

As they sat in the simplicity of the warmth of their bodies pressed against each other, he drowned himself in his love for her. In that moment, he felt as if he had the girl he'd fallen in-love with so long ago. The feel of her trapped him in a trance that seemed to subdue his anguish and reminded him of the way her strength permeated through him, which always had a way of making him feel whole. He couldn't understand how she never understood just how wonderfully crafted she was. From the very beginning, the way she gave herself to him—saved him and taught him what love truly meant, made him fall deeper and deeper. She was made perfectly—for him.

She did not know it then, but the care and attention she paid, when they were nothing more than children, gave him the strength to get through the complexities and demons that plagued his childhood. It was the authenticity of her inner beauty that solidified his love for her—a love that had saved him more than once. Like a beacon of light, the energy she poured into him, so effortlessly, was what drew him to her. And like a moth to a flame, he was bound to her, and needed her with him—always. He needed her back. He needed them back.

"I think it's time that you come home," he whispered.

"Really?"

"Yes. I shouldn't have let you stay this long in the first place. I just…I didn't know what to do. I thought I was going to lose you. And…well…there isn't any reason that you can't finish your care at home."

Squeezing him tightly, she rode the wave of emotions that washed over her. For the first time in a long while, she smiled confidently at their future. "I love you, Benjamin Ezra Lati," she said with tears in her eyes.

Grabbing her face in his hands and staring into the well that led to the depths of her soul, he expressed the vow that was welling within him. And between each passionate kiss, he made his proclamation, "I want you… always. I will never keep a secret from you again. Never, will you leave my side. I love you, Colette Imani-Mae Lati. You are my soul."

And with that, he rose to leave, and his heart swelled at the knowledge that this wasn't their last goodbye, because his wife was coming home.

Benny couldn't stop tossing and turning. The weight of the blanket pressing against him did nothing to subdue him. It was always harder at night; the reality of being without her seemed to plague him more. The empty space where her body once emanated warmth, taunted him, and he couldn't help but reach out. As he stroked the softness of her pillow, clutching it to his body, he smelled her scent that still lingered lightly in the down of feathers inside. It wasn't long before it conjured images of her. Closing his eyes tightly, the long lines of her body as it usually splayed across their bed, danced deliciously in his head. Images of her face cast in the moonlight teased him mercilessly—and he could almost taste the sweetness of her lips.

In that moment, the flapping of blinds echoed loudly through their room. The hard breeze of the cold night air caused them to whip about wildly, springing him out of his spell. Kicking off his blanket in frustration, he stormed off to trap the gust of wind that ended his fantasy of her. One more week—one more week and she'll be home in my arms again, he thought.

"Not soon enough," he scoffed loudly, as his frustration mounted.

It had always been hard to sleep without her. And the clock on his nightstand blaring two a.m., did nothing to help his mood. "Shit!" he yelled. The words escaped his lips as another night's sleep, slowly crept away from him.

Sighing heavily, he began the nightly ritual he adopted since she'd been away. Walking through the space they shared, he allowed it to envelop him in memories of them. Looking across their spacious bedroom, visions of them dancing wildly around unpacked boxes played prominently, as he remembered their first night in their home. A walk through their closet invoked images of her in her wedding gown, as he touched the veil, she purchased to renew their vows. It was a day he would never forget, for it was as if he were seeing her for the first time. He felt so proud to be able to give her the wedding he knew she deserved.

Thinking of what he called their true wedding, always brought joy to his heart, and he found himself pulling out the stack of neatly placed photo albums and keepsakes from the bottom of his wife's side of the closet. Picking up each album and skimming them quickly, he smiled at the visual manifestations of their life together. Looking through them all, as he basked in the glow of nostalgia, he came across a small box of letters. Pulling out the stack, a lone picture toppled out that placed him into a living nightmare.

"I thought we got rid of them all," he whispered, as his mind began the involuntarily journey to memories, he tried hard to bury. Visions of them emerged in front of him, and he knew that he was on the verge of entering that realm where it was hard for him to flee…without her.

His pulse quickened as his anxiety rose, sparking a tightness in his chest that he could not control, forcing him to double over as he tried to catch his breath. *Calm down now, Benjamin. Breath in and out slowly. Try to catch your breath. It's just a panic attack. It'll be over soon if you maintain control.*

But the overwhelming thoughts tormented him, causing his mind to race towards a time he desperately tried to escape. It wasn't long before he lost himself once again to the madness of his past, where memories washed over him and pulled him into the abyss, unwilling to let him go from his pain. Compelling him back to that time, once again.

Casualties of War

The morning light cascading through the window prompted him awake. It had been five weeks since his return home, and his body still ached from the blast that almost claimed him. Reaching for the glass on his nightstand to quench the unbearable thirst his medication encouraged, he flinched at the pain his body radiated upon moving; a result of his last surgery that saw him fit enough to return home.

"Don't do that. Lay back. I got it, love," she said in a groggy whisper.

"Still here? I thought I told you to rest…and I didn't mean in that chair that you've somehow made your bed," he reprimanded.

"You were crying out again. And I didn't want to leave you in case you needed me," she said with a yawn, as she allowed him to sip his water.

"What I need is for you to take care of yourself."

"I'm fine. Is that enough?" she said, as she waited for his cue that he was finished.

Colette barely recognized him now. His once jovial, lighthearted nature was weighed by the anguish and nightmares that constantly afflicted him. The large brown eyes she once spent hours getting lost in, now held sorrow so powerful it drowned her in its misery; tormenting her so, she could hardly keep his gaze.

"Another nightmare, huh?" he said, wishing he could get the images out of his head. Every time he closed his eyes, he could see them—their screams rose in his ears, as their faces blared at him in rapid fire. He had long ceased trying to find his escape in slumber. The fear of summoning their memories was enough to wither him—forcing him into the shell of a man he found himself becoming. Although the sleeping pills put Benny into the sleep his body desperately needed, it did nothing to rid him of the echoes of his ordeal. It played like a movie reel, over and over, as his dreams turned to nightmares.

"I didn't hurt you, did I?" he asked.

The fear in his eyes at the prospect of hurting her, made her take pause. The first night he acted out in his sleep, had terrified her. That night, she awoke to the sounds of his screams and his body violently thrashing about. In turn, she grabbed him so that she could compel him awake. Within seconds, his hands, that were once viciously grabbing at the air, found their way around her neck. His eyes, glazed over and wide with terror, brought forth the image of a creature desperate for release. A crash from a glass they knocked over in their struggle, finally startled him awake, forcing his awareness to the placement of his hands and the fear in her eyes. It was enough for him to ask her to sleep in a separate room and leave him to his turmoil. But she couldn't leave him. Instead, she had taken to sleeping in the chair that was placed strategically near their bed, and at his insistence, kept her distance from him during his nightmares, no matter how gruesome they seemed, until they passed.

"You could never hurt me," she soothed, as she caressed the scar that danced menacingly across his cheek.

He flinched at her touch and drew her hand gently away from his face. Although scarred, the wound had not yet healed, as it had become a constant reminder of what could have been. He could still feel the shrapnel imbedded in his cheek in place of the lingering heat of her hands. When will this end, he wondered.

"Please don't," he whispered to her. His voice came like a wounded child, who had finally conceded defeat. He knew that she was only trying to ease his pain, but he felt that he didn't deserve her grace after all he put her through.

"I'm sorry…I didn't mean… I guess I can't do anything right."

"No, motek. My love, you are doing nothing wrong," he said grasping her hand, "It's just… I can't explain it."

"I don't like seeing you like this, Benny. I hate seeing you in pain. I wish I could take it away for you, because…I just…I miss you. That's all," she said as she struggled to find the words to convey her thoughts. She tried to harness her feelings, but the tears in her eyes betrayed her. For months she thought the worry from the countless surgeries his body had endured, and the physical pain she watched him suffer, would shatter her. But it was the anguish behind his eyes that never ceased, that was becoming her undoing.

It was the way the light in his eyes no longer glimmered at the sign of her presence. Not even their sons could rouse him, and it scared her, because with each passing day, her love did not return.

Falling into an awkward silence, her eyes fell on his bare chest. The once smooth skin checkered with fine hairs, was now riddled with the markings his wounds had left behind. It added a sense of fierceness to his appearance. It had been a year since she had the feel of him, and the tautness of his abs as they strained from the tension in his body, did nothing to help her growing frustration.

All she wanted was his love again, but the man that sat before her now was an empty shell. He was neither good for company, nor comfort. Her gentleness with him seemed to rile his angst. And despite her efforts to gain the warmth of his embrace, he constantly shrank away from her touch. It devastated her.

As if reading her mind, he brought one apprehensive hand to hers, and guided her towards him. The longing in her face, broke him in two. He knew that she needed him, but how could he explain that he felt undeserving of her. She wouldn't look at him if she knew what he did, let alone touch him. She had put on a brave face until now. Her constant smiles and jovial appearance were a façade—a performance she'd invoked especially for him. He saw that now. Defeat spread like wildfire through her body, and he could torture her no longer. "Come…please," he said, reaching out to her again.

Her hesitation to move, deflated him; but with a stifled breath, he pulled her in close and placed her head onto his chest. His arms, once uncertain, settled into a tight embrace, causing them both to finally breathe easy.

"I miss this," she said gently.

"I know. I do too. I'm sorry, Colette. I just… I wish I could make you understand," he said exasperated.

"You know you can always talk to me, Benny. That will never change."

Before he could reply, a knock on the door captured their attention. Moving reluctantly from the comfort of his embrace, she got up to see who was there. Peering on the other side, she could see the faces of the two people she dreaded seeing most.

"Mr. and Mrs. Lati. I didn't know you were stopping by," Colette said.

Pushing past her. They placed themselves on the couch by their son's bed, where she had made vigil. "I didn't realize I needed an appointment to see my son," replied his father.

"It's not that, Mr. Lati. It's just that with his appointments and physical therapies, you might not have caught us," Colette said. She tried to keep her voice even, but the look on his face—the same look of contempt he always had upon seeing her face, was making it difficult.

"So, what? We're not welcomed unless you're here. We have grandchildren to see as well, you know?"

"That's not what she's saying, Abba," Benny chimed in, coming to her defense. He could already see what mood his father was in, and he was not about to deal with it, let alone allow his wife to become a human punching bag. "It's not like you see the kids anyway. I mean, I've been home for weeks now, and this is the first that you've shown up."

"How can we, when apparently, we have to make an appointment to come over?" he replied.

"Are you eating enough, Ben?" his mother asked, trying to change the subject.

"I'm fine, Ima," he whined.

"It's just that you look so…I don't know."

"I said, I'm fine, Ima."

"Is she not making you enough food?" his mother questioned.

"My wife cooks well for me. I just don't have an appetite," Benny replied. He was growing frustrated. This was the reason he insisted on waiting to tell them he was home.

"I bet if she made the things you liked, you'd eat better. I could go fix you something right now. Have you eaten?"

"I said, my wife cooks for me just fine, Ima! There is nothing wrong with her cooking. It's me. I don't want to eat. I'm stuck in this bed until my leg heals enough for me to walk freely. I'm on several different medications that make me fucking nauseous. And I…I can't stop… I can't stop seeing their faces," he rushed out. "So, no Ima, I don't want to eat! So lay off! Alright?! And stop talking about my wife like she isn't in the fucking room!"

"You will not speak to your mother that way. No one asked you to go over there. Leaving your wife and children—"

"Don't act like you give a shit about my wife and children," Benny replied heatedly. "Were you there for them while I was gone? How many times did you visit them? Huh? My wife gave birth to Luke by herself and had a toddler in tow. Where were you? She's lucky that she at least had her mother and Miriam to help lighten the load."

"The better question, son, is where were you?"

"I was doing my duty and serving my fucking country!" Benny exploded.

"And look what good it's gotten you! We would have been better off staying in Israel, if it meant you'd never be here like this. You could have served there, if the need presented itself. Hell, you should have. Now we have to see you… like this," his father stated in disgust.

"Is this what you came here for, Abba? I'm already in enough pain. Why did you have to come here with this bullshit?"

"Look, maybe we should all just calm down a bit. Benny, you can't get yourself worked up like this, my love. How about I go make some lunch, and we can all sit down and relax. And you two can visit with the kids. I'm sure that they'd like to meet you," Colette said, trying to keep the peace.

"I think that's a great idea," his mother agreed. Her accent growing heavier as the stress in the room began to consume her, "I'll help you, Colette."

"I don't want anything from you," Mr. Lati said to Colette pointedly. Turning his attention to his wife he said, "Dina, you go. Make us some lunch."

"How about you stop treating my wife like a lepper, please, Abba? Before I ask you to leave," Benny seethed. "This is our home, and if you choose not to eat the food she makes—"

"Really, Ben. It's fine. I'll make something. That is, if you don't mind, Colette," said Dina, trying to calm the situation.

"At this point, I'll do anything to keep the peace, Mrs. Lati," Colette answered.

"Okay. Very good. I'll show you how to make *kubbeh*. And we can make *ba'be'btamur* for dessert. Come. We can do it together. Do you have any dates?" she asked. Her smile was encouraging and gentle as she rose from her seat.

"I said, you, Dina," his father said. The look on his face was enough to make Colette want to scream.

"Musa *khalas*! That is enough! We did not come here to place more strain on them," Dina bellowed, "All I want is to spend time with my son, his children, and this woman, who is supposed to be my daughter. At least grant me that peace."

"I'm here, aren't I? I granted you that. Don't ask anything more of me," Musa fumed. "I don't want, nor need that woman to make anything for me."

Kissing her teeth, Dina marched herself out of Colette and Benny's room. Her buoyant demeanor was replaced with an ire that left her once softened eyes, marred with fiery anger that made her husband stiffen with remorse. In the minimal interactions she had with Musa and Dina Lati, Colette couldn't help but feel for the woman. She didn't understand how Dina didn't run away and leave the ungrateful lot to their own devices.

"I'm going to go help your mom," Colette said.

"I said that my wife will be making lunch. Perhaps, you should go see to your children," Musa said callously.

"With all due respect, Mr. Lati, but in your house, you can command anyone or anything as you please. However, in *my* home, you will not be telling me what to do. Nor your wife. Now if you'll excuse me, I'm going to help my mother-in-law, and let her finally meet her grandchildren," Colette replied snidely. And with a stroke of his hand, she left Benny in his father's company.

"This is the woman you chose to marry," Musa exclaimed. "You know, in the old country, a woman would never speak to her husband's family in such a manner."

"Well, it's a good thing that we're not in the old country, isn't it?" Benny replied arrogantly. "You come to our home and think that you're going to run shit? You are a real trip, Abba."

"So, this is how you speak to me now? You sound like—"

"Like, what, Abba? Like her? Like them? I rather sound like the people who give a damn about me and what I want, than to sound like a pompous asshole, like you."

"You better watch yourself, boy," he said vehemently. "And if I remember correctly, you had nothing to do with getting this home, you seem to want to put me out of."

"If you're speaking of my wife's prowess in the real estate market, then yes, she contributed the bulk of our down payment. So what?" Benny scoffed.

Despite his father's attempt to emasculate him, he was proud of the woman his wife had become. After eloping, he found that his wife's assertions of his family were true. It wasn't long before his father cut him off completely, and left him alone to fend for the family he created with her. After transferring to State University, the academic scholarships she received, along with his scholarship from ROTC, helped them both to graduate with honors—she with a degree in business management and marketing, and he in psychology. While pursuing his master's and starting his career as a reservist, at the behest of Akal, Colette received her real estate license.

By the time Benny had volunteered to do his first tour, she was making a killing at a high-end brokerage firm, she and Akal worked for. Working effortlessly as a team in a rising market, the money she made, she used frugally. And before leaving for the deployment that had ridden him in the bed, he now found himself in, they'd closed on their beautiful home. If she weren't taking care of me, she'd be finished with her MBA by now, he thought, as guilt began to consume him.

"It should have been you to provide your family with a home. Not her. That is not what we do," Musa scoffed.

"It really drives you insane that she's not the 'gutter trash' you invented in your mind, doesn't it? Or is it the fact that she's the one that's sitting pretty with that business degree, instead of me?" Benny said smugly, his amusement in goading his father evident by the look in his eyes.

"*Al titfos tachat.* Tread lightly, Benjamin. You're not too old," Musa warned.

"For what? You don't. You act as if I'm oblivious to the grudge you have against her," Benny snickered.

"*Yalla.* Fine. You think you want to hear it, but you really don't. She's everything you should have been, and that I wanted from you. And if it hadn't been for her bewitching you, with that ass of hers—"

"Oh, so you noticed. I knew it. She does have a beautiful ass, doesn't she?"

"Enough, Benjamin! When did you become so crass?"

"Me? I'm not the one checking out my daughter in-law," Benny said with a shrug, "I don't blame you. But just so we're clear, sex wasn't the reason I wanted her. It wasn't to spite you either. I could have done that without her, in my sleep. And, Judah isn't the reason I married her, so stop reducing my wife to what's in between her legs. Alright?! Thanks."

"Whatever, Ben. It doesn't change the fact that if it weren't for her, you'd be by my side where you belong."

"I'm exactly where I belong, Abba. The quicker you realize that the better off we'd all be. You can't blame her forever for the decisions I made, for myself," he said. "I really need you to get this. Seriously, Abba… I do. She didn't steal me away. She didn't force or hex me to be with her. I was never going to take part in being who you wanted me to be. Whether my wife came into my life or not; under no circumstance would I have worked for you—or with you."

"I see," Musa said sadly. The hurt in his eyes was fleeting, and it didn't take long for him to lash out against the son he had put his all into. He didn't care what he said. His mind wouldn't allow him to think rationally, because to him, if it weren't for Colette, his son would have never defied him. She was to blame. His son wouldn't be laid up in the bed with his body mauled to pieces in a war he had no business in. She stole his son from him, and he could never forgive her for that.

"You may not have been working for me, but you wouldn't be lying in this bed, needing your wife to help you go piss and wipe your ass!"

"Like, I couldn't have gotten this way had I gotten hit by a fucking car?! Or by some freak accident? Shit happens, Abba!"

"But you didn't, did you? If you hadn't married her, you would have never joined their military, and gone to that place," Musa rationalized.

"If I hadn't married her, I would have never known what love truly is. I would have never learned what it feels like to have someone love me for me, and not for my ability to behave like a damn robot. You cut me off and left me no choice, remember? You!" Benny snapped back. "And for the record, even if I hadn't married her, there was no way I wouldn't have done my duty to serve after what happened to my city."

"You owed them nothing! You don't owe these people—you don't owe this place, anything at all. Nothing! You hear me?! This city doesn't care about you! So why do you care so much?" Musa replied, pounding his fist hard against his chest.

"It doesn't matter what you think, Abba," Benny sighed.

"So, you really think you've done your duty? And what was your reward, eh? Like I said. You owed them nothing. Especially not this," he said, thrusting his hands towards the man, who was still nothing but a boy in his eyes. Despite what his son believed, it pained him to see him this way—broken by the tragedies of war. *What if we had lost him?* Musa shuddered at the thought.

"I owed you nothing either. Look, Abba…I think it's time for you to go."

"Benjamin. You don't understand? The fear? Every night we spent, wondering if you were okay. We were all worried about you. We still are."

"Abba. I'm tired. Why don't you go meet your grandsons? We can visit some more during lunch. Okay? And please…don't disrespect my wife while you're here," Benny said quietly. His spirit defeated, he was tired of having this conversation with his father—a man he once worshipped and wanted nothing more than to please. But time had a funny way of revealing the truth; he realized a long time ago that his father was nothing more than a man, swallowed by his own passions and pride. And it had cost him to lose his son. With each passing moment and transgression against Benny's family, the bond between father and son became undone, with no signs of mending.

"Okay, Ben. Okay. I'll behave. And who knows? Maybe one of those grandsons of mine will become the man I expected you to be," he replied.

"Are you done griping at me, or no?"

"I'm not saying it to be…never mind," Musa said sympathetically, "I'm sorry."

"Whatever. I don't have the head for this—"

"They look like you, you know? Your boys," Musa interrupted.

"So, you have gotten our pictures, then? Interesting," Benny sighed.

"Look, Abba—"

"Yes. your mother showed them to me. Would you mind if I brought them down to the office?" Musa said absently. "Your boys, I mean. I'd really like to show them around. And it's never too early to start them off in a three-piece suit, ya know?"

Looking at the fine lines and smile of his father's face, as it amassed so much hope, brought on so many emotions. On one hand, the boy in him wanted nothing more than to agree to his father's whims; however, the man that he was, could not concede. How could he give in, when his father denied the very essence of who his children were—their mother.

"My children aren't going anywhere without their mother."

"Why? She doesn't need to be there," Musa scoffed. "If you're worried about me getting too busy, I'll have your mother with me to help. It'll be an opportunity to spend time with them and get to know them better. Besides, your wife should be here to help you."

"You'll never stop, will you?" Benny asked.

"Stop what? You know…I don't get you," Musa replied. "I'm finally doing what you want, and you're angry with me?"

"My sons weren't born to become miniature versions of you, Abba!"

"Alright, fine! I won't bring them to the office, but can we at least have them to the house for visits? For shabbat? Someone has to teach my grandsons about their heritage. HaShem knows they're probably not learning anything here."

If looks could kill, the glare that Benny gave his father would have struck the man where he stood. Stifling his anger, he exclaimed, "My answer isn't going to change! Where they go, their mother goes."

"I don't need that woman at my home! Your mother is well-versed in caring for children," he chastised. "Besides, we should be able to spend time with them in peace. I don't need that woman's interference in rearing these boys into the young men they should be."

"The young men they should be?" Benny sneered. "You mean the young men, you'd like them to become?"

"And what's wrong with that?"

"Abba, whatever you're looking for, you will not find it in my children. You're better off looking to their mother for that."

"What is that supposed to mean?"

"My wife is the child you've always wanted. You even said so yourself, in this very conversation. And at the rate she's going, she'll surpass anything you've ever dreamt up, when it comes to me or my children," Benny said matter-of-factly.

"What does any of that matter? It's not like she cares for us—for our family," Musa retorted.

"You really don't get it do you? I chose her because she is everything you've ever taught me to seek in a wife. And she has exceeded my expectations in every way. She's a good woman, Abba," Benny replied.

"Is that so?"

"Yes, that's so. The woman I married is selfless to a fault. The only thing she cares about is family—our family. And since you're my family, you're already family to her," Benny implored. "Look, Abba…truthfully? If it weren't for her, you wouldn't have known about anything that has been going on in my life. The contact you've had with me, is because of my wife and her efforts in trying to keep the peace."

"I see," Musa replied somberly. "Still, it doesn't change much for me, son. I can't be bothered with someone who…I mean…well…she's just so different from us. From what I expected for you."

"And why is different a bad thing, Abba?"

"Look, son, despite what you think, you need a wife that understands—"

"I need her."

"Will you let me speak?" Musa asked. The irritation that danced across his face, could not be masked. "As I was saying, you need someone who understands the importance of…maintaining our traditions. Or at the very least, is willing to raise your children the way they should be raised; and in accordance with our values—"

"Abba, she's the one who goes to shul. Not me. If you haven't noticed, I've been rather busy getting myself into the mess I'm in now," Benny replied. "Trust me, your traditions are safe with her, old man."

"Really?" Musa asked. His interest now peaked, as his serious face relaxed and became transfixed by his thoughts.

"Yes. Really. I've told you before, and I'll say it again…you've misjudged her. And…you've misjudged yourself."

"How is that?"

"You raised me, Abba. And you should trust in the work that you've done—that I would choose someone who's everything you could have ever asked for, for me."

"You're right, son," Musa relented and reflected. "I never thought of it that way."

"Damn straight I am."

His father stood quietly again, as his son's words took hold, and he realized what a fool he had been. Clearing his throat, he asked, "So…what shul did you say she goes to again? And she takes the boys as well? All by herself…without you asking?"

"I never said, but you could go ask her yourself," Benny replied. And before his father could counter, he sent him on his way.

Allowing his mind to wander, Benny found himself thinking of the choices that brought him there. *Maybe my father is right? If I hadn't gone, they'd still be here*. But how could he ignore the call to battle? His father could never understand. None of them did. His family weren't there when the towers fell; instead, they watched the travesty from the comforts of their home—where the sun shone brightly with life, and in contrast to the cloudy skies that consumed his city's skyline with rubble and debris. And the air grew thick with screams of terror.

He had just made his way from the plaza after having a light breakfast, when the first tower was struck. It had become routine for him to pass through its art filled floor on his way to work, to prepare for the long grueling day at his internship. He found that the art and watching the hustle and bustle of the many who worked at the towers relaxed him. He was on Broadway when he heard it. The sounds of the first impact had throttled him. Like others, he found himself frozen and entranced by the scene before him. He never made it in to work that day, because for one hour and forty-two minutes, he watched in distress at the tragedy that had befallen his city.

The gust of fragments that encircled him, when the towers fell, as he hid behind cars, were still vivid in his memory. As the dust settled, he'd taken to giving aid where he could, and it wasn't until he was within the safety of his home, with his wife and son held tightly in his arms, that he was able to unleash his grief for the many that were lost. His family hadn't a clue what those moments were like. So, it was easy for them, he felt, to play spectator in the decisions he made when they had no skin in the game. Even as a child, he had always been someone who tried his best to put duty first, no matter the cost; so, they shouldn't have been surprised when he volunteered to go.

He remembered the day he told them, like it was yesterday. It had been a long day of fighting with his wife, and although she understood his desire, she could not understand his need to fight. To her, they had been lucky—

unlike others. At the time, he had been spared orders to fight in the war, that would eventually lead him to his current state. He had waited over a year to answer the call, and when it didn't come, he decided to take matters into his own hands.

War Bound

Do you know how many would kill to be in your shoes? To have the ability to be home with their families for as long as you have? And you just went ahead and volunteered?!" she screamed. His news had caught her off guard. Throwing her into a spiral of emotions she couldn't contain.

"What do they have to do with me?"

"How about the fact that you're taking things for granted."

"I'm not taking anything for granted, Colette. This would have happened eventually anyway—"

"Yes…eventually! But you didn't have to go looking for it! You didn't even discuss it with me! How could you make a choice like that without consulting me first?!" she shouted.

"I made a choice for myself, to serve my country the best way I know how," Benny shrugged.

"No…no…no…NO! You didn't just make a choice for yourself. You made a choice for me without my input. You made a choice to leave me without a husband, and our son without a father, so you can go play hero," she said heatedly.

"It's not like that. It's not that way at all. I am doing my duty—"

"Duty? Your duty is to me and our son. Your duty was to discuss this, before you decided to make a life changing decision without me. You always do this! You're always cutting me out, like I'm not a part of this…marriage," she huffed.

"Because you act like this," he said, trying to calm his growing irritation.

He wished that she would lay off him and not make things harder than they had to be. It wasn't like he wanted to leave them, but he knew his purpose. He needed to do his part. He wasn't going to sit idly by, while his friends were in the thick of it. He couldn't. Some of his buddies were already there. It was his turn now.

"You're overreacting, Colette."

"Overreacting? I'm overreacting? Really?" she fumed. "You've been sitting on orders for months! Months! Sneaking around to trainings—you lied to me about that too! All so you can wait until the day before you are scheduled to leave… to tell me this? And, you say I'm overreacting? Why couldn't you be like a normal person and realize that you are blessed to not have to go over to that…to that place?"

"I'm not other people," he said simply. His eyes never looking up as he packed his things. Although he was going to be sent out sooner than he anticipated, he couldn't wait to be of use. And while he was cognizant of her uncertainty, and understood her fear, he had to go. She had to see that. She had to accept it.

"Yeah. You're right, Benjamin. You're not like other people. You're the kind of person who has this constant need to prove himself!" she chided.

"Benjamin? Ouch," he said, feigning hurt. "Anyway, I'm not trying to prove anything. This is bigger than you or me. We're needed over there, whether you like it or not. This is my job—"

"You have a job! And a fucking future, here! We had plans. Or did you forget?" she said.

"And our plans will still be here when I get back. I wear the uniform first, Colette."

"You sound like a brain-washed idiot! No! You are Benjamin, first. *My* Benjamin. *My* husband. Our son's father," she croaked. The lump in her throat growing wildly with each passing minute.

"I am all those things, regardless of where I am. But it is still my job—"

"That you didn't have to volunteer for."

"That I would eventually have to do, Colette!" he barked. As she turned her back to him now, he tried his best to even his tone and pacify her. This was not how he wanted things to go. He knew that there would be some resistance from her, but he never imagined that it would become such a hostile feud. He didn't want to fight with her— not when they didn't have much time left. "Don't you remember how I came home that day? Covered in dust? Seeing the crash and the buildings go down—it changed something in me. When it happened—"

"Yes! And you somehow made it home…alive," she returned in rapid fire.

She didn't want to hear it. She was tired of his rationale. All she saw, was the possibility that she was going to lose the love of her life. "Not everyone had that privilege during the attacks. Yet you sit here, like the pompous shit that you are, and tell me that you volunteered to go over there, to do who knows what? What about Judah? What about me?"

"You two will be fine," he assured, "Your mom said that she would keep an eye on you guys, and you have Kami to keep Judah busy. Plus, you'll be so occupied with work that you won't even know I'm—"

"That's not what I meant. What if you don't come back?" she said in a panic. "What then? You'll leave me to raise our son alone?"

"I have set you up to the point that you won't want for anything. You and our son will be taken care of."

"Set me up? Set me up?! Are you kidding me? You think that's supposed to take care of the fact that you won't be here? That I may never see you again? You think I care about money? I make my own money, Benjamin! You know what? I'll kill you myself," she said, picking up a pillow from their bed and tossing it hard in his face. "You're selfish, Benjamin! You're a selfish prick!"

Sensing her anger mounting, he reached out to her, "Come here."

"No. Don't you fucking touch me!" she said, struggling to pull away from him. His strong arms would not relent as he embraced her anger, just as strongly as he embraced her. "I hate you. I hate you. I hate you! If you leave me, I won't ever forgive you. I won't. I promise you."

"Shh," he soothed, trying to calm the beast within her. "I won't leave you, motek. I'll be back."

"You don't know that!" she whimpered, no longer able to hold back her tears. "Please. Just…just come back to me, Benny."

"I promise you. I'll come back to you. I promise. You hear me?" he said, with soft kisses; willing her body to submit to him. And in melding their bodies together to release the seed of doubt that wore heavy on her heart, he planted the seed of life inside her womb instead, once again.

Time stood still as he watched the even rise and fall of her chest as she slept. He had promised her that he would not go to his family's home until she fell to the comforts of sleep. They had spent the rest of the evening after prayers and their Friday night meal relishing in the simplicity of their family—their life together. They took in their son's serenity and prayed that they would have the chance to be with each other again.

His folks had been back in the city for a week and were staying at the brownstone they kept on. If it weren't for his departure, he wouldn't have bothered to see them—their refusal to see his son was enough for him to maintain his distance. However, given the circumstances, he felt that it was only right to tell them in person just in case he didn't return.

The drive to his parent's home had wracked his nerves. It had been over three years since he last saw them. Although he had called and tried to make amends, the neglect and rejection of his wife and son had made it impossible for him to see them. For Benny, the family he created was an extension of himself, and if they weren't accepted, he wasn't interested in being the dutiful son any longer.

As he exited his car, he was greeted by his sister, Nadia, smoking a cigarette. Three years older than him, she had the ferociousness of a velociraptor. She was vile and mean—even as kids he thought her nothing more than an energy sucking leech, who was spawned from the devil himself. A feminized version of him, her round full face carried the same eyes. However, where Benny's eyes lit up by life's joy, Nadia's projected a calculating coolness that made people skittish. Leaving her without lovers or friends. Her dark brown hair was thick with loose curls that flowed past her shoulders. While her full lips were always turned up into a twisted smile—as if she were plotting one's demise. Although moderately attractive, the ugliness of her attitude and demeanor, left little to be desired.

"Look who finally decided to show up," she said snidely.

"I had things to do. You do realize that I have a family of my own, right?"

"I would hardly call that whore and her spawn, family," Nadia said menacingly.

"If you weren't a female, I'd break your jaw."

"Well, look at you. I see you found your place among the natives. Why are you here, anyway? You've already missed shabbat."

"I don't have time for this. Move, cunt," he whispered, loud enough for her to hear, as he pushed past her to enter.

"Hey… you made me drop my cigarette!" she squealed. Her screams muffled by the door shutting behind him.

Entering his parents' home, he could smell the remnants of the sabbath meal his mother more than likely spent hours preparing. Although it smelled of home, the friction he felt as he made his way into the formal living room, where his family sat, made him feel like an unwelcomed visitor. His mother was first to approach—after the shock of his presence wore off, she rushed to embrace him, "Thank you, Hashem, for bringing my son home. I didn't think you would come."

"I did call, remember?" Benny said, burying himself deep in the feel of his mother's arms. He had missed her dearly—calls were not enough.

"What was the point of showing up, if you weren't going to come for Shabbat?"

"Hello to you too, Abba," he said sarcastically. "I did shabbat with my family, as I am supposed to, since I am the head of my own household."

Benny turned his attention to the rest of the family. The time spent away from them had made them all but strangers to him. Following his father's lead, his siblings had taken to ignoring his calls and pleas for solace. Although he recognized their faces, seeing them now, with the look of antipathy held in their eyes, he wasn't sure that he knew them—perhaps, he never did.

His younger sister, Mazal, sat quietly in the chair next to the shelf of books his family had collected over the years. Her head was buried so studiously, that she didn't care enough to escape, to greet him. She had grown so much in the three years he'd been away. Benny had always been closest to her. From the moment she was born, he had taken her under his wing, and he couldn't believe that the little girl who once bustled with laughter as he danced with her on his shoulders, was now a full-fledged teenager.

She was starkly different than he and their other siblings in looks. Her blonde hair that normally fell past her waist, was now cut into a sophisticated bob to mark her transition into womanhood. Her sea green eyes no longer held the wonder of a child, but the mischief of a teenage girl, ready to cause mayhem in the world around her.

"Hey, Mazie?" he said, as the pet-name he had for her, rolled off his tongue with ease, "You've grown."

"Amazing how that happens," she replied sardonically. Her eyes never leaving her book.

"When you decide to choose someone else over family, you tend to miss a few things," said Daud, his older brother. The malice in his voice was something Benny had grown accustomed to over the years. As the eldest of his father's sons, Daud Lati was to be the heir and head of the comforts their father had obtained. But from an early age, their father recognized his inability to be steadfast in building for himself and the family. So, when he saw the drive and ingenuity in his youngest son needed to expand the legacy he worked hard for, he placed his confidence elsewhere. Where his brother was short-sighted, Benny had shown a natural knack for leadership, causing his father to invest heavily in him. However, his brother as the eldest felt more deserving.

"I did choose my family," Benny replied.

"How does that saying go, again? Bros before hoes?" Daud lambasted. The smirk that played across his thin lips, made his spitefulness even more evident.

"Khalas, Daud. Enough," their mother chastised.

Walking away from Benny, his mother found her place by his father's side. Enveloping her arm with his as she sat next to him on their sofa, she squeezed her husband's hand and prayed for strength. "I haven't been able to see my son in years. And I've barely spoken to him due to…this mess you've created amongst yourselves. He is finally home. Allow me my peace with him, please."

"You act as if this is our fault. He made his choice over family when he decided to marry that—"

"At least he has a wife, Daud," Musa said coolly. "By your age, I already had a family of my own—a wife and two children to care for. And I had made my own way by then to where I am now."

"This isn't the stone age, Abba. You act as if you had a choice in marrying her. Forgive me if I'd like to take my time," Daud replied.

"Despite how your mother and I came to be, she is the love of my life. Anyway…what you say doesn't change the fact that we became who we were meant to be…and what I expect you to become. Now, while I may not agree with who your brother married…and believe me, he'll come to his senses soon enough," Musa said confidently. The snort he heard from his pride and joy did nothing to deter him from professing what he thought in his heart to be true. He was not meant to be with that girl—and if it took years for his son to find his place back into the family fold, he'd be ready when he did. "But what I can say is, he took responsibility for his mistakes and did the honorable thing, unlike you, Daud."

"Are you fucking kidding me? Even now, he gets praise for marrying that gold-digging whore?!"

By the time he saw Benny coming for him, it was too late. With his hands securely around his brother's neck, he slammed his body hard as he rushed him against the wall. Standing eye to eye with him, and no longer the little boy that once feared him, Benny overtook his brother with the fury and agility of a leopard. "I want to make something perfectly clear," he said menacingly. "You will not talk about my wife like that again, you hear me?"

"Let him go, Benjamin," Musa intervened, "I said, let him go. He understands you."

Turning towards the sound of his father's voice, Benny noted the amused look in his eyes. He had seen that look more times than he cared to acknowledge. While his father took pride in the way his youngest son handled himself from the wrath of his siblings, Benny had wished he would step in and end their torment of him. Ever since he could remember, his eldest brother and sister had always taken pleasure in the suffering they committed against him. And although he understood why, it didn't lessen the pain and resentment he had towards them, just as their resentment of him never ceased. It wasn't his fault that their father had placed all his efforts into building the child, the son, he thought was deserving. Despite his capabilities and devoted nature, Benny never wanted the responsibilities his father manufactured for him. Growing up, he had always wished his brother would become the man his father wanted him to be. However, at thirty-three years old, his brother was still nothing more than a perpetual fuck-up.

As he stepped slowly away from his brother, Benny was able to get a closer look at him. His years of womanizing and partying had finally caught up to him. The grey that generously peppered his hair and dark circles that overtook his beady eyes, caused him to look older than his years. Taking notice, Benny finally saw the scantily clad young woman that had moved from her place in the corner to be by his brother's side. Her barely-there mini skirt did nothing to hide the leopard print underwear that was available for all to see. And her spaghetti strapped top, couldn't contain the enhanced triple-D breast she was more than happy to sport. Chunky blonde highlights clashed horribly against her naturally dark brown hair and overly made-up face. No longer able to hide his disgust, he snickered at what was obviously his brother's new flavor of the month.

"She's allowed here, and not my *wife*?" Benny said to his father. "And you all have the nerve to call my wife a gold-digger? A whore?" he scoffed.

"I didn't invite her," Musa shrugged.

"Are you serious, Abba? He's allowed to talk about my girl that way? And attack me?" Daud said, feeling scorned.

"Well, did you expect anything less, for the son who is most revered?" Nadia said snidely. Benny hadn't noticed her arrival into the room. And her smug pudgy face, did nothing to release his growing tension.

"I rather be that, than the prodigal son," Benny said, taking a shot at his older siblings. "And you know what, Nadia? Fuck off. I'm sick of you too. Why is it that every time I come around, you two must be such miserable little bitches? Huh?"

"Maybe if you weren't such a suck up and have to play daddy's favorite all the time, you'd be better liked," Nadia said sharply.

"His favorite? Seriously? We're not children anymore. Get over yourselves," Benny yelled. "And for the record, favorites don't get treated the way I have been, okay?

"Are you three finished?" Musa asked. "I love each and every one of you equally."

"If that were true you wouldn't treat us the way you do," said Daud.

"While you may believe that I treated, Benjamin differently—I only fed his potential," Musa replied placidly. "You've never had the head space to take over, Daud. You were too busy with your head in the clouds. No matter how many opportunities and responsibilities I gave you, to show you what's needed to care for this family, you never seemed interested. You were too busy chasing your own…aspirations. You've always been this way."

"And what am I, Abba? Cut glass? Most times, you act like I don't even exist," Nadia stated.

"You?' Musa chuckled. "You may have the smarts, my darling, but you have the charm and personality of a viper. You see… it takes more than intelligence to run a business, my dear. Not to mention, you'd bring us to ruin with your spending habits."

A bolt of laughter startled them all. He didn't think his baby sister was listening to the dysfunction that always seemed to plague their family, but apparently, she was. The glow of merriment on her face, from the enjoyment she got from her father putting her siblings in their place, was the only thing bringing Benny joy.

"Shut up, Mazal!"

"Don't talk to her that way. My patience is already thin with you as it is, Nadia," Benjamin warned.

"Your mother and I came to this country with nothing but our wits. I worked hard to save enough money to buy my first property; and from that very first property, I managed to build our brokerage firm. I promised myself that I would never have children…grandchildren…great-grandchildren even, that would know hunger the way your mother and I have. Ever! And I was hoping that I would have children who would want to help me in building that legacy—but neither of you… Daud and Nadia, ever did," Musa said pointedly. "You've always thought only of yourselves. And when it came time for you to learn, what did you do? You got your license, Daud, and never looked back. Nadia, you couldn't control yourself or your temper long enough to even file paperwork, let alone run an office and deal with clients."

"No, Abba. You have it wrong. Daud and I never had it in us to be controlled by you," Nadia said vehemently.

Ignoring her dig at him, Musa went on to say, "Like it or not, Nadia, but Benjamin has always done what's right. It's his nature. He has always cared about everyone and remained loyal to what is best for our family."

"Loyal, huh? Where is he now, then, Abba? Where has he been? Your precious, perfect fucking son?" asked Daud.

"It's not his fault that he's been bewitched," Musa reasoned, "And it doesn't matter, because he's here now."

"You don't even know why he's here. Why are you here anyway, Ben? Let me guess, she's finally left you, and now you've suddenly come to your senses with your tail between your legs?" Daud jested, turning everyone's attention to his younger brother; whom but a moment ago stood tall and sure, now began to shrink before them.

"Based on that guilty look, I'd say that he's not here to beg for forgiveness and acceptance back into the family fold, Abba," said Nadia, now making her way to one of the chairs by the fireplace, for what she was sure would be one hell of a show.

Looking from his eldest daughter to the face of his youngest son, Musa Lati couldn't help the wave of unease that rushed through him. For some reason, he knew that the news he was about to receive, would break him in two.

"*Ma-kara*? You have something to tell me? Us? Is that why you're here? What's going on, Ben?"

Finally taking a seat, Benny braced himself for the onslaught of anger he knew his words would bring, "I'm…well…I'm going to deploy?" he rushed out.

"Deploy? *Ma-zeh*? What is this…deploy? What does that mean?" his mother asked.

"It means they're sending him to Iraq," came from Mazal, "You're going over there… aren't you, Ben?"

"I volunteered to go, Mazie," escaped him, as his heart sank at the sight of his baby sister's face. The look in her eyes was almost his ruin. And although the heat from the fireplace covered them like a warm blanket, Benny shivered as he felt the coolness of his anxiety wash over him.

"He volunteered? Oh, that's fucking rich! Here, you thought he was coming back on bended knee—only for him to tell you that he's going all the way to Iraq! To fight in a fucking war?!" Turning to his younger brother, Daud said, "Are you out of your fucking mind, Benjamin?!"

"What do you care? You can barely tolerate my presence anyway. You don't have to go, so don't worry about it."

"You may be a thorn in my side, Ben, but you are still my brother," he replied.

Daud was many things, but oblivious wasn't one of them. He knew what war could bring, and the thought that he may lose his only brother, was enough for him to put his resentment and hostility aside.

"Regardless of how I may act, and I'm sorry for that, I do love you, Ben."

"I have to go, Daud. It's my responsibility—"

"Oh horseshit. You're not going. You're not going anywhere, Benjamin," Daud said, slamming his fist against the wall. "Tell him that he isn't going, Abba. Tell him!"

"That's not how it works, Daud," Benny replied. Between the reaction from his wife, and now seeing the worry increasing in the faces of his family, he didn't know how to handle it.

"Then tell me, how does it work, Ben? Abba, please, slap some sense into him," he said, his frustration mounting. "Why are you just sitting there?!"

"It's not Abba's choice, Daud."

"What about your wife and kid?' Daud tried to reason. "What if you don't come back? You'd just go and possibly leave them? That's the kind of man you are now?"

"Don't act like you care about my family," said Benny. "And don't question my integrity. I know what I'm doing. I'm not leaving them. I'm going over there to do my job! To help them—to help my friends. And stop saying that I won't come back!"

"You won't!" his father roared. He had sat quietly trying to process what his son was saying to him, and comfort his wife, who had taken to squeezing his hands so tightly he'd lost circulation in them. Getting up from his chair, he kneeled before his son, and grasped his face in his hands, trying to search for the little boy he once knew. "I didn't come to this country for you to risk your life for…for a war that is not our own. I have seen war. It is ugly. It is vicious. And it is indiscriminate. It would kill me if I lost you, Benjamin. Please. Don't go."

"It's already done. I leave tomorrow," Benny whispered. His father pulled away from him. He couldn't move. He just sat, quietly, stunned on the floor.

"I'm just being the man you've always taught me to be, Abba."

"Tomorrow?! You're leaving tomorrow?! And you all call me selfish? You're an asshole, Benjamin!"

"This isn't the first time I've heard that today, Daud. So, thanks," Benny said, gathering himself from his seat to see to his mother.

"That's because you are an ass!"

"Ima. Look at me please," Benny said, ignoring his brother. But she wouldn't look at him. She couldn't. Instead, she sat solemnly in her seat, allowing her tears to fall freely down her face, as she thought about losing her son. Pressing his face against her cheek as he sat beside her in his father's place, he wished desperately that he could remove her fears. "I'll be back, Ima. I promise. You hear me? Don't worry. I'll be alright. And I'll write and call as much as I can. Okay?"

He didn't wait for her answer. Instead, he began to make his way towards the corridor that led to the exit of his family's home. Stopping him along his way, his brother whispered in his ear, "You come back. You hear me? I need someone to fight with."

"I love you too, brother," Benny replied.

As he approached the threshold of the living room door, he called out to his father and said solemnly, "Abba, I'm sorry I couldn't be the son you wanted me to be."

Making his way to his car, he was almost down the stairs of his family's brownstone, when he felt a sharp pull into her arms. "Please don't leave me with them," she cried.

The tears in her eyes almost broke him. He could never stand to see her cry, and the distress in her eyes would play vividly in his memory forever. "I'll be okay, Mazie."

"You promise?" she asked apprehensively.

"I promise. I'll come back in one piece," he assured her.

"Pinky swear?" she asked.

"Pinky swear," he said grabbing her finger. But it was a promise he would never keep.

The Here & Now

Bringing himself back to the present, he looked back on the memories of the night he had turned his world upside down. It was a trajectory of decisions that brought him to his now; riddled with guilt, as he sat wracked with pain in his bed.

He listened to the light squeals of his children and the bustling of his parents about his home and realized that he could have lost it all. It was a hard truth he could no longer ignore. His father was right. They were all right. He didn't know war. And his romanticization and naivete in what duty truly meant, almost cost him his life.

"I wish I could take it all back. I wish I could bring them all back," Benny whispered, as tears threatened to fall.

The opening of his bedroom door snapped him out of reliving the nightmare he couldn't seem to shake. And he was happy to see the beautiful vision in front of him.

"I hope you'll come down, but I brought lunch to you, just in case you didn't want to," she said to him. Although she hoped that her optimism moved him, the look in his eyes conveyed that he hadn't the energy nor the heart to do so.

"I don't think I'm up to it," Benny replied.

"I didn't think so," Colette said, as she laid his tray of food down. Not seeing the use in staying put, she began to make her way out of their room.

"Wait," he said as he grabbed her arm. Moving his tray to the side, and circling his hands around her waist, he pulled her in closely, forcing her to take a seat beside him. "Are they treating you okay down there?"

"Surprisingly, yes. Your dad won't stop quizzing me about shul, however. I'm starting to think he doesn't believe that I really go. He keeps asking, 'and you did everything? All of it? All on your own? He didn't ask you to?'" she said laughing; mimicking his father's inquisitive nature in respect to her conversion and desire to be part of their faith.

"I would say that I'm shocked, but that's how he is."

"At least he's asking me about myself for a change."

"What else did he ask?"

"Well, he asked about how I finished school and handled things on my own when you were away."

"That was nice of him, I guess. I'm happy he's at least being cordial."

"And then," she said smiling, "He said that from now on, I can count on your family if you're ever called away again. So, I guess you can say, things are beyond cordial, and are going well.

"Great. I think he's finally realizing that he found the child he always wanted."

"Huh? What do you mean?"

"You'll see," Benny chuckled.

"Whatever you're implying, Mr. Lati, it better be good," she replied.

"Let's just say…if he's trying to get to know you, then you've finally gotten on his good side. I just wish that it hadn't taken this long for him to do so. Get to know you, that is."

"Well, as long as it's happening, it shouldn't matter. Hopefully we can bury the hatchet and move forward," Colette replied.

"Yeah. Fingers crossed. And my mom? What about her?"

"She is sweet as usual. But man is she bossy. I was under the impression that she was…timid. However, feisty is more like it."

"Timid?" Benny laughed. "It is hardly the word I would use to describe my mother. She's more like a quiet and reserved…fire."

"I see that now," Colette said. "I'm learning a lot from her, that's for sure."

"And what might that be?" he asked.

"Let's just say that I think I understand what it means to be a lamb in appearance, yet a wolf when it matters."

"Care to explain yourself, Mrs. Lati?"

"Well, while you may be the head, my dear husband, I am and will most certainly be the neck. And you can thank your mother for those words of wisdom."

"I see. And here I thought you were downstairs learning how to make my favorite dishes with her."

"I did. But as she said, I am now her daughter, and she must teach me more than just how to be the perfect cook for you, Benjamin Lati."

"Colluding against me, I see."

"No. Just trying to get to know your folks. The olive branch has been extended, and I don't plan on wasting it. So much so, I invited them to shul with me next week. I think your mom would really get on with Miriam. Although your mom seems soft spoken, they're more alike than one would think. And my mom will be there, so they'll all finally get to meet."

"That's great," he said languidly; her words now quieting, as his mind drifted towards his thoughts. His wife had found her tribe. In his absence from his family, Miriam and his mother in-law had formed a bond through their shared love for Colette. Now his mother would become part of their fold. And although it made him happy, it also shook him to his core. He realized that it was something else he would have missed, had he ended up like the others. A revelation that forced him to shrink back to the feelings of despair he tried so desperately to break free of.

"Oh, I think the boys have taken a liking to your mother. While it could be all the sweets she's been luring them with, I'm going to chalk it up to her sweet nature, instead" Colette said playfully, bringing him away from his thoughts. "They can't seem to get enough of her. I'm so glad they've finally gotten to meet her—them both for that matter."

"I'm not surprised they've taken to her," he said solemnly. His mood no longer light, dampened the brightness in his eyes.

"Hey…are you okay?"

"Yeah…no. I'm just…I'm so sorry, Colette," he said. "I shouldn't have gone there. I should have listened… to all of you."

"Shh. It's okay, Benny. It's okay."

"I shouldn't have gone. I shouldn't have," he said repeatedly, as he broke down in her arms. Tears streamed uncontrollably, as it forced his body to convulse with the weight of his agony that trapped him in his bed of sorrow. And as he grabbed hold of her waist tightly, stealing her breath away, dread washed over her.

"What did they do to you?" she whispered. Her heart aching now, as she thought, *I'll never get him back.*

Hopelessly Devoted

He doesn't want to go," she said in a huff.

Although he made stride in healing physically, the mental trauma he suffered wreaked havoc on their lives. In the months that followed, Benny had spent his time in relative isolation. The visions of the faces of the men he lost, plagued his day, while their screams haunted his nights. Soon, he took to the bottle. And while she stood steadfast in her love for him, the change in him as he slipped deeper and deeper into depression, forced her into his nightmare. One that she didn't think she could endure.

"It's their memorial for fuck sakes," he said. "He owes it to them. Hell, he owes it to himself to be there."

"He's not fit to go, Devon. You don't understand."

"I understand all too well, Colette. I understand what he's going through. Which is why I believe he should be there!" he said angrily.

Devon Hightower was the type of man that would sell his soul, if it meant that he would save others. At a towering six-foot-eight and a calming spirit, he had earned his tag as a gentle giant in their squad. So, it was rare to see him angry.

"I know that already. But what do you expect me to do? I'm trying."

"I'm sorry. Forgive my tone. I just want what's best for him. And I think this will do him some good. It ain't right how he is. Look… it's my job to take care of him, the same way he took care of me. I owe him," he said sincerely, as he unconsciously touched the jagged scar that marred his head through his course curls—a reminder of what could have been.

He sat pensively. His full lips that were once expressive with empathy, were now pursed with regret. His brown skin, once smooth and supple, began to ashen, as his memories came forth. Taking his hand gently into hers, Colette waited for him to return, just as she'd learned to do with Benny. Finally, when the dust settled and his brown eyes regained their light, she said to him, "I know you mean well, Devon…and you've found a way to manage, but Benny isn't you. He lives with so much guilt."

"I know. I just wish he would realize that it's not his fault. None of it was," Devon said. "Look…I should go. Will you see me out?"

Getting up, she proceeded to show him to the door, when they were startled by a loud crash and painful howl, causing them both to rush upstairs. They could hear the clattering and clamor of things crashing against the walls of her room in the distance. The acts of his aggression no longer unnerved her. She had grown used to his violent outburst over his current lot in life. Nevertheless, she refused to allow herself to submit to the explosions that erupted. So, she had begun to put herself within the walls of his rage and try to smother the fire that never seemed to cease.

Approaching her door, she felt the strong hands of her husband's comrade on her shoulder, "I can go," he said softly.

"It's okay, Devon. I got it. He just gets like this, sometimes," Colette replied weakly.

"We'll go together then. Okay?" said Devon.

Her nod of agreement was all he needed to brace himself for what was to come. He had seen it before during his time volunteering at veteran's hospitals—it was one of the reasons he had started his seminary education. He had found peace in ministry. And he hoped that he would someday help others like him and Benny. Standing behind her, he waited for her to find the courage to open the door. The stench of alcohol filled his nose as a large glass bottle shattered against the wall, barely missing her head. Her ear-piercing scream had caused him to instinctually place himself between her and the danger lurking inside, and it tore him apart that it was his best friend who was the offender.

"Alright, brother. I think it's time you settle down now," Devon said with outstretched arms. It pained him to see the sight of the man in front of him. He was no longer proud. Instead, he staggered about the room in a drunken rage. His eyes were red at the rim due to the drink and insomnia he was sure had consumed him. His hair, once neatly cropped, now sat in a matted and disheveled mess. And by the look and smell of him, soap and water had not touched his skin in some time.

"Leave me alone!"

"Come, man. You don't need that," Devon said, referring to the bottle that was pressed firmly in Benny's hand.

"If you came here about the memorial service, you should have saved yourself the trip," Benny replied. His eyes never leaving the sheet of paper clutched tightly in his other hand. "Did she send for you?"

"No, I didn't send for him, Benjamin. He came on his own," Colette said in a huff.

"Benjamin, is it? Whoops. I guess I'm in trouble," he said as he took another swig from his bottle.

"Hey…man, why don't you just put the bottle down. You can shower, and we can sit here and just talk," Devon pleaded with him.

"While we can talk, letting go of this bottle is not on the agenda today, buddy," Benny said, tipping his bottle towards his mate, before taking another sip. "You know what I want to talk about? Whose bright idea was it to go for a second round after we got back? Because I can't, for the life of me, remember what made my dumbass think that going back would be worth it. Hell…even going at all."

He had begun to hiccup now, and she knew that the calm before the storm had already begun. "Benny…baby, why don't you lay down? We can lay together—"

"I don't want you fucking near me," he said cruelly.

"Come on, Lati. Don't speak to her that way," Devon said. "She's your wife."

"My wife?" he said amused. "My wife wouldn't have let me do something so stupid. My wife would have made me stay where I belonged. And my wife would have known."

"I am so sick of you blaming me for your shit! You chose to go! You!" Colette yelled. "Look at you. I don't even recognize you anymore."

"Well…this is it, baby," Benny said with outstretched arms. "Perhaps you never really knew me at all."

The sting he felt radiating from his face did nothing to deter his wrath, and instead of snapping out of his madness, he slapped himself harshly, egging her on more.

"You smug bastard!"

"You see…Devon? You see that? Another woman would have known better. And here I am trapped with an insolent bitch, who couldn't even be woman enough to…never mind…what difference does it make, man? I'm stuck with her."

"Fuck you, Benjamin! The fucking audacity! I swear!" she roared. "No one asked your stupid ass to go once, let alone twice. No one chose that for you, but you. I begged you… you hear me? *Begged* you. Each time. And you did what you wanted to do, like you always do!"

"Maybe you were just too weak to be my neck," he replied.

"You must be describing someone else, because the bitch you're talking about ain't me," she said, reverting to the days that never left her.

He knew what he was doing. He needed it. Craved it. He wanted someone to fight with. Someone to help him release the torment that washed over him in crashing waves that never let up and drowned him into submission. So, he pushed her. Pushed her to those parts of herself she'd rather forget, so that she would join him in his misery.

"Ben. Come on. You don't want to stoop… to this, brother. You're better than that," said Devon.

"Am I? How good could I be if they sent me this? Here. Look at it," he said, forcing the papers into his friend's hand.

"Shit. I'm so sorry, brother," Devon said, reading the papers in his hand. Passing them to Colette, he knew the feelings Benny had, because he had already received papers of his own. Getting the document was hard enough, but he knew that it would be especially so, for someone like Benny. It was a smack in the face to him. All the effort placed—the fight that he had—all that he had given, to be diminished by one piece of paper.

Colette knew it was coming. They both knew. In fact, she had prepared for this day. It was why she had taken to sifting through the packages and mail that stormed their door. Somehow, it had gotten to him and now she had garnered the privilege of wrestling with the aftermath.

"After all this… all that I've been through. I get an eight and half by eleven-inch sheet of paper, that says, 'thank you for your service, you're through," he said as tears flowed freely. Falling to the floor in a slump, he descended into a maniacal laughter beyond his control.

"Momma. Luke is up. He's crying," said Judah.

"I'll be right there, baby," Colette replied, as she tried to maintain her composure. She hadn't heard his small feet tapping lightly through the halls, as she usually did—a measure she'd begun to use to mitigate her children's interactions with their father. Despite her best effort, times like these were occurring more frequently, and she was finding it harder to shield her boys from the wrathful man before her.

"What's wrong with Abba, Momma?" Judah asked. His arms were set tightly around her leg now, as he peered at the man his mother called his father. In his young years, he was not sure of much, but what he did know, was that the man that sat, slumped in a ball in the corner, could not possibly be his father—no matter how much his mother insisted. The fear he felt viewing the vision before him, as Benny thrashed about violently in agony, forced him to conceal himself behind the comfort of her body more. The whimper that escaped his lips, caused her to cling to his tiny body and wrap him in her tenderness. Soon, Colette placed her son safely into the arms of Devon.

"Do you mind looking after them?" she asked.

"Are you sure?" Devon questioned, "I don't want to leave you alone with how he is now."

"I got it. We'll be okay in here," Colette replied, glancing in her husband's direction, as she pushed him gently out the room with her son in his arms. Securing the door, she turned around to face the man who resembled her love. Walking towards him, she crept quietly and slowly, so she wouldn't disturb him. As he became more immersed in his despair, she found her way next to him, and sat aching for a moment where she could bring some semblance of him back.

Wrapping her arms around him, she squeezed firmly, hoping she could breathe life back into him. His resistance didn't last long; and soon, he allowed himself to melt into her. Tucking his body tightly next to hers, he took in her scent. He needed her to draw him away from the shadows that danced in his head. However, he could not find relief in her nearness. Instead, he found her standing in the visions that ravished him, and he could not determine where she began, and they ended. Figments of her blurred in memories of them, taunting him with their knowingness of what he had done. And although he tried his best to reach her so that she could pull him to safety, they would not let him go.

"I can't do this anymore, Colette. I can't," he whispered hoarsely.

Sobs wracked his body as visions of them continued to call out to him. He understood now, why they plagued him so. It was because they knew—they knew that he wasn't supposed to be there. He didn't deserve the privilege of being surrounded by his family, while they could no longer be with theirs. He wasn't a survivor as many had stated; he was nothing more than an imposter. A man unworthy of the life he had. And as he conceded to the call of hades, just as he did to his call for battle, he whimpered, "I want to die—"

"What? No. Don't say that to me," she said.

Fear washed over her, and she couldn't quell the anxiety that had begun to rise. Sitting up frantically, she grasped his face within her hands, caressing his cheek, "You can't hurt yourself, Benny. You can't…you can't do that to me. I can't lose you."

"Like you haven't already? You don't think I know how fucked up I am? That you hate me. I'm no good for you!" he roared. "I just want the pain to stop! I need it to go away. I need to make them go away—out of my fucking head."

"No. No, love. I don't hate you," she soothed, "I love you."

"I keep seeing their faces. Over and over and over again," he whimpered. "It should have been me. I'm not supposed to be here. Don't you get it? I'm not supposed to be here!"

"Benny… listen to me. I love you. You hear me? I *love* you. And I need you—"

"You'd be better off without me. I know you would. You're young and beautiful. You can start again," he sulked.

"Please. Stop saying things like that, Benny. You're scaring me."

"You don't think I scare myself? I can't get them out of my head," he said, striking himself atop the minefield of memories that plagued him. "Everywhere I look, I see their faces. Haunting me. Seeking me out. I can't stand it anymore. They won't let me go. They won't let me be!"

"Maybe if you just go back to the counselor, it could help you. It could help us—"

"They can't fucking help me! No one can!"

"How would you know, Benny? You barely even tried," Colette replied emphatically.

"Try for what?" he said. "No one understands what I'm going through!"

"Then tell me!" she cried. "Tell me. Please. So that I can help you. I want to help you, baby. Please just tell me what to do."

"There is no help for me," he said weakly. "It's my fault anyway. I should have been paying attention. It's my fault that they're not here!"

"Then make me understand. Talk to me, and make me understand you," she said as she squeezed him tightly. "You need to tell me because I won't lose you. I can't. You promised me, forever. And you're going to keep it!"

"Don't let me go," he said, breaking down once more. "I shouldn't have let them go with me."

She couldn't hold him tight enough, and he took hold of her, forcing his body into hers, for fear that he might fade away.

"I won't let you go. I promise," she stated. "I need you. I love you. I won't let go. You hear me?"

She didn't wait for a reply. Instead, she sat gripping him securely, close to her heart, as she willed him every ounce of strength she possessed. Time passed slowly, and as she lulled him, providing the serenity he sought, she wondered when their nightmare would end.

He knew that he had kept her at a distance. Perhaps it was because he did not yet want to lose them forever. Or maybe it was because he felt he was owed the suffering he had buried himself in. But in feeling the unwavering strength of the woman holding him, he allowed himself to submit wholly to his pain. He was ready.

"I don't know what to do anymore, Cole—"

"I know, Benny. I know," she soothed.

"I don't know if I will ever get better. I'm scared that I won't," he said through his tears. "Do you think I can? Do you think I can be better?"

"We won't know unless we try, right?"

"I guess, it's sink or swim, now, huh?"

"Yeah. Listen, Benny, only time will tell. But, I'll be here. Swimming right beside you," she said, stroking his hair encouragingly, "Now talk to me. Tell me what happened…please."

"I don't know what to say. How am I supposed to tell you…tell you…"

"Tell me however you need to. I'm here. Just to listen. If you let me," Colette replied.

"Okay…what if I say it like a story?"

"What? What do you mean?" she asked.

"Like it's not you that I'm talking to. It'll make things…it'll make it easier for me."

"If that will help you…help us…then yes. I'm willing to try anything."

"I guess I should start from the beginning," he said softly. "The day I made the decision that changed the course of my life…our life…forever…"

Brothers in Arms

It hadn't been long since we arrived in the sandbox. And the burden of the promises we made to each other was wearing on my morale. The bonding and brotherhood we acquired during our first tour drove us into a partnership I had never experienced before; compelling us into a promise we were sure to keep. I found love with the men I would call my brothers. A love I had never felt with my elder siblings. The men that swore their loyalty to protect me, did so, as I did them. The security I felt in having them around surpassed anything I'd ever felt with my own family. I felt safe and guarded. They were men who didn't allow their fears to consume them. They used their trepidation as a catalyst to enforce our strength, in undertaking what we had to endure. So, it wasn't an option for any of us to stay behind; a pact was made—one that I would live to regret for the rest of my life.

I remember the day like it was yesterday. The months home had gone by in a blur, and the monotony of life gave way to the realization of how difficult reintegration truly was. In some ways, so much of us was still stuck there—the parts of our minds and bodies that had been conditioned by the heat of the desert sun, was drawn back to the pits of sand that bore nothing but war. For some of us, the contrast of war to our lives had brought new meaning and gave a sense of purpose; for others, it was a means to make a life worth living. In my case, it was a way to filter my reprisal.

After longing to be home in the arms of my wife and children, there was a part of me that couldn't shake the urge to return. I would spend hours fantasizing about what more I could've done. I didn't feel I was much value at home anyway. She had done something I didn't believe capable—she had built a life without me. A life I was only privy to, through photographs and packages. Her success as an agent had bolstered our lives forward into a community, I had now become alien to. And she had made a home for our family—a task I had always thought would be mine. I couldn't quell my resentment. All the moments I felt were mine to hold, were somehow taken from me.

Although she tried to make me feel included, there wasn't much to be done. She'd taken care of it all. Our family. Our home. All that I promised to give her, she already built for herself. And I found myself longing for the grittiness of fiery sand in exchange for the dullness of playdates and diaper changes, that I couldn't seem to get quite right. And I wished that I could exchange the sounds of my city, for the intensity of air raid sirens.

The contrition I felt being home, along with the guilt in wanting to return, put me in a state of isolation. Unlike my brothers, it forced me into the confines and security of my thoughts. While they basked in their ability to master and ease themselves back into the civilian world. So, when I heard those words that night—well, it sounded as if an angel had heard my prayers. But his words didn't come with the relief I thought I'd receive. Instead, it came with a fear and apprehension I should have listened to, because it could have saved us all.

It was the night of our housewarming. After being home for a few months, Colette had put her foot down on celebrating what she perceived to be our achievement. In part, I think she had done so to force a welcoming upon me that she knew I didn't feel part of. I had checked out of the life she'd formulated—where I felt like an outsider looking in. And with the instincts of a momma bear trying to bring comfort to her cub, she utilized my brotherhood to ignite what could be, within me.

The night was young, and the food and drink we gorged ourselves on, set the tone for a joyful evening. Fireflies danced in unison to the flicker of the lanterns she placed strategically around our small yard to light up the night sky. The smell of lavender and mint that permeated from our garden, subdued us into a chatter that brought a sense of calm and tranquility. That was until he spoke.

A wise cracking, self-proclaimed Southern gentleman, Jameson Clarke was the epitome of mischief and mayhem. He was neither a gentleman nor polished, but his crudeness offered up a type of charm that seemed to draw people in. A jack of all trades, he was a MacGyver of sorts, who exuded a bravado that was seemingly made for him. Growing up in a traditional, well-to-do Texan family, he had auburn hair and a ruddy complexion to match the fieriness within him. His desire to leave his small town, saw him to our city for college. In the City, Jameson found himself. His Southern accent comforted by his imbued charm, had put him at ease here; offering him opportunities many of us could only dream of. He'd fallen in-love with my city, he now called home. So, there wasn't any wonder that he ended up being part of our brotherhood; and we understood why he needed to return.

"Ya know, Lati…you really got yourself a good ole place here," he said.

"Wait… was that a compliment? Are you trying to pay me a compliment, Clarke?" I said playfully.

"Now. Now. That wasn't a compliment, sir. A compliment would be saying just how fucking ravenous that sexy ass wife of yours is. That there is a compliment. Saying you have a beautiful place? Now that's stating fact," he said, causing everyone to fall into an uproar of gentle laughter.

"But isn't my wife's sexiness a fact?"

"Nope. It's a compliment because she's attached to your ugly ass. Now, if she were attached to a fine and deserving, sexy and ruggedly handsome person like myself? That would be fact."

"Watch it, Bro," I said, trying to restrain my laughter.

"I mean he has a point there, Lati," said Anthony Jiménez. He was shorter in stature to my and Clarke's six-foot-four frames, but larger in mass. He carried his muscle densely and huskily, giving him a stance that would seem menacing to any foe he'd encounter. He came from the Dominican Republic to New York in his teens, where his family settled in the Bronx. His accent was thick and deep. While his bright blue eyes, curious and alert, were in stark contrast to the dark brown coloring of his skin and dark wavy hair. Overall, his reserved demeanor, complimented Clarke's naturally rambunctious nature—making them closer to each other than the rest of the group.

"Listen to my man, Tony Tone over there, Lati," said Clarke, referring playfully to him by the nickname he'd bestowed upon his best friend. "We all know that he is the voice of reason."

"Look, Lati…all we're saying is that, comparatively, she got the shitty end of the proverbial stick—"

"Fuck you, Jiménez," I said, my irritation mounting at my friends playful jeering, which caused the others to join in with the boisterous laughter emanating from Clarke and Jiménez. With that, I gave one last jab at my brothers, showcasing my feigned anger, "Fuck all y'all, man."

"Oh, come on, Lati. Don't be like that," said Clarke. He rose to his feet and sat on my lap, "We think you're gorgeous. I promise. It's just that your wife is like a fine piece of filet mignon, and you're…well…you're more like a mangled piece of bologna."

The hooting and hollering from the men that ensued had started to pique the interest of the women, causing us to calm ourselves and Clarke to return to his seat, so that we wouldn't be disturbed.

"Okay… in all seriousness, she's a rare kind, Lati," stated Jiménez.

"Yeah. If I were a settling man, I'd like to have a woman as beautiful as your Colette. Plus… she sends the best packages," Clarke said with a wink. The men all nodded in agreement. During their time away, she had sent many care packages to his brothers when they had been down range. It was a kindness they all appreciated, and had earned her the nickname, "Momma C." among them.

"Alright. Alright. Can you all just stop fawning over my wife? Thanks," I said.

"I'm just glad that she took Kalani under her wing man," said Taylor.

He wasn't a man of many words, but when Charles Taylor did speak, his commanding voice would boom and echo with a boldness that made you pay attention. His mother's family had called Bensonhurst home since before the second World War—starting up a small bakery that reminded them of life in their homeland . The copper-colored skin that he sported, spoke of his strong Sicilian heritage, while his green eyes were the only remnants left of his English Scots great-grandfather; whose name he carried.

"I'm sure, Colette appreciates having her for company," I replied warmly.

"You know they've taken up with an older neighbor of ours."

"Yeah. Um…Mrs. Feinstein, right?" Taylor said with a snap of his fingers.

"I met her the last time I was over," said Devon. "She's a trip."

"That is an understatement," I stated.

"Well, if Mrs. Feinstein sounds this fun, maybe I need to exchange my little Filipina companion over there, for her" Clarke said.

"Did you not hear me say, that she is an older neighbor, dude?"

"I heard ya. Old does not mean incapable my friend," Clarke said slyly, "Is she single?"

"Jeez, Clarke. You really know no bounds, do you?" I responded, truly amazed by his coarseness. "No. She's not single. She's married."

"Happily?" he asked, raising his eyebrows suggestively.

"You're relentless." I said with a shake of my head. "I think you need to have a talk with mini-Clarke and figure out a better way to be productive. Meaning something that doesn't involve your dick."

"Lati is right," said Devon. "You know, God don't like ugly."

"Well, isn't it a good thing that I'm pretty," Clarke responded. Making the men and I break into hearty laughter.

"Don't worry. I'll make sure he settles down," said Jiménez. "He can't fight it if everyone's attached. Gotta follow the herd, my guy. I mean…I think Celia might be the one," he said. The air went quiet, as shock reverberated within our group of comrades.

"Say it ain't so, Tony Tone," Clarke said dramatically. "You're going to leave me high and dry?"

"Clarke. My friend. Look around. Look at those gorgeous women over there. I don't think it'll get any better than that," Jiménez said with a shrug of his shoulders. "If you want proof that that's where it's at, look at our man, Taylor. He made it through our time in the pit and came back with a ring to propose to Kalani. And I think he even had you beat on the womanizing."

"Speaking of…we're gonna have to push that wedding date a little earlier than expected," Taylor said coyly. "She's pregnant, guys. I'm going to be a daddy!" He could barely contain his excitement, as the guys and I echoed our congratulations and happiness.

"See. This is what I'm talking about," replied Jiménez, "I'm trying to be a grown-up like you and Lati. *Una mujer hermosa.* A dope ass crib with some crazy little *ninos* running around in it. You boys have it made."

Guilt swept over me in a violent wave. I wanted to feel what Jiménez felt, but I was too far into my isolation, that I couldn't bring myself to appreciate what I had, as much as my brothers seemed to. And as I watched them all speak of the families and life they desired; I couldn't feel more out of place. Noticing my aloof demeanor, I heard Devon's voice, breaking me free from my thoughts, "You okay man?"

"Yeah…no…I don't know man," I said reluctantly, drawing the attention of the rest of the guys. "Do ya'll ever feel…I don't know…out of place, since you've been home?"

As each man, except for Devon, slowly nodded their heads, it was as if the elephant in the room had finally been addressed, making the air feel lighter. I hadn't been as alone as I thought.

"I thought I was the only one," Taylor said tightly, breaking the silence.

"No. You're not the only one," I replied. "And I feel so…so fucking guilty. I have a beautiful wife and two healthy sons, and yet I can't help but feel like I would be more…I don't know. I guess useful…back there."

"Useful, how?" Devon said. "How do you figure you're not useful here?"

"She has her own life, man. She doesn't need me," I rationalized. "She's so busy doing her real estate thing, that I barely even see her. I feel like an afterthought, you know? Like I have to be worked into her schedule."

I watched as he took it all in, and as usual, he tried to make me see sense, "So, what you're saying is that you wish she would have stayed twiddling her thumbs for damn near two years until your return. Is that what you're saying?"

"That's not what I'm saying, Devon," I said, growing frustrated. "I just feel…I feel like she's had this whole life without me. I missed so much. I don't even know where I'm needed…or if I'm needed at all. Hell…she went and made this fucking house into a home… without me. That was supposed to be my job."

"You can't fault her for holding shit down. Do you realize what you got? You have a wife who made sure you came back to a home, bro."

"We were supposed to build together," I said, "Not her just doing whatever—"

"Doing whatever? Was her life supposed to stop? Was she supposed to be trapped in bed, unable to be without you? If she were, you'd have something to say about that too," Devon said irritated.

"I don't expect you to understand, Devon—"

"Oh, no. I understand, nigga. I understand you're fucking tripping," he said vehemently. "See… now you're making me come out of character with this bullshit."

"I hate to interfere in your lover's squabble, gentlemen," Clarke interrupted. "But I was just wondering why Mr. Hightower here, gets to say that word, and well—"

"Shut up, Clarke!" Devon and I said in unison.

"Why don't you just say it, resident shit-starter, and see how that works out for you," I fired back.

"He wouldn't dare try it. Fucking, hillbilly," Devon said with a smirk on his face, forcing us all to burst into laughter.

"See. I knew I could get you two love birds back on the same page," he said, pleased with himself that he was able to relieve the growing tension between us.

"We love you too, you country bumpkin," Devon said.

"I love ya'll Yankee city slickers too," Clarke said, blowing us a kiss. "Now, if only I could get you guys to realize the beauty of a lifted truck… spray painted in the finest camo you ever laid your eyes on—"

"Just say your dick is small, already, man," I said, sparking a roar of laughter.

"Let me have an hour with that pretty wife of yours. I bet she'll tell you otherwise," he said slyly.

"Hey. Watch yourself," Devon and I said in unison, causing us all to swell with laughter once more.

"Look…all I was saying is that you have it all. A good life going for yourself. And there ain't no reason for us to go back there," Devon said.

"You do, man. You have a good life. You all do," Clarke said. "Which is why, you all need to stay back."

"Stay back? What do you mean?" asked Taylor.

"Well…I'm going back—"

"Da fuck you mean you're going back?" Jiménez questioned.

"Now, ladies. Don't get your panties in a wad," Clarke said calmly, "I can't hack it home. I don't have a beautiful girl and a momma who loves me the way that yours does, Tony. I don't have a family like Lati and Taylor. And we all know that I don't have the good sense that the lord gave me, like Hightower, here. I just…need it."

"You don't need it," said Devon. "It's just an adjustment period, we're all going through it, man."

"Look…this is my fate. I was born to do this, and we all know it—"

"If it's your fate, then it's the rest of ours too," Jiménez stated, referring to the pact we made with each other not so long ago. "You're back for mine… for all of ours, remember?"

"When were you even going to tell us?" Taylor said heatedly.

"He wasn't going to," I said as I realized his true intent. It was the same thing I had done to Colette two years earlier, and it pained me to feel what she must have felt at that time. I was gutted.

"I don't want you all to follow me, that's why I didn't tell you."

"Then why bother to do it now?" asked Devon.

"Because he knows it's fucking wrong!" Taylor said in an outburst, drawing attention from the women.

"Shut the fuck up, man," Clarke hushed. "You want them to hear? Look…I don't want you guys to go with me, and I also…well, I don't know if this will be the last time—"

"It's not going to be the last time, because we're going with you," Jiménez stated.

"Yeah. We're not letting you go alone," came from Taylor.

Feeling a sharp tug to my arm, I stood quiet as I felt the warm breath of my best friend against my ear, "You know you don't have to do this. You have more to lose to than I do…than Clarke does. But if you go, I'll be there with you," whispered Devon.

The ringing in my ears became overpowering as I realized the choice I'd have to make. Sure, my adjustment back home had been a trial I had no defense in, and I had thought that returning was what was needed, but as I reflected on the possibility of my family's future without me once more, I could not bring myself to answer.

"Lati…I understand if you don't go, brother," I heard Clarke speak—his voice muffled over the sound of the rapid beat of my heart in my ears.

"I made a promise," I spoke finally, more to Devon than to him. "I have your back. I'll get us home safe."

"I guess I have no choice but to be part of this shit show," said Devon.

"Kalani is going to kill me," said Taylor.

"I have two Latin woman I have to deal with man, you'll be alright," Jiménez said with a light snicker.

"Guess it's going to be a courthouse wedding for ole Taylor, then, huh?" Clarke said solemnly.

"My back for yours," we all responded to him.

"I'll bring you all back safe and sound, and ready to pop out more fine specimens with those beauties over there," Clark said emphatically.

"You damn sure better," I heard Devon say in the distance, as a gut-wrenching panic swirled within me, coaxing me to hear it, and whispering to me to stay home.

The Pit of Contrition

Seven months passed, and the same longing I had to return to the madness I now found myself in, was calling me home. I daydreamed often; about the day I could return to them. How it would be to have my children in my arms, and relish in the little faces that reminded me so much of my own. I could hear their laughter as it invaded my senses, as I assured them of my love.

In time, I had learned to drown out the sounds of sirens and the smell of gasoline from Humvees with fantasies of her. I yearned for the warmth of her arms around me, and it was that desire that made the feel of her so real. I could smell the light scent of lavender bouncing softly from her skin, as I buried my face in her neck. I learned to replace the sting of sand as it swirled in the air, with the delicateness of her hair. And the soft mews of her passion got me through days of attacks and unrest. It was this—the very way in which I had thrown myself in my thoughts of home, that caused the never-ending suffering, I would eventually find myself in.

It had been a morning filled with the same repetitiveness we had grown accustomed to—creating a sense of dreariness we hadn't felt previously. The heat of the sun blared hotly against our bodies, forcing us to constantly seek relief and refuge. The constant flow of fiery air, churning grey powdery sand, was enough to make us pray for rain, to which the universe obliged. And it wasn't long before the callousness of our answered invocations, reared the ugliness of my future.

The low winds that once provided a warm and gentle breeze, picked up rapidly, swirling hot sand harshly against our skin. Clouds of dust charged towards us like a tsunami rushing powerfully from the sea; the speed in which it came, engulfed us into a blighted abyss, forcing us to make our way into our sleeping quarters. The cold we felt as the air conditioning kissed our sweaty backs, was nothing compared to the eruption of sand that soon surrounded us, blackening the once bright sky, as it brought us into darkness. Thunder crashing thereafter, signified the reality of our enclosure. Days went by as the sound of sand and rain pounded against the containers in which we slept, like hornets who settled into their ferociousness, after being disturbed. The storm had stopped everything in its tracks, and we knew that a supply run would be imminent—a mission that would eventually become my worst nightmare.

The storm had brought a sense of eerie calm over me. The dread I felt mounted as I went through the usual routine of running security measures, sparked the interest of Ibrahim. Kahlil Ibrahim was a man filled with the type of insightfulness that Jiménez implied was reserved for a *brujo*; yet to me, he was a man filled with wisdom beyond his years. He was older than we were. Yet he and I bonded over the simplicity and vibrancy of our shared ancestry, as we exchanged language—he in fixing my broken Arabic, and I in teaching him the nuances and lingo of my city. A military man himself, he had been vetted not long after our arrival to work as an interpreter for the base, and he had become a blessing for my morale, because he reminded me of home.

Feeling his presence, I glanced at him as his dark eyes scanned me with a scrutiny I had long since become familiar. The tawny color of his skin had a natural pleasant glow. And as his inspection increased, his hawk like nose rose, furrowing his brows deeply and crinkled his skin. With a run of his hands through his thick dark hair, as he'd always done before making an inquiry, I prepared myself for what was to come.

"*Shakou makou*?" he asked softly.

"*Makou shi*. Nothings up. Really. Promise," I replied with a heavy sigh. The slump of my shoulders as I averted my eyes conveyed my true feelings. He knew that all was not well.

"No…no. You have that look about you again."

"I said, I'm okay, Ibrahim—"

"I don't know. It's not the words you use, my friend, but what your body tells. I'm starting to worry."

"Look…Kahlil," I began hotly, as the heat of my anxiety rose faster than the external temperatures engulfing us. Realizing my defensiveness, he threw his hands up to signify his surrender, as he waited for calm to wash over me.

"It's just that…never mind."

"No. No. Take your time, brother," he soothed.

"You ever get the feeling that something bad is going to happen?"

"What do you mean?" he asked curiously.

"I don't know, brother. I don't know. I just can't shake this feeling," I said. The shiver I felt traveling down my spine, making its way through my body only solidified my trepidation.

"It's normal to feel this way. Look at where we are. At what's happening—"

"But this feels different. Ever since I got here…I don't know," I said with a shake of my head.

"My brother, we cannot control what *Allah* has destined" he said empathetically.

"I know…but…I just don't want anything to happen to you all," I replied.

"I understand. That is why I feel comfortable putting my life in your hands…and if Allah comes to take me home, it will be no fault of yours. I chose this life," Ibrahim replied. "Plus, I know that you will keep your word."

The vow he referred to, was in respect to his son Bassam. He was a bright-eyed little boy who was the spit of his father, and no older than my Judah. His only child, Bassam was his father's pride and joy. After his wife died in childbirth, Ibrahim had placed all the love he had for her into their son. As the only family he had, Ibrahim knew the consequences his son would face if ever orphaned, so I had taken up the task of doing my all to secure Bassam's future if it ever came to be.

Before I could reply, the sounds of Clarke's feet trampling through the mud captured our attention, which was followed by a fervent hug. "Well, look at you, dumplings. You two weasels speaking that Arabic again?" he said with an excitement, I couldn't help but envy. Trickling in one by one, the rest of our brothers began to surround him.

"Didn't you ask me to teach you?" Ibrahim questioned him.

"That was before you cheated at our poker game. No way will I learn from you now. How do I know you'll teach me the words right? You'd probably have me saying things like, 'I like to eat goat ass'," Clarke replied. His laughter now booming in our ears.

"I won. Fair and square, as you all say," said Ibrahim.

"I know," Clarke shrugged. "I just need a free day and then we can start, savvy?"

"Always with the bullshit, my friend," Ibrahim said, trying to restrain his laughter. "You're just lazy. We start on your lessons as soon as we get back. *Savvy*?" His tone was light and imbued that of a father chastising his son.

"Fine, dad!" Clarke said. His mouth pouted and brows crumpling into defiance like a petulant child, was enough to throw our group into a fit of laughter.

"Alright. Alright," said Jiménez, trying to calm our boisterousness.

"Ready to saddle up, bitches? Or nah?"

"What do you mean, saddle up?" I asked.

"Did you think you'd get to have all the fun on this run, Lati?" replied Devon.

"My back for yours, bro-ham. You know the rules," said Taylor.

"You guys don't have to go. I got it," I said.

I couldn't pinpoint why, but doom enveloped me like a silent wave. And for the first time, the mission didn't feel right with them on it. It's one of the reasons I didn't tell them in the first place.

"Nope. No can do. Rules are rules. Even for you, Lati," said Devon. "Let's finish up this sweep. The rest of the convoy looks like they're about done."

"I finished all safety checks, already," I said.

"Alright, let's monkey this shit up," said Clarke.

"Wait, I want a picture before we go," replied Taylor.

It had become tradition. He said that it was because he wanted to remember us at our best, but I felt it was his way of immortalizing us if something led to our demise. Taking my place between Devon and Ibrahim, I felt as the weight of my body drove my feet down deeper and deeper into the muddy sand, making it harder to maintain my balance, which forced me to shift to keep from sinking. It was this moment that increased the gnawing feeling I couldn't seem to shake all day, as I wondered whether this picture would be our last.

Before I could vocalize my concerns, the rallying call that we were mission ready had sounded, and we promptly made our way into our Humvees. We weren't long into our journey before nature in her crudeness had stopped our convoy from moving ahead. The storm had created deep divots of mud within the sand, causing us to stop in our tracks in front of a small village, and splitting our convoy into two fractions. Clarke, Taylor, and Jiménez were in the truck ahead of Devon, Ibrahim, and mine, and we had, like others, stepped out of our Humvees to begin sweeping the area while a team worked to get us moving again.

"Stay sharp, ladies," Clarke said, as we worked our way away from our vehicles to clear our surroundings.

"Anyone else finding this a bit strange?" Jiménez said.

"I know. It seems…quiet," Taylor responded faintly.

The harsh thud of his body hit the ground with a resounding crash, as bullets started to whizz by. Cruel and savage, they came at us indiscriminately, as the sound of their light sonic boom pierced the air, cracking loudly, rumbling through like small bolts of lightning, as we struggled to find cover.

I had become complacent—in the time I'd spent wrapped in my own thoughts of apprehension, it didn't strike me how the normal jeering from children bustling about wasn't present. And I had failed to notice the lack of women hustling through, often making their way around as they mingled amongst each other and completed their duties. By the time I spotted the slight movement in the center of patrons who had long stopped shuffling, as they waited in anticipation for our impending onslaught, it was too late. Taylor had already been hit and was gone. I never had the chance to warn them. I didn't prevent what happened. I didn't stop it.

"Taylor is down! Taylor is down!" screamed Devon. In the chaos he had planted himself in between our Humvee and the one behind us, while I found myself behind a string of barrels with Ibrahim.

"Hey, Hightower… you good over there?" Clarke asked from a distance. Like, Devon, he and Jiménez had utilized a vehicle from our convoy as cover.

"I'm good. Just in a bit of a shit show here," he replied.

"We'll get to you when we can," shouted Jiménez. "You got eyes on Lati?"

"We got eyes on each other. Ibrahim is here with me. As soon as we can, we'll make our way to Hightower," I called out. At that moment, I felt the strong grip of Ibrahim's blood-stained hand on my uniform—blood now poured from his chest and spurted from his mouth, as he struggled to maintain his breath and speak. "Aw, fuck! Ibrahim is hit!"

"I'm sorry, brother," Ibrahim said weakly.

"Don't be sorry. You just hold on, okay? You hear me? Hold on," I said, as I took him into my arms, trying to will the inevitable from happening.

"Remember… don't forget…don't forget… my Bassam. Okay?" he said breathlessly.

"No…no. Khalil?" I cried. "*Khaliq ma'ee.* Think of Bassam. You fight… you hear me?" I said to him, as the rigidity of his body gave way, signaling the departure of his life, as his Allah took him home. Placing his body down gently, I shook my head at Devon to signal Ibrahim's demise.

"Fuck! We lost Ibrahim!" he yelled towards Clarke and Jiménez.

"Shit! How's Lati and the rest of the guys faring?" Clarke asked.

"Lati's okay. Just heavy under fire. I'm not sure about the others," he replied.

"Okay. Try to get him to you," said Clarke.

"You gotta try to make your way here, Lati. I'll cover you," Devon said, directing his attention to me, as he made his way out of his refuge to ensure my arrival safely to him. The rapid fire that ensued forced him to shield himself once more. Watching him, I saw panic light his face, as blood began to seep down into his eyes.

"You okay, Hightower?!" I shouted.

"Yeah. A fucking flesh wound. Good thing, we have these," he said as he began to place his helmet back onto his head, which never made it on. The boom of the *RPG* landing overpowered the sounds of bullets raining down, hitting the vehicle that sheltered Clarke and Jiménez. Its powerful explosion had eradicated the windows, sending debris flying, as it made its way into Devon's head, splitting his skull. It wasn't until I heard the painful screams and rallying cries of Clarke, that I knew Jiménez hadn't survived the blast. His skin scorched and blackened, the result of the blaze that had ensued, only fueled Clarke's thirst for blood. It was this passion to avenge our brother, that caused his death. Charging at them, he didn't make it more than a few feet before his body was littered with bullets that drove him to the ground.

As Clarke laid out the framework of distraction, I rushed myself to Devon's side where I felt the sting of the first bullet I received, fly through my shoulder. Dragging Devon to cover next to the body of Jiménez and behind his charred Humvee, I worked to see if he was alright. Although unconscious, he was still breathing; to which I searched the remains of the truck. Soon, I found the med kit I was looking for, which luckily, was still intact. Working gently, I secured the shrapnel that lingered in his skull, so that I could stop the bleeding.

"Hang on, now, brother. You're not done yet. I can't lose you too," I said, as I prayed to Hashem to protect us.

Lifting him over my shoulders, I worked my way from vehicle to vehicle, as I attempted to get to the front lines of our convoy where they seemed to have stabilized the impact of the ambush against us, where I was met halfway by soldiers who had made their way back to get those of us under heavy fire, to safety.

"Take him…please…" I pleaded.

"He's still alive?" asked the young Private.

"Barely breathing…but he's alive. Take him, now!" I spoke. His unconscious body now transferred over into the arms of the young soldiers before me.

"Sir, you're hit. You should go on ahead with him, so you can be taken back to base—"

"Take him," I said firmly, "He's my best friend. I'll only slow whoever it is that helps me down. I'm going back to sweep through and see who else I can find. Get him back, and then you can come back for me. Got it?" I spoke. My feet planted firmly on the ground, as I ran each step back to the fire I had just escaped.

I didn't last long out there. As I checked for signs of life within the hostility of the guns blasting, I was soon hit by a fiery sting of bullets zipping through my pelvis, as a second *RPG* penetrated the sky, plunging me into darkness.

Welcome Home

It had been a week since the demons of his past came back to haunt him. Gone were the nights he couldn't sleep because of his desires for her. Instead, the nightmares had returned with a vengeance. Visions of what he faced surfaced throughout the day, tormenting him, as they rushed him back to a past, he'd long thought put to rest. They played, over and over in a symphony of regret, as time stood still. Bringing him back to moments of repentance, and to a time when she had become his escape, as he delivered himself from the shackles of his anguish. And as the days of her arrival grew closer, he prayed that she couldn't smell the gloom washing over him. However, as he took in the look of uneasiness in her eyes, he knew that his wish had gone unanswered.

"What's up with you?" Colette asked, staring at him curiously. The week had gone by slowly for her, as she anticipated the fresh start she desperately craved. Now that she made the choice to put everything behind her, she was looking forward to the possibilities of the rest of their lives together—but that excitement waivered upon seeing him. Gone was the light banter she had begun to look forward to. At first, she thought the stress of managing their children and home had finally caught up to him, but looking at him now, the way in which his body tensed, and he wiped the sweat frantically that kissed his brow, she knew better. Now as they sat in the car in silence on their way home, she wondered if she had made a mistake in hoping.

"Nothing. Just have a lot on my mind," he said.

The vague way in which he replied made her raise her brows. Although he knew she was questioning his behavior, he hadn't the heart to bring it to the forefront. To him, she had enough to worry about. While he understood her concern, he wanted the focus to be on her, not him. Plus, he was ashamed. After all this time, he thought himself free of the confines of his past. Yet, there they were, ruling over him, eating away at the strength he reserved for her.

"Care to share?" she asked.

"Not right now," he replied more harshly than intended. The look of sadness that now emanated from her eyes forced him into calm. The last thing he wanted was to rouse her distrust of him and the rebuilding of their marriage—he had to ease the tension that was rising between them. "I'm sorry. I didn't mean to be so abrasive, motek. I just…can't right now. You understand?"

Despite the nod of affirmation, she'd given him, she did not understand. In fact, she did not want to understand. It was this level of understanding she often afforded him, that led them down the path of discontent they found themselves in now. While she would bend to him in this moment, she had no intention of allowing this to slide—she was not going to make the same mistakes.

Turning her attention now to her surroundings, she said her goodbyes inwardly to the place that had forced her to confront her demons. Taking in the mid-November chill, she noted how the leaves had already fallen, cascading their beautiful branches over passerby. She had always thought of them as colorful braids that rained down from the crown of a majestic queen. Nature had a way of amazing and soothing her, and as they approached the long drive on the Taconic Parkway, she knew that it would bring her into the calm she needed, before having to weather the storm she was sure would ensue.

He did not take her silence as defeat. Although her look was serene, the fire in her eyes warned him of what was to come. He tried to prepare himself, but as they arrived into the bustling chaos of their city, and left behind the scenic tranquility of their journey, he couldn't help his growing anxiety. Not even the excitement of the surprise he prepared for her could ease his discomfort. And the apprehension on her face, as he pulled up to their home, rattled his already unsteady nerves.

"Are you okay?" he asked. Turning off the car and pulling the key out of the ignition, he sat patiently for her reply.

"No," she spoke. "I'm just afraid. I'm scared that they will be mad at me. That they won't want me home. You know?"

The sadness vibrating from her shook him to his core. It had been fourteen weeks since she last seen her babies, and although her heart ached to be with them, the embarrassment she felt at being apart from them for so long, kept her glued to the warmth of her seat.

"We've been through this," Benny soothed.

"I can't face them," she said, "I…I abandoned them. I basically abandoned our children."

Tears began to fall freely down her cheeks, causing him to come to her aid. "No. No, Cole. Listen to me," he said, pulling her face gently into his large hands. Staring into her eyes, he wished she would see what he saw. He knew what kind of mother she was—it was the reason that he'd begged her to expand their family. Watching how she was with their sons, how she nurtured them, made him want more children to love and hold on to. It was as if she'd molded his own personal army of love. It completed him. "You were grieving, my love."

"They were grieving too, Benny. And I… I just left them," she replied emphatically. Guilt swept her like a violent storm—one that she was quickly realizing, she may never be free of.

"The kids want nothing more than to see and hold their mother. You cannot beat yourself up for trying to get better. With everything you went through…everything I put you through," he said with a wary sigh. "Listen, I'm not going to let you play martyr here. You didn't let me do it to myself. Now…our children are waiting to hear about your wonderful trip at that beautiful resort you've been staying at. So, make it good."

"Okay. Okay. Just give me a minute," she replied.

Conceding, he decided to step out of the car to give her the moment she craved. Absently, he leaned on the passenger side door, where his wife now sat in anguish. He stood in the chilled night air, allowing it to act as a cloak, as it enveloped him in its cold winds. He hoped that it would be a distraction to his own feelings of inadequacies.

"Pull yourself together. She needs you," he chastised himself.

Seeing movement from his periphery, he turned his attention to their front bay window. There he saw his eldest two sons gesturing their irritation at him for not coming in. As he prepared to text their sons about their delay, he was interrupted by the slight tap on the window by his wife. Looking at her face, as she rolled down the window, he could see that she had cleared the remnants of her tears and touched up her make-up.

"I'm ready now," she said. The look on her face was strained, but it wasn't long before she evolved into the woman his children called their mother. It was a transformation that he had become accustomed to seeing and wanted nothing more than to be rid of. Opening the door, he extended his hand, which she took without hesitation, prompting him into a better mood. Walking hand-in-hand to their door, they were stopped by the familiar face of Sarah Cohen.

"Oh. Hi, Colette," she spoke. "I didn't know you were back home. I was just going to drop off some food for Ben and the children."

Her forced smile laced with a hint of malice did not go unnoticed, as the woman who had been a long-standing thorn in her side, took pleasure in her discomfort. "I arrived today," Colette replied.

"I told you she would be back today. I mentioned it the last time you came to our door. Now, as I told you before…my children and I don't need your help," Benny replied. There was something in his eyes that Colette couldn't quite put her finger on. It disturbed her, causing her to get a rush of wariness that marred her senses.

"Oh. I see," Sarah responded.

Her eyes squinted slightly at Colette, as if she were a speck on her glasses she was trying to see through. Transferring her line of sight towards Benny, the desire in her eyes was unmistakable, causing Colette's angst to increase. "I just thought that it would do the kids some good to have a home cooked meal. You know… since their mother hasn't been home for some time," she said snidely.

He didn't dare meet his wife's gaze. He didn't need to. He felt the burn of her eyes against his skin, and he knew that he would need to find a solution to the trouble that Sarah, was obviously trying to create. This wouldn't be happening had you not let her in, Benny thought to himself. *Why did you let her in?*

Normally, the thought of her made his blood run cold. From the moment his father asked him to take her under his wing those years ago, Sarah Cohen had latched herself on to him to the point that it made his skin crawl. In her eyes they were meant to be. Colette and his children were just pawns to be maneuvered, until she could get her king. And if it weren't for a moment of weakness, where he surrendered the deepest depths of himself to her, he wouldn't be standing there, filled with dread welling in the pit of his stomach, due to her presence.

"My children are and were well fed, by me," Benny said tightly, "Thanks for your concern, but we got it."

"I didn't mean to imply that they weren't. Just that a mother's touch could go a long way—"

"And they have a mother, who just lost her mother in the most horrific way possible. It's something you should understand," he chided, "My wife was entitled to some time to grieve and process—"

"I know. I know. This isn't coming out the way I intended," Sarah fumbled. Turning her attention to Colette, she asked, "How was your trip?"

"Her retreat is none of your concern, Sarah,"Benny said defensively.

The tension in his draw heightened the scar he obtained so long ago. His stance was ominous, forcing Sarah to take a step back. She did not enjoy this version of the man she'd conjured so often in her dreams. She preferred the man who made her days lighter and easier with just the sight of him. If it weren't for Colette, she would have him all to herself. And Sarah couldn't help but wish she would have stayed gone.

Reading the friction in the lines of her husband's body, Colette instinctually pulled her body closer to him, as she always did when his anger got the better of him. In most cases, just the nearness of her would soothe him into submission, but for some reason, it made him swell with a callousness that was unrelenting. It was as if he were trying to protect her, but she couldn't figure out why. Given the uneasiness and brewing strain growing between Sarah and her husband, Colette decided to put an end to their exchange.

"Look, Sarah…it's been a long drive, and we just want to get settled in—"

"You know…I could help, Benny. That way, Colette can get some rest," Sarah said melodically.

Her use of the pet-name Colette had given her husband so long ago, caused rage to stir within her. Despite her attempts to keep the peace with the woman in front of her, Colette was in no mood for games. This wasn't the first time, Sarah had tried her hand at supplanting her, and she had no intention of allowing her to do so now. Especially not in her face or in front of the home she shared with her husband.

"I think it's time for you to go, Sarah—"

"Colette…really…it's no bother."

"No. Really. You need to go," Colette said, as she snaked her body around her husband. "You see, I have children who miss me…their mother. And I have a husband, who I haven't been able to make love to in weeks. So, if you'd be so kind as to go and tend to your own home, and your own husband, I think that would be a wise decision. In other words…politely, fuck off."

Colette's smile was wicked. And she savored the way, Sarah angrily stumbled down their steps and toddled towards her home. The light baritone laugh that radiated from her husband had forced an eruption of laughter that bellowed from her. Seeing her under the illumination of their porch light, her eyes and face filled with joy over the mischief she caused, reminded him of the girl she once was.

"I knew you were still in there," he said to her.

Spinning her towards him, he captured her in his arms. The heat of her body in contrast to the cold that surrounded them, brought his desire for her to the brim, and soon his lips found hers. The stillness of her breath ignited by her hesitation against him, only provoked him more. Coaxing her gently, he took what they both longed for.

Despite her reservations, it was moments like this that fueled the passion she had for her husband. He had a way of commanding her want and need for him. It was enough to make her wilt against him and swell with desire. Pulling herself nearer, she allowed the world to collapse around her, as she delved deeper into the feel of him. If it weren't for the sound of their son, Luke, interjecting, she could have stayed in his arms that way, forever.

"I've found them," he cried out. "You know, if you old people are going to do things like this, you could at least get a room."

The playful look of disgust on his face was enough to make them climb within themselves with embarrassment. "I guess we should get inside, huh?" Benny said, offering his hand.

"Let's go. I'm ready now," she replied confidently.

Upon entering their home, Colette was stunned to tears. While the ceiling was lined with vibrant streamers that rained down in streaks of gorgeous gold, every square inch of the floor was littered with colorful balloons she had to playfully kick to get through. The giant 'welcome home' banner that hungover the archway of the family room had rendered her speechless. The visibility of the love her family had for her was overwhelming. Looking at the gratefulness in their faces at her return, made her happy that her absence had not caused her children undo harm.

"Do you like it, Mommy?" asked Zachary. His soft voice played like a beautiful song, chiming sweetly in her ear, "It's okay, mommy. Don't cry. Oh no. I don't think she likes it."

His face, once filled with delight and excitement, had now begun to sink, causing her to lift him lovingly into her arms. "Oh, no, Zach. I love it! I love it very much. I'm just so happy to be home because I missed you all so much. These are happy tears," Colette said smiling.

It was enough to bring the joy back into his face. After touching her nose to his, she let him down so that she could make her way to his siblings. Reaching her two beautiful daughters, she placed a hand on their cheeks and slowly caressed their faces, taking in the softness and feel of their skin. Pulling them into her embrace, she kissed each of them atop their heads, taking in their scent and relishing the warmth of them close to her.

"How was your trip, Momma?" Nahla asked.

"It was fine, baby. I met a lot of people who were sad just like me. And needed some friends—"

"So, you all became best friends? To help each other?" asked Charlotte.

"The best of friends," she said with a wink, "We hung out. We talked. Did lots of yoga and projects to make us feel better. I hope that's okay?" she said to them. Based on the looks on their faces and nod of their heads, her answer seemed to satisfy her youngest three children.

"You'd be so proud of me. I made most of the meals, Momma," Nahla said, changing the subject. In the time since Colette was gone, she no longer needed to look down, to peer into her daughter's eyes, as they now stood face to face with hers.

"You didn't do them by yourself," Charlotte said, "We helped *Savta* and Bubbe."

"I did too make them," Nahla said defensively, "Even if it was with Savta and Bubbe, I did make them all the same. We got tired of pasta and take out. So they came over to cook for us and I helped."

"I know you did, honey," Colette said. "And I am so proud of you. Both of you, for all the help you must have given."

"Abba tried to cook, but he didn't do a very good job of it," Charlotte whispered.

"Yeah, Momma. If you're going to go, at least leave some food," Nahla replied emphatically, which forced Colette to look quizzically at her husband. His curious response towards her was enough to make her giggle with amusement. He hadn't a clue about what his girls were saying about him.

"Why do I feel like they're complaining about me?" Benny said, coming closer from his spot in his favorite chair. He needed to hear what half-truths his girls were likely telling.

Never one to shy away from speaking her mind, Nahla came forward first. "We were just telling Momma that your food could have been better," she said matter-of-factly.

"Yeah…it could have been better. But at least you tried," Charlotte said sympathetically.

"At least I can always count on your diplomacy, Charlotte. Never lose that," Benny said sweetly. "And you, young lady. Don't ever lose that spunk. You'll need that in law," he teased Nahla.

"Law? I don't remember anything about that during our talks," Colette questioned. She had always known her daughter had an affinity towards it, but like most young ones, she was still teetering between career paths, prior to her leaving. Now it seemed that her daughter had settled on her decision. *So much has changed.* Colette couldn't help but be pained. She'd missed out on much of their lives in such a short time. I'm never going to get this time back, she said inwardly, as her mind began to drive forward her shame.

He recognized that look in her eyes. He had seen it often enough in other women, and throughout their life as parents together, to know what she must be feeling. He himself had had moments of discontent, in respect to his ability to be a father to their children, when he returned home. And just as she'd seen him through it, he promised himself that he would do the same for her as well.

"It's law. For now. But…they did start a program at school recently, and the papers are waiting for your signature. She wanted *you* to be the one to sign them," he said encouragingly. The change in her demeanor pleased him, as she seemed to delight in the consideration.

"So…who's going to ask her?" he said to their children.

"Ask me what?" Colette replied curiously.

"We know you just got home—" Nahla began.

"But can you make your lemon cake?" Charlotte finished.

"Yeah, Mommy. Can you make your lemon cake?" asked Zachary.

"Everyone tried to make it for us, but it wasn't like yours, Momma," said Nahla.

"Hmmm. I don't know guys. Before I decide whether to make it, I do have a question. Would you guys prefer vanilla or lemon icing?" Colette asked playfully. Although she could barely decipher their answers, the rapid responses that ensued made her feel like she was finally home.

"Can we help?" asked Charlotte.

"No can do, little one. This is our time. But you can help eat it when we're done," Luke said, as he tossed her up onto his shoulders, spinning her around as she squealed with happiness. Placing her gently on the couch, he turned to join Colette and his brother in the kitchen, his olive skin now tinged red from his antics.

What started as a distraction for her boys during their father's episodes, had become a tradition she kept on with her elder sons, long after their father's healing had begun. Whenever one of them was feeling down, one or both of her boys would gather up the ingredients, signifying that they needed time with her. As they grew older, she had made it into a bi-weekly event to keep tabs on the changes in their life. Although she'd seen Judah weekly, she hadn't realized how much she missed spending time baking with them.

Luke spoke first, "I'm glad you're feeling better, Mother," he said.

He had finally made the transition to addressing her formally, and she still hadn't quite gotten used to it. *When did he grow up so?* The boy she once held snuggly in her arms, was now on the threshold of manhood; and while proud, she couldn't help but feel uneasy. "I know how much, Grandmother meant to you…she meant a lot to us too—"

"I know, honey," Colette turned to him, stroking his fine honey blonde hair. He looked so much like his aunt, Mazal. He had her eyes and all. "I wish I was strong enough to be there for you all."

"You've been strong for too long, Mother," said Judah.

"Yes. Agreed. Honestly, Mother, we're shocked you didn't take off sooner," Luke said solemnly.

"Look…we love Abba," Judah started off slowly, "And you guys had some great years in between back when…well…you know. But this past year or so? We've noticed."

"And we saw how it changed you," Luke confided.

They were speaking of the one thing she'd feared most. Although she suspected that her sons sensed when things were not perfect between their father and her, she didn't realize just how perceptive they were.

"Listen, your father and I have our problems. But he isn't to blame for this," Colette said cautiously, "I don't want you to blame him for me going there. I don't want you to be angry with him."

"We're not angry with him. And we understand his reasons," Judah said consciously. "We just…well—"

"We want you to be happy," finished Luke. "That's all we want. You both deserve to be happy."

"I am happy…when I'm with all of you," Colette replied.

"All we're saying is that we hope that this will be the fresh start that's needed after this year," Luke said.

And with that, they all went on in serene harmony, putting together the cake they had often constructed before. Mending and binding it together to form a strong structure, just as she hoped she and Benny would do with their marriage.

The day went on seamlessly as she worked to take in all that she had missed with her children. In the time she'd been away, she found that after some things he perceived to be red flags, Judah had decided to prolong his engagement to Primrose and focus on finishing his degree. That was a huge relief to her. She thought it wise that they dedicate more time to getting to know each other better.

Luke had decided to take a gap-year to travel abroad. As her most studious child, she understood why he wanted to do so; he had skipped a grade and spent his entire life, it seemed, trying to be the perfect son. But despite her acceptance of his reasoning, she was not yet comfortable with his choice to go so far away from home. Nahla, however, was trying to nurture her new interest in law. While Charlotte had formed an interest in art. And young Zachary had finally learned to write his name. Yes. She'd missed so much; but as she filled the end of her day with them, wrapped in their warm embraces, and goodnights filled with love, she finally accepted her welcome home.

Winding down for the evening, Benny and Colette made their way to their bedroom that once held so much passion and promise. Now, as she bounded each step, she looked upon it with suspicion; and she couldn't quell the apprehension that began to swell within her as they passed the threshold.

The excitement of seeing and holding her children again waned, and her attention was brought back to the change in her husband's demeanor upon picking her up. Despite his pleasantness throughout her visit with their young ones, she could still see the worry and angst that settled behind his eyes. Like her, with the energy of their children no longer driving their interaction with each other, he sat with an awkwardness that prompted a strange silence, neither seemed to know how to push through.

"You seemed to have kept the place in pretty good shape," she broke first.

"Is that your way of saying that this is still where the magic happens?" Benny jested. Instant regret washed over him. And he couldn't believe how inept he'd become in speaking with his wife.

"Already that's where your mind is," she responded, "I didn't think you would want to."

"Of course, I do," he said, "I always want you, Cole. Always."

"Uh huh," Colette said skeptically. Her feelings of the day's prior events giving way.

"Uh oh," he said, trying to keep his voice even. He knew this conversation would come, but he was hoping they would focus on their reunion, instead. "Look, you just got home, and you have enough to deal with. I don't want to add to it. Can we just enjoy each other for a while?"

Walking towards her. He tried pulling her body close to his, but the pressure of her palm against his chest was enough for him to realize that he wasn't going to get off easily. "Secrets," she scoffed, "I hate that you don't communicate with me, Benny. Again, you're keeping things from me. You still haven't learned. Have you?"

"I know. I know. And I'm sorry. But if I told you, I would've had to betray your mother's confidence—"

"Like keeping it from me helped? And that is not what I was talking about."

"Look. I know that it made things worse, but it wasn't my story to tell. It tore me up inside to keep it from you, and I wish that I never did, because I lost more than I could probably only hope to get back—"

"So, why are you doing it now?" she asked, "Why are you pretending nothing is wrong? When I know for a fact that something is up with you."

"Shit. You're right. You're right," he replied. "I'm sorry…I'm doing it again, aren't I? I'm fucking up."

"Spill it. Now," Colette demanded, "No more secrets. We can't do anymore secrets. You hear me? I want everything out on the table, right now!"

Running his hands through his beard, he sat on the edge of their bed and patted his hand in the space beside him, prompting her to have a seat next to him. "I had an episode," he confessed.

She didn't think she heard him correctly. An episode? After the day he finally told her everything he'd endured during his time at war, it had taken some time before Benny figured out the coping strategies necessary to make life bearable again. She was there by his side, as he struggled to find a regimen that helped him to disarm his demons, and it had been years since an incident occurred.

"What triggered it?" she asked.

"It happened a week ago. I was going through our photo albums," he said, choking up. "And a picture fell out…our last one together."

"I'm sorry, Benny," she replied.

It all made sense now. And she truly was sorry. Sorry that she wasn't there for him and that she assumed the worse. She believed that he truly didn't want her home. She was sorry that his PTSD was something that would never end. It was tied to their lives forever, no matter how hard they tried to stave it off.

"You have nothing to be sorry about."

"But I do. I thought I cleared it all, like you asked me too," she said sadly. Her hand now outstretched, settled on his face, to capture the tears he allowed to flow freely.

"It's not your fault," he said to her. "And I don't want you to worry. I've doubled up on my sessions after work, put more time into my runs in the mornings, and I've had meetings with the guys, twice now this week. All that was missing was you. And now that I have you home again, I'll be okay."

At least he had them while I was away, she thought. She was grateful for them—the group of men who'd become part of his support system. In time, Benny and Devon had accomplished what they had set out to do so long ago. The center they created for men suffering in the same way they were, was a godsend to them all. It helped them work through the troubles of their past, while formulating a bond that aided them in looking forward to their future.

"Was it bad this time?" she asked.

"No…not as bad as it was when…"

"We lost her," she said, finishing his sentence. Her mind wandered to the loss they experienced soon after they'd begun to get their life back. He had taken it hard. The loss of their daughter fractured his psyche, splitting him in two, and sent him back to his place of torment. And while the doctor explained that those things sometimes happened, he was convinced that he was being punished for the crimes he believed he committed. She hadn't taken it any easier—the choice she made to prevent further pregnancies without his knowledge, was done to regain a sense of control. But the act had put them into a tumultuous period. As time passed, they healed. And soon they were able to appreciate the child they lost, and what they felt, was eventually returned to them.

"I hadn't had any real issues since I found out about your mom, you know?" he professed. "That's why her illness…that year…was so hard for me."

"I can see that."

"I wasn't trying to avoid you. I just knew I had to because you would have known. You always do. All the lying…it was too much. And all it did was…it pushed us further apart, and for that, again, I am sorry," he said sincerely.

"I know you are. We'll get through this too. Together," Colette said adamantly. "Sink or swim, right?"

"And always swimming by your side," Benny responded, "I love you."

Bringing her close to him, they laid down on the bed in silent bliss; while interlocking their fingers repeatedly every so often, to remind themselves of the other's presence.

"You want to tell me what's going on with you and Sarah Cohen?" she said absently, breaking the silence between them. She had begun to drift off when her mind was suddenly jolted awake by thoughts of their strange encounter.

"Nothing. I think your absence has sparked some crazy in her. Miserable people tend to like company," he replied.

"Trouble in paradise?" she asked.

"Hasn't it always been." he said. "She doesn't love him. We all know that."

"True," Colette said lightly, "I just wish she'd stop trying to get her grubby little claws on you."

"Jealous?" Benny asked playfully.

"No. Cautious," she said warily, "Anyway…I'm tired. Let's go to bed."

Bringing her body closer beside him, she allowed herself to sink deeper into his warmth. And as she let sleep take her, she hoped the feeling that she was being betrayed, would fade along with it.

Don't Look Back

Feeling the strong tug and drag of her leg towards the edge of the bed, she whimpered, "Benny, no. I'm tired."

"You don't have to do anything," he said. His voice now low and husky with desire, quickly roused her senses. "Just lay there and let me take care of you. I promise, I'll do all the work."

"Benny…I'm serious," she said. Her protests now withered toward defeat, as his soft kisses up and down her thighs began to send shock waves through her body.

"You don't seem like you're serious," he said playfully.

"I'm going to be late for my meeting," she said, trying to squirm away from him.

It had been six months since she arrived home, and as they fell back into the normalcy and rhythm they once had, before the chaos of the previous year took hold of them, the passion they felt for one another had been rekindled and magnified. And they'd both missed more meetings than they cared to admit because of it.

"They won't mind," he whined, "You're the boss, right? Besides, I don't think you really want to get ready now."

Going back to the task at hand, he took his time caressing the curves of her body as he took in her sighs of hunger. His kisses were gentle as he glided his hand methodically up and down her body, causing dampness to seep from her center. "God you're so wet. I need to taste you," Benny said as he drank from her thirstily, causing her to release soft sighs of pleasure.

"Come on. Stop. I really need to get ready," she cried out.

The moan she allowed to escape her lips betrayed her, causing him to mischievously glide his tongue lazily across her soft mound, making her writhe with longing against him.

"You really want me to stop?" he asked coyly.

"No. I mean, yes. Yes. I want you to stop," she whimpered.

"You don't sound very certain, Mrs. Lati," he toyed.

"Last night wasn't good enough for you?" Colette asked.

Although she enjoyed being with him, she couldn't understand how he never seemed satiated. He was insatiable. The more she gave in to him, the more he seemed to want her. Like many nights since reuniting, he had spent the night before, savoring every part of her. And if it weren't for the fact that he finally let her rest at three o'clock that morning, she wouldn't have minded being woken up at six a.m. to make love to him again. Despite her exhaustion, the way that his tongue played rhythmically against her, started to ignite a fire, she couldn't help but bend to.

"Last night was an appetizer. However, it doesn't seem like you want me to stop anyway," he said, as his laughter filled the air. The sight of her body shuddering with need, pleased him; and it roused a fire that made his onslaught heated and deliberate.

"I don't find this funny," she said breathlessly, "Quit messing with me. You've had enough fun."

Despite her protest, she began to give in. Her body now owing its loyalty to him, as she began to move mindlessly to the pleasure that only he could bring. The pressure she applied against the back of his head, guiding him forward, as he took the opportunity to tease her, amused him greatly. "I will never…ever…get…enough of you," he said between each taste of her.

"Then stop teasing me," she grunted.

The provocative movements against her core increased her frustration, as the swell in her body called out to be filled. He played with her masterfully; listening to her body until he brought her to the brink of ecstasy before stopping suddenly and making his way up her torso with soft kisses until he reached her lips. He brushed against her mouth gently, before standing above her, as he tried his best not to burst into laughter at her confused expression.

"What are you doing, Benjamin?!"

"You said you have to go, so I thought it best that we stop here."

"When I'm close? You thought that would be an appropriate time, Benjamin?" she asked heatedly. "Making me late, for… *this*?"

"Yes. Now you can go to work thinking of me all day."

Two can play at this game, she thought. Lifting herself up, she crawled over to him slowly until she was met with his member that was standing effortlessly at attention. Pulling down the grey sweats that covered him, she admired his length as he stood proudly and boldly before her. Painstakingly, she took off her camisole, and tossed it to the side, revealing the mounds of flesh he desperately wanted to touch. As he took in the suppleness of her breast, she stood on her knees and placed his hands against her chest and moaned as he squeezed gently. Wrapping her arms loosely around his neck, she brushed her lips softly against his, coaxing him to surrender to her. Kissing him deeply, she permitted his exploration of her body until his hands settled firmly on her back side. Sliding her hands and body down the tightness of his abs, she stopped when she felt his hardness and commenced to stroking him, as she placed tender licks, teasingly against his tip.

"So, you're going to tease me now?" he asked. His voice, husky with unbridled desire, was music to her ears. Kissing his belly, she smiled to herself as his body trembled with need. The light suction she commenced coyly around his member, while swirling her tongue gently around his fullness, forced a moan from deep within him. Releasing him from her mouth, she sat quietly, trying to stifle her amusement, which was his undoing. Grabbing her neck, he forced her to look at him. "Do it, *right*. Right. Fucking. Now."

"Why?" she provoked, her smile devious.

"Colette…don't toy with me," Benny replied. His breathing increased, forced heavy sighs of anticipation to escape him, as he tried his best to remain controlled. But the look in her eyes and the way that she opened her mouth slightly, exposing her tongue as she glided it over his thumb that had landed across her lips, sent him into a frenzy. As she pulled his thumb into her mouth, he buckled inwardly.

"I know a better place you can put that mouth of yours."

"No thank you," she said, as she released his hand from her neck. Pushing herself back against their headboard, she gazed smugly at him, watching as his jaw clenched tightly. She knew it wouldn't be long before he did precisely what she needed him to do.

"You think you're funny, don't you?" he asked.

He was aching for her, and the way he was feeling, he could no longer control the need to wipe the smirk off her beautiful face. Bringing himself across the bed, he settled on top of her and kissed her lips softly, and languidly so, until his desire fueled his need to possess her. Wrapping his arm around her waist, he lifted her hips until he found his way to her entry. With one smooth stroke, he plunged deep inside her, sounding off her satisfaction of being filled by his need for her, sending them both into bliss. His movements were teasing in nature; the strokes he committed against her, were intoxicating, making her seek him out with a fervor that made his body quake. His manipulation against her was torturous, and Colette could no longer commit to his taunting and suppression of her need to release; a peak he seemed to take pleasure in withholding at his leisure.

Pushing him back gently, she coaxed his body back against their bed and straddled him as she exhaled sweetly, "I want to ride."

The sound of her ache for him, as she lowered herself, consuming him deep within her, and the tightness of her flesh taking hold of him, sent Benny reeling. She fit like a glove—one that was perfectly designed just for him. And as he watched the way her body snaked and coiled, as she grinded against him, he knew that his loss for control was imminent.

"If you keep moving like that, you're not going to get what you're seeking, Mrs. Lati."

"Don't you dare! Hold on for me, baby…please," she whimpered, "I'm almost there."

Flipping her onto her stomach, he brought her body into an upright position to meet his hardness and allowed her to sit upon him. With her back to his chest, Benny spread Colette's legs wide; and with one hand strategically on the small bud of pleasure between her thighs, he gripped her neck lightly with the other. Slowly he permitted her to consume him, as they stirred rhythmically against each other, pushing them to the brink of ecstasy. And with each swirl of her hips, Benny matched her with fervent thrusts and the light stroking of her jewel. Her heavy pants and moans, as she slid down to take him in deeper, told him all he needed to know; he needed her to give in to the calls of her body, so he too could surrender.

"*Ani chayav shetigmeri*. Come for me, motek. I know you're there. I can feel it," he whispered against her ear. "That's a good girl."

With the sound of his encouragement, finally, she let go. The cry of his name, as her flesh constricted around his member, unraveled the knot of lasciviousness that permeated within him. Soon, he too released, as they matched each other's rhythmic manipulation of the other; with a force that made them collapse into each other's arms—spent from the physical manifestation of their love.

"Satisfied?" she asked, trying to catch her breath.

"Satisfied? Yes," he replied. "But am I done with you? Not even close. I have plans for you later."

"Well… that will have to do…for now, because I have to get ready,"

Colette replied.

"No. Lay with me for a bit," Benny said, pulling her close as she attempted to rise from their bed. "I could lay like this with you forever."

"I bet you could," she said lightly.

Snuggling up against him, she watched the rise and fall of his chest, and felt calm wash over her—she always felt secure in his arms. "I was thinking... maybe after Mazal's wedding, we can have a sort of...I don't know... a honeymoon style trip of our own. What do you think?"

His sister's wedding was less than a week away, and he couldn't believe how much time had gone by. One minute she was this beautiful little girl that he'd instantly fallen in-love with. The next, she was engaged and getting married within a matter of months—a revelation he was not quite sure he was happy with.

"Ugh. Don't speak of it," he said.

"Stop being such a baby. She's a grown woman," Colette replied.

"You felt the same way about Kami."

"Yes, and I had to get over it. They don't stay little forever," she said.

Although it was stained by their mother's illness, thinking back on the day of her sister's wedding made Colette proud. There she stood, as beautiful and elegant as a swan, next to Akal in the traditional wedding attire of his culture, before all their family and friends, as she committed her life to his. Now, they were planning for the arrival of their first born, and she couldn't be happier for the little girl she once carried in her arms. "I'm just glad that mom got to see them married, before—"

"I know. I know," he said, caressing her cheek. He was grateful for them all that his mother in-law was able to be there. It hadn't been easy for her, but the strength she exhibited to be at Kami's wedding, was something he would never forget.

"Anyway," Colette said, changing the subject, "If you feel this way about Mazal, then how will you survive walking our daughters down the aisle?"

"My daughters will never get married. They'll be staying right here with their Abba. Forever."

"Selfish. Selfish is what you are. They deserve a love of their own too, you know."

"They have all the love in the world they will ever need in me."

"The love of a husband is something different than the love of a father. And they deserve to know that love, just as I have," she said, as she nudged her nose against his cheek, prompting him to kiss it.

"Fine. I'll relent," he said thoughtfully, "But, I can't believe she went to a *shadchan*. A match maker? Really? And it's all happening so fast. She barely knows him."

"She knows him plenty. They've been friends for some time now. And it was fortunate for them that Mrs. Haddad finally suggested them to each other. You know how shy they both are. They would have never gotten together otherwise. And they're adorable together. He absolutely adores her. He's always been that way."

All that she said was true. Aaron Goldblum had been in-love with Mazal since they were kids. A blind man could see it. He just never had the heart to approach her—until now. And despite his apprehension, Colette was sure that Benny saw Aaron's love for his sister as well. In truth, she wouldn't be surprised if it were him who begged Mrs. Haddad to set Aaron up on a date with Mazal.

"Whatever," Benny said emphatically.

"You're being such a bratty older brother. It's cute. Bratty…but cute," she said, kissing his lips. Rising from bed, she went on to ready herself for the day.

"No. Come back to bed," he said, gently catching hold of her arm.

"Unfortunately, that's not possible. I really can't miss this one," she said. "Your dad will kill me."

"Just tell him you were making sure that his son was happy," he joked.

"I don't think that would suffice. Imagine this…hey…Abba? Yeah. I'm going to miss an important meeting with an investor because your son can't seem to keep his hands to himself. Yup. That would definitely go over well," she responded.

"Oh. The infamous investor," he said dramatically. "Did Akal ever say who it was?"

Although Benny loved Akal, something about this meeting didn't sit well with him. While it wasn't unusual for his wife and Akal to meet with patrons who had interest in investing with their firm, it was the secrecy in who the patron was that seemed to throw him for a loop. And the sudden surge of anxiety rumbling within him, did nothing to extinguish his apprehension.

"No. He hasn't told me anything," she replied.

"You don't think that's strange?"

"I do, which is one of the reasons why I just want to get this over with. It's probably of no real importance, and just someone that he promised to see. But I told your dad, I'd go to make sure they'd be a good fit with the firm," she explained.

After getting her MBA and broker's license, Colette, Akal, and Musa bought out the previous owner. And with the clientele she and Akal had established previously, they created a successful brokerage that eventually branched into several areas of the real estate market.

"Can we meet for lunch then?"

"For actual food this time?" she asked. The smile on her face couldn't be helped as she thought about the fun they had during their last lunch date.

"I can't make promises," Benny said.

"Well then…I'll keep it in mind and see if I can pencil you in."

"I see," he responded. "All I know is, I better not have to come find you."

"I said, I will try. We're not all privileged to come in whenever we feel or in accordance with our clients' whims, Mr. Lati."

"I'm going to be bored at home without you," Benny sulked.

"No sessions today then?" she called out to him from their closet.

"Nope. It'll just be me. All by my lonesome."

"Great. Since you're not in a rush, come help me find something to wear."

The Devil's Proposition

Standing outside her company's board room, Colette gave herself a once over before entering. Although it complimented her, she wasn't sure about the cream-colored dress her husband chose. It was purchased by him not too long ago for a date night. Under those circumstances, she would've worn it, gladly; but the way it laid against her body like a second skin, made her feel semi-exposed. She hoped that at the very least, her attire wouldn't offend their potential financier. I'm sure my darling husband chose this for himself, for lunch time, she thought wickedly. Taking a deep breath, she mentally prepared herself and opened the door, but there was nothing that could prepare her for the man that sat smugly in their office chair.

"Hello, Colette," his deep baritone voice echoed in her ears.

"Akal…could I talk to you for a second?" she said.

"Is everything okay, Colette?" Musa asked. The look on his face conveyed that he was not pleased with her perceived rudeness.

"It's fine, Abba. I just need him for something right quick," she replied. "Akal. My office. Now, please."

"I'm right behind you, sis."

Walking into her office, she couldn't believe the idiocy she'd just walked into. "Out of all people, Akal knows that I don't want to have anything to do with that man," she vented to herself. Anger and fear washed over her—its power, callous and unforgiving.

"Look…Colette," Akal started, bursting into the room. "I can explain—"

"What in the actual fuck, Akal," she roared. "Why is *he* here? Why didn't you tell me it was him?"

"Will you keep your voice down?" Akal said, trying to calm her. "Do you want, Musa to hear?"

"You should have thought of about that before you invited that man here?"

"I didn't invite him, Colette," he said. "It was your father in-law."

"Are you kidding me? First, he's not interested in more investors because we don't need any. Then he sets this meeting. So, what is about him that's changed his mind? Why that man? Why now?" she said. "So much for my darling father in-law being a silent fucking partner!"

"Musa didn't approach him. It was the other way around. He contacted your father in-law, and I guess the price was right enough to get him a meeting," Akal replied, "Apparently, he was rather pushy. You of all people know how that man can be. So, they met up. And Musa seems to like him well enough—"

"They've already met? Since when? In all the time we've had this company—been working here, these two have never had any interest in meeting with one another. So why now? I don't get it."

"Yes. A few months ago. And he's been in contact with him ever since. He's in his ear, Colette."

"Why didn't you talk Musa out of it, Akal? Why didn't you make something up, so that I wouldn't have to deal with that asshole?"

"I tried, Colette. Trust me. I did. But we both know how persuasive he can be," he said to her.

That, she knew. Dominic Toussaint had the venomous charm of a serpent—and his command for attention was only surpassed by his ability to capture your desire to be near him, something she had come to know all too well.

"Listen…I don't know what he's up to, but I don't have time for it," she said. "Can you please let Musa know that I won't be attending the meeting."

"Come on, Colette. He's not going to like this."

"You know who's not going to like this? Benny. My husband. Your best friend," she said vehemently.

"What am I supposed to say?" Akal asked.

"I suggest you make something up. I'll be in my office. Tell, Stella to let me know when he leaves. And close the door behind you, please," she said to him. That he did, and she spent the next few hours trying to figure out how she was going to get Dominic Toussaint out of her life again.

A knock at the door jolted her from the work she had busied herself with, until she received word that it was safe for her to leave her office. Thinking that it was her secretary, Stella, she did not expect the tall masculine figure, who now stood smugly at her door.

"So, you got Akal to do your dirty work for you? I expected better from you, Colette," he said, as his full lips sat in a mocked pout. The light French accent he sported, she once considered endearing, now grated at her nerves.

"What are you doing here?" she asked. Her irritation mounting. She couldn't believe his audacity to show his face after all this time—and what a face it was. His espresso-colored skin was smooth like satin, and illuminated his almond shaped, hazel eyes. The strong jaw he sported complimented his high cheek bones, which flattered his Nubian nose. By conventional standards, one would call Dominic Toussaint a very handsome and desirable man.

"Ouch. I take it that you're still angry with me," he said amused.

"What do you want, Dominic? I don't have time for your games."

"Why, you, of course," he said.

He allowed the words to play over in her mind and watched as it sent her reeling. He couldn't help himself. He took pleasure in tormenting her—after all, it was she that still haunted every moment of his life, since the day she chose to be with *him*. He still couldn't understand why she would want to stay with her mess of a husband. The revelation that he would not have her by his side, was more than he could bear. It was a decision that broke his heart and forced him back home.

"Still an arrogant smart ass, I see," Colette fumed.

Dominic Toussaint was a man of many things, but the settling kind, he was not. Before her, he was happy with his life of philandering. The times he'd seen Colette in passing were insignificant, lending neither a chance to get to know the other. But when his father asked him to close out of the small American real estate company that began his family's legacy, he had not intended to stay long—that is, until he truly saw her. The fact that she was married was of little consequence to him, considering whom she was married to.

"What I meant was…there is no one else I would rather work with on this…small endeavor."

"Not interested," she replied.

"Not interested? How could you say that to the man that gave you your start?"

"Your father gave me my start, and if I remember correctly, we made him a very, very rich man in return. I mean…wasn't it this very firm that paid for that fancy French boarding school you went to? Now, if you'll excuse me…I have work to do," Colette said, feigning interest in the pile of papers that sat on her desk.

Augustin Olivier Toussaint was not born a man of means. He was the son of a Haitian mother and French Philanthropic father, who'd met at the resort his mother had been working in, while his father was looking into some investment opportunities in Santo Domingo. His mother thought she had found her soul mate, but with the discovery of her pregnancy with Augustin, the married father of three ended the relationship, leaving her to rear their son on her own. After immigrating to the United States in adulthood, Augustin sought out his father to get his birthright, which he received. Taking with him both money and knowledge from his French father, he developed the company that Colette now maintained ownership of, which he'd given her, upon following his decision to live out his dream of living in France. It was this very same business that afforded Dominic Toussaint his arrogance, as well as his privilege.

"You are very beautiful when angry," he said.

"Look, I've already told you that I have no interest in working with you. Ever," she began, "I don't know how you weaseled your way into my father in-law's good graces, but we don't need, nor want your business, so go."

"Doesn't seem like Musa agrees," Dominic shrugged.

"Does your father know you're here, harassing me?" she asked.

The look on his face at her jab, struck his ego, slumping his shoulder momentarily as he absorbed her blow. It was the only entertainment she found from her exchange with the man who almost ruined her life. She learned long ago, that despite the airs that Dominic put on, he lacked the secure confidence and ability to be on his own. Unlike her Benny, he was much too in-love with his father's money, to become his own man.

"I heard about your mother. I'm sorry about what happened," he said, changing the subject. And he was genuinely sorry. He had grown quite fond of the woman he believed would eventually become his mother in-law, despite her reservations about him.

"You don't get to talk about my mother," Colette seethed.

"And you don't get to talk about my father. Deal?" he asked. "Can I sit?"

Not waiting for a reply, he sauntered over his brawny body, which sported broad shoulders tapered into a slim waist, making him appear taller than his six-foot-two frame, into a chair.

Rolling her eyes at his rudeness, she wondered how she ever found herself attracted to such an infantile soul. "A deal would be you taking your ass back to Paris, and staying there," she said with a sigh.

"Must you be so cruel?" Dominic asked. "Come on. Be nice, *cherie*."

"I am not your darling!"

"Okay. Okay," he said. "Look. Truth? Dad has finally given me an opportunity to show what I'm made of. And there is this investment that I want to look into, but I need your help."

"Talk to Akal. He can handle it."

"Akal isn't as beautiful to look at," he said playfully. "I need you."

"What you need to do, is fuck off."

"Such awful words, coming from such a pretty mouth. Absolutely filthy," he said. The arrogant look in his eyes were like a dagger to her nerves, and she wanted nothing more than to lay a strong pop across his handsome face.

"I know," she replied. "My husband absolutely loves how I use it."

Why did she have to mention him, he thought. Benjamin Lati was the only man who could make his blood boil more than his father; because he was the only person who had ever gotten in the way of him getting what he wanted.

"I will never understand why you chose him over me. Are you even happy, Colette?"

"You don't understand because you don't know what love is," she stated.

"You think so, huh?" he scoffed. "Perhaps I don't know what love is, as you say, but I do know what desire is, and I will always want you," Dominic replied.

Rising from his seat, he walked over to her like a panther in the night, stalking his prey. He wanted nothing more than to ease the tension in her mouth, that was hot with anger, with the warmth of his. It was a need that was just as strong as it had been the first time he had a taste of her sweet lips, twelve years ago. Coming face to face with her, as he sat on her desk, he absentmindedly brushed his thumb across her lips, taking in their velvety feel. And as he grazed the plush sensation of her full breast, he was startled with a piercing pain in his groin, causing him to cry out. "Fuck! Why did you do that?!"

"I can't believe you would have the fucking audacity to touch me, Dominic!" Colette said, angrily. She could still feel the remnants of the weight of his testes in the palm of her hand. The squeeze and pull she gave to them was more than enough to send him staggering away from her. "Maybe you'll leave now."

"Is there a problem here?" Stella asked. The older Black woman in her employ who was always pleasant in nature, had now taken the stance of a lioness ready to pounce. Colette hadn't noticed her arrival in her doorway; for she was too busy enjoying the spectacle of the man writhing in pain before her. But as always, she was grateful for her presence.

"Everything is fine. Mr. Toussaint was just leaving," Colette said.

After getting his bearings, Dominic stood to leave the office of the woman who had once been his dream. "No matter what you believe, Colette. I do and will always love you," he said. Leaving her heavy with fear.

Love Everlasting

The light stroke down her spine startled her, causing her to spin around cautiously to face the person behind the assault, only to be drawn into the strong arms of her husband.

"Geez, Benny. Why do you always do that? You scared me," she said.

"Why are you so easy to startle?" he teased, grasping her hand. With a slight jerk of her arm, he said, "Come with me."

"Where are we going? Are you crazy?" Colette asked.

"To answer your first question, you will see. And the second? Well, you already know the answer to that," he replied, as he pulled her into a coat closet, locking it behind him with a devious smile.

"Benny, this isn't funny. We have to go," she said frantically.

Mazal and Aaron had just finished signing the *ketubah* and were more than likely fast on their way to the *chuppah*, as Benny and Colette should have been. She could still see the joy on Aaron's face when he approached Mazal for the *bedeken*. The love he had in his eyes for the beautiful young woman Colette had grown to love as a sister, was all she needed to give her blessing to their union. They were only at the start of the marital rituals, and she was already entranced by its beauty. It reminded her of her own wedding—a vow renewal that Benny and his parents insisted they have. And she had been glad of it. They all worked together to put on a wedding for her and Benny that was just as beautiful and lavish as Mazal's was seeming to be. It was his parents' way, she suspected, of showing their remorse for the early years of their relationship.

"Apparently, we have about ten minutes before the wedding procession begins, so I was thinking—"

"Slow down, cowboy. It'll take a lot more than ten minutes to get what you want done."

"If you let me finish, you would know that I am referring to teasing you senseless. Afterall, you can't walk around in this dress, and think that I won't be coming for you…all night," he whispered lustfully.

"Ah. So, it's the dress, then?"

"No. It's this wonderful…beautiful…person…and…body…wearing this fucking dress," he said, kissing her gently, "If it's one thing my sister did right in marrying this guy, is that she got you into this dress."

"Ugh. You're still mad? She's allowed to live how she wants, Benny," Colette said.

"I just…she's so much like me, you know? I didn't think she would… buckle," he replied, referring to his sister's sudden change into *orthodoxy*.

"We women do crazy things for love," she whispered to him. "I know I did."

"Look, she's on the fast track to making partner, and I don't want anything to mess that up for her."

"Ah, so it's okay for me to fall into the wonderful world of modern orthodoxy, but not your sister?"

"That's not what I mean, smart ass. You're…different. You've always had a knack…for this life. Our ways. If you weren't, I would have never supported your conversion," Benny said. "Mazal is… I mean…she's radical. Unorthodox. Okay, honestly? My sister is a total ball buster."

"And she has just the man by her side to help her be the radical and zany, ball-busting woman, we love so much. He's patient. Kind. And he loves her for who she is. He knows exactly what kind of woman he is marrying. He's known it since they were kids. He also knows that your sister is every bit of… well…you," Colette shrugged. "And look at you. You've found your place. So will she. Don't worry so much. She will find a happy balance, just as I did. Also, she has Aaron by her side. He doesn't expect her to be anything less than herself, and for that, she is willing to give him the life he has always wanted with her."

"Look at you. Still in-love with the idea of love," Benny said.

Pulling her close, he kissed her deeply, and she felt heat rise within him, causing her to create distance between them. No matter how much she wanted to immerse herself with the feel of him, she couldn't afford for them to lose control on Mazal's day.

"Whoa there, buddy. Keep that to yourself," she said.

"Do you really want me to?" he asked sneakily.

"Don't even think about it. Anyway," Colette said, changing the subject, "I wouldn't count your sister out. She did put me in this, didn't she?"

Taking her hand to admire the vision before him, he was happy that his wife and sister had designed a dress that would live on in his fantasies, forever. In the onset, the long-sleeve, floor length gown was conservative comparatively to modern standards; but the way the satin material clung closely to her body, left little to the imagination, making it daring and avant-garde in their sphere. The plunging line in the back of the dress, sat firmly above her back side, accentuating her round bottom. It left her back exposed through the diamond chain that hung loosely down her spine. It's emerald color and her crimsoned red lips, complimented the beauty of her silky mocha colored skin and the old Hollywood waves of her luscious locks. She was a vision.

"I still can't believe she did it. And that you agreed," Benny said. His wife's dress was in stark contrast to the beautiful white, conservative, long sleeve princess gown, his baby sister was wearing. "You're going to be the talk of temple next week."

"As Mazal wanted me to be," she replied, "If she couldn't do it, one of us had to, she said. And what kind of sister would I be if I didn't oblige every whim of our beautiful bride?"

"Come here," he said wickedly. Tugging her gently to him, he toyed with the diamonds that laid softly against her back, sending shivers down her spine. "I love you so much, Colette."

He began to lean in to take hold of her lips when they were interrupted by the sound of harsh knocking at the door. "Benjamin? Colette? I know you're in there," called Musa.

A man that rarely missed a thing, he had watched his son sneak off with his wife. Having been a young man himself, he decided to let the two have a moment to themselves. However, as time slipped away and came closer to the procession starting, he thought it better to bring the two back to reality.

Unlocking the door, Benny allowed Colette to face his father first, and the impish look on her husband's face as he indiscreetly adjusted himself, sent a wave of embarrassment through her.

"I would expect this from, Benjamin. But you, Colette? I expect much better. You're matron of honor. Hurry. Get along now," Musa said playfully, thoroughly tickled by the color that stained his daughter-in-law's cheeks.

"Sorry, Abba," she replied, scurrying away.

"You have enough time, son?" Musa asked. His hearty laugh alluding to his amusement.

"Come on now, Abba. What do you take me for?" Benny said, "Not even close."

"Better luck to you all tonight then. Now, let's go. I have a daughter to marry."

Finding her way back to the rest of the wedding party, Colette took her place with the bride and sea of bridesmaids that littered the hall, as she watched Benny disappear into a room that held the men.

"I see, Abba found you in the closet," Mazal said.

"You knew?"

"Everyone knows," she laughed, "And here I thought your dress would be the talk of the evening."

"I still think this dress was a bad idea—"

"Don't deflect, babes," Mazal said, "We both agreed."

"You decided. Not me," Colette corrected her, "Therefore I did not agree."

"Well, I wanted everyone to know that just because I am settling into a life of marital bliss, it doesn't mean that I have to stop being grown and sexy. Even if it's through you," she said, "Don't look at me like that. It's you and my brother's fault that I'm like this.

"Me and Benny? I'm sure you came out of the womb full of mayhem."

"Yes. And I wouldn't have it any other way," Mazal said lovingly, "Now, fix my dress. The music is starting."

"Such a demanding child," Colette said playfully, "There. Your dress is fixed, your highness."

"Thank you, Colette. So much. For everything," Mazal said sincerely.

"Don't mention it, kid. I love you. You look beautiful. Now, let's get you married."

Haunted

Colette had been to many weddings before, but the beauty and simplicity of the vows stated between the two betrotheds in front of her, captured her heart. They stood before their audience under the cascading roses of reds and white that ornately adorned their chuppah and began their new chapter; one that Colette hoped would be filled with love and joy. Watching the young couple, moved her, and reminded her of the splendor and humility marriage could bring. Feeling his presence, she was captured by the look of adoration and gratitude in her husband's eyes. And as the *seven blessings* played on in the distance, she settled into a fantasy filled with the possibilities of what her and Benny's future held.

The shattering of the glass broke him from his trance, prompting him to yell, "*Mazel Tov*!" While he couldn't believe that his baby sister was now married, he hoped that she would be as happy with her husband as he was with the woman that still transfixed him, from across the room. He couldn't wait for the recessional to end, so that he could grasp and feel the warmth of his wife—his bride, within his arms. Finding her through the crowd, he placed his hands about her and wrapped her up in his embrace. Locking their hands together, they stood back and watched the newlyweds take their time in *yichud*.

"Do you remember how we spent our yichud?" he asked seductively.

She remembered it vividly. It was the time they were able to spend with each other, with no one else around, after becoming husband and wife, once more. The moment had been absolute bliss—enabling them to break free from the confines and stress the wedding and planning had brought them.

"I do remember. But I'm doubtful they'll do the same. Not everyone has their mind in the gutter and on what's in their pants, Benjamin Lati. Besides, we were already married. They are just entering the world as husband and wife. This is their time to finally rejoice in becoming one."

"True," he agreed, "Is it me, or did watching them remind you of our own weddings? You know…I'd marry you a thousand times if I could," he whispered softly against her ear.

"Me too," she responded. "However, I'd have to disagree."

"Disagree about what?" Benny asked.

"While our elopement was…fine. There was something about standing under the chuppah before everyone that made the experience almost… magical."

"I can see that and I wouldn't trade it for anything," he said.

"Neither would I, my love. Neither would I," she said, hugging him close.

"So, you ready to go in? I want to see what you guys did for the reception."

"You didn't sneak a peek?" she asked. "So, you do have self-control, after all. Shocking."

"Oh. You got jokes?" he said. "And if you must know, I have self-control with everything but you."

"Aww. Don't be mad. I still love you, no matter how much of an insatiable beast you are," she soothed, "Now, shall we go? I want to show you what it looks like before Mazal and Aaron come out."

"They haven't seen it yet?" he asked.

"No. Ima and I wanted them to be surprised," she said with excitement.

Colette and her mother in-law had taken great pains to ensure everything was executed according to Mazal's specifications. With Kami on the design team, she was sure that the young bride would be delighted in how it all turned out. "Alright. You ready to see it?" she asked.

"Yes. However, all I know, is that it better not be better than what we had for our wedding," Benny joked.

"Oh, hush up," Colette said, grabbing his hand and leading him down to the reception area.

The long hallways and grand ceilings of the mansion on the Gold Coast of Long Island the women had chosen was filled with grandeur. As they entered the great hall, they were led by velvet white carpet that lined the aisles between long glass top dining tables, that were decorated with tall rose-colored candelabras. The long, thin candle sticks were lit to illuminate each guest in a serene aura. In between each candelabra, small vases were filled with floating flowers of the same colors that were draped across the couple's chuppah, while garlands of roses of red and white hues, hung between stringed lights over the bride and groom's table, and throughout the high ceilings of the ball room. The white starlight dance floor, staged with a monogram of the couple's initials, laid between the guest and bridal table that was decorated with a white floating chiffon tutu skirt; while candles of varying size adorned it. It was magnificent.

"Geez, Kami has surely done it again," Benny said.

"I know. Your mom and I had so much fun planning with Mazal and Kami," she said, giving her sister a wave.

As the event planner, she was busy making sure everything was perfect for the bride and groom. Colette smiled at how serious her little sister looked with her headset on, working to ensure that Mazal's special day went on without a hitch. She was happy that she took a chance and invested in her sister's event planning business—the eye that Kami had, made everything flow beautifully. Colette couldn't be prouder.

"This is marvelous, Cole. It truly is," Benny stated, "And by the looks of it, I think Mazal and Aaron think so too."

Glancing over at the jaw dropped faces of her sister and brother in-law, there was no doubt in her mind that they were happy with the imagery before them.

"This is absolutely stunning," said Dina, as she approached Benny and Colette. She and her husband were the ones to walk the newly wedded Goldblums into the ballroom to see the splendor of their reception hall. And as Mazal and Aaron made their way to express their gratitude to Kami, Mr. and Mrs. Lati decided to make their way to Benny and Colette.

"I can't believe everything Kami has done," said Musa.

"She was here all night, I believe," Dina replied to her husband. "We're truly grateful for all the hard work she's done. I wish your mother was here to see it," she said, directing her attention to Colette.

"Thank you. I wish she were too. And I'm sure that Kami would be glad to hear it," Colette replied, "Now if only she'd take some time to relax and enjoy everything with the rest of us."

"Agreed," said Dina. "Colette, why don't you show the men where our table is, and I'll go have a chat with Kami about the importance of enjoying the fruits of her labor."

"I'll come find you guys later," Benny said.

"Are you okay, my love?" Dina asked him. "You seem distracted."

"I am distracted. By my stomach. I'm going to get a small bite before cocktail hour ends," Benny said, kissing his mother on her cheek. "Do any of you want anything, before the rest of the hoopla starts?"

"No. I'm good," Colette said.

"I'm fine, Ben," said Musa. "Now, if you'll excuse me, Colette and I have a date with our seats."

Linking her hand with his arm, Musa allowed Colette to guide him to their family's table, while his wife and son went on their own adventures. Pulling out her chair, he watched her graceful movements, as she sat down, placing her hands delicately in her lap. Sitting in the seat beside her, he said, "I don't think, Ben will mind if I steal his seat until he gets back."

"Knowing his stomach, he'll be there for a while," Colette chuckled.

"You're right about that," Musa responded.

"So," she began, "I've been meaning to ask you about the Brightwood Community Development—"

"No. No, talk of business today," he said, "Besides, it's up to you and Akal now to figure things out."

"You haven't officially retired, yet, old man," she joked, "What happens if we need your guidance? Then are we allowed to call on you?"

"Colette, my dear…it's been a long time since you've ever needed my assistance. Plus, I have complete faith in your and Akal's abilities," he said confidently.

Musa Lati looked forward to this moment, since the first day he'd arrived in country. Through her, he turned his father's small souvenir stand into a thriving real estate brokerage. He was grateful to her. And as the grandchildren she'd borne him trickled in, he hoped that she knew that she had given him more than he ever imagined. In the eyes of Musa Lati, his retirement had been a long time coming, and would be spent enjoying the rest of his life with his family.

"I'm glad that we have your vote of confidence," Colette said, "But… why…never mind."

"No. Say what's on your mind, dear," he coaxed.

"Why meet with Dominic Toussaint, then? We don't need his money. Nor do we need to work with him. So why entertain him?" she asked.

"Well, my sweet girl, you never turn your back on a snake," Musa said thoughtfully, "A man that would betray his father, is a man I needed to finally meet."

"Ah. I see. It isn't about investing with him at all," she reflected.

"No. Not at all," Musa replied. "Retiring doesn't mean that I won't protect you and our family. His father basically handed us…more specifically *you,* the keys to his kingdom, because he couldn't, or rather didn't want to do anything more with it. Nor did he want to give it to Dominic. And it was more than likely because he saw the same thing in you that I see every single day…as a wife...mother…and businesswoman; you handle everything with dignity, grace, and ease. I am truly blessed to have you," he said to her.

"Abba—"

"With that said, we have no real interest in Mr. Toussaint, other than to see what he's up to. It's the least I could do for his father, when he asked me to arrange the meeting," Musa winked.

"Oh you," she chuckled, patting him on the hand. "I should have known you had something up your sleeve."

"Look, Colette…I know how uncomfortable he makes you. And I don't like the way he looks at you either. I noted that during our meeting."

"I didn't think you noticed," she responded nervously.

"I notice everything. Including the tension, he created between you and Ben, long ago," he spoke, "I'm not sure what happened, but listen… you're more than my son's wife; you have become a daughter to me. You and Kami both. I would never work with someone who would jeopardize my family's well-being. Family comes before business. Always, my dear. If I learned anything over the years, it's that."

"Family before business," Colette said in agreement. "Does…Benny know?"

"Do I know what?" he asked.

Engrossed in their conversation, they hadn't realized that Benny had made his way back into the reception hall with the trickling in of guests, eager to find their seats.

"That the investor we met with was Dominic Toussaint," Musa stated flatly.

"Oh? Interesting," Benny replied. "Colette neglected to tell me that our old friend, Dominic was back in town. Pray tell…what does he want?"

The tautness of his jaw and venom in his voice was not overlooked by her, and she braced herself for the fury that now lit behind his eyes.

"She didn't tell you, because he isn't relevant," Musa said calmly.

"I'm just curious why she neglected to tell me who our visitor was."

"Perhaps it's because she had nothing to tell. Your wife had other business to attend to, so Akal and I met with him instead."

"So, does this mean that we will be seeing more of our friend, Dominic?"

"You won't be seeing anymore of him past tonight."

"Tonight?" Colette asked, unable to hide the panic in her voice.

"I figured this would be an excellent place to turn him down," Musa replied. "Plus, his father was unable to attend, and sent Dominic in his place."

"Great," Benny said sarcastically, "As long as he keeps his distance, we'll be fine."

"I'm sure that we will all have a great time and show our best selves, for your sister's wedding celebration, no?" Musa said. Satisfied by the nod of his son's head, he rose to allow his son his rightful place beside his wife, so that he may address his wife as she approached their table; pulling out Dina's chair, Musa turned his attention to her, leaving the couple to themselves.

The rigidity in the lines of her husband's body did nothing to put Colette's mind at ease. And as he leaned closely into her, she was hyper-aware of the heat of his breath against the nape of her neck, as it caused the light dust of hair on her arms to rise. "We'll be talking later," Benny whispered.

His declaration of their impending squabble was more than enough to distract her from the entrance of her sister and brother-in-law. And as the couple shared a kiss before taking their place on the dance floor, she wondered if today, would be her last kiss with her husband—her love.

Pathway to Division

"Shouldn't you be the one dancing with your wife, little brother?" Daud asked. He had just finished taking a spin around the dance floor with his own wife—the energy he expended had made him seek respite, which now found him sitting at the table with Benny and Nadia, nursing his drink. The years had been kind to Daud; like his siblings, he'd relieved himself from his father's expectations and had come out the better for it. For three years he traveled—his eyes opened to the possibilities the world had to offer him, and it changed him. His final destination landed him on a *kibbutz*, where he not only found his wife, but a new lease on life, which had done wonders for his relationship with his family—especially, Benny. Now as he observed the look and mannerisms of his younger brother, and the distance he formulated between he and his wife, he knew that something was gnawing at him.

"My wife is entitled to dance with whomever she pleases," Benny answered defensively.

"Is everything okay, Ben?"

"Everything is fine, big brother" he replied. "I don't want to monopolize my wife's time. That's all."

"Trouble in paradise?" Nadia taunted.

"I'm not in the mood for your games today, cunt!" Benny responded nastily. Unlike the changes Daud and Benny had experienced over the years, the bond between he and his sister, Nadia, continued to be strained. As time passed, her misery engulfed her, causing her to seek solace in the maliciousness she delivered endlessly to those around her.

"Oof. Sounds like our little brother isn't in a good mood on such a joyous occasion, Daud. Why do you think that is?"

"Leave, him alone, Nadia," Daud defended, "You know…I liked it better when you were being quiet. Colette, dancing with Akal is indicative of nothing."

"Someone has to keep him company if his wife won't," Benny said, tipping his drink towards Kami. She had yet to relent to the idea of enjoying the wedding with the rest of the family.

"And we thought Colette was bad," Daud laughed, "Kami, really is quite the busy bee."

"Always. Just like her sister," Benny responded.

"I still need to speak to her about the *Bris*," Daud said absently.

"Yes. My first nephew. I can't believe it," Benny replied excitedly. While he loved his nieces dearly, he couldn't wait to meet the newest arrival; he would be the first boy to arrive in their family since his own sons were born. "However, I'd wait on that conversation with Kami if I were you."

Although she seemed to be thriving, the young woman who was like a sister to the two men, was certainly a bit too overwhelmed to speak on her thoughts about another upcoming event. "Trust me, I have no intensions on talking about it tonight, brother. But I am…I don't know—"

"Nervous?" Benny finished.

"Yes, I'm nervous," he stated. "How did you…you know…do it?"

"I didn't do anything. It was the *mohel* who…you know…snip, snip," Benny replied, using his fingers to indicate a cutting motion. He knew the apprehension his elder brother felt, but he couldn't resist the urge to mess with him.

"Really, Ben?" he scoffed.

"I'm only joking, Daud. Geez. Your son will be fine. Plenty of boys have been circumcised. It's a rite of passage we've all been through…for generations… okay?" he said. "Besides, your real worry should be the fact that you will now have four under five years."

"Don't remind me," Daud said, "This is what I get for starting so late and having to play catch up with you."

"What?!" Benny demanded. While he had tried to ignore her glare, the long-winded sigh of irritation she exhaled at the bonding between the two brothers, fueled his anger.

"Nothing. I'm just wondering when we'll be able to go one moment without you two making yourselves the center of attention," Nadia replied.

"How are we making ourselves the center of attention?" Daud asked.

"I don't know. Perhaps it's the fact that you're spending more time talking about yourselves than you are reflecting on the fact that our sister is now a married woman."

"Like you really give a shit that Mazal is married. You couldn't even be bothered to help her plan," Benny said.

"Perhaps it's because your wife stole my place as Matron of Honor, Benjamin."

"No one stole anything from you," said Daud. "Mazal just didn't want to be miserable while planning the most important day of her life. If you'd acted more like a sister, instead of a dejected witch, our wives and Kami wouldn't have been the ones doing everything you should have been doing for Mazal."

"You two think that you're so perfect, don't you?" Nadia replied. "At least I'm not the one popping out babies like my life depended on it. Are you sure you're trying to play catch-up, Daud? Or are you just trying to prove that you can have a life just as great, if not better than Ben's?"

"Shut up, Nadia! Did it ever occur to you that some people enjoy being parents? They don't just leave their kids to fend for themselves, like you," Benny said vehemently.

Although his sister had gained two wonderful girls through her first and second marriage, respectively, she lacked the empathy and love needed to raise them. Instead of the compassionate and unconditional admiration for her children, he'd seen from other women, his sister couldn't be bothered with mothering. Settling down didn't seem to work for Nadia; it only enforced her rage against a life she could never fully submit to. Her desire to find a man who'd submit to her whims, left her without the love her siblings had found with their partners, and now on her fourth marriage.

"At least I understand my limits, Benjamin. Perhaps it's something, your dear, Colette, should take notes on. Then she wouldn't end up…needing a *vacation*," Nadia said nastily.

"What is wrong with you?" asked Daud. "She lost her mother. A woman who was family to us all. And all things considered…she's allowed to take a break."

"It's okay, Daud," Benny said. "Let's not feed into her misery."

"All I know is that she better keep my and your wife's name out of her mouth…and her games," Daud replied.

"She will. If she knows better. Because I am sure her husband would love to know where she currently spends her nights," Benny said pointedly.

"Well, I see a nephew of mine I've been meaning to have a talk with.

Particularly about the joys of marriage," said Daud, rising from his seat. "Care to join me brother?"

"No. I'll meet you there. I have some…business to attend to," Benny said, stalking off.

The perplexed look of his brother and change of his sister's demeanor ignited Daud's anxiety. The overt arrogance that danced across her face, let him know that he wasn't the only one who had noticed the change in their brother's expression.

"Don't do anything stupid, Nadia. I'm warning you," he said, before heading towards Judah.

With a dismissive wave, she ignored the departure of Daud, and lent her focus to Benny. Something about the pensive look on her little brother's face, caused her to take pause and lie about in wait. Like a vixen stalking her prey, she followed her brother cautiously into the garden, where he seemed to be following the strides of another. The lush leaves of the emerald evergreen shrubs placed neatly about in a maze, casted shadows against the illumination of the outdoor floor lanterns, making it harder to be seen. While the bellowing of the shrubs in the wind, silenced the footsteps of those who walked within.

Finding a place within his vicinity, she awaited the exposure of the figure who was now causing her brother to thrash about wildly in the distance. The friction in his body, complimented the wildness that raced through his eyes, and it wasn't long before the figure in question exposed herself, as she attempted to give him comfort. Seeing the woman next to him, Nadia knew that she had more than enough ammunition to ignite the form of entertainment she'd been craving all night. And with that she went off to find her victim.

Ghosts of the Past

Approaching the woman who would help her take part in the melee she hoped would ensue, Nadia couldn't help feeling vexed by the look of careless abandonment that seemed to run rampant through her eyes. Each step that she took filled with joy as she twirled and rocked to the beat of music amongst the group of women who had embraced her into their sisterhood, made Nadia hot with anger. It was the same feeling she felt when in the presence of Benny. And just like her brother, Colette had seemingly overtaken her place among her friends and family, causing a spark of hatred for her within Nadia.

Grabbing Colette's hand, Nadia hung on to it tightly as she pulled her through the crowded dance floor towards the doors that led into the garden of the mansion that had housed her sister's wedding.

"Wait. Nadia, where are we going?" Colette asked.

"Ben wanted me to grab you. He has a surprise for you," Nadia replied.

"Oh goodness. This better be a chaste rendezvous," Colette replied.

Despite her reservations, her husband's call for her meant that he was no longer angry with her, and a sense of relief settled within Colette's core. However, as she found her way through the winding maze and heard the familiar voice of her husband booming with anger, she was no longer cast in a spell, and in awe of the beauty and opulent scene of bountiful flowers and evergreens surrounding her. And although the view of them enclosed together under the radiance of the twilight night air did weaken her resolve, what she heard sent a wave of fury boiling inside her, she'd never experienced before.

"I don't understand why you're treating me this way," she said., "After everything I've done for you, Benny. I was there for you…for your kids. She wasn't."

"Don't call me, Benny. I've told you before not to call me that. It's not reserved for you," he fumed. "I never asked for your help, Sarah. You imposed yourself on me and my children, just as you do with everyone around you. And stop acting as if I allowed you into my home."

"And before? Was that me imposing myself onto you? Or was that you in need of me?" she asked.

"That was a mistake, I regret ever making with you, Sarah," Benny said vehemently, "And it was no fault of my own. You're lucky I didn't kill you for what you did!"

"So, I was a mistake to you?" Sarah asked, "I can't get the taste of you from my lips. But I was a mistake? I don't understand—"

"What part of, I love my wife, don't you get?!"

"You were never supposed to be with her!" she exclaimed. "It was supposed to be me. From the moment I saw you, I've been in-love with you, Ben. When I came here, I thought I had found the one I would grow old with, in you. If it weren't for her… I'd be the one you'd be holding at night. This baby would be yours…ours!"

She took his hand and placed it gently against her womb. The look of disgust as he wrenched his hand away from her violently, caused her to double over in pain. "You listen and hear me well. Whether I was with my wife or not, I would have never, ever been with you, Sarah. Never!" Benny stated. "You were just someone I was supposed to show around. Integrate into the community. You know this! You were never going to be my wife. This obsession you have with me… this …this fantasy you've had, even after all this time? It's fucking sick, Sarah. I will admit that I made a mistake. I shouldn't have led you on, but you came for me…you sought me out and manipulated me. You almost destroyed me—my life. I could never love someone like you. And I will never leave my wife. She is who I want—who I will always want with every fiber of my being. Not you."

The mist of tears that now crept its way to her eyes, did nothing to move him. He couldn't even feel sorry for her. Although he knew he had faltered, the things that Sarah Cohen had done to him were irreprehensible, and he would be glad when she would relent and release him from her clutches.

"Benjamin, please," she begged.

Catching hold of his shirt, she proceeded to pull him in a tug of war he had no intent on playing. Turning to address her hold of him, he did not expect the presence of the woman who had now come in between them. Soon, he was startled by the hard resounding note of the slap that came across his face, as he came face to face with his wife. "All this time you've been harping on my indiscretions and you yourself have been busy," Colette said.

"Cole…motek… you don't understand. It's not what it looks like," Benny tried to explain.

"It's not?" she said through tears. "What is it then? Did you fuck her, Benjamin? Answer me!"

"I think I should leave," Sarah said.

"No. No ma'am. You don't get off that easy," Colette said, blocking her. "I thought after all this time, you'd get over this infatuation with my husband. I thought that we had finally gotten past whatever weird fixation you have on him, and we were becoming friends. No. That wasn't it at all. You were just busy plotting behind my back. To do what exactly?"

"You don't deserve him," Sarah said harshly.

She didn't know what came over her, but like the force of a hurricane, Colette gripped tightly around the base of Sarah's throat. Enclosing the space between them in a fit of rage, she said, "I swear, if you know what's good for you, you'll stay the fuck away from my family. I don't deserve him? The audacity! You don't deserve your husband, who loves you."

Releasing her slowly from her clutches, seething, Colette turned and began trotting towards the party, as her husband's voice crying out for her in the distance fueled the tears that were threatening to spill. Passing by the figure standing in the shadows, their smile filled with wickedness sent shivers down Colette's spine.

"I should have known you were up to no good."

"I was only trying to help," Nadia shrugged.

"You really are a miserable bitch," Colette replied, brushing past her, as tears blurred her vision. Making her way inside, she headed towards the bathroom to pull herself together. Barricading herself in a stall, she was unable to control the wave of emotions that swelled within her, as she mulled over the conversation, she wished she had never been privy too. She'd been happy in her ignorance, and now that she knew, her mind began to scrutinize the actions of her husband and the woman who couldn't seem to let go. It was all starting to make sense to her now—the uneasiness and evasiveness her husband had when addressing anything pertaining to Sarah had suddenly become clearer. It had been due, not in part to his dislike for her, but because of something more ominous.

"How long has he been lying to my face? Was she the reason for his distance when my mother was sick," Colette whispered, as she allowed her mind to run rampant and exhaust all avenues of what could have been.

She couldn't believe that she allowed Sarah back into the fold of her friendship, knowing now that she was the one who'd added to the distance that unfolded between her and her husband. When she came to her, Colette had clung to the olive branch, Sarah offered, not knowing that it was laced with hatred and fueled by jealousy.

"She was using me to get closer to Benny. To my husband," she scoffed.

As she allowed herself to delve deeper in thought, she was startled by the boisterous laughter of women trickling in. Their happiness was like a sword, seeped with acid, cutting her like a hot knife through butter. Trying to drown out the noise of their giddiness, she was awoken from her despair by the familiar voices of her friends, Lisa and Talia. Like, Miriam, the two women had taken Colette under their wing.

The women settled in, waiting for the bathroom to clear before they spoke, but the words that flooded their mouths sent shock waves through her. "At some point, we're going to have to talk to Colette about it, Lisa," said Talia.

"I know…I just…How do we tell our best friend that we think her husband is cheating on her?" Lisa replied.

"I'm not sure. But if we don't say something soon, I don't know what I will do to Sarah," Talia began, "Every time Colette turns her back she's in Ben's face. It's ridiculous. How does Colette not notice?"

"Talia, we are only now seeing things for what they are…and given everything, Colette has gone through this past year, I'm honestly not surprised," said Lisa.

"Which is why we need to tell her," Talia said vehemently.

"Can we think this through, please?" Lisa asked. Out of the friends in Colette's circle, she was always the most diplomatic, while Talia was spirited and impulsive.

"We don't have time to sit here and think this through, because I am sure that evil little ninny is up to something with our best friend's husband," she said. "It's one thing to help out…we all did our part when she was away—"

"It really broke my heart to see her in that place," Lisa said sadly. "I wish I could have done more to help Anita."

"Look, you did all that you could, Lisa. She was in the best hands when it came to you. But, can you stay focused, please?" Talia asked, snapping her fingers. "What happened to Colette can happen to the best of us. And it's not like Ben helped matters."

"That's not a nice thing to say, Talia. Ben is her husband. He loves her. And it wasn't easy for anyone involved—"

"He was a shit for what he did, Lisa. He never should have kept that away from her."

"So, I guess that makes me a terrible person too, then, huh?"

"No. You were Anita's doctor; you didn't have a choice—"

"I was and am, also Colette's best friend. I should have said something too. So, if Ben is guilty of making things worse, than so am I. So lay off."

"You know…whatever," Talia said. "Think what you must in respect to that, but it doesn't change the fact that I saw them—"

"Saw who? What?" Lisa asked.

"I saw Sarah and Ben coming out of a bar one night. *Late*," Talia emphasized. "And Sarah didn't look very happy. It seemed like they'd been fighting."

"When was this?"

"The night before Colette found out her mother was sick," she replied.

"It doesn't mean anything, Talia."

"No. But we both know that this is something that we don't do with other people's husbands. This is not our way. Sure, we've all heard things, but we just don't do things like this to each other. Or at all," she responded. "And how do you explain the way she looks at Ben? Huh? How she's always trying to touch him? Be close to him. Every time she thinks Colette isn't looking. It's disgusting. I've never seen such a thing. So, if you think that Sarah has just been trying to be a good friend to Ben, you're delusional."

"I'm not saying that at all. What I am saying is, although I do think Sarah is being sneaky and vile, I don't think Ben would ever do that to Colette. He loves her too much, Talia."

"Lisa, love or not, men do stupid things," Talia said, reflecting on her own husband's affair. "And regardless, at the very least, we need to make Colette aware of Sarah's behavior. Goodness, I wish Miriam was here, she'd know what to do."

"Miriam is awaiting the birth of her first grandchild. We are not going to bother her with this, Talia. So don't even think about it."

"She would want to know what's happening with Colette!"

"She would also kill Ben! And considering we don't know the extent of what any of this means, we should really be careful of what we say," Lisa said evenly. "Let Miriam enjoy her time in Israel with her family until we know more."

"I don't understand how you can be so—"

They were interrupted by the charging in of a bride who no longer wore the face of an angel shot by cupid's arrow, but of a hellcat looking to ruin. "*Ani horeget otah.* I'm going to *kill* her. Where is Colette? Have you two seen her?" Mazal asked.

"No. Is everything okay, Mazie?" asked Lisa.

"I wish," she replied, "I really need to find Colette. She needs to get her ass out there right now."

"Let me guess…Sarah?" asked Talia.

"Yes. How did you know?" Mazal asked. "Do you know she's out there blubbering like an idiot? About how it should have been her to marry my brother, instead of Colette? To anyone that will listen, no less. She's going to get the rumor mill started, and I for one will not let that cow do so, especially not on my wedding day!"

"You would think she'd get over it already. They never really dated! I was there when it happened. She acts like he was in-love with her, and Colette stole him. But the moment Ben saw her at Ezra's place, Sarah never stood a chance. And to be honest, even if he didn't see Colette that day, he still wouldn't have been with Sarah. He was going to end things soon anyway. Look… I mean, I like Ben just as much as anyone else, but Sarah's acting as if he's some sort of divine being she can't seem to escape. It's madness," said Lisa.

"Tell me about it! Seriously, it was like, what? Twenty-years ago. When is she going to stop?" Mazal replied, "And my idiot brother is acting like a bull in a China shop. If he acts out against her, he's going to make himself look more guilty than Sarah has already made them out to be. So, I need to find Colette. She's the only one that can calm him."

"Who's out there with him now?" asked Talia.

"Daud is talking to him. And Abba is trying to get Sarah's husband to take her home without him feeling slighted or wondering what the issue is," she stated. "How can he be so oblivious to how creepy his wife is with my brother, is beyond me."

"Oh. I'm sure he knows," Talia said. "We all know that Oded is just happy to have someone."

Although kind, Oded Cohen was not a man one would find attractive by conventional standards. A portly man, his tiny beady eyes were empty behind the thick glasses that dressed his round face, as if the light had been snuffed from out of them. He did not dress smartly like the other men and was never left without a stain on his shirt or crumb in his long dark beard. And while he adored his wife and the children she bore him, she wanted nothing to do with the man she felt was forced upon her.

"You don't think it's true, Mazal? Do you?" asked Lisa.

"Of course not!" she said emphatically. "Look, while I think my brother may have been overly friendly, or perhaps even flirted a bit to blow off some steam, he would never cheat on Colette. Never!"

"That's not what I've been gathering from some that I've spoken to," said Talia.

"They're talking already?" asked Mazal.

"It's as if Sarah is trying to make it blatantly clear that something is going on between her and your brother," said Talia.

"Or she's just trying to cause a rift between Colette and Ben," Lisa suggested.

"Look, ladies…the point is, that if we don't get her to shut her trap and mind her own household, she really will cause an issue between Ben and Colette, and I won't have it," Mazal said.

"So…did everyone know but me?" Colette asked. They had not heard her come out from the stall. And as they took in her disheveled appearance, they couldn't help but pull her in.

"We're so sorry, Colette. We didn't know you were in here," Lisa spoke first. Her hazel eyes were cast in a shadow of grief for her friend, and she couldn't help but draw her tightly into her embrace. The scent of jasmine on her person washed a wave of calm over Colette, as she allowed her friend to comfort her.

"I'm glad she was in here. Now we don't have to tip toe over this mess," said Talia. "I'm sorry, Colette. I don't mean to be insensitive. I'm just infuriated by Sarah's boldness. As if she doesn't know how to behave. She has a husband of her own. I don't understand why she keeps going after yours!" Her fury was growing just as fiery as the red in her auburn-colored hair, which highlighted her alabaster skin.

"No. You're right, Talia," Colette said weakly. "It's best that it's out in the open now."

"You need to get out there before she says something else out of turn," Talia said, "She doesn't know the real reason why you were away, right?"

"No. I don't think so. The only people that know are you all, Miriam, Judah, Luke, and of course, Benny," Colette replied. "Kami doesn't even know. I didn't want her to worry, all things considered."

"Yeah. Abba and Ima don't know either. They just know that she needed some time away, because…well…you know," Mazal said. "We didn't want to worry them. And it's not like any of us would say anything to that wench."

"At least we don't have to worry about that," said Lisa.

"Says who?" asked Talia, "Now don't look at me like that. We don't know exactly what's going on between her and Ben, now do we? What he may have shared with her."

"Do you always have to be so cynical, Talia?" Lisa asked.

"She's right," said Colette.

"You couldn't possibly think that my brother would choose her over you? Or share something so…intimate. Come on, Colette. You know better than that," cried Mazal. "After everything you both been through?"

"That's precisely it, Mazal," Colette said. "Look at everything we've been through. At every turn, it'salways been…something. Sure, we've had moments of peace. Times when we've been able to enjoy our happiness. But really… we've never had a break. Maybe he just wanted something easier. And to see…to see what it would have been like had he not chosen me."

Colette had thought of this during her time in the stall because it was a feeling she'd known all too well herself. It was something that almost cost her her marriage, not so long ago.

"Now you're just uttering bullshit," said Mazal.

"Mazal, really?" said Lisa. "When did you get such a potty mouth?"

"Oh, get the stick out of your ass, Lisa. This isn't the time to be delicate," she chastised. "She's talking nonsense, and she knows it. My brother lives and breathes her. I'm not about to let her think otherwise, because of Sarah Cohen and her weird obsession. And for the record, my potty mouth comes from her and Ben. If you don't like it, take it up with them."

"Okay. He loves her. We get it," said Talia. "But what are we going to do about this…mess?"

"If I weren't in my wedding dress, I'd kill her and piss on her grave," Mazal fumed.

"Mazal!" Lisa chided.

"Yes! A good *kaffa* is really what she deserves. A nice smack to that ugly face of hers," Talia said, "But how will that help the situation with Colette?"

"Look…guys. All I want to do is just go to my hotel room and forget about everything until morning," Colette said. "Do you mind, Mazal? I just need…some time."

"I wish you would stay," Mazal replied tenderly. "But I understand. I'll detract from your absence as much as I can. And I'll send Ben to you in an hour or so? So, you can talk? After I give him a piece of my mind, of course."

"Mazal, please. Don't bother. Just give me a couple of hours. Please?"

Colette said. "Also, I'm so sorry. I didn't want your day to be this way."

"It's okay. I understand. None of this is your fault. It's that witch's fault," she replied. "Now I have more reason to make her life miserable."

"You really are wicked when you want to be," Colette teased.

"Only for my sister," she replied.

"I will call you all later when I figure everything out," Colette said.

Taking a breath, she steadied herself before opening the door. And although she felt the eyes of her friends burrowing into her back, she dared not look at them, for fear that the pity in their faces would force her collapse.

Walking down the great hall, Colette took in the grand archways. There she found peace in the familiarity of the passageway's cobblestone walkway. A simplicity in time she still longed for. Taking her time through the halls, she permitted memories of them to flood her senses. She could feel the heat that the touch of his lips, brushed slightly against hers, left from the kiss that started it all. Even now, the electricity that sparked violently deep within her, at the thought of his touch, told her all she needed to know. Despite what she had learned, come what may, she was not willing to be without her husband.

Tears fell freely as she took comfort in her despair, which was disrupted by a man who was now standing dangerously close. She hadn't noticed him at first through the fog of her cries, but he had not gone unnoticed by the man standing in the distance, helplessly watching the exchange between them.

"And here I thought that weddings were supposed to be a joyous occasion," came the baritone voice of the one man she'd rather not see.

"What are you doing here, Dominic?" Colette asked.

"Right now? I'm checking to see why there are tears staining your beautiful face," he said, as he gently wiped her cheek.

"Don't," she said, taking hold of his hand. "Please…don't overstep your bounds. I don't need shit from you too, today."

"I'm sorry. Forgive me," he said.

"That's it?" she asked. "Since when do you accept defeat so quickly?"

"When the woman that still holds my heart, looks like she's having a rough day," Dominic replied, "Please. Don't look at me like that. Contrary to what you think, I really do love you, Colette."

"You love no one but yourself," she scoffed.

"Your skepticism wounds me," he said. "You have no idea how much I wish you would have left with me."

"I would have never chosen you, or anyone else but him," Colette replied. "You people really don't understand, do you? It will always be Benny and me."

"People? What do you mean by people?"

"Don't worry about it. It's none of your concern," she said. "The fact is, I made my choice. Live with it and move on."

"How can you ask me to give up on someone, I love?"

"You don't love me, Dominic!" she yelled. "You love the idea of me. Of having me on your arm…like a trophy. Of what I can do for you. You don't see me…only what I could help you build in your name."

"That is where we have to agree to disagree, *mon coeur,"* he said plainly, "While I will admit that it may have begun that way, I must confess that I couldn't help but fall in-love with you."

"Whatever. I don't have time for this. I need to go."

"What happened? You would never dare leave Mazal's wedding like this unless something went wrong."

"Don't pretend like you know me, Dominic," she stated.

"I know you well enough to know that your lips taste like honey."

"I was wondering when the real you would make an appearance you egotistical, smug bastard! I really don't need this right now, especially from you," Colette said, storming towards the door.

"Alright. Alright. I'm sorry. Okay?" Dominic said, "I can't see you off like this. What can I do?"

"What do you mean, what can you do? You can leave me the hell alone, that's what you can do," she said heatedly.

"I want to help," he said, "What can I do to help you? Come on. Don't be quiet now."

"Fine. Can you call me a ride?" she relented.

"I have a better idea," he said, "We can take my car. My driver is still parked out front."

"Excuse me? We?"

"I promise you; I won't try anything. I will take you to your hotel and just keep you company for the ride. Scout's honor," he said, crossing himself.

"Okay. You're lucky I'm desperate," she said, "But no funny business. You hear me?"

"I won't try anything. I promise," he said, as he helped her down the stairs and into his car. All the while, the pain of the man watching them had sent gut wrenching blows to his psyche, trapping him in a past he had long thought forgotten. And like a thief in the night, his breath was stolen from him as he watched his wife leave with the man that was almost their downfall. Somehow, he had pushed her into Dominic's arms, again.

Sides of a Coin

"So, are we just going to sit here staring at each other?" Colette asked. It had been some time since she sat across from the man who was supposed to be her deliverance. While the comfort of her seating had remained the same, he had changed the colored walls from its pastel blue, to a vibrant serene yellow, that seemed to capture the light radiating from the summer sun through the room's large windows. The lilies placed strategically throughout, complimented the new color scheme of his office, placing a soft smile on her face. "It's nice to see that the lilies are still making an appearance."

"What are you doing here?" he asked.

"Am I not entitled to a session when I need one, Doc?" she asked.

"I'm not sure a session with me would be in either of our best interest. Things didn't exactly go…well… the last time," he said carefully.

He was never one to deny someone in need, and he didn't want to upset her. However, she had a way of seizing him in a web of desire, he was sure would be his ruin. It had been some time since he faced her this way, and he was already overwhelmed with emotions he could not quite place. She'd changed since the last time they met under these circumstances. She was no longer a timid woman filled with uncertainty. Instead, she carried the determination of a honey-badger, ready to fight for what was hers. Noting the haughty look on her face, he wondered if the uncertainty that reflected through his eyes amused her. She's going to be the death of me, he thought.

The light shift in his seat as he avoided her gaze, did nothing to detract from his bemused appearance. He was nervous; and it was this revelation that sent a sense of power rushing through her, as she basked in his discomfort—a feeling she had not felt in the weeks since Mazal's wedding. The snubs from her husband had forced her to seek comfort in this way, as doubt, once again, reared its ugly head in their marriage. This time around, she refused to submit to its cruelty, and promised herself that she would not allow what had happened the year before, to transpire again.

Like a butterfly, she'd transformed; and it was the realization of the power she possessed that ignited her painful reawakening within the folds of her chrysalis, bringing forth the woman that now sat before him. She now understood that within her, she held the power and keys to their castle. And she would no longer allow herself to be a transient participant in her own life.

"That was a different time, Doc. I was…different then. I assure you, you have nothing to worry about," she said tightly, "Now, if we can start."

"Will it be, Mae this time?" he conceded.

"Whichever you prefer, Doctor," she said, letting the words roll off her tongue listlessly, causing her voice to lower into a melodical song. The expression on his face at the change of her tone, made her almost squeal with delight; while the slight adjustment he made to his pants to hide his longing, revealed himself. Gotcha, she thought inwardly. He had given her the ammunition she needed.

"Look, I'd prefer if we drop the act, Colette," he said.

He couldn't feign his irritation any longer towards the woman who always seemed to have a way of getting under his skin, the way no one else ever could. From the fit of her chiffon creamed colored blouse that clung tightly to her torso, to the way her legs crossed to expose her mocha-colored thigh, and the dark-rouge placed perfectly across her full lips, he didn't think he would be able to maintain his decorum. Everything about her set him off, and he was certain she knew it too.

"My, my, my. If I didn't know any better, Doc, I would think that you were angry with me," she said. "And to think, I thought that I could rely on your…expertise, to help me figure out a solution to my…dilemma."

"Can you get on with it," he said crossly, "Just tell me why you're here to have another session, after so long."

"Aren't you aware, Doctor?" she asked. "What does it say in your little notes, there?"

"Stop toying with me, Colette—"

"You know…come to think of it…I think I would prefer to be called Mae," she teased.

"This isn't a game!" he bellowed.

"I'm glad that you agree," she said arrogantly, "I don't think that my husband ignoring me is a game at all. You know, it isn't nice when a woman experiences distance from the man she loves."

"Maybe it was something you did that put him off," he said nastily.

The headache that was once a dull pain in the back of his head, was now threatening to throb in full force. His workload had increased tenfold in recent weeks. As people became more and more aware of the need to relinquish themselves from their traumas and terror, he had become scarce in his own home, as he tried to impart a sense of serenity in the lives of his patients. In turn, he felt trapped by his inability to free himself from his own anguish; so, he was not in the mood for the antics of one, Colette Lati. And he wanted to get to the purpose of her visit, sooner, rather than later.

"It's nice of you to assume, Doc. How do you figure it was something I did?"

"Look, Colette…I mean Mae, or whatever you'd like to be called today. I might be wrong, so please correct me if this is the case… but based on what I know thus far, your husband may have a perfectly good reason for the distance you claim exists between the two of you," he said.

"And what might that be, Doc?" she asked salaciously.

"Can you please stop calling me Doc, that way?"

"I'm sorry. Is doctor better?" she asked. Noting the way, he rubbed his temples, she wondered if his patience was waning. "Am I bothering you?"

"Yes. Yes, you are bothering me," he said.

"How so? This is your job is it not. To help your patients?" she asked, "My…where is your professionalism, sir?"

"I swear, if you don't stop fucking around—"

"And you'll do what, Doc?" she replied, "Are you going to have me again in your office, as you've done before? If so, I am more than happy to assist you, if that's the case."

"Dammit, Colette!" he roared, rising from his chair, "I have real patients to deal with. I don't have time for your bullshit."

"Now. Now. Sit down, Doctor. Behave and be a good sport," she taunted. Sitting patiently as she waited for him to take his seat, she couldn't mask the blissful expression that danced across her face. Once he settled, she began again, "As your patient, I have just as much right as anyone else to receive the full benefits of your…services. And don't you worry, darling. It'll be just you and me for the rest of the day."

"Excuse me? Want to run that by me again?"

"Oh. Right. I didn't tell you," she said, feigning ignorance, "I took the liberty of booking you for the entire day. So… are you ready to start? Or do you need more time to pick your jaw up from off the floor?"

"You know what, Colette—"

"Mae. I told you, that I was sticking with that one. Or at least I think I'm going to stick with Mae, today. I don't know. Maybe I'll feel like…switching it up," she said.

"Fine. Can we just get this over with?"

"Thank you. I thought you'd never ask," she said, "Now… where was I. Oh. Yes. So, my husband is being an ultimate asshole, currently. Despite me explaining to him that nothing happened between me and Dominic, he keeps avoiding me."

"How do you figure he's avoiding you? Maybe he's just busy," he stated.

"Listen. There isn't any amount of busy in the world that would keep that man from having me, with my legs spread like an open buffet, darling" she said, low and slow, as she watched him nervously swallow the large lump forming in his throat. "Now, I figure he's either avoiding me because he's actually guilty, or because he's truly angry with me, and doesn't want to submit."

"Submit? Submit to what?!" he scoffed. He was unable to hide his angst any further, and decided it was best to take his kid gloves off and handle her plainly. Who does she think she is, he wondered.

"Why…submit to me of course," she replied.

"Something tells me that the man in question, would hardly submit to you, or anyone else for that matter. Especially if you're saying that he may be angry with you," he said harshly.

"First, let me make one thing perfectly clear—he is a man who melts like butter every time I am in his presence. The very thought of me makes him vibrate with longing and a thirst that only I can quench. He is a man that loves me with every fiber of his being and lives and breathes me. So, yes…he submits to me, just as I submit to him," she said sensually, "Any questions, Doc?"

"No," he said sheepishly. The hardness in his pants now pulsing just as much as the pounding of his heart. "But if your marriage is as you describe, then it's safe to say that he is angry with you, no?"

"Or, he feels guilty," she said confidently.

"What does he have to feel guilty about?" he huffed.

"Well…something about fucking a woman who is borderline insane with yearning for him, certainly rings a bell," she said hotly, "And guess what? Don't worry, I'll give you a hint…it wasn't me!"

"Do you have proof of this?" he asked, "Because that is a huge accusation without any proof. If your husband loves you as much as you say, why would he stoop to being with someone who isn't you?"

"You know. I'm glad that you asked, because the reason why he's angry with me is because he believes I've cheated on him. And guess what? He doesn't have any proof. Would you look at that? He has exactly what you said. An accusation…without proof," she said slyly. "So, how is it that he has the right to be angry with me?"

"Well, are you sure that you didn't?" he asked, regretting how non-sensical the words were as soon as they left his mouth.

"Excuse me, sir, but for someone so astute, you really can be quite daft," she said snidely, "Look. If there is one thing I do know, it's who has been in this sweet cat of mine. And I assure you, it wasn't Dominic Toussaint."

"And how does your husband know there hasn't been anyone else?"

"Don't insult me. It's not becoming of you," she replied plainly, "If I wanted to fuck Dominic or anyone else, trust me, I could. But I did not. So, shall we move on?"

"Have you ever been with him?" he asked.

"Have I ever been with whom?" she responded.

"Dominic! Have you ever been with him before?!" he said fervently.

"We've gone over this already, Doctor," she replied tightly.

"Well. Humor me…again."

"I really didn't come here for this," she said.

"Trust me. This is necessary," he stated, "I mean…we both know that you have a knack for storytelling. So…humor me. Tell it…again."

Crossing her legs meticulously and slowly to allow his gaze access to what she knew he wanted most, she sat up straighter in her chair to draw him in. "Alright. I'll bite. I have nothing to hide. But I'm going to need your eyes up here," she said, coaxing him to meet her scrutiny. Satisfied that she had his attention, with an upturn of her lips to expose a radiating smile, she began, "I guess I should start at the beginning. To a time when loss was plentiful for me, and I thought I would lose him forever."

The Price of Lilies

They say time has a way of healing all wounds, but for Benny and me, it only seemed to exhaust our despair. Of the four years since his return from the war that shattered him, three of them were spent in relative bliss. He had found his way through his demons in the men that shared his nightmares. The support group that he and Devon founded had done wonders for him, and gradually we fell into a routine that seemed to set us on a path to normalcy, until we found ourselves in a pit of contrition, once again.

He had fallen in-love with travel. For Benny, surrounding himself with the wonders of the world had become therapeutic. Being in a foreign land allowed him to forget. "*I can be anyone in the world. I don't remember any of the pain when we're away. I can escape*," were the words he'd often say as he drowned himself in the beauty and discovery of the faraway places we'd find ourselves in. So, when he asked me to go on a summer-long adventure to celebrate his impending start into an established practice, I agreed.

We'd worked diligently to reach the depths of the wanderer within him. Behind the scenic walls of cities, we lost ourselves in the spirit of wanderlust. We never spent more than a few days in one place, giving us a nomadic lifestyle we never knew we craved. It was something we both found freedom in. The spontaneity that each day brought us, had us enraptured with one another, as we became each other's constant, in a midst of scenic views that often changed before we reached nightfall. From the lush and vibrant beauty of Tuscany through the vast hills of the Scottish Highlands, we wrapped ourselves in the serenity of ancient cities that boasted imagery of cobble-stoned walkways. Reminding us of what started it all. And in its simplicity and splendor, our bond became steadfast with each night that we spent wrapped in each other's arms, as we melded into one, finding one another, once more.

It wasn't long before things changed—within six weeks of our travel, I realized that I was pregnant. And while Benny had found redemption in the child that nestled in my womb, I only felt apprehension. Despite the prosperity and trust we now found in our life together, I couldn't help the overwhelming fear that would not cease in consuming me. For those past four years of aiding Benny's recovery, I had lived it, tiptoeing through his pain. A pain that only seemed to fill me with uncertainty of our future. And for some reason, even then, as we listlessly allowed ourselves to be carried through the vastness of the world, I wondered when or if, he'd succumb to his demons again.

While Benny relished in the prospect of new life, the sinking feeling I felt was realized soon after our arrival home, with the sight of crimson red that stained our sheets. With the stillbirth of our child, I found myself a marked woman, meandering my way through my days limply, as I mourned the loss of our baby. A girl. A first for us. We named her Lily.

I found myself wondering why. Why then? Why that way? It was said that sometimes those things happened. But they weren't supposed to happen. At least not to me—not to us. You see, those things weren't supposed happen to two people who had lost so much; who'd endured a dance at the edge of hell, and like a phoenix, rose from the ashes, to become stronger than before. But it did happen. And when all was done, over the span of a year and a half, I'd walked within the safety and shadows of grief, while Benny had become consumed by his.

With her loss, came an eagerness to rebuild a life he now staked claim to, but it came at the price of his sanity. Although the flash and flicker of her fluttering heartbeat seemed to subdue and rejuvenate him, the emptiness of the dull black and white color of the screen, put him in a trance that was marred with suffering, that I couldn't seem to tap into. It was a pain whose only cure was the sound of horses galloping in his ears, that played rhythmically from the heartbeat of another— a life he needed to grow inside me. But it was something I was unwilling to give. And it was my unwillingness to add on to our suffering, to see him drowning in the madness of the apparitions of children that would never be, that became the catalyst to our world being shattered completely by the presence of Dominic Toussaint.

The day I finally got to know the man behind the cool smile and debonair suit, was a day like many, I'd now found myself having. It had been almost two years since our loss, and although I had resumed my wifely duties, Benny was now growing wary of our inability to conceive again, causing a wave of tension and hostility that seemed never ending. He was no longer an unwilling participant wallowing within his sorrow, but began to immerse himself within it. Covering himself in a veil of anger that would not cease. His belief that he was being punished by the divine for his crimes against the souls he'd loss, were now replaced and seeped with the pain at my inability to give him what he believed he was promised. And I found myself weakening from the constant barrage of his scrutiny. To which I'd taken up a routine of washing myself in the tears of my sadness, as I had been doing that day in my office, I encountered Dominic.

It was supposed to be one of the happiest moments of my life. I'd finally reached the point where I would be given the keys to my own kingdom, and I found myself no longer able to bask in excitement. Instead, I'd become filled with the insecurity our current state found us in, when he walked in. Although, I had seen him in passing before when his father was still head of our office, I did not know much about the man behind the smile. Like most men of leisure, he spent his days surrounded by beauties, rather than the duties of work; so, our interactions were minimal and formal in nature, until that day.

"Everything okay?" he asked. His voice deep and pleasant, vibrated the light French accent he had acquired during his time spent away at school. I didn't know how long he'd been leaning against my doorframe, but based on the inquisitive look in his eyes, I deduced that he may have gotten an earful.

"It's fine. I mean, I'm fine," I replied sheepishly. The wave of emotions that were now imbued on my face, was not convincing.

"They don't seem like happy tears to me," he said, "It seems more like trouble in paradise."

"Excuse me?"

"I'm sorry. I didn't mean to overstep. May I?" he asked, as he took the empty seat that sat in front of my desk. "I didn't mean to overhear, but it was honestly hard not to—"

"Can we not?" I interrupted, "What I discuss with my husband is neither appropriate for discussion nor any of your concern."

"Okay. Fair enough. But I will say this…a woman of your caliber, should never wear her beauty with anything other than a smile," he said. "Look. Let me take you to lunch. You can sign the papers to solidify the change of ownership, and we can talk."

"I really don't think that's a good idea, Dominic. Why don't you just leave them on the table, and I'll sign them and have Stella fax everything to your father," I replied.

"No. That won't work for me. Contrary to what you are saying, I think you need a break from this office and a good listening ear, and I'm just the man for the job," he said lightly.

In most instances, the arrogance sported by the man who compelled me with his invitation, would have had me seething, but there was something about the exuberance and confidence of his smile that made me feel at ease. And despite my hesitation, within the hour, I had found myself in his eager hands.

Sitting in the large café, sipping my coffee, I began to enjoy the company of my lunch partner. His light conversation and witty banter were in stark contrast to the taxing conversations that had become my norm with Benny. He had a walk that exuded the confidence of a man that had never experienced the weight of the world on his shoulders; and it was this buoyancy that seemed to attract all to him. There wasn't a step that he took, or movement he made, that didn't grasp the attention of some unwitting woman. They flocked to him. And seemed ready to risk it all for the chance the the sharply dressed man sitting across from me in their arms.

His tailored suit was the color of teal and hugged his body perfectly, accentuating every pulsation of the muscles it held on to, and brightened the specks of green that lit up his hazel-colored eyes. His hair, neatly cropped, was just as glossy as his skin, which was captivating in its espresso hue. And although filled with the cockiness of a peacock rattling its feathers, he was generally good natured. I was transfixed by him. It was as if he put me in a slumber of serenity, I did not want to escape.

"So, now that we've gotten through all of the hoopla of office politics and document signing, you want to tell me why you had tears staining your beautiful face, this morning?" he asked.

Taking a breath, I mulled over the weight of allowing Dominic to be privy to such information. Despite our jovial exchange, there was a part of me that felt sharing the issues between Benny and me would be perfidious. But as I sank under the weight of my burdens, I succumbed to the warmth of his smile and spoke of things that should have never left the covenant between husband and wife.

"We're just going through a rough patch right now," I said. I tried to make my voice even, but the look in his eyes did something to me. He didn't glare at me with the same scrutiny that was often veiled in sympathy. It had become common after the loss of our daughter. They drowned me in the suffocation of their pity—choking me with a physical manifestation of the grief I tried desperately to relinquish. The contrast of his gaze held me, bolstering strength that seemed to resonate from behind the mask of arrogance he usually donned.

"I'm sorry…that was bullshit. It was complete and utter bullshit. I'm sorry," I whispered.

"Don't apologize."

"Sorry. I just didn't mean to be so crass. I'm just…over it all, I guess," I said tightly.

"Hey, didn't I say not to apologize?" he said, placing his hands on top of mine. They were wonderfully warm and heavy. It felt like a blanket, enclosing me on a cool autumn day. The velvety feel of them were soothing, while their weight made me feel secure. "You don't ever have to apologize for being yourself. Not with me. Ever. Besides, I rather enjoy hearing such damning things, coming from such a beautiful mouth."

Pulling my hand away, I unconsciously placed them against my face to hide the rise of color that now tinged my cheeks. I could still feel the weight of his hand hot against mine. The smile he had, turned into a fascinated smirk that made him more enticing, forcing me to relax and release an obnoxious snort.

"I'm sorry. I don't know why I'm behaving this way," I began. My laughter was all consuming, which seemed to please him more. "Forgive me. I'm normally more put together than this, and not as…erratic."

"I thought we said, no apologies," he said playfully, "This was obviously something you needed. Sometimes laughter is the best form of medicine, and I'm glad, that whatever I did, allowed me to see your gorgeous smile. This does include your snort by the way."

"Gosh. Not the snort," I said, unable to hide my embarrassment. "I haven't done that in some time. Really, I'm usually better at being a human… and less… I don't know…crazy."

"I love crazy. And please, allow me to say this… you're welcome for gifting you the experience," he replied.

"Well, aren't we full of ourselves?"

"Am I though? I would rather refer to it as…confident," he shrugged.

"To be fair, there is confidence and then there is downright arrogance. They are two entirely different facets of being."

"Look, I'm just a man who knows what he deserves. And I take what I want. When I want. How I want it. Wherever I want."

"Hmm, interesting. Spoken like a true male. You are far beyond conceitedness, sir. I think we should add a touch of egotism," I said. My displeasure plastered clearly across my face.

"Ouch. Tell me how you really feel," he stated. "You know…I've never had anyone call me out like this."

"What do you mean?" I asked.

"Most women, because of my status, ignore my antics. But you," he said leaning in closely, his accent heavy against my ear. "You don't seem to shy away from telling me your true feelings. Nor do you hide behind feigned niceties when you find something to be crude or unacceptable. And I never thought I'd say this, but I think I like it. I'm grateful for this time with you."

"You're welcome. I guess?" I replied.

"You don't seem confident in your reply."

"It's just that, your back-handed compliment was kind of confusing."

"Back-handed compliment? How so?" he asked.

"Well, on the one hand you seem to be praising me for taking you to task on your…egotism, for lack of a better word," I said openly, "Then on the other hand, you're essentially calling me rude for chastising you. So, which is it?"

"Which one is what?" he asked. His brow now raised playfully, alluded to the mischief that boiled within him.

"Do you think I'm being rude, or do you appreciate my candidness?"

"I appreciate that you're not afraid to speak your mind to me," he began, "As I've said previously, it's not something that I am accustomed to, but it's certainly something I would love to experience more. Who knows? I might become a better man because of it."

"Well, I've always been someone who is ready to lend a hand when needed," I said, "Especially to lions who need a bit of…taming."

"Careful, Colette…you may make a fiend out of me, yet."

"Why do I get the sense that I am already dancing with the devil," I said lightheartedly. Although he smiled, it never reached his eyes—instead, they filled with desire, I now realized I missed, taking my breath away.

"Maybe you are, but I'd be a happy one if you could be my guardian angel," he said slyly. And although the look on his face indicated his nefarious intensions, there was something about it that made me gravitate to him more, instead of remaining steadfast in my guard against him.

"I'm sure you'll find your own guardian angel, eventually," I said, not wanting to detach myself from the feeling of being wanted just yet. "Out of all of the beautiful women that seem to grovel at your feet, you'll find someone that will become your everything."

"Yes. Perhaps. But I know for a fact that they won't be as wonderful as you," he said, "It's why I can't seem to understand why you were so upset today. Or rather, why he upset you."

"Ah. Doubling back to the question at hand, I see."

"I was never one to take no for an answer, easily," he replied, "So, what gives? I know that we've never really spoken before, but—"

"That's because you, sir, are too busy being a playboy." I joked, "If you would have spent more time in the office, we might have been good friends by now."

"You're calling me out? Again?" he laughed. "Look, I will not deny that I am…well…was a bit of a rake, to which I am definitely regretting now in this moment, because I would have definitely wanted to spend all of my time with you."

"Does that work on all the ladies, or do you think that's the only effort you have to make with me?" I said smugly.

"Ouch. Like a snake, she bites," he said dramatically. "But guess what, my little viper? If I were truly running game on you, you'd know it."

Chills rushed down my spine as the words of his confession resonated. "Well, as a married woman, I've seen, heard, and done it all already. So, your little games won't phase me."

"Is that a challenge?" he asked.

"No," I replied, "Not a challenge at all. Just a reality check for you."

"Okay," he said, shifting in his seat. There was a subtle change in his gaze, as if he were trying to calculate his next move. "Well, that's enough deflecting for you…spill it."

As I wrestled with whether I should further unload my burden on a man that I had only now become familiar with, he sat slyly across from me as he waited patiently for me to speak. And it was his patience that encouraged my descent into the madness of my world. I had expected him to falter, but with each word of my suffering spilling from my lips, his eyes never wavered, nor cautioned the removal of the consideration he paid me. At the end of my exchange, he took on a calm that I'd never seen in him before, causing me to wonder if I had delved too deeply in my candor. But as he sighed deeply and placed an even smile on his face, I began to feel at ease again.

"I am so sorry," he said, taking my hand once again. "I know you're probably tired of hearing it, but it's what I can offer."

"Thank you. While I have grown tired of those words, I am grateful that you listened," I stated. "You'd be surprised at the number of people, whose help only consists of their opinion. I don't want their unsolicited advice on how things can or will change, and I don't want their benevolent exchanges."

"I see. You don't want to be pitied. I understand," he said sincerely.

"No. And I honestly…I don't know if I even want more children," I said. The tone of my voice seemed to startle him, as if he were now seeing me for the first time. "You know, each time that we conceived, I cried. Not from happiness…but from fear."

"Wow," he said. "Forgive me. I'm sorry. That didn't come off the way I intended. I just always thought… I mean at least from what my father has said, you love being a mother."

"Of course I love being a mother. My children are my world. But it doesn't mean I want any more…at least not right now," I said.

Relief washed over me as I exposed myself to reality. Things were difficult, always had been, it seemed for Benny and me; and with every hurdle we crossed together, I felt like I was doing so by the skin of my teeth. I had two children I already felt I raised alone, as their father wallowed in the depths of his misery, and now, despite the hell we currently found ourselves in, I finally had a semblance of the man who had captured my heart, and I wasn't ready to let him go.

"Look, my husband and I have been through a lot, and we have only now begun to get back on track… to a point. I don't need the stress of a baby upending that," I reflected.

"What about you?" he asked.

"What about me?"

"You speak a lot about your husband. Your fears for him. But what are you afraid of Colette?" he asked. "I get the feeling that your fear of having another child has more to do with you, than you trying to protect him."

"Now, who is calling who out?"

"It's only fair," he said.

"Um…well…I guess," I started, "I'm afraid that if I have another child, I might have to watch that child suffer in the same way Judah and Luke have. I'm scared that I might have to raise more children with a man that they may come to fear."

"But isn't he well now?" he asked.

"Yes. He's doing okay. All things considered. But it never goes away, Dominic. Never."

"You can't live your life in fear of someone you love. You shouldn't have to walk on eggshells," he said emphatically.

"I know I shouldn't have to, but I do, because it isn't his fault that he is this way. You don't understand what he went through. Look, I know that it is a fight and will continue to be, but it is one he will never have to do alone, as long as I breathe air," I replied tightly.

"I hope he understands just how lucky he is to have someone like you. And I get that I could never understand what he's been through, and truthfully, I hope I never will. But…you shouldn't have to suffer because of it, and neither should your children. Are you cold?" he asked.

He didn't miss a thing. Although I was not cold, I nodded my head, and took his jacket about my shoulders. Something about the way he spoke those words to me, had given me a chill.

"Anyway, there's more to that."

"More to what exactly?" he asked.

"More to what I was saying. You see…I don't want…I also don't want another child because I want to be able to finally enjoy something for myself. Everything that I've done has led me to this day. This moment. Where I am finally able to reap the rewards of everything I've worked hard for. And I just want to enjoy it. Even if it's just for a moment," I rushed out.

"So why don't you tell him that?"

"Because like you, Dominic, my husband is a man that doesn't take no for an answer, easily. Also, I feel like he just wants a chance to be the father he always wanted to be," I replied. "I don't think I can deny him that. Or that I should."

"Yes. But that shouldn't come at your expense. You don't have to please people all the time, Colette. It's okay to say no, and not feel anything about it," he countered.

I could feel my face tighten with tension, as helplessness washed over me. I began to look hard at the fact that I was never an active participant in much of my life with Benny, or with anyone else for that matter. I had become a pawn—easily moved and pushed by the whims of others. I never really thought of my own needs, nor desires. Suddenly, it occurred to me why I felt no desire to expand our family—I needed to find myself. I needed to breathe. Just. Breathe.

"You may be right, Dominic. But I am his wife."

"You're also your own person."

"Yet still, I am his wife, and the woman who loves him. Also, he would never understand any of this anyway," I said.

"He should understand or consider you, as much as you're considering him," he replied.

"You don't get it. You're not married, Dominic."

"Look, Colette…I don't have to be married to realize that sometimes you must think of yourself and what makes you happy. We only get but so many rotations around the sun. Don't let anything spoil your years."

"He used to be like you, you know? Living life just for the feel and thrill of it. He made me feel alive, then."

"I find that hard to believe," Dominic replied. "I'm sorry. That came out rudely."

"It's okay. I sometimes don't believe it either," I said sadly. "Look, overall, I just want to enjoy our time together, and I don't want to jeopardize his—"

"Love shouldn't come at the cost of you living," he said compassionately. "You're allowed to want more, and given how wonderful you are, I'm not sure why you don't demand it."

"Geez. Look at the time," I said. I had been so consumed with our talk that I hadn't noticed that the lunch rush had ended, and I felt myself needing to escape from the scrutiny of the hazel-eyed man in front of me, before I unleashed my true secret. "I really should get back to the office."

"Would you like me to take you back?" he asked, conceding to my rapid change of pace.

"No thanks," I said, "I think I'd rather walk. I have a lot to think about. You know, it was nice chatting with you. I wish we could have done it sooner, and more often. You're easy to talk to."

"Maybe that can be arranged," he replied.

"I'm sorry?"

"I still have other business to attend to, so I'll be around for a while. Maybe I can pick you up next week for lunch again? What do you say?"

From the care he took, to the way he spoke candidly, reminded me of the man, Benny used to be. In some weird way, it felt like I had a piece of my husband back. And although I knew I should have ended our moment there, to not give roots to the seeds being planted, I wanted more. I needed more.

"You know what? I think you have a deal," I said.

"Atta girl. I'll call the office next week to set it up," he said. And with a slip of my body into his warm embrace, I started on my path with Dominic Toussaint.

Fractured

All I'm saying is that you've been spending entirely too much time with that man," he said; his voice echoing from our closet as we dressed for the company's annual Winter Gala.

"Benny don't start, please," I said exasperated.

Expressing his displeasure in my newfound friendship with Dominic had become his favorite pastime. And I was becoming irritated by the constant onslaught of heated exchanges about my choice to engage with the man who'd become my confidant.

"Look, all I want is for us to have a good time."

"My question is, why does he need to even be there, tonight?" he asked. "The company belongs to you, Akal, and my dad. The Toussaints are no longer part of the business, therefore he shouldn't be at the gala."

"His father was the one who started the gala, Benny. It is a tradition that we are upkeeping, so of course Dominic would be invited," I said. "Listen… it's good business. That's all. If you don't like it, well, talk to Akal."

"My only issue is that he's never been to one before, but all of a sudden he's coming now?"

"Are you implying that he's coming this time because of me?"

"Yes," he said, peaking his head out, "Bow tie? Or—"

"I'm a sucker for bow ties, you know that," I replied with a smile, admiring the way his shirt hung loosely open, revealing his firm torso. His hair and beard recently cut, had lent him a look that was both dapper and endearing.

"Bow tie it is," he said, disappearing back into our closet. "Look, Cole, ever since your trip to Paris—"

"Which I begged you to come on," I said matter-of-factly.

"Yes. You did, but I was booked, and I couldn't move my sessions. You know this," he replied, "You should have rescheduled."

"Reschedule? With Albert? You know how particular he is," I said, referring to the man who had now become the bane of my existence.

Albert Gagnon was a man who loved adventure just as much as he loved his wineries. He was a sweet and kind fella of sixty-three, but with his marriage to the beautiful and twenty-something, Chloe-Marie, he had become rather tart in his quest to please his young bride, who had an unquenchable taste for luxury. She was his second wife and came to him when he was still grieving the loss of his first, Jacqueline, who'd been the love of his life. But unlike Jacqueline, who lived her life sharing their blessings with others, Chloe-Marie would rather wear it on her person, and see it, in what she deemed as prime real estate.

As a longtime friend of Dominic's father, Augustin, I thought taking on the timid Albert as a client would be easy. But I did not account for the callous and salacious nature of his new bride. She ran us both ragged with her desire to obtain what she deemed worthy of her taste, which was in stark contrast to the simplicity that Albert craved, making the once reticent man, hostile. If it were not for the assistance of Dominic and his father, I would have never been able to manage such a nettlesome two.

"Dominic and Augustin saved me out there. I wouldn't have been able to find the properties for those two to see next week, otherwise. Also, he was kind enough to show me around the city. Had you been there, I'm sure Dominic would have showed us around."

"I'm doubtful I would have been included in you two traipsing around the City of Light…or should I say, of love," he said vehemently. "Now…you're either being willfully ignorant, or you're just blissfully blind, but that man wants you. It's as plain as day."

"I think you're overreacting, Benny," I said.

The heat of his words choked me with a truth I'd longed sensed, made me spin on my heels to catch my breath on the chaise at the end of our bed. In the months that followed our first lunch, Dominic and I had taken to our newfound friendship like fish to water. What initially started as random lunches when he was in town, had culminated to long talks over the phone and messages sent throughout the day. And with my arrival in Paris, came a confession that made me just as wary of his presence at the night's gala as Benny seemed to be.

I was finally at the end of my trip, and I desperately wished for a quick passing of the day, so that I could get ready for my flight back home. It had been a tedious day of looking through homes that may be suitable for viewing for Albert, upon he and Chloe-Marie's arrival to New York. And I was ready for a quiet evening, when I was invited to dinner with Dominic at his father's new flat.

The place that Augustin Olivier Toussaint now resided, was fixed with the same grandeur its owner exuded. Like Augustin, his home boasted a mixture of old and new, in a level of extravagance that one might find in a well to do, Parisian flat. It's coffered ceilings, raised high to add a bit of flare, extended the grand chandeliers that hung in the formal sitting areas. They bounced their specks of light across the rooms, along with the illumination of streetlamps flashing through the window. The neutral color palette of cream and white, allowed the tapestries and fresh flowers to set off a soothing ambiance against the sophisticated motifs that adorned the walls; while the gilded antique furniture gave a level of opulence that I had only recently grown accustomed to. It was all magnificent, and when I was asked to stay and depart for my flight from there, I allowed the lure of the mid-century style furniture and luscious crown canopy to garner my acceptance. Putting my mind at ease, I settled for an evening filled with the company of the man who had changed my life.

We'd enjoyed a light meal of tapenades, roasted chicken, and potatoes—coupled with great conversation and wine. I allowed myself to bask in the company of my mentor to relieve the stress of my week with the Gagnons. I learned a lot from the man who was now sitting across from me, and it was great to see him in his element. Unlike Dominic, he emanated a sense of stateliness that wasn't forced—his confidence, although steadfast, was bridled by his humility, giving him a sense of grace that one would find in a man of his caliber. He was like Dominic in look and stature, but his hair, that was once the color of ebony, had become dusted grey, as if touched with a fine powder. It contrasted well against his dark-amber-colored skin, making him appear dignified. And the lightheartedness of his banter made me feel at ease, just as it always did.

"I'm so glad that you took me up on my offer, Colette," said Augustin. "For a moment there, I thought your hesitation to my invitation was due to my son turning you away?"

"Turning me away? I'm not sure what you mean by that," I said confused. By this time, we'd settled into the sitting room for the evening, as we awaited our café granita that Dominic had volunteered to oversee, since the staff were let go for the evening.

"My dear, you know as well as I do that my son isn't one to remain dedicated in things that no longer suit his interests," he said, "So, I thought by this time your friendship would have long dissolved."

"Forgive me, Augustin, but I'm not sure I understand."

"You are not the first unavailable woman that my son has sought out for a dalliance. It's a sport for him, my dear."

"Augustin, what Dominic chooses to do with or to other women is of no concern to me. We are friends. Nothing more."

"Friends is such a peculiar word," he said thoughtfully, "And no matter how you have defined your friendship, Colette, I'm certain my son's perception is in stark contrast to yours."

"Dominic has never done anything untoward, if that is what you are suggesting."

"Colette, I would not be worried as I am, if he had," he said cautiously. His accent was deep, as he slowed his words into a tone that became fatherly. "That is what I would have expected from him. Or at the very least, I thought, he would take your status as a married woman who is in-love with her husband, to do what he does best, and leave. But he hasn't yet. And this is what concerns me."

"Augustin, I think you are grossly mistaken," I insisted.

"No. I don't think I am. Since you two have begun together, I have heard nothing but your praise, and knowing the young woman you are, I thought nothing of it...before. But this past week I have spent in your company, has shown me otherwise. I see the way he looks at you, and more importantly, I see the way you look at him. And he is a man that is not for you," Augustin chided.

"I think I better call it a night," I said contentiously.

Although I respected and loved him, there was something in his words that made me want to flee. Sure, I knew that I had opened the door to Dominic's affections, but I couldn't yet admit that I was guilty of desiring the kindness and attention he paid me.

"Colette, I don't mean to offend, and I have long thought of you as the daughter I was never privileged to have. I wouldn't have handed over my business to you if that weren't so. But I also know and love my son," he said pausing. It was as if he were trying to make me see truth in what he said. "I know things are not well with Benjamin, but what I do know is that the love between you two is pure and true."

"I wish what you say was easy to believe, Augustin. I really do. But sometimes—"

"Listen my dear, I may be a man of few words, but I am a man of experience, as my age permits me to be. From what I've seen, the trouble you two are having is due to your inability to stop life from getting in your way. And while you two still have some work to do regarding your relationship and each other, there is no denying the love you feel for one another," he reflected. "I say all this because… again, I know my son. And you do not want to be caught in his fire. A serpent's mouth can be sweet when it wants to lure you into its grasp, but its venom will leave you lost and wounded, all the same. Do you understand what I'm saying?"

"Yes. I do," I said sheepishly.

"Good. Contrary to what he believes, I do love him; but I also know who he is, and I will make no excuses for him. Please, don't let Dominic destroy what you've built thus far," he said. Patting my hand lovingly, he rose from his stately chair.

"Where are you going?" I asked.

"I am not as young as I used to be, *chéri*. I'm off to bed. Just remember what I said," he replied, caressing my cheek. "I'm sure he will be in here soon, and if I've calculated things correctly, he'll make you an offer you must refuse. He's predicable that way. *Bonsoir*."

"Good night, Augustin," I said meekly, "And thank you."

"Not a problem, *cher*. It's always a pleasure."

Silence surrounded me, echoing the loneliness I felt as I submerged myself in guilt. The conversation that transpired between Augustin and me made my head spin. I realized now that I was playing with fire. Igniting and stoking the flames of Dominic's adoration for the chance to feel wanted again. However, I knew deep down that Dominic wasn't alone in his newfound affection. I, myself, had fallen for the man who I allowed to become my lifeline.

Things were easy with Dominic, and I didn't have to stifle myself when around him. I was swept in a swell of independence I had never experienced before; and it was intoxicating. With him, I felt wild and free, as if floating on air, no longer shackled to the sense of duty that had long consumed me. My body screamed in a rebellion that only Dominic seemed to hear, and I found myself craving more and more of him each day. Even so, I knew the comfort I permitted myself in wanting the freedom he posed was wrong. Despite this, knowing that I needed to distance myself from my sweet temptation, stirred me. I wasn't sure I could let it go—the thrill of him, and what he allowed me to be—unapologetically me.

It wasn't long before my thoughts were permeated by the sound of feet shuffling against marble floors. He appeared without our desserts in hand, and no longer filled with the spirit of mischief he often held behind his hazel eyes. Instead, he was shrouded in a look of despondency that made me want to draw him near, and I caught myself trying to reach out to him. Maintaining my distance, we stood trapped in a contentious battle I didn't have the strength to face. Soon his deep melodious voice broke through the stillness, echoing the tension he held.

"I want to make two things clear," Dominic said. His body, long and lean lied limply against the entry way of the sitting room. "Firstly, my father was wrong…I would never do anything to harm you, let alone ruin you. I could never hurt you or make you feel as though you'd have to choose your desires over me."

"I'm sorry that you heard that. I know things are problematic between you two, so it gives me no pleasure to be the cause of any issue," I said sincerely.

"Sadly, that ship has sailed," he shrugged, "And to answer your question, yes…I heard everything. I wanted to know if you and Papa wanted whipped cream, when—"

"Again, I'm sorry, Dominic. He's just concerned that's all. He thinks that there is something illicit going on between us, but you and I know better," I said, clinging to my dress nervously to keep from covering the heat that rose in my face.

"I thought I told you that I don't like apologies, especially when it comes to you," he said gently. "And as I said, harming you is never my intent… having you however, is. But not in the way he's saying."

"Dominic, I—"

"Please, don't say anything," he replied. "I have wanted you since the moment I saw you, but I respected your position in my father's office, as well as your place by your husband's side. But I admit that when I saw you in your office that way, saddened, it made my desire for you escalate to a magnitude that not even I could fathom. I saw an opening, and I am a man that never turns down an opportunity. So, I guess that leads me to my last point…I do want you, Colette. And I have fallen for you, even though I shouldn't have."

"I'm married, Dominic."

"And yet you're not happy with him, are you?"

"What I am or not with my husband is none of your business," I said tightly.

"Oh, but it is, mon coeur," he said, "As long as every thought of you burns inside me, you, being in his arms instead of mine, will always be my business."

"I think I better I go to my room—"

"No. Sit. I just need you to hear me. I'm staying at the hotel that the gala will be held in," he said, "I will be leaving my room key for you at the front desk. At midnight, I expect you to be there—"

"You're out of your mind!" I said, fury now overtaking me. "You expect me to come to your room…to do what? To fuck?"

"Don't be crass! And don't be a child," he chastised.

"Who do you think you're speaking to?!" I bellowed. "You say to me, don't be crass? Yet, you're demanding me, a married woman, join you in bed? The nerve of you!"

"I can't wait for you any longer—"

"Wait any longer?" I scoffed, "You can't be serious. I have a husband. A family. We are only friends, Dominic."

"Friends don't look at each other the way we do," he said fervidly. "You feel something, Colette. I know you do. And perhaps neither I, nor you, may know exactly what it is that you feel for me, but I know that there is something between us. So, I am not willing to wait any longer to have you the way my desires intend for me to."

"You've said that already, but what you fail to understand is that I am married!"

"To a man that no longer makes you burn with desire the way I see you light up when you look at me—"

"You know, I'm surprised you can even stand in the doorway with an ego that big," I mocked. "Contrary to what you believe, I do love Benny."

Rubbing his hands along the light stubble that covered his face, he smiled a smile that hades himself would envy. "My room. Midnight," he said fiendishly.

"You're wasting your time, because that is something that will never happen," I said, my anger mounting.

"That may be, but I guess we'll find out soon enough, won't we?" he replied. "I will no longer subject myself to breathing the air of a woman I can't have."

"And you won't have to. I love my husband. I will never choose you over him," I stated.

"As I said before, we'll see. Midnight. Him or me. Your choice. But you're going to choose," he said, turning his back to me, his light steps echoing his descent.

Staring at the remnants of his presence, I became drunk with anger from the proposition he offered me. He was cruel to force me to choose in this manner. To force me to throw away the freedom I found in him. My mind ran dizzy with the thoughts that now flooded my mind. Soon, I would have to face my torment, and trade my peace for the servitude I'd begun to bear. Rising from my seat, I braced myself against the weight of my reality, as I grappled with the choice I had to make.

It was a decision I had to make that evening, as I was brought back to the home I shared with my husband, preparing myself for the gala I now dreaded. Where I now stood, staring at my face transfixed in our full-length mirror, trying to relinquish the memory of my night in Paris with Dominic.

Looking at my image in the scarlet form-fitting floor length velvet gown, anxiety swept over me like a strong gusty wind. *What is the matter with you? He's nothing more than a man, Colette.* Taking a breath, I focused on readying myself for what I thought would be a beautiful night out with my husband, until the unthinkable happened.

"Benny, can you hand me my earrings? They're on my vanity," I called to him.

"Which ones are you referring to, love?"

"The gold teardrop ones your mother bought me for my birthday last year."

"I don't see them," he said, "Are you sure they're not in one of the drawers?"

"No, Benny…don't worry about it. I'll get it," I rushed, trying my hardest to retrieve what I needed concealed. However, I knew by his eerie silence that he'd found what was hidden.

"Do you want to tell me what the fuck these are?" he asked, holding the small compact that had been my freedom.

"I… I was going to tell you, Benny. I swear," I said, hanging my head, weighted by the guilt that now gripped me.

"How long?" he asked as the redness in his face already exhibited the change of tide I needed to prepare myself for. "How long have you been hiding this from me?"

"Benny, can we just sit down, and I'll explain, love. Please—"

"How long have you been taking birth control behind my back, Colette!" he roared.

"If you'll let me speak—"

"There's nothing to talk about," he fumed.

His rage rising, he paced the floor to curb his anger. With his stride strong, masking his stagger, I knew that I wasn't going to get through to him. His brows furrowed as the tension in his jaw grew, masking his face in a menacing glare that I could not escape, as he realized the extent of my deception. "You've been taking them the entire time, haven't you? That's why we haven't conceived since…"

"I'm so sorry, Benny," I said, trying to grab hold of him, to which he swatted. Pulling away from my grip, sharply, he stifled a fury, I had yet to become privy to.

"How could you do this to me? You know how badly I want another child."

"I was trying to protect you…us. I was scared that—"

"Scared of what?! I've been better. I am better!"

"You can't fault me for being concerned, Benny. You told me yourself that another loss would break you. That you didn't know how you'd get through it. Why would I risk that?"

"It wasn't your decision to make for me! I know what I said. But I also went to my meetings, partnered up so I wouldn't be alone by myself with my thoughts on my runs—I did everything to make sure I would be good for you and the kids," he said emphatically.

"You're right. It wasn't a choice to make for you. It was a choice I had to make for myself."

"So, you're admitting that you're selfish? Great. Good to know," he said sarcastically.

"Selfish?! Really?" I replied hotly. "From the moment we've been together, I have done nothing but try to please you! And often, at the expense of myself."

"Oh, come on, Colette. It's not like you to play martyr," he said nastily.

"And maybe that's the problem, Benjamin," I responded. I could feel the intensity of my rage choking me into surrender, as the warmth of my tears began to cascade down my cheeks. "I tried…I tried for you. More for you than for me. But we lost her. And I know that you want a second chance… but you don't understand how it feels, you're not a mother."

"So, because I'm not a woman…not you, I'm not in pain? I don't feel it as strongly as you? Is that what you're saying to me? I can't possibly feel the pain of losing our child, Colette?" he asked.

"That's not what I'm saying at all. If you would just let me speak—"

"What?! There isn't anything that you can say to me! You lied! You're a liar and a thief. You have literally stolen my chance of being the father I know I can be, away from me!" he yelled.

"Do you have any idea what it's like for me? You pushed me just as you always do. Do you know what it's like to have your child ripped from your body? And then be unable to do anything to breathe life into them?" I pressed.

"It happened to me as well, Colette. You don't own the patent on losing our daughter."

"I never said that I did," I replied, "You want me to consider your pain, but you don't even acknowledge that it happened to me? That I'm the one that must carry the burden and blame? I failed to carry her! They don't look at you the way they look at me."

"Why is it always about what other people think, with you?"

"Why do you never think about me?!" I screamed, "Do you even care about the toll that it has taken on me? The toll it took on my body. You didn't even care to ask me if I was okay with trying. You just assumed."

"Assumed? Because you gave me any indication that you never wanted to?"

"Like you would have listened? You're barely listening to me now," I sneered. "Then I had to watch you inch closer and closer to how things were before. It tore me apart."

"Stop it! You don't get to use that as an excuse for what you did."

"Why can't I? You have no idea what it's like to watch your children be afraid of their father. You haven't a clue how much it hurts me to see you that way. And I didn't want to risk it happening again, for something that isn't meant to be."

"You know what? I'm tired of being treated like a pariah, Colette! Like I'm this broken burden of a man," he raged, "You know what, perhaps you feel like you'd do better without me. Is that it? So you wouldn't have to be the wife of me…your husband…the helpless invalid. Is that why you talk to him?!"

"No, that's not it. You're putting words in my mouth, Benjamin."

"Don't lie to me! You've done enough of that already," he said, "You want him, don't you? That's probably the reason you don't want to try again."

"I told you why I don't want to try again, Benjamin," I said warily, "Why can't I just want you to myself for a while? Have me to myself? Just for a little bit. Like we were, that Summer before all this?"

"Nah. Don't try to spin this shit."

"I'm not spinning anything! You're being irrational!"

"No. You know that he wouldn't want you fat bellied," he said maliciously.

"You're right. He doesn't want me barefoot and pregnant like you seem to need. He wants me to be me. Unlike you, he doesn't push me to do or be someone I am not. Or do things I don't want to do. He listens to me. And he wants me for me," I replied. "Dominic is the man you used to be. The man I thought I'd fallen in-love with, but I realize now that he's no longer here. He's been replaced by a tyrant instead!"

The flicker of hurt that plastered across his face, was enough for me to quell my anger. And as he took to our closet, I sat quietly on our bed, washing myself in the remorse that now overtook me, until he came out with his suitcase in hand.

"Wait…. what are you doing?"

"What does it look like I'm doing? It's obvious that this was all a mistake."

"Are you serious? You can't be serious. This isn't the time for games, Benjamin."

"I won't be going to the gala," he said matter-of-factly. "I'm sure you'll find an excuse to tell everyone. I'll see the kids tomorrow evening when I come for the rest of my things."

"Benjamin…please. Be reasonable," I pleaded.

"Just so you know…there is nothing you could say that will make me forgive you," he said.

His words pierced me like daggers. The venom in his voice reverberated throughout my body, reminding me of just how callous he could be. "Go to him. Perhaps he will make you happy, Colette. The way I never have."

Into the Lion's Den

Entering the ballroom, I made my way through the guests who had long become a fixture in our lives. Making my rounds within the sea of family and friends who were enjoying the night's event, I allowed myself to relish in the winter wonderland we were all transported to. The room, cast in lights of blue and white, afforded the feeling of being captured in an ice castle under the Northern Lights; while the white linens and tall vases filled with course powder to simulate snow, reflected the lights that bounced about from the large white snowflakes and chandeliers that hung from the ceilings. The bare, faux winter trees and ice sculptures laid strategically throughout the hall, enclosed us in, as if we were wrapped in a forest. It was magical and created a stillness within me. Yet despite the beauty of the night, I could not share in the happiness of the other patrons, as my mind drifted off to Benny's last words to me.

Finishing my mulled wine clutched tightly in my grasp, I went over to my table to sulk in my fear of what may come. Distracted by my thoughts, I didn't notice her presence until I felt the subtle weight of her hand, tucked gently under my chin. "You mind telling me what's wrong?" she asked.

"There's nothing wrong with me, Momma. I'm fine," I said. The furrow in her brows creased the smoothness of her skin in a manner that didn't hide her scrutiny. "Look at Kami over there, bothering the planner."

"I don't expect her to be doing anything less," my mother said, "But don't try and change the subject. You and I both know that you were never good at lying, especially when it comes to me. Now…talk to me. Come on, Coco Bean."

"Okay. So, what am I in for? Chastisement? Sad news? Or will this be a happy talk about how wonderfully proud you are of me?" I asked.

Her smile, radiant and fine, exuded a wisdom and sense of knowing I hoped to attain one day with my own children. Over the years, our relationship had transformed into a friendship, I long came to cherish.

"I come in peace…with a bit of scolding," she smiled. "Don't worry. Think of it as moral support."

"Ah. He called you, didn't he?" I asked. It had become a long-standing tradition for Benny to involve my mother in our squabbles when he felt jilted. If he couldn't get me to fold through the depths of my weakness— my love for him, he sought it in my love and respect for her.

"Of course he did, Colette," she replied.

"I seriously hate it when he does that. He has no right to include you in our affairs."

"He does when you're being foolish," she stated.

"Momma…please."

"Don't Momma, me, little girl. If you weren't acting as if you weren't a married woman, your husband wouldn't have acted out the way he did," she said.

"And now the scolding begins," I said; my eyes rolling heavily, displaying my irritation.

"Don't you sass me. You're not too old to get beat," she replied mockingly.

"Mommy, you don't understand what's going on."

"Oh. So, it's Mommy, now? You really are in deep shit then."

"Are you going to listen to me, or are you going to ignore me like he does?"

"Don't do that, Colette," she said, "I don't get in the middle of y'all mess unless I feel like you've both gone over the deep end. And it seems to be the case now, with you messing around with that man."

"I'm not doing anything with Dominic!" I protested. Fuming, I called a member of the wait staff to my table to grab a drink off his tray.

"Hello, Ma'am. How can I be of assistance to you?" asked the pretty young woman, carrying the tray of drinks that were now becoming increasingly inviting. It's rich crimson color of liquid courage was just what I needed.

"What's in the glass?"

"It's a holiday margarita, ma'am. Would you like one?" she asked.

"I'll take two," I replied.

"I don't want a drink, Colette," said my mother.

"I never said one was for you, Momma," I said irritated, "Now, don't look at me like that. At the rate things are going, I see that I'm in for a long night, and I might as well enjoy it."

"Don't get crazy. You still have responsibilities and things to oversee."

"I know what my responsibilities are, Momma. I don't need constant reminding about the things I need to do, should do, or take care of," I snapped.

With a raised eyebrow and pursed lips, she gathered herself forward in her chair, and smoothed out her ice blue-colored gown that contrasted well against her unblemished mahogany skin. Her position now strong and upright, created a magnified stature against my tall frame, making her appear as if she were elevated on a pedestal, forcing me to cower.

"Now, I know that you're grown," she said thoughtfully, "But it doesn't mean that I'm going to stop being a mother and mothering you. So, take my meddling as a sign of me caring, and not a sign as me…well…meddling. You get me girl?"

In the years since I'd become a mother, my own had changed the way in which she'd once been with me, as if I had become privy to some secret society that altered the way we navigated our world together. She had become the woman who I always yearned for, and as I gazed into the hurt trapped in her almond shaped eyes, set upon high cheekbones so very much like mine, I became remorseful of the tone I had taken with her. "I'm sorry, Mommy," I said like an admonished child. "I just wish everyone would understand that things are just…well…they've always been hell for us. Even in the beginning. You know that."

"I do. But you made a vow, and it shouldn't be taken lightly."

"But at what expense? How much of myself do I have to give?" I asked.

"Marriage is compromise, Colette. It is two people learning to submit and bend to each other. It is not a life filled with one's will to exact their own whims."

"Then how come its only me doing the compromising? My turn is over, it's his turn now," I said fervently.

"So much resentment, baby girl, you have coursing through that body of yours. You keep it up, and it's going to eat you alive," she chastised, "Now, he's done his mess. Made choices and decisions that didn't suit you, I can agree with that…but you made your bed, and you had a part in it too."

"How, Momma? How did I make my bed? By standing beside him even when I probably shouldn't have?"

"And what is that supposed to mean, Colette?"

"Why should I have to suffer because of what he went through?"

"Now that's not fair, Colette. You know it's not."

"No. What's not fair is that everyone expects me to do for him…protect him… *love* him, but where has he been when I've needed him?" I asked. Hurt washed over me, and I found myself wanting to go to my place of tranquility. "Where was he when I was alone with his children, wondering if we would ever see him again? When I lost my baby, Momma…he did nothing for me. Nothing at all, but try to get me pregnant, like I'm chattel! He didn't think about how I felt. Not then. Not ever. And the only thing I ever do is put him first. No matter how it hurts me, and I can't do it anymore."

"Yet it doesn't change the fact that you should have told him this, before doing what you did. Birth control? Really? Without talking to him? That is your husband, Colette.

"So much for it being my body," I said.

"Now don't you get smart with me, girl," she reprimanded. "In all honesty, you should have told him every time you felt overwhelmed or slighted. Not go to the extreme that you did without consulting him."

"I didn't want to hurt him," I said sheepishly, "I didn't want to risk—"

"I know, Coco Bean. I know. But what good has keeping all of this bottled up done for either of you?"

"Nothing," I shrugged, "But it still doesn't change the fact that everything I've had to go through was because my husband is a selfish brat."

"That you chose," she said matter-of-factly, "And he knows who he is. What do you think he's been saying to me? He realizes that he's entitled. That he hasn't always been the best husband. And although his intentions were good, he still messed up, but he's willing to try."

"If he's so remorseful, then why hasn't he shown up to fix things himself? He called you. Damn coward. You know he packed his bags to leave me and our children, Momma. The ones he claims he wants to be a father to. Not like he could muster it, anyway," I fumed. "Look, I don't buy it. I don't buy that he wants to mend this—whatever this is anyway. And, as I've said before, he should go to his own mother. It's not like he doesn't have one. He shouldn't be pestering you!"

"Now you listen here…the moment you said I do and became his wife, that man became my son. And if he sees fit to call me to sort the two of you out, then so be it. Don't be mad because he loves me too. Jealous little girl." she said. The smile on her face contradicted the firmness of her tone. "What? You can't share? I share your love with him. And he loves you, Colette. He truly does."

"He's drowning me, Momma! He makes it so I can't breathe."

"Since when did I teach you to be weak, gal? Buck up!" she censured. "Things aren't perfect, but they can be fixed. For the smart people you two are supposed to be, a box of crayons seems to have more sense. How y'all have careers where all you do is communicate and work through problems with or for other people, and can't even talk amongst yourselves, is beyond me."

"You say this like he listens to me, Momma," I replied, "He doesn't care about me, he only cares about himself."

"Oh, he cares alright. If you heard him tonight, you'd know he cares," she stated. The look in her eyes lit with amusement at what she considered an absurd statement from me. But she didn't understand how stifling living with a man like Benjamin Lati could be.

"And I've said it once, and I'll say it again…I didn't raise you or your sister to be fragile-ass women, who just can't even. You have a man that you can make listen to you. And he is willing to. Trust me. I've seen enough in my life to know that he will. He ain't like most of the men that we've come to know. He cares. And I know that he may not be the best at showing it all the time, but you got a good man, Colette…despite his ways."

"It shouldn't be this hard. With Dominic, it's never this way. I say what I want…do what I want," I explained.

"Does that make sense to you? In what world do you live in where we can always say and do as we please?" she asked, "That kind of freedom? The freedom you'd get with a man like Dominic, is not what you want, baby girl. And it will come at a price that you will not be able to pay."

"But love shouldn't hurt this way—"

"Has Benny hurt you, or has life thrown you what it's gonna give the two of you and caused you pain?"

"It's not just life, Momma. It's the fact that he never considers me or gives me a choice."

"It sounds like you need to put your big girl panties on and open up your damn mouth, to me. He's a man, Colette… not a mind reader. An imperfect man, that so happens to have made some mistakes; and it's not as if you ever spoke up. I know you in that way. You can't eat shit and then wonder why you're drowning in sickness. Okay?" she said. "You married a man who is completely different from you. Different culture—religion—way of being. And you expected what? Perfection? Look…talk to him. Tell him how you feel. Tell him what you truly want. Tell him…your husband, what it is that you need! Hell, go to counseling. That's all the rave now, isn't it? We didn't do that in my day. I wish we had, though. Would have saved a whole lot of misery. But please, just talk to your husband. You make him listen, Colette. You have more power than you realize over that man. Do you hear me? You have power. More than I've ever had. His love for you, is your power—you can make him listen. You can get him to bend the way you need him to, just as you have done for him. He can and will bend too."

"That's not true, Momma. Why can't you understand?" I asked, as I allowed myself to be washed in a wave of calm as her fingers ran lightly through the cascading curls atop my head. It was a tactic she had long mastered, to make me unwind myself from whatever torment that struck me, "What does it matter? He doesn't want a life with me anyway, anymore."

"Coco Bean, if your husband didn't want you anymore, why did he come to me?" she asked, pausing to allow her words to sink in.

"I don't know why he does the things he does, Momma."

"It's because that man adores you. He doesn't want to let go, just as I know you don't."

"I'm just so tired. I'm tired of everything being so difficult with him," I said incensed.

"It's hard because marriage isn't a fairytale, baby girl. You feel like things would be easier with Dominic, don't you? I know you do. But let me tell you something, little girl…it'd be one in the same, except worse—"

"How is anything worse than what I've already been through with Benny? And then he decides to leave me? Like I'm the one at fault?" I asked fuming—the consciousness of Benny's indiscretion finally resonating with me. He left me. Despite every sacrifice I'd made for him, he deserted and pained me in a way that no one ever had—that Dominic wouldn't.

"I know that this isn't your fault, Colette. But it does take two," she said cautiously, "However, I do know what having a hard life with a man like Dominic feels like, who loves the idea of you and what you could give him… that is far worse than anything you could ever imagine and experience with Ben. Dominic is the type to see your potential for how it benefits him, not because he sees you. Could he love and care for you? Perhaps. But he will grow tired, just like he does everything else in his life. Once the chase is over, he will always look for something bigger and better, and then where will you be? Hmm? I know men like him. Now, you let go of what you think you're missing. You let go of that man."

"I know what I'm doing, Momma. And according to my husband, I am free to do as I wish," I said hotly. The drinks, coupled with the sadness and loss I felt at Benny's decision to leave, were drawing me further away from reason.

"Now you listen to me now…Dominic ain't for you. You hear? My momma always said if you lie down with dogs, honey…you're bound to get fleas," she said tightly. "Shit. Speak of the devil."

Turning my head to the man who had garnered her attention, heat rose within me as he came into view and walked towards our table. His hair, cropped shorter than usual, complimented the light stubble he sported; while the perfectly fitted Italian, powdered blue suit, intensified the brightness of his espresso-colored skin. The top few buttons of his dress shirt were left open, revealing a soft down of hair on his solid chest. It was the suit I'd picked out for him while in Paris, and he looked damn good wearing it.

"Hello Colette," he said. His voice, silky and smooth, was coated with desire. His eyes were amorous in nature, sending a shiver down my spine that made me shudder.

"Well, don't you look nice," my mother's voice came faintly, as I drifted off in my admiration of his person. "You look like you belong in the backdrop, instead of at our table."

Although his choice in clothing did make him stand out in the myriad of dashing men, dressed smartly in their black suit and ties, I know that my mother's intent was to elude, not so subtly, to the fact that she did not desire his company. Keeping his eyes locked with mine, he pulled out a chair and sat beside me, ignoring my mother's slight against him.

"I can't say that I can take credit for my appearance," he said, "Your daughter picked this out for me during her trip to Paris."

"I see," my mother replied. "So, are you staying long?"

"Momma," I squealed. I tried to protest, but the drinks had taken effect, lending a light buzz, I had no intention of disturbing.

"What? I just want to know how long he intends to stay here. It's not a difficult question, is it Dominic?" she asked slyly.

"You know, if I didn't know any better, I would think that you were trying to get rid of me," he said. The smile plastered across his face, while dazzling as they exposed a pearly white grin, did nothing to mask the testiness of his gaze. "However, to answer your question, I'm here for as long as I'm wanted...and needed."

"Uh huh," she replied, "And where is the new strapping young thing you usually have attached to your arm? Your father has always spoken of your insatiable need for a different woman every month, so I'm curious to see what kind of girl you've chosen to claim."

"Kind of girl? Are you implying that I am without taste, Mrs. Brown?"

"When it comes to looks, I've heard that they've all been…wonderfully crafted," she said, "But you can't deny that some have been a little...uncouth."

"That's because they were only meant for the night," he stated honestly, "I am not ashamed of the man I once was."

"Once was?" she asked accusingly.

"My, my, my, Mrs. Brown. Considering that our understanding of each other is one that has only been acquired through passing, you surely are… opinionated of whom you perceive me to be," he said, trying his hardest to remain elusive and centered. I'd seen this in him before, when trying to evade his father's scrutiny, and it was evident that he was growing guarded and perturbed by my mother's insinuations of him.

"Dominic, I notice that your father didn't come in with you," I said trying to change the subject. "Will he be attending this evening? I'm certain that he said he would be here when I spoke to him last."

"I don't need to know you like I know…well…Ben, to understand what kind of man you are, Mr. Toussaint," my mother said snidely. I could tell she was drawing her line in the sand with him. She was trying to make sure that Dominic knew that he would never have the keys to her castle—or rather to me.

"To answer your question, mon coeur, my father will be arriving shortly," he said to me, "As for you, Mrs. Brown…let's cut to the chase, shall we? You and I both know who I'm here for, and I will make no apologies for that."

"Well, unfortunately for you, she is someone you can't have," replied my mother.

"Excuse me, sir…may I?" Dominic said. Grabbing two drinks from a server, he placed one in front of me.

"I don't think she needs that. She's had two already."

"Three if you count the mulled wine," I said pointedly.

"Well, isn't it a great thing that she's a big girl who can choose for herself," Dominic said.

"I don't believe that I was asking you, Dominic. I was referring to the server."

"I'm a grown woman, Momma. It's fine. It's a party. And if I want to have another drink, I will," I said hotly, growing tired of the hold and rule over my life, that others seemed to have, more than myself.

"She's right. It is a party," Dominic stated, holding his drink, as he awaited me to drag my own against his. Taking a satisfying gulp together,

I ignored the hostility in my mother's gaze, just as Dominic did. We sat for a while in an awkward silence, finishing our drinks, when I noticed the uneasiness in my mother's charcoal-colored eyes.

"Everything okay, Momma?"

"It looks like I'm up. I guess they're ready to make the announcements and give the awards, so they can really start their partying," she said.

Following her line of sight, I saw Stella beckoning her to come. It had become tradition to announce how much we raised during our galas. On this night, it was to go in part to the local veteran's hospital this year, as well as a home that Benny and Devon renovated for homeless vets. It was a project that he was extremely proud of, and he wasn't even around to see what the gala was going to offer them.

Usually, my mother was more than happy to discuss the achievements my company had attained, but something about the way she held on to my hand before departing, made me conscientious of what I now realized was fear.

"What is it?" I asked.

"Just remember what I said, Colette," she said standing over me, her lips now close to my ears, so that only I could hear, "You don't want fleas."

"Momma, it's my life," I whined.

My body was now wrought with anger, as I tried my hardest not to feel like I was being coerced by a puppeteer. Despite the comradery my mother and I now maintained, there was something, like with Benny, that never seemed to change. They had a knack for dictating how my life should be. And with the alcohol I consumed, I couldn't help the rise of rebellion boiling inside me, "Who knows…maybe I'll like fleas."

"I hope you know what you're doing, little girl. I really do," she said, leaving me to my own devices.

"Fleas?" Dominic asked.

"Don't worry about it. Do you want to go out into the lobby or something? I need some air," I said to him.

I was becoming overwhelmed by the awareness of those who surrounded us; their questioning stares as they whispered about Benny's absence and Dominic's presence and proximity to me, made me uncomfortable. And as I was not scheduled to impart my words to the slew of men and women draped in their finest wears until the end of the night, I made my escape.

Making our way to the lobby of the hotel, I could feel his eyes on me, as he trailed behind—it was as if the heat of his desire was burrowing a hole in my skin, summoning me to meet his gaze. Wrapping his arm around my waist, I allowed myself to lean into the firmness of his body as we came upon a seated enclosure. Taking a seat a few feet away from him on the soft love seat sofa, I watched as the lights on the tree danced rhythmically to a beat of their own.

"You like the holidays?" he asked, breaking the silence between us.

"Like is an understatement. It's always been my favorite time of the year. The snow…the lights…it always makes The City look so magical. You know?" I said dreamily, "And then you get to snuggle close. Make love to the roar of a fire—"

"Then why isn't he here with you?" he asked bluntly.

"So, you've noticed?"

"How could I not? He never leaves your side. And I know he wouldn't miss tonight. So, what happened?"

"He's not coming," I said cautiously, "Apparently he would rather not have anything to do with me at the moment."

"And why is that?" he asked.

"He found the birth control I've been taking."

"I thought you discussed it with him already," he stated.

"Obviously, I didn't."

"You should have told him, Colette," he said. His tone no longer gentle, was reproachful, and his eyes were concerning.

"So, I've been told," I said angrily, "What is it with everyone? Are you on his side too?"

"I am always on your side, Colette. It's just that you should have," he said, stopping short of completing his sentence. Following his gaze, I saw the hardened eyes of Benny peering over me.

"I need a moment with my wife, if you don't mind," Benny said nastily. His voice dripping with bitterness, was ominous and absent of his usual cheery nature, causing me to take pause.

"I thought you weren't coming?"

"I decided otherwise," he said. His tone was still laced with malice, as he stared Dominic down. "I need to talk to you, Colette. Now!"

"You should have done so when I tried speaking with you earlier, and you decided to walk out the door with your bags, Benjamin," I retorted, "So, don't come demanding me to do anything."

"I don't have time for this, Colette."

"I don't think she wants to go with you, Benjamin," Dominic said.

"I'm sorry, but was I fucking talking to you?" Benny replied. His voice just above a whisper, was domineering and eerie. I hadn't seen him this way in some time, and I knew that it was best for me to subdue the changing tide within him. Getting up from my seat to create distance between the two men, I grabbed Benny's hand and escorted him down a hall until we found an empty conference room, leaving Dominic behind.

"What do you want, Benjamin?" I said exasperated, unable to care about the hostility his glare conveyed to me.

"I was coming here to apologize, but I see now, that it was a moot point," he replied.

"Excuse me?"

"I'm not here, and the first thing you do is go to him?" he asked.

"First of all, you weren't here because you had a fucking tantrum and left."

"A tantrum? Since when do you speak to me this way?" he asked, "And I wouldn't call what happened a tantrum. I have every right to be angry with you, Colette."

"Just as I have every right to be pissed with you over your little tantrum," I said dismissively.

"Stop saying that!" he yelled.

"What would you like me to call it, then? A tizzy? Hold on…wait…how about a conniption?" I taunted, "Whatever the fuck you decide on, it was still a fucking tantrum!"

"So, me being angry at the fact that you lied to me and stopped us from conceiving, is throwing a tantrum, Colette? You really are delusional," he scoffed.

"No, Benjamin. Running off instead of talking it through and telling me that we're done, and to go be with Dominic, is a fucking tantrum!"

"To which you were more than happy to do," he retorted, "Look, this isn't getting anywhere. I shouldn't have come."

"What are you going to do? Run away again? Is that it? I get to have the pleasure of dealing with all your shit for years, Benjamin, just for you to jump ship at the first sign of a problem?"

"Oh, that's rich. That is rich coming from you," he replied.

"What are you going on about?"

"How many times did you break-up with me at the beginning of our relationship? Every time things got hard; it was the first thing you'd do."

"Really? You're bringing up what happened when we were kids? For what? Was this some sort of reprisal for you? What happened then was different, and you know it!"

"How? How was that any different? For someone who has a problem with me 'jumping ship,' as you say, you certainly started the trend," he said callously.

"Let's get one thing straight, Mr. Lati…I broke up with you then because you weren't man enough to do what was needed with your damn family. And I didn't appreciate how you treated me because you couldn't deal with their harassment and scrutiny. I didn't like how you acted towards me then, and I'm getting sick of it now," I seethed, "Your actions caused our break-up."

"Just like yours has caused ours now!" he yelled.

"Oh, really? So much for your fucking apology then," I said heatedly, "What are we doing, Benjamin? If you're done… if we're done, then why are we here?"

"We're not doing anything. It was a stupid misstep on my part to think that you would own up to your mistake," he replied. Looking into his eyes, I could see that his pride wouldn't allow his words to convey what was in his heart, and I couldn't stand it any longer.

"I'm done, Benjamin. I don't have to put up with this any longer. I have gone above and beyond for you and our marriage. It's time that I focus on myself," I said, turning to walk towards the door.

"Where are you going?" he asked, grabbing my arm harshly, "Are you going to him? Well fuck you then, Colette! I don't need you. Nor do I want a woman like you."

"Let go of me! You're hurting me," I said. Pulling myself from his grasp, I charged towards the door, as I tried to drown the pain of his verbal attack.

"Go back to your little boyfriend!" I heard him say, as the doors slammed loudly in my ears, unable to obscure the cruelty of his words against me. Stumbling down the hall, I collapsed against the threshold of the lobby—the agony of his words made me weak in the knees, and sent a fiery wave of fury through me, when I felt the strong hands of Dominic steadying me.

"I saw you as you came out. Are you okay?" he asked.

"I don't know why I care, or why I even try," I spoke.

"I thought I told you that the only thing that should be on your face, is a smile," he said, wiping the tears that burned my cheeks.

"Can we get out of here?" I asked.

"Wherever you want to go, we can go. My car is out front. I am at your beck and call."

"Your room," I said.

Taking hold of his collar, I placed my lips fervently against his and kissed him deeply. His lips, firm and smooth, tasted of sweet melon, and the fullness of them covered mine in a rhythmic dance that scorched my belly.

And despite my apprehension, I leaned into the desire I felt for him in that moment, so that I didn't have to feel the lashing of my pain.

"I…I want to go to your room."

"Colette…are you… are you sure?" he asked. The shock in his eyes, vibrated through his body, causing a wave of tension that made the feel of him hard and sturdy. He was like a statue, tall and firm, and it forced me to lean into his strength.

"I'm sure," I replied.

Taking his hand in mine, I walked with him toward the elevators, and as we waited for it to come, we settled into a peculiar silence, as the uncertainty of our decision took hold. Stepping onto the elevator, we distanced ourselves on opposite ends of it, as we awaited our arrival to his floor. And as the effects of the alcohol, I consumed dissipated, and the rage I felt turned into longing for the man whose heart I believed I no longer possessed began to pass, the chiming sound as we passed each floor felt like a clock ticking down to the end of everything, I thought to be true.

With each step to his room, my anxiety sweltered like a desert heat as it rose through my body. Entering his suite, the light scent of cinnamon and lavender permeated the room, lending an air of tranquility. The rose petals dusted across the marble flooring were the color of crimson, signifying the passion he seemed to imbue—while champagne sat in the parlor. Its bottle covered in mist, sat in a crystalized ice bath, meant to assist its chill, looked inviting; yet I couldn't bring myself to have a glass. It was as if his hope for the night had summoned me there, and it was this realization that swept over me and brought forth a mass of guilt.

Brushing his body close to mine, the craving to be touched by him amplified my shame, and I found myself backing away until my body reached the hardness of a wall, trapping me within his grasp. Now face to face, we stood in the stillness of our desire, moving closer until his mouth found mine. Softly, tenderly, his lips possessed me, and were laced with an anxiousness that flooded his body. He moved with a sense of doubt that I did not expect from a well-seasoned man, such as himself—it was as if he were afraid that I might falter under the weight of his desire. Gone was the urgency he exhibited in his words. Instead, they were replaced with a placidness that insisted that I maintain a calm within me, as he coaxed me into accepting the warmth of his tongue into my mouth.

Closing my eyes, I allowed the sweetness of his kisses against my neck to pull me into ecstasy—but as I fell into the depths of my desire, my mind drifted to Benny, and I no longer felt the firm hands of Dominic caressing and cupping the weight of my breast, but the feel of my husband's lips pressed against my body. As my mind raced and replaced the erotic manipulation Dominic played against me, with the sensual feelings I'd often experienced with Benny, the raking of his hand up my thighs, made me call out the name of the man my heart still possessed.

"Benny," I said breathlessly, unable to stop the words from escaping, causing him to stop his assault against me. Looking beyond the veil of shock that cloaked his face, I could see his pain, which quickly morphed into anger.

"I finally get to taste you…to have you…and you're thinking about… him?" he said, "What is it about him?"

"He's my husband, Dominic," I said, "And I love him. I truly do. I'm sorry. I can't do this. I thought I could, but I can't."

"Sorry? Yeah. You're most definitely sorry," he said viciously, "I knew I should have just had you and be done with it, but I thought we could be good together."

"Had me and be done with it?" I said fuming, "You smug, pompous bastard! How dare you?! What makes you think I would have ever given in to you?"

"Hmm, let's see… are you currently with your husband right now, or were you just with me only moments ago, with my hands all over you?" he asked, nastily.

The sound of the slap I'd given him, resonated in the air, causing him to cup his cheek. "They were right about you," I said ardently.

"Right about what exactly? About the fact that I want you. You knew that already," he stated, "You couldn't deny it even if you wanted to. You were supposed to be like the rest, a trophy to mount—but then I thought that maybe, with your wit and poise, we could be something great."

"You never wanted me for me, Dominic…just what I could give you. Just as my mother said. I can't believe I've been so foolish. God, I have to find Benny."

"Why do you keep obsessing over someone who clearly doesn't even know what to do with you? He doesn't know what you're capable of, Colette. And he doesn't see the fire and spirit of a woman who wants something more," he raged, "All he sees is a fucking milk maid—someone whose only purpose is to bear his children and share his bed. He doesn't see you."

"And you do?" I asked, "You literally just equated me to one of your many whores, but you know me? You're the one that knows what I want? What I need?"

"I know that I can give you more than he ever could. You've known nothing but misery with him. You said so yourself."

"Don't you dare twist my words. You don't know shit about the life I lead with my husband."

"I know that unlike him, I can give you the excitement and freedom you crave," he said snidely.

"Then you don't know me at all," I scoffed, "I am free. It may have taken me awhile, but I realize that now. And I am free to choose the wholeness... the completion, I feel, when my husband looks at me. Even when things are going wrong, he makes me feel that way. Even the way the light brush of his beard against my cheek, makes me feel home. These are things that you will never know…or ever feel, because you don't have any idea what it is to love someone the way that Benny and I love each other."

"Love each other? You can't even tell him how you really feel, and you call that love?" he ridiculed, "How does he love you when he railroads your desires?"

"I'm not going to talk to you about my marriage!"

"It's never stopped you before," he retorted.

"So, what? You were just listening to me to use it against me? Is that it?" I said angrily, "Hear my sob story so that you can get into my pants? I thought you were my friend, Dominic. But you were just using me."

"And it's still more than what he's doing for you now," he replied, "Explain something to me…since when does a man, who is in-love with a woman, stifle them? Takes the very essence of who they are from them—"

"Shut up!" I yelled.

"And doesn't even realize when she is in pain? Or is falling for another man?"

"Stop it! You know nothing about him…and you sure as hell don't know anything about me. And I would rather be the wife and mother of the children to Benjamin Lati, than deal with a conceited dickhead like you!" I said bolting.

He blocked my path as I tried to make my way towards the door, and the anger that once played like a beautiful symphony on his face, was now masked with a sense of urgency I'd never seen in him, "Listen to me, Colette…if you walk out that door, you'll be making the biggest mistake of your life. I don't make the same offer twice," he said.

"The only mistake I ever made, Dominic, was allowing myself to supplant my husband…for a man I should have never bothered with in the first place," I said hotly. "I was foolish. Stupid. I see that now. Get out of my way. I need to find my husband."

"Colette…wait. Please. I didn't mean it," he cried.

Reaching the door, I opened it to come face to face with the last person I expected to see. With eyes crazed and body taut, he stood his full frame in a determined stance, ready to pounce, "Move, Colette. Now!" Benny said, pushing past me, forcing me to trail behind him, as I found myself back into the lion's den.

Burning Coal

"Into the lion's den? Really? You don't think you're being just a tad bit melodramatic?" he asked, bringing his forefinger and thumb together for emphasis.

"Well, I've always had a flare for words and expression, and considering what happened afterwards, it was definitely like being in a lion's den," she replied, "I mean, what else would you call two grown men fighting like toddlers over a woman that doesn't belong to either of them, Doc?"

Watching the proud and knowing look dance across her face—a look she often had when she knew she was testing his patience, made him want to take her. He never could stand how separating herself from him made him feel, which always caused an urgent need to reclaim her, so that she understood where she belonged—with him.

"Why do you do this to me?"

"I have no idea what you're talking about, Doc," she said. Her smile was radiant as she basked in his uneasiness.

"Stop playing around, Colette," he said.

"Listen, I'm only calling it as I see it," she said evenly, "And from where I was standing, it was absurd how Dominic and Benny—"

"Can we stop putting on airs?" he sneered, "I'm growing tired of pretending."

"Well…I don't know, Doctor. Are you going to behave?"

"Dammit, Colette! You're seriously pushing it!" he yelled, "And if you cross and uncross your legs like that one more time, I swear—"

"What?" she asked, "What are you going to do, *Doctor*?"

Letting her legs relax slightly, she allowed some visibility to the tunnel he longed to have but hadn't the guts to claim. Unlike her, he couldn't dismiss what happened, nor could he ignore what he saw—it was too painful for him and opened wounds he didn't care to explore.

"Why do you insist on torturing me this way? The night of Mazal's wedding wasn't enough for you, was it? You had to stir the pot more and dredge up memories I would rather forget? And for what?" he asked. "If I wanted to talk then I would have. I can't do this right now. Just go home, Cole. Please."

"Cole? So, I guess you're throwing in the towel? Are you declaring defeat now, Doctor?" she asked coyly.

"Is this a game to you?" he asked, "Using my practice like this? And for what? What purpose do you think this will serve?"

"The same purpose it served before, Benjamin," Colette said, "I will not have what happened before, happen to us again. I won't have silence and secrets ruin us, like it almost did. Just what? A year ago? No, thanks. I rather just nip this in the bud right here and now," she said matter-of-factly.

"Sure. If you say so…"

"And for the record, I wasn't the one who brought up the past. You were. Or did you forget that it was you that asked me to speak about that night, as if we haven't gone through it and moved on already. It was years ago. Years! And since then, we've obviously re-built what was broken between us, until—"

"You act as if doing this worked out so well the last time," he mumbled under his breath.

"Excuse you, Benjamin? Care to speak up, love?"

"I was saying that it's not like it worked out well for you or us the last time—you coming here like this."

"Oh. You're speaking of my nervous breakdown? That little thing," she said waving him off, "It had nothing to do with our sessions, love. But everything to do with losing the love of my life."

"The love of your life?! Okay. What am I, then? Chopped liver?" he sulked.

"If the shoe fits, hun," she said playfully.

"Whatever," he dismissed, "Either way, you really think that not speaking for a few weeks is going to cause some catastrophic end to our marriage, Colette? I'm angry with you. Yes. But this isn't like before…I'm not carrying a huge burden that would destroy you…destroy us."

"No. You're correct about that part," she said snidely, "Perhaps, because this time, your secret got out before it could truly marinate and eat away at you."

"And you? The first sign of trouble and you sprint off to that asshole?" he retorted, feeling the heat rise in his face. The grin that graced her lips, fueled his irritation. "Why are you laughing? This isn't fucking funny."

"I'm laughing because you're jealous of a man I want nothing to do with, and that to me is hysterical, especially considering you were doing who knows what with Sarah," she replied. "How many times do I have to say that nothing happened, Benjamin? He dropped me off at the hotel, and we sat in the lounge talking to Judah and Primrose. We've been through this already."

"I don't know what happened on the way over, just like I don't really know what happened in his hotel room that night."

Taking in the seriousness of his tone and poutiness of his lips, she couldn't help the roar of laughter that escaped her mouth. For everything that Benjamin Lati was, there was still something deep within him that didn't accept her love and loyalty—it was as if he were always waiting for her to come to her senses and turn away from him. She couldn't help but think how ridiculous it was, because for everything they experienced and endured together, she couldn't be without him.

"Oh, come now, Benjamin. Don't insult me," she replied, "A five-minute car ride is hardly enough time for me, love. But you of all people should know that already."

"Really? That's all you have to say?"

"What do you expect me to say? I'm not going to entertain you accusing me of something I didn't do, neither back then nor now."

"Because you're so innocent, right?" he scoffed, "If I remember correctly, you let that man touch you before, so what am I supposed to think? Huh? How do I know that you wouldn't kiss him again…if not more?"

"Ugh! Would you like to get a time stamped video from the hotel? Perhaps, from the hall as well? You know what? Maybe, I should have fucked him, then you'd have something to chide me about," she snapped.

The pained look on his face, caused her to instantly regret the reckless way in which she spoke. She didn't mean what she said—in-fact, the moments she shared with Dominic had always been her biggest regret. She could still remember the look in his eyes when she saw him on the other side of the threshold of Dominic's hotel room; the pain and anger that radiated behind his eyes, made her feel even more treacherous than the act of her betrayal itself.

And although she experienced bouts of his rage during those moments when the sting of his past swelled inside him, she had never seen him as enraged as he was when he trampled Dominic. It had taken everything within her to separate the two men, who had sat brewing in the blood and fury their fisticuffs had led them to. And contrary to what her husband might believe, there was nothing more she would love to do, than to erase every moment she shared with Dominic Toussaint. Like many before her, she had fallen prey to her own weakness, and instead of cleaving to her husband during their time of need, she allowed herself to become complicit in a scheme that almost destroyed them.

Looking back now and how far they had come since, she understood where they'd gone wrong, and it was what led them down their current path. With that, despite how his accusations of her loyalty to him inflamed and amused her, she knew that reassuring him was what was needed most, to get back to who they'd once been before their secrets and lies crumbled them.

"I'm sorry. I shouldn't have said that."

"It's fine," he lied, "You were just sharing how you really feel, apparently."

"You know that's not how I feel about him," she soothed, "I didn't mean what I said. I was being petty. I know how he makes you feel, and I hit below the belt. I'm sorry."

"I still can't believe you ever considered being with him."

"It wasn't him that I wanted, Benny. I know that now. And truthfully, I knew it then. But as I've said before," she replied, "He let me realize the woman I needed to become. Unfortunately, I lost her this past year. I lost me. I know I did. And if I may, he also reminded me of who you were before… before life changed you."

"I am nothing like that asshole!" he said heatedly.

"You're right. You're better. And you're mine," she said.

Reaching cautiously, she grabbed his hand and waited for the pull she expected to occur, but when its rigidity surrendered and relaxed into hers, she hurried herself over to close the distance between them.

"We both know how much I love you and how much I regret—"

"And yet, you still went with him again," Benny said.

He couldn't place why he felt defeated, but the feelings of inadequacy that seeped through his reasoning gave him a visible slump that compelled her to brush her hand lightly across the coarseness of his bearded cheek. He knew in his heart that his wife, the very essence of his soul, wanted no man, other than him. Truthfully, the night he found her with Dominic, sparked a change in them, that afforded them many years of happiness, and the courage to eventually have the family he knew they were meant to have. But seeing her with him again, and having to deal with Sarah, had incited parts of himself he thought he was long rid of.

"I regret getting into the car with him as well, especially since it hurt you. But you must understand what seeing you with her did to me," she said, "Look at me please…nothing happened between him and me. Not then nor now. You know this to be true."

"I know. You're right. I do," he conceded, "But it doesn't change how seeing you leave that night with him in tow, just—"

"Brought back so many bad memories?" she said, finishing his sentence.

"Yeah. I thought I pushed you away… like before. And that this time, you were going to be with him…for good," he said candidly.

"Never. I would never do that to you. To us," she said vehemently, "And, I'm hurt that you would think so little of me, knowing how hard we worked since then, and now even…that you would think that I would throw it all away. For a moment with someone I don't want. Who I never truly wanted? You know that's not me, Benny."

"I know. And I'm sorry," he said, "But just the idea that I had given him another opportunity to take you away from me…well…it's made these past few weeks unbearable. Wondering…waiting…for you to tell me that you couldn't take us anymore. I couldn't stand it. I know things were getting better, but things have changed. We've changed you know… since she's been gone."

"I get what you mean. It's like there's a wedge between us that we can't seem to close?" she reflected, "It was the same way for me last year, you know? That's why I started these sessions with you. I didn't know what else to do. I saw you spiraling. Then the distance. I was afraid that it was becoming like before. That something happened. Triggered an episode. You know? It was never a game for me, Benny. I was just afraid that I was going to lose you, and I guess, perhaps I was right."

"What are you talking about?" he asked.

"My mother's illness wasn't the only secret you were keeping from me," she said sadly. "Why her? Why Sarah? Of all people? You know how much she wants you and despises me. I thought after all this time, she would have gotten over you. And to think, every time she smiled in my face, it was only so she could use me to get closer to you. At least Dominic was transparent."

He knew that he had to tell her, but the hurt that marred her delicate features made him want to hold back. Although nothing truly transpired between Sarah and him, what did occur had caused a ricochet of events that almost cost him his wife, more than the secret he kept about her mother did. Even now he hated himself for what he did—how his weakness had tarnished the beauty of the intimacy of their union. Despite how he felt about her connection to Dominic, it was nothing compared to the consequences his actions had led him to commit.

"It was nothing, motek, truly. Can we just move on from this?" he pleaded.

"Hold up. Hold up, now. You can't be serious?" she said angrily, "You can sit there and interrogate me about something I didn't even do, but I'm not owed an explanation?"

"I'm not saying that—"

"Then what are you saying, Benjamin? Because from where I'm sitting, I'm calling bullshit!"

Ah. There she was again. The one that stirred his loins and made him feel alive. He had taken note of how she emerged nowadays. No longer with caution, but with ease, reminding him of the girl he once knew. He'd missed her in those moments. Times when he didn't seem to know her or himself. Making him wish that they could go back to the kids they once were—free of the struggles and straps life seemed to strangle them with.

Hearing the snap of her fingers and seeing the veil of intensity in her eyes, he knew he didn't have long before her persistence for knowledge and understanding would get the better of her. Knowing her current mood, he was certain she would lose the wherewithal and patience she had mustered for their session, to tolerate his inability to be forthcoming. How can I buy myself time, he wondered.

Time would allow him the privilege of laying down the facts she sought, in a way that wouldn't lend cruelty to the infection he knew would tarnish their bond. Either way, he understood that the words he needed to speak would change and devour her, as well as the essence of who they were.

"It's getting late, why don't we go home and talk about it then?"

"For what, Benjamin? Why can't we discuss it now? That's what we're here for, isn't it?'"

"That's what we're here for? Really? All this time, I thought it was just a means for you to monopolize my time for bullshit that we could solve at home," he said feigning irritation. He had not meant to be defensive, but what else could a man on borrowed time do.

"Monopolize your time? Are you serious? Perhaps if you were taking care of home, I wouldn't have to come to you like this in the first place. You fail to realize that me being here isn't just my problem, it's ours!"

"How is it mine? I don't have any issues. It's you…with the melodramatic bullshit!"

"Melodramatic bullshit?! Okay. So, we're back to this again? It was all just my imagination, I guess. That year and what followed, was just what? A prolonged hallucination?" she said sarcastically, "All the time you spent distancing yourself from me, so much so, that you eventually landed yourself in her arms, didn't happen at all? Great. Noted. Considering that fact, I should probably check myself in again, since I'm obviously just delusional."

"You have no idea what was going on. What I went through."

"You're right. Just as you have no real understanding of what I was going through! I felt like you were slipping away from me!" she replied, as the pain of the past came rushing at her. "I didn't know what to do, Benny."

"You think I don't know what I put you through? You think that it didn't hurt me? You didn't have to see—"

"See what?" she said. She watched as his eyes closed in agony against the memories that plagued him, and it tore her apart that he was still shutting her out.

"Nothing. Just forget it, Colette. Please," he begged.

"Why won't you let me in, Benjamin?" she said hotly, "How can you say you love me, when you always keep me at arm's length? I'm not some delicate flower that will wither—"

"You don't understand, Colette. It'll ruin everything," he said tightly.

"Look, all I know is that everything that's happened in the past year or so, that has been ugly, has led us here. And I for one am ready to let it all go so that we can move forward from this point of contention in our lives, just as we have done before," she said gently, "Can we make a different path together? No more secrets. Please. Explain to me why you were in the garden with her at Mazal's wedding? Tell me why she was saying those things to you."

"Why do you keep mentioning her? She's irrelevant!"

"Why do you keep deflecting?! Every time I mention Sarah, you get defensive. What's the deal?" she said fervently, no longer able to control herself, "I am and have always been transparent with you. Stop the bullshit, Benjamin! You're not being fair to me!"

"Can we just go home, and then we can talk about it? Please, Cole," he said, feeling defeated. He hoped he could appeal to that place inside her that melted and bent to his whim, but the fire that burned behind her eyes, as if it could trample a forest, told him otherwise.

Despite his pleading, she refused to allow herself to fall prey to his persuasion. And the franticness in his words, in his attempt to quell her, ignited a sense of distrust, she'd never felt in response to the boy who was now her husband, causing her to stand and distance herself.

"You know…never mind…you're right. I think I should go," she said, trying to hide the sting of betrayal she felt by the person who was her everything. She was halfway from exiting, when she heard the heaviness of his steps booming behind her, followed by a forceful tug, that soon had her face to face with him.

"Where are you going?" he demanded.

"I would tell you, but you seemed to have gotten beside yourself," she replied, eyeing the tight hold he had around her arm until he loosened his grip. As she pulled herself away from him, he secured his arm around her waist, forcing her back until she was pinned against the door she tried to place between them. "Let me go. Now!" she squealed and contorted herself to no avail, "I'm just doing what you asked me to do. You wanted me to go, right? So let me leave, Benjamin."

Although he hadn't meant her any harm when he first grabbed hold of her, the urgency he felt with her attempted departure felt like a punch to his gut. While the delivery of her words was calm in nature, he knew his wife—she always took care with her words, and her lack of inclusion of him when deciding to leave, didn't go unnoticed. It caused a crippling panic that now placed him in the stand-off he now found himself in with her. The amber-color that tinged her chestnut brown eyes, filled her irises with flecks of gold, as her eyes burned hot with rage like lit coals, and he knew that she was not ready to give in. *I pushed her too far. How can I fix this when I need more time?*

"I don't feel like doing this with you right now, Benjamin," she said. She was exasperated. The struggle between them had left her winded and her ego bruised, because despite her efforts, she was unable to free herself from his grasp.

"I'm not doing anything, Colette. You're being foolish."

"What exactly is foolish about doing what I've been asked to do by you? You want me to stop questioning you and go home? Well then let me go, so I can get out of your hair!"

"I never said for you to go home. I said we should go home and discuss this. As husband and wife. Just ourselves. Benny and Cole. No airs," he said evenly. "I want nothing more than to tell you…to explain to you what you want to know and put your mind at ease; but I'm afraid."

"Afraid of what, Benjamin?" she asked.

The curiosity that caused a crinkle to furrow in her brow, expressed a fear that seemed to take hold of her, and he couldn't bring himself to say what she was longing to know, and it tore him apart. I can't protect her. Why won't she let me protect her, he thought inwardly.

"I don't think you'll forgive me."

"You slept with her, didn't you?" she asked, averting her eyes, unable to face what truths she may hear.

"No. It wasn't like that," he soothed, "You have to believe me. I've never wanted her, and I could never do that to you."

Her audible sigh of relief was his undoing. He couldn't keep up this masquerade—one he created, to shield her from the pain he knew he would have to commit against her. Despite his pledge to protect her heart, his omission of the truth was destroying her faith in him, and he couldn't allow it to go on any further. To him, there was no reason for his deeds to weigh heavy on her heart. And regardless of the consequences he'd have to endure, it was time to relieve her of the torture his secrets enacted against her.

The pained look in his eyes did nothing to alleviate her distress. Although she began her quest with confidence, she realized now that she may no longer know nor have the loyalty of the man before her, and it tore her apart. Every beat of her heart resonated the minutes passed, which seemed to echo the stillness of silence that swarmed between them.

"Let me go! Now! I'm going to be sick," she said, frantically trying to free herself and running towards the bin near his desk. After releasing the contents of her lunch into his trash can, she sat quietly, allowing herself a moment to catch her breath.

"Is everything alright, motek?" he asked. The contortion of her face and her once vibrant appearance, now ashen and pale, told him that there was more yet to come.

"What do you think?" she replied, before relieving herself once more.

"Are you getting sick?" he asked, "Here, let me help you."

Jerking her body away from him, she pulled herself to her feet, dismissing him—the concern in his voice doing nothing to subdue her anxiousness. "I want to go home," she said weakly, "I won't bother you anymore."

"Okay, let me get my things and we can go."

"No, Benjamin. I think its best that I go alone."

"I can't let you leave. Not like this—"

"You're the reason I'm this way!" she said heatedly. Her discomfort steadily growing into a rage that couldn't be controlled, "Why does it always have to be so hard with you? Why do you make it so hard?"

"I'm only trying to protect you—protect us."

"No! I am so sick and tired of that excuse. You're not trying to protect me, you're not trying to protect our marriage, you're only trying to protect yourself!" she shrieked.

He tried to counter her, but the words wouldn't come, because in his heart he knew she was right. Every time he kept a secret from her—it wasn't to keep her safe—it was to shield himself from the possibility of losing her. A mistake he now realized, had caused them more harm. In truth, his attempts to keep her close to him by omitting the cruelty of their reality, had almost cost him her adoration. This time, he decided to put his faith in her love for him, instead.

"I'll tell you," he relented, "Just promise me that you'll come home with me now."

"Fine," she agreed. Noting the crimson and yellow hues beginning to cast across the sky, she knew he would have nowhere to run. "But you'll tell me on the way home. Take the long way. Going through Chinatown alone should give you plenty of time. Clocks ticking. Start now."

"Now? Like, right now?"

"Yes," she said grabbing her purse. "Either we do this now, or I'll take a taxi home. The choice is yours."

With a heavy sigh, he put on his suit jacket slowly as he prepared himself to speak about the woman who had become the bane of his existence. At least she can't walk away from me while in the car, he soothed himself.

"Okay. Shall we? I guess I'll be taking a note out of your play book…or should I say, out of my old one," he replied. Opening the door, he began his story, "It was the day I found out her cancer was spreading…"

You Can't Outsmart a Fox

"I'm sorry, Lisa. But what do you mean it's spreading? I thought you said everything was under control?" I asked.

"This happens. Sometimes we think we have a handle on things, and then they spiral," she said. Her dark hair shaking with the disappointment that danced across her face.

"No. I'm sorry, but I can't accept that. The last time you checked, you said things were looking well. And now you're telling me that it's spreading. How?"

"The last time we met, I said that the tumors in her lungs were shrinking. The others, however, were neither increasing in size, nor decreasing. Things change. And cancer can sometimes be unpredictable," Dr. Navarro said gently. "Look… at this point, our only choice is to either attack this thing more aggressively—"

"No," I heard her say faintly. The sound of her voice projected just as weakly as her physical state.

"What do you mean, no?" I asked. The compression of her words weighed heavily on my chest.

"Ben, I won't do it," she said.

"Momma, no. You can't give up, now. You have to fight this—"

"It's stage four, Ben. It's in my brain now. It's over."

"No. No. No!" I spoke. I could feel my head shaking, but the stress of her defeat began to take me to that place that held so much pain, and I could feel myself becoming unrooted.

"I can't do this anymore," she said weakly, "I'm tired, son. I'm so tired."

For six months I held out hope. She was going to beat it, just as she had before—a knowledge I hadn't known. Her battle had been silent. The days she pretended to be enthralled in new hobbies and ventures, were instead, spent circumventing our family's ability to discover the truth about her illness. And when she had fallen into remission, things went on as they were, until the day her cancer returned, and she sought me out to aid her in evading the woman who held my heart.

As the months passed, I learned to hold on to the spirit of her past—if she made it into remission before, she could do so again. It was something I convinced myself of, because without her, I knew that my love would cease to be. And I couldn't let that happen. Not when we had come so far and found each other again. So, I became part of her scheme, and defied my instincts to tell my love. I used my mother in-law's former remission to rationalize my deception. And I watched as my wife's mother withered away with each cycle of chemo. What was supposed to heal her, instead, trampled her body and determination. Now as I sat before her, watching her hope dwindle as she came to terms with her mortality, I felt the intensity of the aftermath of my secrecy creeping forth. Like a thief in the night, it was there, ready to steal the joy I'd cultivated with my wife. I wasn't ready. I needed her to fight. Not only for herself, or my children, who loved her deeply. Nor for me—the man who thought of her as his own mother. I needed her to fight for the woman who breathed her very essence and strength from her. A woman—who seemed so frail and small now. I needed her to fight for her.

"Ma, please?" I pleaded, "Can we at least give it a try? You know I'll be there every step of the way. Just like I promised."

"One more round. That's all, Ben. I mean it," she said. "That's all I got in me. I don't want to live out the rest of my time being sick. The chemo…it's just too much. I'm tired. I just want to live the last of the time I have left in peace with my family," she said, grasping my hand.

The tight grip she once had, now grasped me listlessly, signifying the toll her journey had taken on her body. The once vibrant woman who nursed my wounds alongside her daughter with a vigor and love that only a mother could muster, was unable to angle her head towards my face. Her mahogany-colored skin had lost its luster some time ago. And as I stroked her cheek gently and took in the gauntness of her face, for her sake, I knew that I had to respect her decision; but I couldn't let go. I still held out hope.

"Okay. Okay, Ma. If that's what you want," I said trying to hide my fragility, as I submitted to my reality.

"It's what I want, son," she said, squeezing my hand as tight as she could, as if she were willing me to accept her fate, just as she had.

Accepting the nod of my head, she rose slowly from her place beside me. Her movements were nervy and languid, and as she reached the door, she gripped it tightly to steady herself. Reaching out to her, I used my body as a shield to prevent her fall. I had long become a means of aid—using my frame as a vessel to bring her to and fro—an act she still rebelled against. Swatting my hand gently, she said weakly, "I got it, you sit back down. Now if you'll excuse me, I'm going to go visit with Barbra and Gail while I'm here."

"I'll come with you, Ma," I replied.

I was overdue for a visit with Ms. Barbra myself, since she'd been admitted into the hospital. Although she still had her faculties, her cancer had ravished her, just as it had done my mother in-law. Despite the intensity of her illness, Barbra had the spirit of a mare. In the short time we'd spent with her, she'd become a friend to my mother in-law and I both. She had come of age during the free-love movement of the 60s—a product of the son of an English gentleman and his teenage housekeeper. The sight of her pale skin in contrast to her mother's tawny color, was enough to infuriate the man she would come to know as her grandfather. I remember her saying, "As father told it, Grandfather was so furious that he cast Mother out. During that time, it was unseemly for a man of Father's station to fall for someone like Mother. So, Grandfather paid her a small sum to leave with me. But it wasn't long before Father came after her. He left quietly with Mother and I in tow. It was some years before he saw Grandfather again."

Her parents stayed together and eventually settled in their Brooklyn brownstone, until a drunk driver stole their lives when she was eighteen years old. She lived in their home now with her daughter, Abigail, whom she had at the tender age of twenty-two, with her college sweetheart, Samuel. He was killed in action during the Vietnam War. He meant the world to her, and as she put it, "was the greatest love I'd ever known." And she could never bring herself to marry again. During rough days, I came to look forward to Ms. Barbra's stories. She had lived a life full of love, loss, grief, triumph, and adventure. And like my mother in-law and Abigail, she'd found the resilience to carry on, in a way, I'd still yet to master.

I became in awe of them and enthralled in the tales they told. Tales of their conquests and defeats. Beautiful women, who were all so different. Yet they shared similar stories that were probably experienced by many women since the beginning of time.

And with the knowing exchanges between the two women before me now, something told me that I would be taking a rain check on a visit with

Ms. Barbra and Ms. Abigail.

"No, Benjamin. You stay here," my Anita said, "I believe she has something to say to you."

"Why do I feel as though I'm being ambushed?" I replied.

"Please, son," she pled, "Do it for me?"

As she trudged out the door, I didn't understand why, then, but I felt my fight go with her. "So, what do you want?" I said with more animosity than I intended.

While her deep-set hazel-eyes held remorse, they couldn't hide the quiet indignation resonating behind them, "What I want isn't relevant, but what she wants is, Ben," she replied.

"I really don't have time for this. Right now, I should be up there with her, hanging out with Ms. Barbra and getting an earful. Her visit is over. So, I'm going—"

"Ben, please," she said grabbing my hand. "I need you to sit. And I also need you to listen." She didn't release her hold until I settled back in my chair. One, that just moments ago held so much promise. But in that moment, it acted as a prison. Holding me hostage so that I would face a reality, I was not yet ready to surrender to.

"What, Lisa?! What do you want from me?!" I snapped.

"Listen, Ben…we've been friends for a long time…and this is just as hard for me as it is for you, because I love you all. You…Colette…the kids. And you know how much I love and care for her. But Anita…she's done. She's been fighting this disease for some time, and now it's run its course."

Looking at her now, one would never know that she was once a shy and reclusive bookworm. When we first met during our undergraduate years, I knew that she would be brilliant. Her attention to detail and innovation was admirable, and we developed a partnership that saw the both of us through those first few years of school, where childhood makes way to adulthood. Despite a bond developed through shared interest, her connection and friendship to my wife and the rest of our family made our relationship steadfast. It was one that grew to transcend the confounds of what could have been a season in time. And as much as I respected her knowledge and skill, it did nothing to ease the turmoil brewing inside me. I could not bring myself to accept what she was trying to convey to me.

"No. No, no, no, no, no! You're not understanding what you're asking of me, Lisa!" I cried.

"I understand just as well as you do, Ben," she said resentfully, "You think this is easy for me? You of all people should know otherwise."

"And you should know that I'm not giving up on her. I can't, dammit!"

"Ben, this isn't one of your servicemembers from your support group or a patient from your practice," she said slowly, as if she were calculating her words. "Anita is terminal. The best thing we can do, is to do what she's asked."

"So… you're telling me that I'm supposed to give up on the woman who has been a mother to me? Who loves my children? Gave me my wife? I don't know if I can, Lisa. And what about, Colette? Things are already…" I started, unable to finish my words. The lump in my throat grew wildly as I tried to mask my fear and subdue the tears that threatened to fall.

"You wouldn't be giving up on her. You'd be allowing her to live her last moments as she sees fit, and with dignity."

"What about what you said before? About attacking it aggressively?"

"It wouldn't do anything. At best it may prolong things a couple of months, but it isn't the way she wants things to be—"

"She'll do it. I'll make sure of it."

"Dammit, Ben! You're being a selfish prick!" she raved.

"No. I'm trying to save her life!" I said incensed, "You don't get it, do you? I need her to get better. I didn't go through all of this to watch her throw in the towel now."

"You? Now I see why she came to me first," she replied harshly, "She knew you'd pull this crap! Just like she knew she was getting worse."

"Came to you, huh? So, I was right? You two were in cahoots with each other. To do what? Make me wave a flag of defeat?" I said mockingly. "I hate to break it to you ladies, but I don't scare nor give in easily. She of all people should know that."

"This isn't your choice, Ben."

"Look, I'm just trying to understand something here, *Dr. Navarro*… you've always spoken about how hard you fight for your patients…how you encourage them to fight…and now—"

"Using formalities now, I see," she said. I could tell that I hurt her, but I could'nt see past reason. In those moments, I felt as though she held my future in her hands. It was a loss of control; I was not ready to concede.

"How else would you like me to address the woman who isn't going to bat for my mother-in-law, like all of her other patients?"

"You know what, as your friend I would just like to tell you that you're being an asshole, and you're not being fair…to neither Anita nor me," she said fuming. "Look, she isn't just my patient, Ben…Anita is like a mother to me…my friend. And as her friend, I must respect her wishes, even when I don't want to."

"And as her doctor?" I asked.

"Considering how things are going, it would still be the same, Ben," she sighed. "Truthfully, I never should have taken her case to begin with. But I thought I could fix it and make her better again, just as before. It was foolish of me. And now we're all paying the price for it," she said sadly.

"I just thought that you would want to fight as hard as I—"

"That isn't fair, Benjamin! You're all my family… especially since… look, Anita is just as much a mother to me as she is to Colette and Kami. The girls are my best friends. No matter where I've been in the world, that woman has always looked out for me, and Colette and Kami have always accepted me. So don't you dare act as if this isn't hard for me too. You think I don't know what you're going through? I'm deceiving them too. The two women who are more of a sister to me than my own. And they may never forgive me. So don't think for a minute that you're the only one being swallowed up by guilt, here."

In my heart, I knew that she was right—that I wasn't being fair to her. The woman I called my friend. For as long as she could remember, Lisa's sexuality had been a fire burning within her that she had tried her best to quell. But the stringent way in which she restricted herself, sparked a need that thrashed inside her recklessly—like a budding flame trampling through a forest. Like me, her inability to let go of the love and life that excited the very fiber of her being, caused her to lose the cover and safety of her family, to which she found within the home of Anita and her daughters. Within the shelter of Anita, she got through medical school and went on to have a successful practice with her wife abroad in Lisbon. But the call for home was too strong, and she was drawn back to our city, conveniently when Anita became sick the first time.

"She's my mother too, Lisa. I can't lose her. And, what about Colette…" I whimpered. Tears burned my vision, as I tried my hardest to come to grips with what was happening.

"I know, Ben. Out of all people, you know that I get it. But do you understand what you're asking her to do?" she asked softly. "She shouldn't have to live the rest of the moments she has with you…with all of us, in misery. Now, she's giving you one round, and that's one too many if you ask me, all things considered."

"How long does she have?"

"Ben…look, why don't we focus on how to spend the rest of the time that we have with her—"

"I said, how long does she have?"

"Six months. Maybe? If we're lucky," she whispered. Her voice was barely audible. And the aversion of her eyes was enough to make me bolt. Getting up, I heard the faint sound of her voice echoing through my consciousness with the sound of the door closing behind me, "I'm so sorry, Ben," it came, numbing my body and weakening my knees.

Making my way to the waiting area, my desire to hear stories of the past had waned with the weight of Lisa's words. Six months was all I had to prepare for a loss, I wasn't sure I could endure. Reality hit like cut glass against my skin—stinging me with the searing hot edge of the time I could not control. *Six months. Colette will only have six months. She'll never forgive me for this*. The words crashed and swirled in my mind, causing me to become dizzy, as my breathing increased harshly, signifying that my anxiousness would soon spiral, causing me to lose myself. *Get a grip, Ben. Think. What can you do? There's nothing. Nothing. There's nothing you can do*, echoed again and again, like a melody playing the roughshod truth I was desperately trying to avoid.

"Ben? Ben? Are you okay?"

The words came lightly. Breaking through the fog of panic that rapidly engulfed me. Turning my head towards the voice that reverberated through my dread, I found myself staring back at an unexpected, yet familiar face. "Sarah?" I uttered confusedly. My voice cracking under the strain of the impending fate of my family—the weight of which, made me feel as though I was being crushed from within.

"Are you okay, Ben? You don't look so good," she asked, placing her hand atop mine, the weight of it lightly pressed my hand deeper into the armrest, I had not realized I clenched so harshly. *When did I get here?*

At some point in my haze, I had made my way into the chair that now sat beside the one she had planted herself in. "I saw you walk in. I tried getting your attention, but you seemed… I don't know. Geez, you're sweating bullets. Oh no, you're not the one who's sick, are you?" she asked.

"No. Anita is," I said absently.

In my moment of weakness, I had betrayed the secret I'd held onto, sending shock waves of guilt through me. However, with the release of my words escaping the bounds of my mind, I began to feel lighter. And with the weight of my shackles harboring the truth finally undone, I sat as my breathing evened and the haziness that had me transfixed in a spell of pain lifted, making my vision clear enough to see the relief dance across her face.

"*Baruch HaShem*. My stomach dropped. I thought that you were—"

"No. I'm fine. But although I may not be sick, my mother-in-law, whom I love dearly, is ill, so a sorry would suffice," I snapped. The disgust I felt at her insensitivity must have cloaked my face tightly, because she spoke in haste, trying to remedy my irritation.

"I…I didn't mean anything by it, Ben. I care for you. That's all. Our families are friends, so of course I wouldn't…look, I'm sorry you're going through this. All of you. How is Colette taking it?"

The tears that threatened to fall were instantaneous, as the sound of her name invoked a wave of emotions that rattled me senseless, rocking me in a slumber of fear and panic, I had not experienced in years, "She doesn't know—"

"What? What do you mean, she doesn't know? How does she not know that her mother is sick?"

"She doesn't know, okay? Anita made it perfectly clear that Colette and Kami couldn't know until she saw fit," I bit out. My emotions getting the better of me, the swell of it grew uncontrollably, threatening to swallow me whole and pull me under. "Anita…well…she thought…she thought she would beat it this time. You know? And I was stupid enough to believe it would happen. I should have told her. I should have told Colette. Now everything is messed up."

"Ben you're not making any sense."

As if possessed, my mouth poured out the secrets that bounded me to the treachery I felt I'd bestowed upon my wife. I spoke of the months of helplessness that held me tightly in its grasp, as I watched Anita struggle to hold on to the life she knew, and the future I now knew would never come. I told Sarah of the toll it had taken on me—my secret. How it weakened me and turned me away from the feel of my wife's touch. I couldn't help but push Colette away; because how could I accept such love and tenderness, when I kept the truth of her mother's illness from her. How could I enjoy the feel of my wife's touch, when the very sight of her delicate face, seemed to tighten the grips of my guilt around my neck like a noose. Forever constricting, tighter and tighter, as the weight of my conscience pulled me down as heavily as a body swaying lifelessly from the gallows. In time, my only relief came from being away from the one person who had always made me feel whole; and it caused a friction so deep within us, it made me shudder.

My agony flowed as my words echoed my pain—the changes in me had made me complicit in the destruction of my wife's confidence, causing her to now pull away from me, in turn to me turning from her. And as I confessed my grievances to Sarah, I became committed to the idea that Colette had knowledge of my omissions. In my mind, I was sure that my love knew just how far I'd gone in betraying her—to hide her mother's truth. A truth that had not shielded her as I hoped, but instead, hung a shroud between us that I could not see a way through. And I knew that was why she no longer melded into me. It is why she no longer sought my gaze. She didn't even accept my touch… at least when I had the strength to seek her out. It was why I felt her walking apprehensively towards our future. I wondered now if the way her head hung low was because she knew that the enigma that held me captive, was destroying me, as I had been destroyed once before. My words revealed my façade of certainty for what it was, as I speculated whether I had scared her away from me—this time for good. And as my tongue released my anguish, my mind began to hold on to the possibility that we would not come back to each other. It made my heart weep, for I knew that the cost of my silence had not been worth the trouble it caused.

With each word that passed through my lips, I felt the panic and angst leave my body, as I passed along my burden, "Now you see. You see why everything is fucked? She barely looks at me, and when she does, it's like she's waiting for me to lose it. Who knows…maybe I will. Maybe I'll finally buckle," I said with a shrug. "I can't. I can't do this anymore."

"So why don't you just tell Colette? I mean…It's not your responsibility, really. It's her mother after all."

"No. I can't. I gave my word to Anita, and I intend to keep it," I replied, "And you better not tell Colette either."

"I would never do that, Ben. I couldn't betray your confidence in that way. You know how much I value our friendship," she said, "But as your friend, I must tell you, you can't go on like this. Let someone else take the reins. I wish I could. I mean, Anita does have a husband you know. You shouldn't have to do this."

"No. No way. That asshole has done enough."

"I don't understand," she said softly.

Although I could tell she was prying, the weight of my worry wouldn't allow me to practice restraint, "He lost that opportunity when he decided to dishonor their marriage," I said disgusted, "Piece of shit! While she's sick, nonetheless!"

"No!" she squealed. Shock washed over her face when she realized what my words implied, "Surely, Ben, this isn't true! They've always seemed so… so solid. In-love."

"Yeah. I thought so too," I said resentfully, "But, imagine after hearing the news that you are no longer in remission, you see the man who is your husband…the father of your children, with another woman?"

"I don't…I don't know what to say," she replied.

"He crushed her. So much so, she didn't even bother telling him about her condition, so she did the next best thing…she told me. Now here we are. Drowning in this shit show," I snickered. My laughter filled the air, as the bitterness that resonated inside me turned to tears, that long needed to spill, to which she caressed my cheek and wiped them away.

"I'm sorry, Ben. You shouldn't have to go through this," she said empathetically, with a tenderness I'd never seen from her before. For a moment I allowed myself to feel the warmth of her touch, until the guilt of my submission to the feel of the weight of her hand, collided against me as cruelly as a winter's storm.

"I'm sorry," I said, removing her hand abruptly, "I don't know what came over me."

"You don't have to apologize, Ben," she exclaimed, "I understand." The compassion that welled in her eyes just moments ago, turned into despondency—and I was bemused by the obvious change in her demeanor.

"You know, all this time I've been talking about my problems…but I didn't think to ask you, what brought you here. And I'm sorry about that. I'm not usually this self-absorbed… at least, I'd like to think that I'm not," I rambled. "Oh goodness, I hope that you aren't sick, Sarah. Is that why you're here?"

My sudden shift in concern seemed to appease her, causing a glow of satisfaction that set her eyes ablaze. "No. It isn't me, thankfully. We are in the same boat, it seems. I thought you would have concluded that already."

"I'm not sure that I follow," I stated.

"Really? But I received the basket you sent," she said. It wasn't long before she realized her mistake, and her eyebrows furrowed together in displeasure, "I see. I would have thought she would have at least told you what's been going on before signing your name to a gift."

"As I told you, I've been busy and we haven't been at our best, so either it escaped her, or she just didn't bother. Either way, you can tell me now," I said evenly, as I realized that Colette had already saw to Sarah and her family.

"It's Isaac… he's the one who's sick. And I, like you, are the one who is stuck dealing with this mess," she said angrily, "But at least I'll be free of him soon. It won't be much longer now."

"While I understand why you feel the way you do, I am not stuck, as you've stated. I made my choice to be here for her, because I love Anita, just as I do my own mother," I said as heat rose to my face.

"I'm sorry. I didn't mean it that way. But you of all people know… I mean, I'm sure you've heard…things," she said softly. Her eyes casted downward to hide her pain. The burden of being attached to Oded Cohen was no secret. Although her husband was as kind and docile as a lamb, it was his father that remained an issue for all, which is why I understood her relief that her time with him was coming to an end.

Once a stately built man, Isaac Cohen had become just as round as his pliable son. But unlike Oded, the former Cohen's height and angered disposition, made his stockiness more menacing. Even as a child I did not like the man. And as I grew older and noted his cruel ways and foul manners, I learned to despise him just as everyone else did.

He'd been a long acquaintance of both our fathers—Sarah's and mine. Growing up together in Israel, the men that Sarah and I had come to know as heads of our respective households, had spent their boyhood trying to be a family to a friend, whose childhood left him the scarred and dubious man I'd come to know. Isaac's life had been harsher than most. He hadn't the gentleness of a mother's love, nor the guidance of a father's heart. His mother left the world before he reached his second birthday. And as my father stated, she'd worked herself into an early grave due to Isaac's father's inability to maintain a livelihood. He was more interested in an opium pipe than he was in providing for his family; giving way to Isaac raising himself the best way he knew how.

Despite the guiding hands of my father's family, spending his formative years in the cradle of the streets, rather than the warmth of his parents' love and protection, made Isaac a cruel and callous man. He was the type that demanded respect and yet gave none. And he ruled his wife and children with an iron fist and discipline that brought on Oded's passive nature. This allowed for the destruction of his and Sarah's marriage. Like everyone else in his family, Isaac's need for control drove Sarah into submission with a viciousness.

The first time Isaac's heavy hands landed across her cheek, bruising her skin, made Sarah run into the comforts of my family's home, where she had gained the care of my mother. She awaited what she thought would be a swift extraction. Instead, her father's words were crushing, as his sensibilities of providing her with a good match and maintaining the family's name, outweighed her need for an escape. And although initially, Sarah believed herself capable of being with someone like Oded, she realized that her ability to maintain propriety with a husband who would allow such cruelty against her, was a life she wouldn't be able to endure. So, from the moment her father refused to grant her sanctuary, her disdain for the man she called her husband, grew to a hatred that would not whither.

And without the protection of her husband, Sarah found herself in a misery that only seemed to lighten when she indulged herself in her craving for being menacing herself. It was as if the distraction of everyone else's life, served as a passage to freedom that was not her own. She lived through them all—playing them like chess pieces on a board that only she was master of. In time, she'd grown to manipulating those around her to suit her need for escape.

"I understand. I will say that I hope his illness has softened him a bit. Made it easy on you all… you know? I find that most people at the end are reflective during this time. At the very least, they want to make amends for the things they've done." I stated.

"I wish I could say that were true. If anything, it's made him more merciless than he's ever been. It's like he's angry with us for reaping the consequences of decades of chain smoking and heavy drinking," Sarah said bitterly.

"May HaShem grant you all peace during this difficult time."

"We'll have peace when he's gone," she said more to herself than me. A sense of tranquility washed over her, as she reflected over the thought of being rid of the man who'd been the source of her suffering, for the better part of fifteen years.

"I wish I had more to say that could help, but what does one say under these circumstances? How are we to cope watching someone wither away like this?"

"We can always lean on each other," she suggested timidly.

"I don't know about that, Sarah," I replied.

Her intentions may have been well meaning, but there was something in the urgency in which she said it that caused me to take pause. Although the expression, time heals all wounds may apply to many, the history between Sarah and me, made any semblance of a relationship beyond common courtesy, a dubious one.

"Seriously, think about it, Ben. Who else would empathize with what we're going through, better than we can?"

"While I see your point, I still don't think it's a great idea. I've already shared too much as it is."

"Look. Open your phone—"

"Excuse me?"

"Open your phone. I'll put my number in, and if you ever need to have a chat, just text or call," she said eagerly, holding out her hand to grasp my device. "Come on, Ben. There isn't any harm in having it. We can honestly help each other."

Although her acts of kindness previously had always been sinister in nature, given the circumstances and the toll my secret was taking, I considered it, "Maybe…if things get to be too much…it might be good to have someone who understands, to talk to," I said.

As I cautiously handed over my phone, I spotted Anita in the distance. She looked weary. Her eyes were solemn and seemed to be holding back tears. Excusing myself, I walked over to the woman who'd captured my heart, just as her daughter did decades ago.

"She's gone, Ben. She's gone," she said as she wept.

"Who's gone, Ma?"

"Barbra. We were just talking… and then she…"

Taking her into my arms, I held on to her tightly, trying to take her pain away, "I'm sorry, Ma.I know she'd become a wonderful friend to you. A friend to us both. I hate this…this disease. It's not fair!"

"I know, son. I know. But she's in a better place, and at least I got to say goodbye. I only wish you were there to say your goodbyes too," she said.

Pausing in her tracks, she wiped away her tears. Her face, once marred with grief, was now masked with a fierceness of protection that only a mother could muster. It wasn't until I felt the heavy weight of an object piercing my back that I realized my mistake. In my rush to see to Anita, I had forgotten my phone with Sarah.

"Hello, Anita," Sarah said lightly. Never reaching her eyes, the smile on her face caused my mother-in-law to scowl in scrutiny, as she tried to gage her motives. "Are you okay? You look unwell."

I buckled under the weight of her gaze, as the study of Anita's eyes locked with mine—cutting deeply, as she tried to examine whether I had shared our secret. "I suppose anyone would look sick walking around here. But since you want to be nosy, I just lost my friend," she said tightly, "I'm guessing you're here with Mr. Cohen? I heard from my daughter that he was unwell. How is he doing?"

"I'm sorry that you've lost your friend. In respect to my father in-law, well, he's terminal," Sarah stated.

"I'm sorry to hear that. My prayers are with you and your family—"

"Don't be. It is HaShem's will," Sarah said callously.

"Still, it is never easy to lose a loved one," Anita replied, "Ben, it's been a long day, we should be heading back home. I promised Gail that I would help with the funeral arrangements for her mother."

"Of course. It's not a problem. Can you just give me a moment, Ma?"

Raising her brows and scanning her eyes between us, I was sure that she would give protest. But my fears were quelled by the sound of Sarah's voice, "You know, it sure was nice running into you today, Anita. I do wish you better days," she said casually. Turning her attention towards me and with a wink, she said, "Here, Ben. I think this is yours."

Taking my phone back into my hand, I tried my hardest to keep my wits as the tension between the two began to rise due in part to Anita's peaking curiosity, and Sarah's amusement at my discomfort. "Thanks," I replied, "I didn't—"

"You must have dropped it after showing me pictures of the kids," she said blithely. It was in this moment, in the way she lied so easily, that I should have made it my last encounter with Sarah Cohen—a decision I didn't make, and one that I grew to regret later. "Don't be a stranger. Remember… anytime, Ben. I'm hear if you need me."

Watching her saunter off, I felt the heat of Anita's piercing eyes against my back, "I never liked that heifer," Anita stated venomously.

"I know, Ma. I'm not very fond of her either."

"You be careful with that one, now. You hear me, Benjamin? I don't know what she's up to, but if it's anything like it's been before, you need to watch yourself."

"I got it, Ma. I promise," I said soothingly, pulling her hand to rest on my arm, "Come on. Let's get you home. I think there's some ice cream with our names on it."

Revelations

"Pull over," she said with a calm so eerie, it made him shudder.

"Wait? What? Pull over? Why? I haven't even finished—"

"I don't need to hear anymore, Benjamin. The fact that…you know what…just let me out."

"I'm not pulling over. Not right now. Not while you're like this," he said gesturing towards her. The fury in her eyes made him tremor with fear, for if she were this angry at what was currently revealed, he knew that he would lose her forever for the things she did not yet know.

"Benjamin, I mean it! Either you pull over now, or I will be out of this car at the next light," she said. Her nostrils flared wildly, and the amber flecks in her eyes shone brightly, letting him know that he should not tempt his temptress and test her bravado.

"Okay. Okay," he said holding his hands up defensively. Pulling into the next available spot, Benny ignored the loud blaring horns chastising his abrupt departure from the steady flow of traffic behind him. Removing her seatbelt quickly, he had not been at a full stop before she darted off; forcing him to rush in a frenzy, so that he didn't lose her through the landscape of mature trees and winding mazes of pathways, in the park he now found himself next to.

As he made his way through the crowd, he took in the lushness of the place that was once their sanctuary. There were many times he found her there, belly in hand, as if comforting the life they created together. He never heard what she whispered to their eldest son during those times, but he imagined it was filled with promises that he knew she'd long fulfilled.

Following the familiar path, he found her at the clearing below the castle, where they would both go to find peace—her hands wrapped around herself, as she always did when she needed comfort.

Approaching her from behind, he brought his hands lightly about her shoulders, testing her to see where her fury lied. "I thought I'd find you here," he whispered.

"I really wish you wouldn't do that," she murmured.

"Do what?" he asked knowingly, pressing his body against hers, so that they may gain strength from each other. But instead of sinking into him, she moved abruptly, forcing him to stumble forward from losing the stability of her frame, "Can you at least talk to me, please, Colette?"

"Oh, now you want to talk. How extraordinary. I wonder why that is?" she said. Her sarcasm, rooted in pain, lent her mouth a snarl that made her appearance ominous as she faced him, forcing him to recoil.

"Come on, Cole. Don't be that way."

"And what way might that be, Benjamin?"

"I understand that you're upset, but I hate it when you're mad at me. You know this," he whimpered.

"How could I not be? You shared with her, something that should have been shared with me long before I'd become privy to what was wrong with my mother. I mean…all this time you've been telling me that you kept her condition away from me because you were trying to protect me… and come to find out… you told her? Of all people? That bitch?!" she raged. "No, darling. None of this was to protect me at all. It was for you. The way it always is."

"What's that supposed to mean? Of course I did it for you."

"Bullshit, Benjamin! Ain't no way. There's no way," she fumed. "Outside of your need to be a fucking noble martyr of duty, everything you did related to me and my mother's illness, you did it for you! I can't believe what I'm hearing right now—you know you've always had a selfish streak, but this is beyond what I could ever fathom."

"Look, I'm only doing what you asked me to do. And instead of allowing me to finish so that we can move forward from…whatever this…this is, you're lashing out at me," he stated.

"Why would I let you finish? You told me everything I need to know. That you didn't care about me. Not truly. In fact, I'm not sure that you've ever cared about me at all."

"I wish you would stop saying that. The only thing I ever do is think of you."

"No. You don't think of me because you care, Benjamin. You think about how my suffering impacts you. How it would break me. And not because of what it would do to me, but what it means for you. What you would lose. You're so scared of not having the perfect wife, that you treat me like I'm a fragile piece of glass. As if I'll break," she sneered.

"I don't know what to say, Colette," he whispered, feeling defeated. He knew there was legitimacy to her words, and he hadn't the gumption to defy what she said, neither could he find the words to placate her.

"I just don't understand. After everything we've been through… all that I've given you and tried to be to you… for you…you still couldn't give me the only thing I've ever wanted. You couldn't trust me—believe in me. That I love you and would always do everything in my power to be with you, no matter what happens," she said vehemently. "But the only thing you've ever done was take my love for granted. Because apparently, no one loves more than you, right? No. Not as strongly. Not as deeply. We're all so easily tainted and disloyal. Everyone else crumbles under the strain and pressure of the world and would leave you because of their weakness. Is that it? But not you. You're special. You're not like us imperfect, feeble souls. No. Not you. Not, Benjamin Lati. You know, you got some real abandonment issues that your ass needs to work out."

"I don't believe that. I don't believe that at all, Cole. I know that you love me. Truly I do."

"You could have fooled me. Why else would you always cut me out?!" she said sadly.

The coolness of the air and heat of her anger caused her to shiver, and he reached out to her, "Come here, let me hold you—"

"No. Don't touch me, Benjamin!"

"Please. Don't be stubborn, Colette. You're obviously cold. The sun has set. And it's only going to get colder," he tried reasoning with her. "Can you at least take my jacket, motek?"

"Don't you motek, me," she fumed, "I'd rather freeze. Fuck you very much."

"Really, Colette? This is childish! You're being completely unreasonable. Just take my fucking jacket," he replied.

"You didn't say, please."

"Can you at least take my fucking jacket…*please*?" he repeated.

"No," she said nastily, "Like I said, I'd rather freeze than to take anything from you, you asshole."

"You are really trying my patience," he said heatedly.

Taking his jacket from his person, he walked over, wrapping it around her forcefully and pulled her tightly into his arms. The man that he was, could never allow his wife to sit in discomfort—so she was going to take his chivalry, whether she wanted to or not.

"You're so infuriating!" she criticized.

"You're right about only one thing," he said cautiously, waiting for her body to release tension, "I didn't trust that you would come back to me, if you lost yourself the same way I have…in the past. And it's not because I don't trust that you love me, Cole. It's because, I know what it's like. I know how it feels to watch someone you love…care about…leave you. I know what it's like to watch someone die. It eats away at you. Swallows you whole, until there's nothing left. And I thought, why would you come back to me, if I was barely able to come back to you?"

Her body relaxed in his arms, as the words he spoke resonated and comforted her into a quiet submission. Finally, breaking the tension between them, she spoke, "I'm not like you, Benjamin. And I don't mean that to make you feel less than. I know that you've been through things that I can't even imagine. So, I know why it was hard for you—"

"And you haven't? You act as if your life has been easy, Colette," he whispered passionately in her ear. "It is because I know what you've been through, and the… the loss that I've had to endure…that I knew exactly what was coming for you if you knew. I couldn't let you feel that kind of pain, love. I couldn't risk losing you in that way. Destroying you like it did me. Look…truthfully? I just couldn't watch you, watch her die, okay? I couldn't. That's a level of pain I couldn't bear. Seeing you in that way."

"It still wasn't your choice to make, Benjamin. You took away time that I will never get back."

"And I know that now. Trust me. I do. Which is why, as we've discussed before, I will try my hardest never to shut you out like that again," he said softly, "But let's be real here, Colette—this wasn't just my decision. It was also your mother's choice to keep you in the dark."

"You didn't have to go along with her and help her do it either."

"I had a responsibility to your mother. I gave her my word—"

"Who cares?! You're always speaking about your duty to this person…or that person, or something or another. What's right. What's wrong —"

"It's who I am, Colette! You know this already. From the moment you've known me, you've known this to be," he said, the tension in his body growing as he felt the need to defend his character.

"If it's who you are, then how come it never applies to me? What about your duty to me? Your wife!" she hounded. Looking up at him, she found that he would not meet her eyes.

"The only thing I can do is say sorry, but I don't know that I entirely am," he said. His voice barely audible, he braced himself for the eruption he knew would come.

"What?! How can you not be sorry, Benjamin?!" she raged. Breaking herself from him, she tried to restrain her fury.

"Can you hear me out for a moment, please? Don't jump to conclusions, motek. I'm begging you," he pled.

"This better be good. You got one chance to explain yourself. Just. One."

It took a moment for him to find the right words, and even then, he was skeptical of their merit, "Cole," he said hesitantly, "While I am sorry about the pain it caused you…I think I would do it all again, because she wouldn't have had anyone else, love. I mean…she…she didn't have him. And she didn't want you and Kami to spend the time you had with her, waiting for her to die. Being afraid every day. She wouldn't allow it. If I didn't agree, there wouldn't have been anyone there for her. And even with me there, it was hard."

"And she could have had me too, you know? Had you given me the chance to be there for her, I would have been there. For you both. You know this. Instead, you told that wench! You allowed her to have what belonged to me!" she replied. "Why her? Out of all people, you chose her to tell. You had so many other options, and you told her? About my mother's illness. Things about us. That was personal, Benjamin! You let her into our lives in a way, she never should have been."

"I don't know why I did. I knew better. I did," he said frankly, "But there was no one else, and I was struggling. I felt myself buckling under the pressure. And so, I pushed you away. I know I did. I wasn't strong enough, Colette. I can admit that. But with the distance between us and seeing Anita that way, I slipped up."

Something in the way he said those words made her take heed. "*I slipped up,*" resonated in her head, and caused the hairs on the back of her neck to stand, sending a chill down her spine. Despite his fervent denial of any wrongdoing previously, the aversion of his eyes away from hers, and the way in which he rubbed his forefinger and thumb together—the way he always did when nervous, trapped her in fear.

"What did you do?" she seethed.

"I don't know what you mean," he replied.

Seeing the rise and fall of her chest, and the fire in her eyes, caused his voice to shake and breathing to stagger. With each passing moment, the quiet that grew between them became like a calm before a storm he was not ready to weather. With a change of her expression, he watched the gears of her mind churn towards the assumption he knew she'd long made, and he knew he had to get ahead of it before her theories spiraled out of control.

"Don't patronize me and insult my intelligence, Benjamin. You know perfectly well what I mean."

"Cole. Please. It's not what you think."

"Now where have I heard this line before? I can't believe you. You lied to me. Right to my face," she said, storming away from him.

She didn't get far before her knees grew weak and folded her towards the ground. The vertigo had come on suddenly, and her body collapsed swiftly into his awaiting arms. She was lucky he'd been behind her to break her fall with his rigid frame. The moment she began creating the void between them, he'd been steady on her trail, picking her up briskly, and placing her on his lap as he sat on a nearby bench.

"Here. Let me help you," he said gently, "What's with you today?"

"You! Do you think this has been a cake walk? You're stressing me out! Now let go of me. I don't want to be here with you anymore," she yelped, struggling against him.

"You could barely walk moments ago. You think I'm going to let you just up and leave? At this hour nonetheless?" he replied.

Scanning the dark skies, she hadn't noticed the night creep upon them. But she was happy for the breeze it afforded her—casting her in a cool blanket that eliminated the heat inching harshly up her body and shocking her back to her senses. She only needed a moment to get her bearings, and then she would be off; to where, she was still uncertain, but she knew that it could not be with him.

Prior to this new revelation, she'd begun to concede her anger against him. Although he shared a level of intimacy with Sarah, that should have been reserved for her, it was his duplicity in everything that transpired between the two of them that was breaking her in two. Forcing her mind to run rampant with thoughts of him and Sarah. *What else isn't he telling me? Do I even want to know?*

"Colette, did you hear me? Are you still dizzy?" he asked.

His concern seemed foreign to her now that she knew of his deceit. She reflected on the many times she'd seen them together at one event or another. She'd been in a haze of defeat then—a time when his secrecy became the veil that divided them, and they no longer sought each other out. Yes. It all made sense now.

The distance he created that found her at his office, conjuring Mae, she now understood, was invoked by stolen glances between the two, when they thought no one was watching. It's what drove him away at night, to which she suspected was into her arms. Her thoughts swayed to her husband, held, and cradled in the lust of a woman who yearned for him since the moment she saw him—it tore her apart. And she wagered, that their affair was the reason for what she captured that night at Mazal's wedding. She saw it now—her haze undone.

Gently, she released his arms from around her waist. Standing, she allowed herself time to be sure of her stability, so that she wouldn't have to rely on him further. Stable now, she removed his jacket and placed it gently in his lap and turned away from him, so that he couldn't see the tears threatening to stain her cheeks.

"Where are you going?" he asked.

"Home. I want to go home and be with my children," she replied.

Although she treaded lightly, her foot seemed weighted, heavy almost, as if they didn't want to leave him. Despite the dread she felt with each stride she took, she knew that getting to their children, would melt it all away. With them she would have peace. At least for the night.

"Our kids, you mean," he said defensively, "They belong to me too."

"I'm not interested in playing semantics with you. You know what I meant," she said heatedly, "Now, if you'll excuse me, I'm leaving."

Grasping her arm, his pull of her towards him was magnetic. Filled with an energy of desperation, she didn't have the vigor to fight. Instead, she allowed herself to be swept away in her anguish and buried herself in his shoulders, as she let her tears flow freely.

"Please don't cry, Cole. I can't stand it when you cry," he begged, "Let me take you home."

"How could you? How could you do this to me, Benjamin? Why wasn't I enough? Haven't I been good to you?" she cried.

"Let me take you home, love. We're not far," he said as he lifted her into his arms, "At least let me do that. I promise, I will drop you off and leave. I won't stay. Okay?"

The light nod of her head gave him the assent he needed to trudge forward to their car. Her tears rained down heavily, like hot coals, burning the exposed skin of his neck, crushing him and withered his façade. *She's going to leave me. It doesn't matter what she hears now. I know she's made up her mind.*

"Put me down. I can walk," she sniffled.

Placing her down gently, he settled into a comfortable pace beside her, back to their car. Once inside, he watched her through the window. The streetlights gleaming through the dark of the night, gave him a clear view of her reflection. And like a ghost, it haunted him.

It wasn't long before the silence, sprinkled with the soft sighs and heaves of her sadness, became too much for him to endure and fueled his growing desperation. *I have to fix this. I have one shot. I will not lose my wife,* played heavily in his mind.

"I just wanted to say…um… I know in your mind you believe you've figured out what happened between…um… Sarah and me. I was the same way when things transpired with you and Dominic. And clearly…I was…I was wrong."

"I don't want to hear it, Benjamin. Please. Just leave me alone"

"I can't do that, motek," he responded frankly, "The same way you needed me to trust in you, is the same way I need you to put faith in me. In us. I need you to trust that I would never hurt you in that way."

"I don't know if I can do that, Benjamin. You've been lying this entire time. How can I possibly trust you?" she replied.

"I was afraid. With everything that's happened…I didn't know what to do."

"So, you did sleep with her."

"No. That's not it, Colette."

"Then what happened?! Why would you be so afraid to tell me if you didn't sleep with her? I don't understand."

"If you let me explain, then you'll understand why, okay? Will you let me? For real this time? The whole way through?" he asked.

Although she was apprehensive, the nod of her head gave way to a pressure release of uncertainty, as she braced herself for what she was about to hear, "Go ahead. Not like I'm going anywhere anytime soon."

"Okay," he began, "After your mother's last round of chemo, things quickly took a turn for the worse. Together we concocted the story that she was going to take that trip she had spoken about, and I would go by and care for her. With each day that passed… I don't know… but the weight of it… everything, it was too much. And I felt… I don't know, out of control. We weren't doing well. We barely looked at each other then, so I started talking to Sarah. Only on the phone. To blow off steam, you know? It wasn't until you showed up on your first visit as…Mae, did I see her in person. That was the day your mother decided that she was going to tell you girls… that she…

that she was sick. And I…I was afraid that you would hate me once you knew. So that night after shabbat…you remember? I was already not doing well. I was a dick…I know I was. It's because I thought…well…never mind. Then dinner happened. And that was a disaster because Miriam and I started butting heads—"

"Jesus, Benjamin! Just spit it the fuck out!"

"Okay. Okay. Let me start from the beginning of that day…"

Laid Bare

"From the story you tell, I'm not sure why you're here," I said, placing the notepad in my lap. It was all I could do to diminish the fire burning inside me.

"That was only our beginning, Doc. If it were the whole story, I wouldn't be here," she stated.

"I guess, I should try this again—your marriage seems to have a decent foundation. So, what is actually lacking?" I said feigning curiosity.

I wanted to reach out to her—to let her know that I'm still here for her, even though she couldn't see it. If only she'd realize that my love for her was uncompromised; in-fact, the opposite was true. It was my love for her, that brought us here, and my inability to say so, tore me apart.

"I think the better question is: What changed? And to answer your question? Well, that is another story for another session," she said lightly, "Is there anything else?"

"Why Mae? Why that name?" I asked, breaking the silence between us. Although I was aware of the family name she chose, and the story of the woman it belonged to, I couldn't help but wonder why she didn't come to me as herself.

"Mae is everything that I am not. I need her in order to get through…this."

"What's so wrong with being yourself?"

She closed her eyes, and the breath she took seemed to ignite the strength needed to face the demon before her—I just never thought it would be me.

"She is neither confident nor able. She has neither strength nor courage. She is nothing. At least nothing… to him," she said sadly. The pain in her eyes at the thought of losing my affection for her, broke my heart. Confidence that took years for her to gain, I was shattering. *How did I let it go this far? I'm breaking her. I wish I could tell her. I wish I could fix it. Tell her now, you idiot!*

"Mrs. Lati—"

"Mae. I really would prefer if you called me Mae, Doctor."

"Mae," I corrected myself, "I believe that perhaps we should focus on healing you. The *real* you."

"Oh no. I have to go," she said, standing abruptly.

"But we still have more time for our session—"

"I'm so sorry. I really must run. Today's the sabbath, and I need to get home to get everything ready. See you next week," she said on her way out the door. The woman she called Mae, was no more.

Watching the sway of her hips move in her fitted dress, I wanted nothing more than to grab her and press my body against hers. As the weight of her mother's illness dragged me further into the abyss and her glances became more fleeting, I had taken to sleeping away from her. Our talks, once long and contented, were now languished. It had been sometime since we'd been this close to one another, and despite my distress, my need for her never waned. And while her proximity fueled my loins, her sorrow fed my vexation. *It's gone too far. She thinks I don't love her anymore.*

The sound of my phone ringing tore me away from my thoughts. At first, I welcomed the respite from the images playing in my mind, but the voice on the other end of the line forced me back, like a riptide, drowning me into a trap I couldn't seem to free myself from. "Ben," she called faintly, "It's Anita."

"Oh hey, Ma," I replied.

Although she put on a brave face, she was growing weaker each day. The luster that once captured her beautiful face, was now gone completely. And the magnetism in her voice gave way to a shallow hoarseness that exposed her frailness. I'd taken to spending my evenings with her—an act, that while it brought me great joy, furthered the divide between my love and me. Looking at the hour, I realized why she called; I was so enthralled in my thoughts after the session with my wife, that I'd lost track of time.

"I'm sorry. I know I'm late. I'll be on my way soon. Don't start that episode without me—"

"No, son. That's not why I'm calling," she said. The heavy sigh that escaped, seemed to make her breath more ragged and labored.

"I hope you're not moving around. You're supposed to be resting," I chastised, "I'll get the plants when I arrive. I was thinking about getting some of that kettle corn you like. What do you think?"

"She doesn't need you to come over, Benjamin," his voice blared through the phone, causing my temperature to rise and incite my anger.

"What is he doing there?"

"Now son, don't start," she pleaded, "Do you hear me?"

"I'd do anything for you, Ma. But there better be a good explanation as to why that asshole is there with you," I said heatedly.

"He is my husband, Ben. The father of my children—"

"He is no father to my wife! And all things considered, let's just say, I'm thankful for that, because that means she won't miss him once I get to him."

"What did you say, boy?" he spoke. His voice amplified as his irritation mounted.

"Oh. So, he is on speaker? Great. When I see you, I'm going to kill you for what you did to Ms. Anita," I said vehemently.

"You always were an arrogant, self-righteous little bastard," he exclaimed, "Why don't you stay out of my marriage and worry about yours!"

"I wouldn't have to worry about your marriage and take care of your wife, if you weren't busy sticking your old wrinkly dick into anything that moves! And to think, I respected you… looked up to you—"

"Benjamin, please! That's enough!" Anita said in earnest.

The pain in her words sent shock waves through my system. Like a bucket of ice crashing against my skin, it sent me back to my senses, "I'm sorry, Ma. I didn't mean to upset you. It's just that…never mind. It doesn't matter. I'll be on my way soon, and on my best behavior. Promise," I said carefully, trying my hardest to remain calm and not disturb her peace.

"I don't need you to, son. That's why I called. And that's why he's here," she said hesitantly.

"I don't understand."

"It's time, Ben. It's time we tell them."

Panic surged through me. It pierced me with the heaviness and sharpness of a bull's pointed horns—knocking the wind out of me, as my mind worked to try to delay the inevitable. This day was one I suspended in my thoughts; one, I believed I could will myself through. My own belly of the whale. Yet there I was. Faced with reality. And still, I could not resign myself to her fate, "Why?" I asked. "I'm sure we can wait a week or two. Just until I figure things out."

"We can't wait, Ben! We can't wait any more," she said, "I can barely walk without help now. I don't have any fight left in me. I need to tell my girls, so I can spend this time with them. We did all we could, son."

My heart sank. In a moments time, our lives would be ravished by the harshness and cruelty of her illness, and I had not prepared my love for it. "She's going to hate me," I whispered.

"Oh, no. No, son," she said, "I don't intend her knowing your part. It was my choice to leave her in the dark."

Her voice was low and in a tone of a mother trying to lull her child to sleep, but I could find no solace in her reassurance, "It may have been your idea, Ma, but I also decided to keep it from her as well. And I know my wife—"

"Then you should know, that if anything, our girl has a forgiving heart. And a loyalty to you and our family that is unfathomable," she soothed. "Look, Ben…I've seen a lot in my time on this earth, and I have never seen a love as great as the love you share with my daughter. You will be fine. You'll see. You both will."

"How much time do I have before you tell her?" I muttered.

"I want to tell her as soon as possible, but to be honest, I'm not sure. I don't know how to go about it. How do I tell my baby girl that she won't have her mother anymore?" she whimpered. Although she tried to be stoic, I could hear the sob threatening to escape, "This is why I called you. So, we could talk about how and when to tell her."

"It should be now if you ask me. Call them girls now and get this over with!" I heard him say in the background; the sound of his voice grated harshly at my nerves.

"Did anyone ask you, Kevin?" she replied, "Because I sure as hell didn't."

"And you said you didn't have any fight in you left, Ma?" I laughed.

"For him? I surely do. Just because he's here, doesn't mean that I forgave and forgot. I'm only doing this because my girls will need their father. Otherwise, he can go to hell," she said, exhibiting the same fire I'd seen in her daughter—a fire I feared I may have extinguished. "Listen, I'll try and hold off til tomorrow, alright?"

"I don't have much of a choice, now do I?" I said solemnly, "Are you okay with him there? He doesn't know what you need…your meds and everything else."

"We knew you'd be this way. Lisa sent someone over, so don't you worry about me. You just take care of our girl. Love on her…on each other, the way you used to," I heard her say in the distance. My mind now distracted by the finality of her words. Her voice, delicate and bright, was designed to detract from the inevitable, did nothing to calm me.

"We're at the end, aren't we?" I asked. It was a question I posed more to myself, as I could not stomach the answer, but her audible sigh confirmed my suspicion, "I'm going to go, Ma, if that's okay? I'll see you tomorrow, yeah?"

"Yes. I'll save that episode, just for you."

I'll see you tomorrow—while such an inconspicuous statement to make, seemed silly now. I didn't understand before, but as I stood in the depths of her mortality, I finally understood the meaning of the adage, 'youth is wasted.' People—so hopeful we are; living in our perceived invincibility and dreams of tomorrow, not realizing that for some, tomorrow will never come. And in that moment, I realized that she may not have tomorrow.

"Ma? Wait," I called out.

Reading the urgency in my voice, it was as if she knew from whence my panic came, "Don't worry. I *will* see you tomorrow. You just do what I say now, ya hear? Come back to each other…the way I know you can," she soothed. "I love you, Benjamin. I love you, son. Now get yourself home."

"I love you too," I said to the click of the line.

My body, now limp, played to the tune of emotions that would not allow me reprieve. My throat clogged, reverberated my turmoil as my tears drenched my face. I welcomed it. It was the rush I longed for—a relief that while inexplicable, projected an inconceivable fear. It made me feel alive again—human. It was what I'd been missing that past year. And I knew the only thing that would make me feel whole, was the feel of my love's weight pressed against me. Yet I could not bring myself to make my departure to her. Instead, I found myself walking towards the cabinet, intending to bide my time, and drown my sorrows. Unlocking its doors, I reached for a glass and the decanter that had become my comfort, "It's good to see you again, old friend. At least you've always been here for me," I laughed harshly.

"And here I thought, I was your best friend."

"What?" I said absently.

Although his voice seemed faraway, it startled me from thoughts of her. Chugging the golden-hued liquid, I relished in the warmth it washed over me. Its sting in my throat, offered a much-needed distraction from the impending conversation, I would've much rather not had.

"You sure you really need another?" he asked, peering at the contents of my glass.

"I didn't know you were still here."

"I'm just checking in. I got a call from Ms. Miriam, wondering where you were, so here I am."

"If meddling were a sport, she'd be a champ," I sneered.

"She means well, Ben," he replied, "You're lucky to have her. I mean, so many women in general, who love and care for you."

"Yes. If only you knew how untrue your statement truly was," I heckled. My laughter now resonated within the room, as I reflected on the irony of his words, as the alcohol began to overtake me.

"So, it's true then?" he asked.

"That I'm the biggest asshole on the planet? No? I guess that's not it," I jested. "Well friend... you need to be more specific."

"Well, Miriam seems to think that…look, I can't believe I'm going to say this, but then I saw Colette as she was leaving, and she looked…off—"

"Will you stop rambling and come out with it, please?" I huffed.

"Are you cheating on her?"

"Why would you ask that?"

"Miriam said that you two haven't been… you know…in some time. And that you've been coming home late often or not at all, and I know you're not here. You've been acting weird too, brother. Then I saw Colette's face today as she left—do you really think you need another, Ben?"

"I don't need you to babysit me, Devon. Okay? And to answer your question, no. I am not, nor have I ever cheated on my wife, contrary to what Miriam might believe," I said heatedly.

This was the last thing I needed. Although I appreciated the woman that was Miriam Feinstein, her presence often grated at my nerves. There was something about her carriage that exuded a semblance of disdain for me. And I knew that she believed me ill-fitted for my wife—an outlook that she took every opportunity to exercise. She was also quite influential over Colette; so, if Miriam believed that I was cheating, then I could be sure that Colette may too, which infuriated me even more.

"Honestly, the next time you have a chat with Mrs. Feinstein, I'd be grateful if you told her to mind her own fucking business," I fumed. "Her son's googly eyes for my wife, doesn't make me any less her husband."

"Look, I'm not getting in the middle of you and Ms. Miriam," he said, "But what I do need to know is, what's the problem, then? It's been a weird year, and things seem to have gotten worse within the past few months. You think I haven't noticed it too? Usually, I try not to get involved, but when I get a call and see you like this—look, you haven't touched a bottle in a long time, friend. This isn't you. It hasn't been for awhile now. Over a decade even. Talk to me. Please."

Taking a swig of the liquid weighted in my glass, I allowed myself a release of my defenses, "I haven't been cheating on Colette, Devon—"

"Then what the fuck is going on, Ben?"

"Anita is sick," I answered.

"What do you mean, she's sick? And what does that have to do with what's going on between you and Colette?"

"I've been taking care of her, which is why I haven't been home—"

"All this time?" he asked skeptically.

"Are you going to let me speak, or are you going to keep interrupting?"

"My bad. My bad. Go ahead, brother," he relented.

"She's... Anita," I began. It was difficult to contain my emotions; the certainty of her demise, never seemed to get easy to face, "She's terminal, Devon. She um...she has cancer."

"What?! No. Not, Ms. Anita," he said solemnly, "This is a joke, right? You're fucking with me."

I allowed him a moment to process, but as I watched my friend go through the motions of accepting Anita's fate, I couldn't help but think how Colette's face would look when she heard the news. Would it contort with disbelief, like him? Or would she collapse from fear? The possibilities seemed endless to me, which made them more frightening.

"I wish it were a joke, Devon. I wish this wasn't happening. I haven't been cheating on my wife. I love her. You know that. I've been spending all my time helping Anita; taking her to her appointments, cooking for her, cleaning. I've been doing everything, man."

"I see why you're...well...never mind. I mean...what I'm saying is, I understand. This is a lot to undertake for the two of you. But what I don't get is why would Miriam and Colette think something is up. Or that you're cheating?" he pondered. By the scrunch of his nose, followed by the widening of his eyes, it was evident that he'd figured out our secret. "She doesn't know, does she? Colette doesn't know that her mother is sick?"

"No. She doesn't," I said matter-of-factly, while nursing the drink that had begun to feel lighter in my hand.

"How could you keep that from her?!" he exclaimed.

"It wasn't exactly my choice, Devon. When Anita called me, she made it perfectly clear that she didn't want anyone to know."

"That doesn't matter, Ben! Colette is your wife. You don't keep something like that away from her. This will crush her."

"You don't think I know that?"

"Well, this explains why you've been such a distant asshole. The guilt's been getting to you, huh? And as it should! Because this is bullshit, Ben."

"I didn't have a choice!" I fumed, "She didn't have anyone else, Devon.

What was I supposed to do? Tell her no?"

"She has a whole-ass husband, Ben! And two daughters, who clearly don't know their mother is sick!"

"She doesn't have a husband. Her husband was too busy cheating on her with some bitch," I waved off, "And apparently, he's been doing so since the last time she was sick."

"What do you mean, since the last time she was sick?" asked Devon.

"This isn't the first time. She was in remission. It came back…and now we're here. Look…don't look at me that way. I didn't know the last time. She kept it to herself then too," I scoffed. "I only agreed, because I thought she would get better, like before, but—"

"Say no more, brother. I get it," he said faintly, "This is a fucking nightmare."

"Yeah. One that I can't seem to escape."

"I hate seeing you this way. Defeated like this. But if you don't tell her, and I mean soon, at the rate you're both going, it'll ruin the two of you."

"Well, I don't have much of a choice when it comes to that either, because in the next twenty-four hours or so, her mother will be telling my beautiful wife, that she's going to die," I said. The anger in my voice did nothing to showcase the true bitterness I felt.

"I think you should be the one to tell her, Ben. Get in front of this. Let her lash it out with you."

"Anita prefers that I didn't. She thinks that I shouldn't say anything at all," I replied.

"Look, Colette loves you. And let's not get it twisted, you lucked out because she's merciful. You should tell her first. It'll ease the blow, Ben. At the very least, she'll understand why you've been this way. And that you still love her and haven't been unfaithful," he said confidently, "But if you wait… and she finds out later…I don't know, brother."

"Well, that makes two of us," I said.

Gulping down the rest of my drink, I allowed myself to feel its numbness wash over me; taking me away to a place of solitude, where I could hide, even if it was from myself. Picking up the decanter, I was prepared to grace myself with another drink, when I felt the weight of his hands lifting the contents of my serenity away from me, "Put it down, brother. You don't need it. You have me," he said.

Taking me into his arms, I allowed myself his embrace, and as he pulled me into his comfort, the rumble of emotions swept through me with the fury of an avalanche. He allowed me a moment to relieve myself from the weight of my turmoil, then whispered, "Enough with the mushy stuff. Let's get you home. I'll drive. If we leave now, you might make dinner. I know that they're waiting on you either way. Cool?"

Breaking away from him, I used my hands to vigorously swat the tears that stained my face, "Okay. Let's go. It's now or never," I resigned.

Standing on my doorstep, I longed for the will to cross the threshold of what I used to consider my castle—a place I'd always found life, love, and wonder. Now, as I stood there, the effects of the alcohol slowly running its course, left me weak at the knees. I could not pass. I couldn't go to them.

Although Devon tried to be a distraction during my ride home, his energy and attempt to maintain a bright mood, did nothing to dispel the overwhelming anxiety that brewed. Now as I stood before my doorway, peering out into the street, the sense of impending doom rose to the brim like an erupting volcano, making it harder and harder to breathe.

"I can't do this," I heard myself say vaguely, as the wooziness of my attack took over. Turning my head, I caught a glimpse of my daughters through the corridor. Their laughter, bountiful and fine, exhibited the absence of my unrest from their knowledge. It was enough to capture me and deliver my resignation to the unyielding storm raging within. *Just breathe. Breathe, Ben. It'll pass. It'll be over soon. Just listen to the girls.* Surrendering to my restlessness, I welcomed the night air against my cheeks. As its coolness clashed with the heat that washed over my body, I heard the opening of the door. And the soft sound of a small voice, drew me back to reality with a sudden crash.

"Abba! You're here!" squealed Charlotte. Lifting her into my arms, I embraced her carelessly. In that moment, she'd become my lifeline. "Abba, put me down. You're squeezing too tight."

"Hi, Abba. Where have you been? You're late," Nala scrutinized.

"I'm sorry, honey," I said, placing Charlotte down. Turning to Nala, I tried to veil the remnants of my attack, to no avail.

"Okay, but where were you?" she asked again.

"Well, aren't you a nosy little goose—"

"Abba, are you okay? You're shaking," she asked.

"I'm okay, doll. I'm just cold," I replied, "Let's go inside. Okay? Go on."

Walking behind them, I watched them bounce about carelessly with an excitement I couldn't rally, as I tried to level my breathing and gain control over my faculties. Their laughter was infectious, and I found myself smiling at their joy, despite my deep-seated pain.

"Abba is here!!!" they both screamed.

Scooping up Charlotte, I buried my face into her soft cheeks to keep from faltering from the weight of her gaze; it felt like an iron piercing through my flesh, forcing me to face my guilt once more, which threatened to swallow me whole. However, the look of lovingness from my youngest girl was enough to get me through—her laughter, enhanced the beauty in her elegant face, which I allowed to capture me in a moment of gratitude for the limited pleasure it afforded me. Her curls were soft within my fingertips, and the light touch of her head against mine, soothed me back to a time of surreal content. "Neshama sheli," I whispered to her.

"Hey. What about me, Abba?" said Nala. Despite their lack of genetic connection, she seemed to have the spirit and fiery nature of their mother. It was as if Colette had willed it into her, and I couldn't wait to see the powerful being, she'd eventually grow into.

"You know I could never forget my beautiful doll. You look magnificent today. Come. Tell Abba about your day," I said.

I was content to be in the rule of their magnetism—it settled me into serenity, subduing the panic that overtook me. That is until I caught sight of her pained face, once more. And it forced me to avert my eyes, unable to speak the words we both needed to hear.

Into the Fox's Den

Sitting away from her during dinner was torturous, but it was necessary to maintain the composure I needed. Tension welled within me, as I tried to work my way through the evening; an evening that was filled with the laughter of those I held dear, except from the one I needed to hear it from most. I watched as the couples in our home delighted in each other's company—a feeling I yearned for. Every fiber of my being screamed in agony for her adoration.

Watching the way the Feinsteins lovingly held on to each other, and the stolen glances between Kami and Akal, made me want all that was lost and missing. I need the light back in her eyes and the feel of her warmth. I need her back, sprang through. And it was with this proclamation that I decided to tell her. In the darkness of the night, when all that was left was just the two of us, I would win back her heart.

Turning my attention towards our daughters, I relished in their innocence and allowed myself to be immersed in the energy of my household. For the first time, the heaviness of my discontent waivered. The quest to mend what was broken, made me feel whole. And I no longer felt alone among the people I loved dearly, that is, until I heard her voice, sinking into my resolve like a blade.

"So, Ben," she began, "Do tell…why were you so late to dinner this evening?"

Looking up at her, the critical way in which Colette's eyes washed over me at Miriam's question, brought the rigidity back into my body. It snaked its way up my spine, tightening its coils about my frame. And I sat, tension filled, as if I were preparing for battle. My hope now fading. The look in her eyes, although softer now, did nothing to hide the echoing suspicions of her cohort, forcing me to face the consequence of the depths of my deceit once more.

"While you are certainly a light in our lives, Miriam, where I was, prior to entering my home, is none of your concern," I said tightly. Tearing my gaze from my wife, I tried to gather enough decorum to keep the peace. Waiting for the children to leave, I said, "Look, Miriam, I'm not going to do this with you tonight."

"Do what exactly? I just asked a simple question, dear. You see, I find it incredibly odd that you were so late," she said coyly. The cunningness of her eyes was my downfall. I knew that she was on the prowl. To her, she had uncovered the truth in what she believed to be my shame, and it tore me, because for all I had done, she would dare question my integrity in my home.

"I was at the bar with some colleagues, but again that isn't any of your business, now, is it?" I lied.

"Well, it is the business of your wife, and since she can't seem to muster up enough moxie to ask you, I'm doing it for her. There isn't any reason for a married man with children, on a night like tonight, to stroll in smelling like a bar," she spat.

Seeing the look on my wife's face, disheartened me. Her disappointment, though apparent, was marred by panic and defeat, causing disdain to well inside me. *How could she think so ill of me? She doesn't even look like she wants me anymore.*

"Perceval," I called out to him. Although my voice was even, it did nothing to hide the tension and my brewing fury, which was evident by the shift in his demeanor and clearing of his throat.

"Honey… perhaps we should leave this to the two of them," he said rising from his seat.

"No. I. Will. Not! I will not sit by and watch this train wreck," Miriam stated firmly. Her intentions clear, she sat firmly in her place, ready to spar against me.

"Miriam. It's okay. Really. I can handle it. Just let it be," Colette stated.

"I'm sorry, Colette. But I will not sit by and watch this train wreck," she replied. Turning her head towards me, she said with a pointed finger, "And, you?! The least you could have done was give your wife a call. What about saying hello to her when you entered? Can you not do that anymore, even?"

"I didn't realize I needed permission to go to the bar for a fucking drink. Excuse the hell out of me. In fact, I think I could use a drink right now. *May*

I please have a fucking drink?" I stated. The last question was laid pointedly towards my wife; the double entendre worked its way to unnerve her, just as her visit and the events of the day were breaking me. Here I sat before her, ready to reunite us, and she seemed unwilling to see me as I am. *Then what was the purpose of your visit, my love? What was the reason if you can't even bear to look at me now?*

"Don't use that language towards me, young man," cried Miriam.

"Oh. I'm sorry, didn't ask the wife's permission first. May I please use the word 'fuck'?" I said looking towards her.

"Benjamin, please," she begged. Her look of mortification only fueled my resentment and rage more.

"Please, what?! All I want to know is if I have your permission to use the word 'fuck' in my home. Or do I need permission to even do that?" I seethed. "Fine. May I please have permission to ask your permission to use the word, 'fuck'?"

"Ben, really. Calm down, son," said Perceval, "I know that you're angry, but there is really no need for—"

His attempt to appease me did not stir me, for if it weren't for his meddling wife, I could have had mine wrapped tightly in my arms—a fools wish now.

"And there really isn't a need for your wife to interfere. Colette and I are fine," I replied.

"Oh, really? Do you know that she is seeing a shrink? I had to hear it from Sarah Cohen, for crying out loud," said Miriam.

The look in her eyes said it all. *She knows. She's known all along. If she's been speaking to Sarah, then she knows. She was just messing with me today. For what? To see if I'd confess... so she could leave me?*

"Ben, why don't we go into the study, son? I'm sure a bit of scotch could do us both some good. Give everyone a moment to cool off. What do you say?" I heard him say faintly. His voice was barely audible over the ringing that began to boom loudly in my ears. Staring into her eyes, I tried to find a semblance of hope within them. And with the lowering of her gaze away from me, a rush of panic swept over me like a heatwave, and I could do nothing but flee, leaving the crashing slam of the front door behind me.

Walking towards my intended destination, the night air felt like a shield against the fury threatening to beckon forward. It cooled me, trapping the heat of my anger that increased with each matched step

I'd taken. I was long aware of her company; the heaviness of heel studded footsteps, did nothing to hide her presence behind me, despite her attempt to be discreet. I did not want to see her, for she was likely the reason I was in the predicament I found myself in.

"Why are you following me?" I fumed.

"I'm…I'm sorry. I saw you come out, and you didn't look well, so I thought I'd see if you were okay?"

"Did you tell her?"

"Tell who?" she asked. Although she seemed unaware of my meaning, I couldn't put anything past her.

"Did you tell my wife what was going on, Sarah? How could you? I trusted you!"

"What? I wouldn't do that to you, Ben. You told me not to say anything to her, and I gave you my word. I didn't tell Colette anything about what's going on. Why? What happened? Is everything okay?"

"Never mind," I said, turning away from her, and resumed my walking, to which she followed, steady on my heels.

"Ben. Ben, wait. Please," she said grabbing hold of me. "Tell me what's going on."

"I don't want to talk about it, Sarah," I said harshly. "Just leave me alone. Don't you have better things to do? What are you doing out here anyway at this time of night? It's Shabbat!"

"I'm on hiatus," she smiled coyly, "I've decided that joining the circus would be far more appealing and beneficial to me.

"And what's that supposed to mean?" I asked.

"Not even one smile? I thought we at least made a breakthrough, in respect to our friendship," she jested.

"Look, Sarah. I'm in no mood for games."

"Okay. Okay," she said, throwing her hands up, "I was on my way over to drop off dessert, when I saw you, and here we are."

"Great, and now that you've checked on me and said your peace, you can go," I said, charging off again.

"Let me come with you. I can keep you company," she said cheerfully, throwing away the package in her hand into a nearby bin.

"The place I'm going to is no place for you, Sarah. Just go home. Please," I said, increasing my stride.

Seizing the top of my sleeve, she pulled me towards her, "All my life I've had people telling me what to do, please don't be another one, Ben."

"The last thing I need is for anyone to blame me if something happened to you. You know better. You're a wife and a mother—you shouldn't even be out right now. And then what if someone sees? The gossip that would ensue…Sarah, please just go home."

"Why won't you let me be a friend to you?" she whined, "I know where you're going, and I'll be fine."

"What are you doing? Have you been following me?" I asked incensed.

"Park Slope is a small place, Ben," she said timidly, "And for all you know, I want a drink too."

There was something in the way she spoke, that raised the hairs on the back of my neck. It was my body speaking to me, but I was too far gone to listen, "Whatever. You're a big girl. Do what you want. But just give me—"

"Don't worry. I'll give you space," she said sweetly, "And when you're ready to talk. I'll be here."

"Fine," I said.

We walked side by side in a comfortable silence until we reached the bar, where she stopped abruptly before walking in, "Hold on a minute," she said, pulling me aside. "Let me fix myself up a bit."

Hiking up her long skirt, she allowed the elastic band to hover over her breast and stripped herself of her long-sleeved shirt, stuffing it into her purse. She removed her headscarf, letting her hair down, and used it as a tie above her waist to create the illusion of a short dress.

"Why do I get the feeling you've done this before?" I asked, entranced by her daringness.

"Follow me," she said cheerfully.

Trailing behind her, I noticed the slight nod between her and the other patrons, as we made our way through the relatively empty bar.

"Hey, Drew," she said lightly, "It's quiet tonight."

"I was wondering when you'd show up. The usual?" he asked.

"I don't know. I think I'm going to let my friend decide," she replied.

"Oh, hey there, Ben! I didn't realize you two knew each other!" he said happily, "What a small world. Two whiskeys then? Double? Neat?"

"You know me too well," I said.

"Coming right up then, Ben," he replied.

"So, that's what you drink, huh?" she inquired.

"Sarah, what's going on here?" I asked.

"Nothing. I'm just having a drink with a friend."

"You know what I mean, Sarah."

"And I meant every word of what I said earlier. I no longer care to have anyone tell me what to do. I'm making my own way now. Becoming a new woman," she shouted. Her boisterous nature seemed forced and unnatural; it was evident that she was out of her element, no matter how hard she tried to mask her uneasiness.

"Well, here's something I thought I'd never see," I said to her.

Her smile was now radiant, and I realized that she wasn't trying to fit in, she was trying to impress me. "Hey, Drew…keep'em coming. It's going to be a long night," I said.

"I didn't realize you liked whiskey that much," she said, nursing her drink.

"Well, since I intend to forget tonight…I'd say, I'm off to a slow start," I said, tapping the edge of my glass to signify that I needed another, which I downed shortly after receiving.

"It was that bad, I take it?" she asked.

I waited to feel the warmth of the alcohol overcome me and dull my senses. She didn't push me to speak, for which I was grateful. She just sat, patiently, and watched me—quietly, like a scientist observing a subject. I wondered in those moments, just for a minute, what it would have been like, had I not walked away from her and into the arms of Colette, that day, years ago. I knew that things would have been easier in the beginning—perhaps, in that moment, even. *What if I caused a ripple effect of misery, by choosing for love, rather than practicality? What does it matter? It's too late now.*

Dismissing my thoughts, I hung amid the fortitude the honey-colored liquid seemed to grant me. And it was during my fourth round, that I was finally ready to oblige her request. "Well… my life is in shambles, as you know."

"Yes. I am aware," she replied.

Her words, although unsuspecting, seemed exacting in their tone, as if trying to encourage me to share more. And with the liquor weighing down my faculties, my lips spoke the secrets inside me, freely, "Anita gave me the call today—"

"The call? I'm not sure, I understand. What does that mean?" she urged, seeing my apprehension.

"She's dying, Sarah."

"I think that's already been established," she said absently. After taking in my body language and the contempt in my eyes, she quickly changed her tune, "What I meant was…I don't know what I meant by that at all. I'm sorry, Ben."

"If I were you, I'd watch myself," I said defensively.

I didn't come to my place of refuge to quarrel; all I wanted to do was forget. And if she was going to force her presence upon me, the least she could do was allow me to vent.

"Like I said…I didn't mean anything by it. I'm just trying to be a friend… like I have been, okay?" she lulled "Now that we've cleared that up, why was her call so important?"

"It was…it was," I hesitated, the emotions that had been overpowering during the day, paralyzed me, forcing me to take another gulp of my drink, "Basically, she was telling me that it's time. It won't be much longer now, so she's going to tell Colette soon."

"I see. Well, no wonder you're here."

"No. That part, although I am resistant of… truthfully, I've longed prepared for. I also resigned to telling Colette myself—get ahead of it all, ya know? But then Miriam was over with her meddling, and everything turned to shit. My anger and impulsiveness got the better of me, honestly. Now I'm here," I stated.

"Oh…"

It wasn't noticeable at first, but something in her eyes changed. I couldn't place it, but my words seemed to cause tension to rise between us. So much so, I could cut it with a knife. Noting the change in her demeanor, I asked, "Are you okay?"

"Nothing's wrong. I'm just not used to whiskey. It's a bit stronger than wine," she said as she stared at the contents of her glass.

"I can see that. You haven't finished it," I said, "You don't have to keep up with me, you know. I think I'm part of a different kind of party."

"Good," she laughed, "I was trying to be a good sport, but this isn't for me."

"You care for a glass of wine, then? You look like a red kind of girl," I said. Turning my attention to Drew, I shouted, "Hey… can I get a glass of *port* for the lady."

Her energy changed, and the tautness in her body dissipated quickly, and was replaced with a thrill that lent a softness to her face, "Thank you," she replied.

"Why are you so happy?" I asked.

"No reason really," she said playfully, "I just never had a man order me a drink before. You're the first."

"Come on now. Not even Oded? Your husband?" I asked skeptically. The world was hazy now, and I gave myself over to the numbness and giddiness the alcohol afforded me, as it gave way to a more joyous mood.

"He's never taken me out. At least not like this," she said, "All he cares about is shul, and that man."

"I'm assuming that we're speaking of the elder, Cohen?" I asked. "It's a shame. You're good company. It's his loss though. I'm happy to be the first."

There was a gleam of joy behind her eyes, as if she'd been awakened from a pleasant dream, "I'm happy you are too," she said, placing her hand on mine. It was larger than Colette's—and although the weight of it felt foreign, I didn't remove it, causing her to lean her head against me.

The hours passed, and we sat in harmony, distracting ourselves from the worry of our present. We people watched and made-up stories about their lives, ones that we would never know. And it reminded me of Colette—in the way we used to be.

"I'm enjoying this time with you," she said.

"Me too. I really needed this," I replied, "It's been so long…so long since—"

"You've had someone this close?" she finished, "It's the same for me."

"So, you miss it too?" I asked.

"Hardly," she replied, "Oded isn't exactly the best when it comes to… well… to that."

"Well, that's unfortunate," I laughed, "But I didn't expect anything more from him."

"And what is that supposed to mean?"

"He doesn't exactly come across as suave, now, Sarah," I replied, "Look, while he is a good man, I'm just sure that he lacks—"

"The ability to make a woman weak in the knees?" she said. "I bet you don't have that problem."

"I couldn't tell you. I'm not on the receiving end of myself, now am I?"

"Yes, but Colette doesn't seem to have a problem. She always has this glow about her. She seems…well satisfied," she said, swallowing hard. "I mean… if the longevity of your marriage is any indication."

"Then I could say the same for you, Sarah."

"You could, but I don't look at Oded the way she looks at you."

"The way she used to look at me, you mean? However, a love of a woman doesn't always indicate her satisfaction in the bedroom. That, you get from her mood, the way she walks, and the brightness of her smile," I said. I stared at her intently, causing her to shiver, the same way that Colette used to. What I would give to have my wife again, I thought.

"Still, she at least loves you. The only thing I got from Oded… well, I'm still trying to find out."

"You need another glass?"

"No. I think I'm good," she answered. "Hey, Ben? Do you ever…do you ever wonder what it would have been like, had we stayed together?"

"Well…we were never really together," I replied, "But…I mean, perhaps it would have been easier if we did date, all things considered. However, that's just speculation, right? We'll never know for sure."

"But don't we? Look at how miserable we both are."

"Just because we're unhappy now, doesn't mean that things won't get better, Sarah. Colette and I have been down hard roads before—this isn't our first rodeo," I said.

"Yeah, but not for me," she said heatedly, "It will never get better for me."

"If you're so unhappy, why don't you leave?"

"You act as if it isn't too late for me now," she said, "And what will people think? I couldn't bear it. You know what they would say. How I'll be treated. I'd lose everything."

It was clear that she was disheartened, and I wanted to lighten the mood so that we could return to our moment of solitude, where our sadness had been replaced by camaraderie, "Well, you're here now. How about another drink?"

"No. I don't need another drink," she said, "And you surely don't need another either."

"Fine. Then what do you want to do?"

"I want to talk about why you left me. You have no idea what it's done to my life—"

"Okay… first, I didn't leave you. We were never together. We were friends, Sarah. Just friends. I showed you around—"

"So, you're going to act as if we never went out? Dated?"

"I did my father a favor. You were new to The City," I replied. "I know what it's like to be different… to be an outsider, so when my father needed someone to look out for you, I did."

"I wish you never seen her that day. Then we would have had a chance. And I wouldn't have to be with him. I hate him, Ben. I hate them all!"

"Are you daft?! There is no way we would have been together. You never stood a chance, with how much I love my wife. Whether I saw her or not, I still loved her then, just as I love her now. I would have walked to the ends of the earth to find her again. We. Would. Have. Never. Happened!" I exclaimed. "Look…you act as if you didn't have a choice in the matter, Sarah. You didn't have to marry, Oded, in the same way I didn't have to marry Colette—"

"I had no choice, Ben," she said faintly.

"Who forced you, Sarah? No one did," I replied. "Look, I know that things weren't stable for you here, but it's not like your family put pressure on you to be with Oded."

"You don't understand."

"Then make me understand. Because at a certain point, we all have to take responsibility for the decisions we've made and make the best of it," I stated. "So, tell me, please…why did you marry the man if you didn't want him?"

"Because I wanted you," she whispered. Her eyes were closed tightly, as if she were willing herself to breathe, to release the pressure mounting in her body. "You have no idea how much I loved you. And how much I still do. I wanted…no, needed to be close to you. Marrying him was my only way to stay here. I figured eventually…you'd grow tired of her. Tired of being someone who wasn't like us. That you would leave her. That you'd realize that she wasn't meant for you, so that I could have my chance."

"Come now. I think that's the drink talking," I stated dismissively, trying to diffuse her delusions.

"Why do you do this? Why do you ignore the way I feel about you, Ben?"

The tears that pierced her eyes began to cascade down her cheeks, and I unconsciously swiped away at them. For reasons I could not understand, nor explain, I felt liable for her pain, "Please don't cry, Sarah. We're here to have fun. To forget. Not to dwell on the past."

"It's easy for you to say. You got your happily ever after."

"Considering I'm sitting in the very same bar, right next to you, tells me otherwise. I mean, you despise your husband, and well, I'm willing to wager that my wife hates me," I laughed.

"And I'd wager that she does not in-fact hate you."

"You almost seem confident enough in that to be convincing. However, I think she knows. So, in any case, I'm pretty sure that after tonight, she won't forgive me. But what I can't understand is how she found out in the first place," I said curiously. The look of contention on her face made me understand, and it brought about my rage with it, "What did you do?!"

"Ben…calm down. Please. Before you get angry with me, I didn't say a word to Colette."

"Then how does she know, Sarah? How did she find out?!"

"Can you let me explain…please?" she begged, "I didn't talk to your wife. I only…I only spoke to Miriam about us spending time together, that's all."

It came to me like a flash of light. *What happened today wasn't because Colette found out about my involvement in concealing her mother's illness, it was because she thinks I'm cheating.* I knew Miriam, and I certainly knew

Sarah, and her implications in telling the former of our talks were clear—she wanted Miriam to believe that I was being unfaithful. She knew that she would tell Colette.

"How could you?!"

"I don't know what you mean," she said timidly.

"You understood precisely what you were doing when you spoke to Miriam. What is wrong with you?! Spending time together? Outside of seeing you at the hospital, we haven't seen each other. So, talking on the phone is now 'spending time together,'" I said heatedly, raising myself out of my seat. I felt sick to my stomach. All this time I'd confided in the one person who was dead set on ruining my marriage completely.

"Ben. Please. Don't walk away from me," she said.

Her grip on my shirt incited me more, forcing us to dance in a tug-of-war, I found myself losing. The effects of the alcohol caused me to become unsteady on my feet. "Get your hands off me, you, crazy bitch," I whispered snidely in her ear. "It's bad enough you've caused chaos in my home, I'm not about to let you embarrass me here."

"At least let me help you. I'm sorry, Ben. Really, I am—"

"Your apology isn't good enough! I swear, if you've ruined things between me and wife, so help me."

"Ben…please don't leave me. I'm sorry," she pleaded.

"If you've been good enough to find your way here often enough for Drew to know who you are, then you can find your way home," I said, as I turned on my heels, and staggered my way to the bathroom.

Getting through the door of the empty room, I splashed water on my face to sober myself up. Inspecting my reflection in the mirror, I looked at the man before me, and I didn't recognize him. He had aged much in the past year. His hair once sprinkled with a dust of grey, had now acquired deep stains of the colorless hairs at his temples. His eyes, while still sharp in nature, gained lines that were indicative of his sadness rather than the grace of growing older.

"What are you doing here? You should be home with your family," I said to him, as I plopped myself down on the toilet seat. Leaning back, I found myself drifting, as my wary mind and body willed me into darkness.

I don't know how many moments passed, but through my haze I could hear faint sounds from above, "*What do you see in her that you don't see in me? Is it because of what she does to you? Like this?*" the voice said to me.

Blinded by my stupor, my mind summoned visions of my wife. Her almond, chestnut-colored eyes peered back at me, as the feeling of warm flesh wrapped around my member, surged through me. The heat of her body pressed against mine, caused a flame to flicker, as I allowed her to take control. She'd always been my destiny. Seeking me out, she'd finally come to claim me. Rescue me. Saving me once more.

Although the weight of her breast was different and seemed foreign in my hands, I thrusted forward, sinking myself deeper into the swell of her. Reaching to grasp her bottom, I realized how much I'd missed the feel of her beneath the palms of my hands. However, it did not feel of her—it did not feel of my wife, and it caused a wave of panic, that was confirmed by the soft moans and sound of her voice, "So, this is what she stole from me," she said against my ear, crashing through the fog that surrounded me. "Now I know why she doesn't want to give you up. Oh, Benny. I've waited so long for this. You feel so good."

The sound of her voice broke through the shadows I tried to escape to, sending waves of fear through me. Oh, please, no. Goodness, no! Please, tell me this isn't happening, I pleaded into the abyss that once soothed me, as I tried to bring myself back to consciousness. *Just open your eyes, Ben. Open them. It's not her. It's not Colette. You idiot! You didn't lock the fucking door!*

Peering back at the creature, whose weight and heat I did not recognize pummel against me, I became wracked with sickness. Pushing her harshly, my vigor forced her hard onto the floor. I couldn't hear the words she spoke to me, as my mind reeled from her assault and my body emptied its contents from my belly. I did not meet her gaze; instead, after I released all I had within me, and wiped myself free of my tears, I turned away from her pleas and screams, and found my way home.

Retribution

I messed up. How could I have been so stupid? I should have never gone with her. Why didn't I stay home? I've ruined everything, played over and over in my mind, as I made way through the place that no longer felt like home. It was quiet now, and the only sounds heard were the soft sounds of our children snoring in their rooms.

With my vision still shrouded by the haze of my drinking, I made my way into our room, but I did not see her there, and for that I was grateful. I couldn't face her after what I'd done. My body still felt soiled from Sarah's assault, and I found myself dumping my clothes into the trash and stepping into the shower to remove the feel of her. I could still sense her, and the vile stench of her smell permeated my nostrils, making me sick and weak at the knees. And no matter how much I scrubbed, I still felt unclean.

Going to bed, I laid in the twilight of night when I heard her come in. The lightness of her stride signified her need to not disturb me; except, I wanted nothing more than to have her come wrap her arms around me. The sound of the water called to me, as thoughts of her nakedness played within my mind. I needed her, just as one needed air. I needed her closeness and warmth to sooth me and erase the feel and images of the night's affair.

Following the soft sounds of her moans as the water worked its magic to release the tension of her body, I waited for her to finish. The pain of my ordeal was overwhelming, and I could contain it no more. I needed my wife to comfort me, but in coming face to face with the coolness in her eyes, rage began to consume me, as the night's events came tumbling towards the forefront. *If it weren't for you... all I wanted to do was protect you, and you question everything I am. Everything I've been, based on the whims of others.*

Tossing her towel, I watched as she quickly covered herself, as if I were not worthy of a glimpse of her naked flesh, which burned away at me, "Why did you invite that woman here?" I said tightly.

I needed to lash out, so that I could feel anything other than the red-hot anger and disgust my naivete brought me. Yet, she would not relent to my need, and charged onward into our closet, instead. It only goaded me more, "Why. Did. You. Invite. Her. Here?"

"When do I ever invite her? She invites herself, and it's not like she's not welcomed," she said gently.

"Says who? Who says she's welcome here?" I asked. If it weren't for you and that meddling woman, this would have never happened to me, sprang through my head.

"Come on, Benjamin. Not tonight."

But I could not hear reason. I had to fight. I needed to. If I didn't, I knew I would be ravished by the flame burning inside me, like hot magma, "Don't fucking 'come on, Benjamin', me. For once, I would like to come into my house without some bullshit. With some peace."

"It's not us who disturbs the peace in our home, Benjamin," she retorted. There she was. The woman I knew was there all along. The one I wished would have come to me long ago, so that I could lay my entire heart in her hands and be done with the pain I was suffering.

"What I mean to say is, we all want you home. And it would be nice if you would just spend a bit more time—"

"I spend time with our kids, Colette," I said, feigning ignorance, and hoping she would say the words I needed to hear.

"Well, then, it would be nice if you'd come home and spend time with me. I need…I need you too, you know?"

Her sincerity and tenderness sent a chill down my spine, and I realized that the care in which she spoke, meant that I'd been wrong all along. *She doesn't know. She doesn't know anything at all, and I let that woman touch me.*

The truth of her knowledge hit me like a ton of bricks, and I found myself buckling under the weight of my mistake. Guilt rushed me like a tsunami, making me sink deeper into the weight of my rage; forcing me to lash out against her, "Here we go. Here. We. Go. Go on. Tell me how I'm being such a shit to you."

"I don't mean it like that!" she said, "I just want to have my husband. You don't talk to me anymore, and you're drinking again—"

“Don’t fucking start that shit, Colette!” I roared. Her words hit me like daggers and increased the magnitude of my shame.

“Can you calm down please. You’re going to wake the kids,” she said. Walking away from me, she charged through our closet, grabbing her night gown, as I trailed behind, “Why do you always have to yell at me? I’m not asking for much, Benjamin.”

“You shouldn’t be asking for anything. You want for nothing. You have a beautiful home, cars, a nice expense account,” I said deflecting.

“That’s not what’s important. I want you,” she said, reaching to caress my cheek. My humiliation forced me to pull away from her. Turning away from me, she walked into our room and got into bed, to which I followed suit. As if possessed, she cocked her body towards me to release the turmoil that sieged her, “You know, it’s not like you got all of this by yourself. If it weren’t for me, you’d still be a snot-nosed little punk trying to figure out a way to get out from under his father’s thumb! I shouldn’t have to beg my husband to want me!”

The tension between us illustrated the embodiment of our woes, and although deep down inside I wanted to turn to her, the indignity committed against me wouldn’t allow it, and I acted out on the resentment I’d held onto for so long, “You’re right. No wife of mine should have to beg to be fucked,” I replied.

“Benjamin?” she whispered. The silence between us was deafening, and as she made a run for the door, I felt myself grabbing her, forcing her back onto the bed.

“Benjamin, please. Let go of me.”

Her pleas did nothing to subdue me. The cruelness of my world set its talons upon me; creating a monster that could no longer be compelled. *It’s her fault. If she had only told me sooner that she loved me, I wouldn’t have ended up there. That woman would have never laid her filthy hands on me.*

The sound of the slap across my face, brought a ring to my ears that stung me back from my thoughts, “You hit me? Are you out of your fucking mind?!” I raged.

“Benjamin, please. Just let me go,” she begged.

And for a moment, the look in her eyes seemed to calm the monster that wielded me, but as my mind sprung some semblance of clarity, memories of her came to surface; the feel of Sarah’s body upon me, and the coarseness of her hair as it raked against my cheek, summoned the creature once more, and I could do nothing else but seek serenity in the familiar. I needed her body against me—to replace the feeling of loathing and disgust that roared within, because of what Sarah had done. I needed to feel something other than the pain of my suffering—I needed my wife.

I heard nothing. And I no longer felt the vile feel of Sarah's flesh, as I sought the warm depths of my love, granting me redemption. I took her and allowed myself to be swept away in her, just as I'd done many times before. But the moans of shared pleasure never came, her body, rigid and tense, never bonded with mine. And after feeling the damp warmth of her tears, I realized what I had done; in my need to relinquish myself from my misery, I'd subjected her to the same anguish I wished to forget, and it tore me apart.

Wrenching myself from her body, I couldn't look at her as she walked towards the bathroom we shared. The sounds of the water that once drew me to her, reminded me of my own need to cleanse myself from my shame, and it pushed me deeper into my despair. Lifting myself from the bed, the hopelessness that ravished me, acted as a beacon of wrath that tore away from me—my screams in the wake of the destruction I had caused, became my only companion. I lost her. My wife—my love, was no longer mine.

Without You

They arrived in front of their home some time ago, and the quiet she maintained, burned hotter than the tears that streaked her face, and pierced him like a hot knife. He dared not look at her. The hard rhythmic breathing escaping her lips, was enough to let him know to keep his distance.

Opening the car door, she charged into their home with her husband hot on her heels. The feeling of his presence sickened her, as the gravity of his words weighed heavy on her mind. When she sought the truth, she never imagined that this would be her reality; a husband whose betrayal extended beyond the bounds of separating parent and child.

Reaching their bedroom, she tried to shuffle through its threshold and shield herself from his onslaught of lies. But she was no match for his strength; and she lost the fight of sealing him off from her, "You can't just shut me out, Colette," he shouted, preventing her escape.

"You let me pass, right now!"

"I will not," he responded calmy, "Not until you talk to me."

"Talk to you about what, exactly?" she seethed, "From where I'm standing there is nothing to talk about. That bitch can have you."

"You don't mean that," he said.

"You don't know what the fuck I mean. You barely even know who I am!"

"I know exactly who you are—you're my wife. The woman that I love with all my heart—"

"How…how dare you even say that?!" she raged, "You didn't even realize that I had no idea what was going on. And the only thing I ever wanted was you. Through it all, I only wanted your love, you sorry piece of shit!"

"Colette… motek…you don't understand," he stated, "You don't understand what it was like for me."

"What it was like for you? What about what it was like for me?! Do you think it was easy for me watching you spiral? Drinking again? And acting as if I didn't exist?"

"Look, I know. But you don't get it, I did it—"

"Hold on, let me guess? You did it all for me?" she alleged, "If you were doing it all for me, you would have given me your heart, instead of your back."

"You always have my heart, Cole."

"No. I'm the one you lied to and whose heart you've broken into a million pieces, once again."

"You're the woman I've loved since you were a girl," he tried to reason, "The only one I've ever loved."

"Pack your shit!"

"I'm sorry, what?" he asked in disbelief.

In all the years they'd been together, she'd never asked him to leave. The words seemed foreign to him, and yet the intensity in which they flowed from her lips, alarmed his senses, causing him to take immediate defense, as she pulled away from his clutches. "You can't be serious," he said.

He noted the look in her eyes, as she increased the space between them, and it made him shudder. Although she was now without tears, the contortion and quivering of her lip signified her anguish and growing derision. The sound of thunder crashing through the night sky startled her already wracked nerves, causing him to reach out to her, making her recoil at the feel of him, "You don't get to touch me anymore," she said. Her voice, barely above a whisper, was calm and contrite, betraying the misery that swelled within her. "Um…I really need you to go, Benjamin. I don't think the kids should see us like this. And I…um…I think it would be best, so that we could think about our next step forward in raising our children—"

"Wait. What are you saying?" he asked.

This was the one time he was grateful for Miriam's meddling hands. He had shot her a text, long before their arrival home, asking her to watch over their young ones. His children were blissfully unaware of the war raging between their parents because they sat soundly asleep at their Bubbe's home. If they overheard what transpired, they would be just as confused and hurt by what she said, as he was now. "You're not saying what I think you're saying, are you?"

"We don't belong together, Benjamin. Look at us," she said emphatically, "We're fools. We've always been so. And we were fools to think—"

"So, you're telling me that you want to throw our marriage away?"

"You've said the same. You said it when you told me about you and her. That things would have been easier if we weren't together. If you had chosen her, right? That you sometimes wonder? Well," she said with a shrug, "You don't have to wonder anymore."

"There is no me and her," he said, drawing her near to him, ignoring her resistance of his touch. "Look at me, Colette. There is only you and me. No one else. And wondering, during a vulnerable time, doesn't equate to wanting. Because I want you. I always have. And I always will. Until my last breath, it will always be you."

"It doesn't matter. She's had you," she said tearfully. Gripping his face and peering into his eyes, she searched the depths of him to find the untainted love she once knew, "Why didn't you just stay home? Huh? Why? If you would have just spoken to me, instead of assuming—keeping your secrets. Your lies. This wouldn't have happened."

"Don't you think I know that? Don't you think I played that night over and over in my mind? I know I shouldn't have been there with her," he said trying to maintain his composure, "But I didn't choose to sleep with her, Colette. I didn't make the choice to go with her in that bathroom, the way you chose to go to Dominic's hotel room. She forced herself on me when I wasn't even conscious enough to protest!"

"How do I know that's the truth?" she demanded. "I heard the things she said to you. It doesn't sound like someone who's been with a man that didn't want them, Benjamin! How can I possibly believe you?"

"The same way I believed you."

"Barely. Were we not just in your office with you accusing me of sleeping with that man?"

"That was my insecurities talking, just as it's yours speaking for you now. But deep down in your heart, you know that I did not choose to be with her! Just as I know in mine, you were never with him."

"Do not sit here and try to minimize and tell me how I feel, Benjamin Lati. You have no idea!" she fumed.

"Then tell me. Please. Speak to me. Yell. Fight. I don't fucking care. But don't say those words again. Don't ask me to go. Don't imply that it's over, because it will never be over—not for me. Ever. Especially not over some stupid bitch, who can't seem to leave well enough alone."

"She has taken what can never be returned to me, Benjamin."

"No. What she had was not me. What she took was something that she could never keep, because I belong to you, just as you belong to me, Colette."

"That's not what I mean," she said, her voice wavering. "She…she's the reason you did that to me. She's the reason you, my dear husband, stole my—"

"Cole… listen. I was hurt. I…I was confused. I didn't mean it, and I regret it every day, since it happened."

"You punished me for what she did to you, Benjamin! You blamed me for her assault against you, and hurt me in return," she said, her face stained with the shame of that night. "How am I supposed to live with that? I can forgive you, her transgressions against you, but I cannot absolve you of what was done to me in her name. She took the very essence of what was pure in our love, and trampled it! Still, even though we've been intimate since, you know it hasn't been the same. What happened that night…what you did? There's this...wedge between us that will never go away. And now that I know…"

"Don't you think I beat myself up for it every day?" he asked. His heart swelled with sorrow that wouldn't cease, as he tried to hold back the tears threatening to cascade down his cheeks, "It kills me every day that I hurt you that way."

"It doesn't change what happened, Benjamin."

"No!" he said, unwilling to accept defeat. "We did not come this far, just for you to say this to me. All the work we put into rebuilding what we've lost that year? No. If you forgave me once, you could do it again—"

"That was before I knew that it was because of her!"

"What difference does it make?" he huffed, "It was done. I couldn't take it back then, and I can't take it back now."

"It was easy to forgive when I thought that it was because…"

"It was because of what? Explain to me, please. I don't understand, Colette," he begged.

"When I thought it was because you were drifting again…that maybe something triggered you and you needed to find your way back to me. With all the drinking and distance…the nightmares…you know? I just thought that you weren't yourself. That you needed to find your way home—to me."

"You're right. I wasn't myself at all. That wasn't me, or rather, that isn't who I am. You know this," he pleaded. Her hand swept across his mouth to quiet his pleas. And as the weight of her hand lingered, he closed his eyes wishing that the feel of her warmth was under different circumstances.

"Can you please just let me speak?" she asked. Her voice had an air of calm now, as if she had mulled over the decision they were about to face, which swept a wave of fear through him.

"Yeah…um…go ahead," he said hesitantly.

"You violated me…degraded me…because she…hurt you. And I don't think we can ever be the same because of it," she said slowly. The words rolled off her tongue deliberately, playing against her mind like the beat of heavy drums sending charges to her heart, causing her to recoil in pain.

"I didn't…I didn't mean to. I was hurt. And I wasn't thinking," he began, but the look of veiled anger dancing across her face, stopped him in his tracks. He didn't want to acknowledge what she said, but the truth was that he had her that night for the sole purpose of releasing himself of his shame. "I'm sorry. You're right…um… I wanted you for the wrong reason. I…I… took you, for the wrong reason. But I was angry at myself for letting her get the best of me. I'm a man, right? Something like that isn't supposed to happen to someone like me."

"That part wasn't your fault. You can't blame yourself, for something she did," she stated.

"But I could have prevented it," he insisted, "Every fiber of my being screamed at me to tell you what was going on. Hell, to stay away from that… that woman. And if it weren't for everything, I've done…the decisions I made about your mom and her, we wouldn't be here right now. I know that, and I'm sorry. I'm so very sorry, motek."

Heat swelled inside her, causing an inferno of emotions that racked her body in turmoil, and she wanted nothing more than to escape from it. Rising from her place, she took her stride towards the door with an intent that caused him to dart behind her. Seizing her within his grasp, he tried to calm her to no avail, "Let me go. I want to leave!" she screamed, "I can't be here anymore."

"I can't do that," he said, "I won't."

Pulling herself from him, she attempted to flee once more, but the solidity of his arms enveloping around her waist prevented her from leaving and forced her into his embrace, "Let go of me," she said, struggling against him. The loud resounding slap to his face, followed by the pulsating blows to his chest, did nothing to deter his hold on her. Instead, he stood quietly, taking each strike of her fists until she collapsed against him, drowning his shirt with her tears.

"I'm not going to let you go," he whispered against her ear. "I can't let you go. It'll kill me, Colette."

"Like you've done to me?!" she screeched.

Her words devastated him. Despite their history, he never believed he would be the cause of pain of this magnitude, and it crushed him. Releasing her, he stepped away slowly as the weight of her words registered, crashing down on him like a bucket of ice, numbing his senses.

"You really feel that way, don't you?"

"Don't you understand? You were the one person I believed in—that I thought would never do that to me. Use me in that way. And I can't forgive you for that, Benjamin. I can't. It wasn't grief. It wasn't what I thought at all," she said. In her need to rationalize their mess, she paced the floor, trying to will the understanding of his actions into her mind. "It was ego, wasn't it? You couldn't face what was done to you. So, you what? Needed me to hurt with you?!"

"I…I don't know. I just…I just didn't want to feel her presence on me anymore. And the guilt of what I allowed to happen. I wanted to feel the love of my wife again. To feel you. It had been so long. But I was angry at myself. I was also angry with you. And with the drinking…again… I can only say that I am sorry," he said wearily. "I've ruined us, haven't I?"

"I know what you want from me right now, Benjamin. But I can't give it to you."

The silence culminating between them was deafening, and he could no longer stand in the presence of the woman he knew would soon break his heart, "I think I'm going to go. I'll be back to get my things tomorrow evening. Whatever you want me to do, I'll do it. I don't want to hurt you anymore than I have. We can figure everything out with the kids, later," he relented.

Unable to watch him leave, she turned away from him, so that she would not see the pain in his eyes, for she knew that it would ruin her. Listening to the weight of his heavy footsteps descending towards their threshold, she waited for the slam of their bedroom door before she allowed herself to crumble into a heap on their bed.

She didn't know how long the tears had beat harshly down her face, but the weakness and soreness of her body told her that it'd been some time since she had begun to mourn the end of her marriage. Save for the sounds of her soft sniffles, the room was filled with a quiet that magnified his absence, making her feel more alone. "Why can't the world leave us alone?" she whimpered.

As if sensing her distress, her phone vibrated with his name appearing on the screen. Opening her phone, she read over the message he sent:

Motek. You don't have to reply. I know I said I would let us go, but I can't give up on what we have that easily. If there's still a chance...any chance at all, please come to where it all began. I want to give you time to think this through. So, I'll be there. Sunday. Half-past twelve. Waiting to see your sweet face. And every Sunday after, if you don't show up. I'll be there until you do. I love you always, Benny.

Shutting her phone off, she gave way to the tears that welled in her eyes as she pondered his request. What should I do? I don't know what to do, resounded in her mind as she drifted to sleep.

Ani L'dodi V'dodi Li

It was the fifth time she checked her appearance in her rearview mirror, "Come on, Colette. You can do this," she said to herself.

In the moments after their exchange, Benny had kept his promise to her. After he left, he'd gathered his things in the dead of night, when he knew she'd be with Miriam and their children. And he stayed away per her request. The story they devised for their children pertaining to his absence, had given her time to deal with the aftermath of the night she decided to let him go.

Three months had passed since she last saw him. And although the time that passed lent her a sense of fortitude, she couldn't find peace in her loneliness. With each night spent sitting alone in her bed, she'd found herself searching for remnants of his essence, until one day, she knew what she had to do.

Considering the hour, she sat in uncertainty. "Third times a charm, right," she whispered.

The first time she made the trip, was a month into their separation, and despite her desire for him, the anger that leeched its way inside her would not allow her to go to him. When she attempted a second time, she couldn't make it on the road, and had convinced herself that they were better off never seeing each other again. Now she sat once more, in front of the place that started it all, "Alright. It's now or never," she said.

Opening the door, she stepped onto the paved roads, and took in the fresh cool air. Taking in a long-lingered breath, she waited for calm to wash over her. Smoothing out her clothes, she took time to enjoy the familiarity of the scenery in front of her—the changing colors of the flowing leaves, had always been her favorite thing about the small town that housed their begining.

It wasn't long before paved roads became cobblestone walkways surrounded by stone buildings and passageways. They were living memories; filled with the moments she and Benny shared. Everywhere she turned, she could see them and who they once were—laughing and looking into each other's eyes with a longing that could only be quenched with a kiss and the warmth of each other's arms. She missed those parts of them. And it was the memories of who they once were that drove her to the doorsteps of the place, she knew, she should have been to months ago. She at least owed him that.

The weakness in her knees as she traipsed down the corridor had her praying for strength. Reaching the entryway, she faltered, and the reservations that she felt had her turning on her heels. She was halfway down the hall when she felt the light buzzing of her phone on her hip. Reaching into her pocket, she grabbed the item she'd been seeking, and before she could sound off her greeting, the light chime of a familiar voice came through, "Quit stalling, my girl."

"How did you know?" Colette asked with a sigh.

"Although I may not be your mother, I know you," she replied.

"I don't know what to do. What if he's not there?"

"He told you that he'd be there, every Sunday, right?" she soothed, "And if it's one thing we know about him, is that he keeps his word, especially when it comes to you."

"I made him wait too long. I know I did—"

"Colette…listen to me. He may not be my most favorite person, especially after all that mess with Sarah. I still can't believe her. I always knew she was up to no good, but that?" she sneered. "You did nothing but try to be a friend to her…for years, and she pulls the most insidious act. I'm so glad they've moved to Monsey."

"I wonder who managed that," Colette giggled.

"A woman never reveals her secrets," she laughed. "Well, since you're still unsure, I have better for you if push comes to shove—"

"Stop it. He's married," Colette chuckled. "I would say shame on you, but I know it wouldn't do anything to change that mouth of yours."

"You're absolutely right. Chastising me would do nothing. I am who I am. And at my age, I do and say as I please, without apology," she said lightheartedly, "And for the record, he is not happy. I feel it in my bones."

"You leave them be. He chose her, you know. And you have that gorgeous grandbaby to love on."

"While I agree with your last sentence, I know a young lady who could have given me some beautiful grandchildren as well."

"You are relentless," said Colette, "I can't with you."

"Okay. I'll behave. I promise," she replied, "Now, back to you, young lady. As much as it pains me to say this, the one thing I am certain of is that Benjamin Lati, is truly and madly in-love with you. He'll be there, my love. I promise you that."

"I still don't know what I'm going to do. What I'll say—"

"At least you're there to figure it all out. That's a start, isn't it?"

She allowed the words of the woman behind the call to sink in—and just as the words that were spoken proclaimed, she knew in her heart that her husband loved her and wanted nothing more than to see her face, "Thank you. Thanks for the pep talk."

"Don't mention it. It's what I'm here for. As long as I'm around, I'll always be here for you," she assured her. "Okay, I'm going to leave you to it."

"Miriam…wait," Colette called out to her, "I just wanted to say… although you may not be my mother, I couldn't ask for a better surrogate. I love you. Thanks for being you."

"I love you too," she replied tearfully. "Now, stop chit-chatting with me, and go to your husband."

Hanging up the phone, Colette took a steadying breath and walked back towards the door that held so much promise and fear. Pulling the handles, she heard nothing but the slamming of the doors behind her, as she stepped inside the empty auditorium. Taking in her surroundings, she noted the changes that were made since their time there; but as she walked down the aisle towards their meeting place, her attention was brought to the emptiness that surrounded her.

Reaching the stage, panic wracked her body as she swept the large theatre. There was no trace of him there. And as she stood there for what felt like an eternity, her fears began to turn into reality. Shamefully, she turned away from the stage that housed the beginning of their story. But as she started the trek back up towards the heavy doors that held her exit, she heard the harsh rush of footsteps behind her.

"Cole. Wait," he called.

He came from the back of the stage, concealed by the curtains that had once been their retreat. And as he made his way towards her, the relief that washed over her face was instantaneous, extinguishing his fears. Taking in her appearance, he noted how the red scarf around her neck highlighted the amber flecks in her chestnut-colored eyes, while the cream-color of her tweed coat, brought out the suppleness of skin so smooth, he had to fight the urge to touch it.

"I didn't hear you come in. I was looking around for a bit. Do you know they still have the old piano back there?" he said.

The awkward way in which he smiled, made her remember the boy she once shared so much with—but gone was the boy she'd fallen in love with. He was now replaced with a man who stood naked before her. Raw in his emotions.

"I wouldn't know. I haven't been back here in some time," she replied.

"You're right. That was a dumb question to ask, wasn't it?"

"No. Not in the least," she said, "How many times have you been back… behind the curtains, I mean?"

"Every time. It brings back so many memories, I can't help but walk around there. Do you want to look?" he said, reaching out his hand to her.

She couldn't speak—instead she placed her hand hesitantly into his and allowed him to lead the way. His stride, although tense, was purposeful, and outside of his limp, he strutted gracefully to the stage steps and led her across to the piano behind the curtain they had often concealed themselves in.

"I can't believe it's still here," she said, admiring its condition. He stood back, watching, as she took a walk around the mahogany wooden instrument and allowed her hands to run across its ivory and ebony keys, "It's still so beautiful."

"Just like you. Shall we?" he asked, beckoning her towards him. "I don't know when we'll have a chance to do this again."

"Can you help me up?" she asked.

Her closeness brought with her a light scent of lavender, which permeated his senses. He didn't speak. Instead, he cautiously took liberties with her body—grabbing her, so that he was able to feel the indentation of her curves pressed against him. Climbing up behind her, he sat with his back against the wall and hers firmly against his chest, as they used to do, so many years ago. It was a moment before he spoke.

"I've missed this," he began, "Just holding you."

"I thought you weren't going to come," she confessed.

"I've been here every Sunday, as promised, hoping that you would come to me. I'm afraid, Cole," he whispered.

"Why are you afraid?"

"After everything that's been done…and since you've waited so long to come… I guess I'm wondering, why now?" he exclaimed.

She could feel the pulsation of his heart beating rapidly against her back, signifying his anxiety as he awaited her response, "I don't know why I'm here," she said thoughtfully, "But I do know that I still love you, Benny."

"But I've hurt you—"

"As have I," she said. "We've both made mistakes, Benjamin. We've both done wrong to each other."

"Not like that. Not in the way that I've hurt you," he insisted.

"I…I can't contest that."

"I know that you're still angry—"

"I don't know what I am, to be honest. I'm…confused. You know?" she confessed.

"I was supposed to protect you. Give you the life that I promised you. I wasn't supposed to be the one to cause you so much pain," he said. His body convulsed as he became choked with emotion, causing her to shift so that she could see his face.

"Benny. No," she said, placing the tips of her fingers against his lips, "Despite what happened, you've given me everything I could've asked for. Don't detract from that."

"And what about what I did?" he demanded, "How can you forgive me for that, when I can't even forgive myself?"

"Because life isn't easy—the way that you want it to be," she reflected. "Marriage… love… well, it's complicated. I realize that now. It isn't something that falls into your lap with instructions. You got to work at it because love isn't enough. No matter what we've been told all our lives, I know that it isn't enough. Look, I do love and care for you, but—"

"It doesn't mean you want to be with me," he finished. Dread washed over him, overwhelming his senses. Although she showed up, he wasn't sure that he'd won her heart.

"I'm not sure what I want, Benny. On one hand, I don't want to lose what we had—what we've built. On the other, I know that love—"

"Isn't supposed to hurt," he finished. "Not in the way that I hurt you."

"Yes and no. I know that what was done, wasn't you. And it's not something you'd make a regular occurrence."

"No. Goodness no. One and only time. It was fueled by my pain and shitty decisions. And I'd leave before I ever hurt you like that again, Colette."

"I know that. You don't have to convince me. But you're right. Love isn't supposed to hurt. And we've had a lot of hurt. So much so, I don't know what to do. I don't know if this is right—if we are right, together."

"It's been too much" he spoke, "Too much. I get it now. And I guess…

what I did…was the straw that broke us."

"What you did was wrong, Benjamin," she whispered, "But I forgive you. I know you didn't mean it. And for that, I forgive you. But…"

"I know. I let her touch me in a way that only belongs to you."

"You didn't let that wench do anything. She forced herself on you!"

"The same way I did you," he said solemnly.

"Are you *trying* to convince me to end our marriage?" she asked.

"No," he said. The smirk on his face did nothing to hide his anguish, and lent him a look so tragic, she couldn't help but draw him closer to her.

"I just feel so guilty. About everything. And even though I want nothing more than to have you back in my arms, like I used to, before all this, I don't know if I ever will, Colette. And it scares me."

"I know. I've had my fair share of feeling this way—even throughout our years together. And I feel that way now. Confused. And uncertain," she said, "But a part of me is also not willing to throw it all away over a mistake. During a time when things were so unclear…for both of us. And I've made similar mistakes too, Benny. Look, I just…I just want this to be over already, so that we can move on with our lives. Whatever that means."

He could do nothing but look into her eyes. Pulling her closer to him, he felt the soft brush of her hair against his cheek, to which he buried his face in it, "I'm so sorry, motek," he said. "It pains me to think that I could have lost you."

"I will always be here for you," Colette said.

"But where do we go from here?" he asked.

"I'm not sure, Benny. I'm not sure," she whispered.

The look in his eyes rallied her senses, and she allowed her cheek to graze lightly against his. And as relief swept over them, they allowed the magnetism that flowed between them, to pull them in the direction they'd yearned for. Brushing his lips against her neck, he guided himself hesitantly towards the warmth of her mouth. The feel of her lips against his was intoxicating, carrying him into a euphoria that calmed the tension in his body.

She folded into him, as his hands wandered over her and worked with a familiarity that consumed her. The security of the easiness of their attraction settled her core, but the veracity of her uncertainty and their surroundings struck her with a vengeance, "Wait," she panted.

"You don't want to. I'm sorry," he began, "I don't know what I was thinking. I just miss you so much."

"It's not that," she lied.

"Then what is it? What's the matter?"

As the grips of her deceit stifled her breath, she unleashed the worries of her heart, "I'm sorry. I wasn't truthful. You're right. I'm not ready. I mean…I don't even know what…what this is. What we're doing? Do we—are we even together? We can't—"

"I understand," he said. "There's no rush. We can figure it all out."

"Thank you," she replied.

"I only want you to be happy," he said sincerely.

She smiled at him, relieved by his show of restraint and civility. Changing the subject, she jested, "I'd also like to note, that we're in the middle of an auditorium, anyway. I wouldn't call this the most optimal place to… well… to do that."

"In the back of a theatre. We are in the back of the theatre, behind curtains," he corrected.

Although he understood her apprehension, he was hurt by her uneasiness. However, he had no intention of pushing her further than she was willing to go. If he was to have her back, he wanted her fully—whole, and solely his.

"Don't play semantics with me, Benjamin Lati," she said. Turning around to break their connection, she rested herself against him and relished in the refuge he provided.

"I guess we can wait, then," he said with a shrug.

"How did you swing all this, anyway? Having the theater free like this, I mean," she asked.

"I asked the headmaster to lend it to me."

"And what if I would have never come?"

"Well, it pays to be a regularly donating alumnus. And I would have paid to clear it until you came back to me. No matter how long it took. And I know that we haven't figured things out yet, but you're here, and that's enough for me, for now," he stated. "Plus, they built a new theatre a few years back, which you would know if you came with me to visit more often. They only use this one for practice now."

"You minx," she said playfully, "You knew all along how to play this."

"I did no such thing," he said slyly.

"Anyway, just to let you know, I leave being the best alumnus up to you."

"You don't miss it? Seeing it all? Taking a stroll down memory lane?" he asked.

She smiled at the way he spoke of the nostalgia of their place. The place that started it all. He seemed so at home amongst their memories.

"How often do you get back here, Mr. Lati?"

"Well, often enough to remind myself of how much I could never be without you by my side," he said, squeezing her tightly. "And I need you to know that I would do anything to ensure your happiness—no matter what it is."

The gravity in which he spoke made her shudder, and instantly she knew, "It was you. You were the one that made them move."

"I can't take all the credit. I had a little help."

"Wait…you're telling me, that you and Miriam, worked together?" she asked skeptically, "I need to go outside, because surely pigs are flying as we speak."

"Hey, now. Miriam and I have developed a bit of an understanding," he said.

"And what is that supposed to mean?"

"It means that I told her everything… including what Sarah did to me… and what I did to you because of it," he said. She could see in his eyes that it was a struggle for him to speak—placing her hand against his cheek, she stroked his beard to coax him into carrying on. "Together we spoke to Oded and let him know what happened, and that if he didn't want the community to know what his wife has been up to, he should find another place to live where she'd have…better support."

"I suspected it was Miriam that made it happen, but I didn't have any idea that you were involved as well."

"As I told you, I will do anything to ensure your happiness. The last thing you need is to ever see her face again," he said vehemently. "I love you more than life itself, and I won't risk anything or anyone, coming in between us again."

"Thank you," she said. Tilting her head up, she brought his head down for a kiss.

Breaking away from her, he leaned his head against hers, savoring the kiss she bestowed upon him, "Um…Cole," he said hesitantly, "I know that you want to forget this, but…can we, um…can we do counseling? For real this time? Devon said he'd help us find someone if we want."

"Yes. I'd like that," she said. "But—"

"You don't have to say anything. I know you can't make any promises. I don't expect you to. I just need to know, that you'll at least try your best… just as I promise to try mine. No matter where it leads us."

"Whatever it takes. At the very least, I owe it to my best friend," she replied.

"Sink or swim, huh?"

"Yes. But I prefer to swim," Colette replied, "Now, can we get out of here? I'm starved."

"Only if it's at our place," he said.

"Wait…it's still open?" she asked excitedly. "I've been dying for some pizza and a glass of *merlot*."

"Come on. Let's go," he said.

Walking hand in hand, they took in the sights of their former stomping grounds and appreciated its vibrancy and aura, "I can't believe how so much has changed, and yet, is still the same," she said as they reached their place. Looking at the bright red booth, it was as if fate knew they needed it.

"Do my eyes deceive me?" called a voice behind her, "Colette, love… look at you!"

"Oh, my goodness, Sal?!" she said, walking into the outstretched arms of the older man, "It's so good to see you!"

"It's good to see you too. You're still as beautiful as ever," he said, kissing her cheek.

"Aww. Thank you. And you're still as young as ever."

"Ah. You still know how to make an old man happy," he said playfully. "Come. Come. Sit. Your booth is empty. I'll send you your usual right away."

"Add two glasses of red with that, Sal, would you please?" said Benny.

"Of course, kid. Coming right up."

The wink of the older man who had become a friend to them both during their adolescence, didn't go unnoticed. And as she allowed her husband to take her jacket and she sat in her usual spot, she confronted the man sitting before her, "I'm guessing you had a hand in this too?"

"What makes you say that?" Benny asked coyly.

"He most certainly did," said Sal, placing their glasses in front of them. "I'm just happy that you've finally come to visit. Next time, bring the kids. It's been such a long time since I've seen them. The boys are full grown by now."

"Will do, Sal," she said, "And I promise that I'll also come by to see you more often. I've forgotten how much I love this place."

"That brings me such joy. So much joy," he said. The smile that danced across his face was contagious, and she found herself basking in his happiness, as his blue eyes twinkled with joy. "I'm so glad to see you guys still together. You don't see couples like you much anymore. Ugh. The two of ya! Since you were young ones!"

"Until forever," Benny said staring at her intently.

"I can't with you two," Sal said. "I'll leave yous alone. We'll catch up after you're done eating. That okay?"

"Of course," Benny said. His eyes still on his love.

"Can't even take ya eyes off her," Sal said. "I can't. I just can't. The two of you make me miss my Angela. I can't wait until she comes home."

"Oh. No. I was hoping to catch up with her," Colette said.

"Don't worry. You come back and visit when she returns. Okay?"

Like them, Sal and his wife, Angela had been childhood sweethearts. When they were kids, Benny and Colette would watch the elder couple often, hoping that they would have an inkling of their love. And as she watched the white-haired man light up at the thought of his wife returning to him, she couldn't help but ask him, "Sal, how do you guys make it work after so long?"

"We don't let life get us down. And whenever it does get hard, we try to remember the love we have for one another. That gives us strength. You have to choose each other. Every time," he said with a smile. "Now, I got to get back to the kitchen. But I'll be back to visit with ya."

"Okay, Sal. Thanks," she said to him.

Benny didn't hear the man as he left their table—his focus had shifted from his wife's eyes down to the fullness of her breast popping through her white cashmere sweater. He didn't notice it before. He'd been too distracted by her presence after being away for so long, that he didn't heed the story her body told. However, now as he looked at her, he realized that the glow radiating through her smile spilled a secret she didn't know she possessed, "Cole… I don't think you should have that glass of wine."

"Why? Do you know how long it's been since I've had a glass?"

"Well, I'm certainly hoping it's been a while. However, why is that?"

"Truthfully?" she asked.

"I don't expect anything less."

"The stress of everything… of not having you around, has made my stomach so wonky," she said, "So, I haven't had a taste for it."

"And you don't find that a bit suspicious?"

At first, she didn't find it suspicious at all; but as she mulled over his words, it hit her like a ton of bricks. She couldn't remember the last time she had her monthly visit, and with the stress of everything going on around her, she didn't think anything of it. Staring at the wide brimming smile on her husband's face, she knew what he was thinking, and he had never been wrong before.

"We're too old for this, Benny. What are we going to do?"

"Apparently, we're going to be parents again. I'll take that," he said taking her glass of wine. "Looks like you're going to be driving us back home."

"Driving back home? You haven't been home in months. And we still haven't—"

"If you think I'm not coming back home now, you are sorely mistaken," he said.

"And how exactly will that work, Benny? We haven't even decided if we're back together."

"I'm sorry," he said sincerely. "Look, you don't have to worry. I'll still respect your space. But while we don't have to decide on anything pertaining to us, I don't want to miss out on anything with this baby."

"We don't even know if there is a baby," she scoffed.

"Have I ever been wrong?" he chuckled.

"This isn't funny. We are too old to be having another kid!"

"Well, if I'm calculating correctly, based on the last time we've been together, it's just a little too late either way. You've always carried small, except when it comes to here," he said smugly. Touching the brim of her sweater, he allowed his finger to lightly glide across the swell of her breast.

"Stop that," she said, swatting his finger.

"I'm surprised you didn't notice," he smiled. "Or that you haven't felt him or her, yet."

"Maybe it's because I've been a bit distracted with other things, no? Fuck! And this is why we're in this predicament now," she huffed, swatting his hand again. "Seriously, stop it!"

"I can never keep away from you," he said.

"I can't believe we're doing this again."

Pulling her in close, he kissed her gently on her lips and then laid her forehead against his, "We'll be fine. It's just someone else to love. Ani L'dodi," he said. His breath warm against her cheek. "I am my beloved, and my beloved is mine."

"I don't know if I can," she replied.

"It doesn't matter. I know us. And you'll always have my love. There is no one else in this world that I want, but you. We'll take it one day at a time."

"But what if all that's happened, is truly the end of us. I couldn't bear to—"

"Never," he said passionately, "It will never be the end for us. Forever and always, Cole."

“Benny, this is crazy!”

“It always has been,” he whispered, “And we’ve always worked it out to become stronger than before. From childhood…”

“I guess we’ll see,” she replied.

“Say it. Please. I just need to hear you say it.”

“Until forever,” she whispered.

Acknowledgements

It's been a long six years and it has been one heck of a ride. As a writer, I've had millions of stories pop into my mind, but not all have had a chance to be put to paper. This journey has been a long and hard one for me, and like Colette and Benny, life always seemed to get in the way of seeing this story through. If it were not for my family's encouragement, *Diamonds out of Coal* would have never come to fruition. I am so grateful for your words—filled with the best of love, reassurance, and grace, as I've worked on this story.

To my husband, thank you so much, for all the countless days and nights you poured into me, when I thought I couldn't do it. You are an amazing cheerleader, and I couldn't have done this without you. I am forever indebted to how much you believe in me.

I would like to thank my mother. Although you are no longer with me, there isn't a day that goes by that I don't still hear your voice, rooting for me. You will forever be a driving force in my life.

Ms. Angela Nelligan—my very own, Mrs. Feinstein, I thank you. For your wisdom, love, and kindness. Heaven most certainly received an angel when they got you.

Many thanks to TSgt. C. Davis. and Captain B. Rotimi, and all the servicmembers who were of great help but wished not to be named. Thank you so much for being my eyes. I am so thankful for your guidance and all that you do for our country. As a military spouse, I wanted to get your stories—triumphs, losses, and experiences, right. I couldn't have done this without your openness. I appreciate you all for the hours you spent answering my questions and giving me honest feedback. I hope the world realizes what a treasure you all are.

Tex. Thank you so much for letting me into your world. I will forever be grateful for your insight and candidness. You are an amazing person and friend. The world needs more humans like you. Always look ahead. We all need your light and love.

Finally, thank you to my children. You all don't know how much of an inspiration you are to me. Like your father, you are my muse. I am the fortunate one—I get to be your mom.

Author's Note

Hello Readers,

What a journey it has been! First, I would like to thank you all for taking a chance on my very first novel. As a writer, it has been a wonderful and sometimes trying experience. I hope that you enjoyed your time getting to know the Lati family. When I started this novel, I had no idea where I wanted to take it. But as I wrote I realized that, in many cases, as readers, we miss the greatest protagonist of all—relationships. So, I decided to write what I believed to be an honest take on what marriage can become when life and we (humans) get in its way. Although I know this book may have been difficult for some to digest, I truly hope that you enjoyed their story. For those that may have experienced or are experiencing the struggles Benny and Colette faced, I see you. Resources will be provided for you on the following page.

If you were wondering if Benny and Colette's story is finished, I am here to tell you that it is not. As you are reading this note, I am currently working on the second installation of this series, which will be titled, *The Color of Pearls*. It will continue to follow Benny and Colette's journey as they try to mend their marriage; and explore what love, loss, and friendship means during the Jim Crow South. I can't wait to share it with you all. So, be on a look out.

If you didn't know, I am also an independent author of children's books. So, if you've enjoyed my novel, take a chance on one of my books for young readers. You can find the titles on my website **www.NGKraiembooks.com**, as well as my blog **Libraries, Bookstores, & More**, where I visit different towns and cities and explore what literary wonders they have to offer. It's a travel blog, made lovingly for bibliophiles. You can also find me on *Facebook* and *Instagram* under **NGKraiem**.

Again, thank you so much for your time and support. I hope to share more stories with you all soon.

Help & Resources

If you or someone you know is struggling, you are not alone. Please contact one of the helpful resources listed below. You matter.

Suicide & Crisis Lifeline
988

National Sexual Assault Hotline
1-800-656-HOPE (4673)

Grief and Loss
1-800-395-5755

If you enjoyed this story, scan the QR code below!

About the Author

N.G. Kraiem is a mom of four children and a military spouse. With a Master in Human Services, her love of children inspired her to gain her second Master Degree in Teaching. She is often taken away from the classroom to live out the adventures of military life with her Airman and children. In her spare time, she loves to travel and write about the many libraries and bookstores she sees along the way.

This is her first novel.

Milton Keynes UK
Ingram Content Group UK Ltd.
UKHW010913271223
434976UK00001B/96